For Casey,

keep smiling; it's majestic x

Heavenly Realms
Empyrean Falling
By Jonathan Goss

— Jonathan Goss
(615) 300-3074

Empyrean Falling

Heavenly Realms: Empyrean Falling

Written by Jonathan Goss
Cover Design: Renegade Zero, "renzero" (via Fiverr)
Editor: SJS Editorial Services

Published by Jonathan Goss, Nashville, TN
Copyright © 2019 Jonathan Goss

All rights reserved. No part of this publication may be reproduced, distributed, or transmitted in any form or by any means, including photocopying, recording, or other electronic or mechanical methods, without the prior written permission of the publisher, except in the case of brief quotations embodied in critical reviews and certain other noncommercial uses permitted by copyright law.

Publisher's Note: This is a work of fiction. Names, characters, places, and incidents are a product of the author's imagination. Locales and public names are sometimes used for atmospheric purposes. Any resemblance to actual people, living or dead, or to business, companies, events, institutions, or locales is completely coincidental.

Printed in the United States of America
ISBN 9781792701542 (Paperback)

Empyrean Falling

For my brothers.

Empyrean Falling

Index

Preface	5
Prologue	6
Tome I: Nightmarescape	19
Tome II: Dawn of a Dark Prophecy	79
Tome III: Empyrean Falling	186
Epilogue	383
Glossary	392
Acknowledgments	400

Empyrean Falling

Preface

    We can't fully grasp what lies beyond this vale of tears. How much of it is real and how much of it our holy books got right will remain a mystery. The angels are no exception. Symbolic, masculine, luminous, preternatural, they move through the pages of the Word in a multitude of forms and functions. Yet they always remain powerful. They always have a mission. The mere glimpses we catch of them on those pages have left indelible impressions.

    But that's not enough for a story. Do not regard this novel as canon; creative liberties must be taken to fill in the gaps. And a deeper story lies behind the curtain of those arresting biblical scenes. Pavilioned in terrestrial settings, costumed in anthropomorphism, we can slip past the unfamiliar superficialities and grasp what lies beneath: the thoughts, passions, faiths, loves and fears which reside within the denizens of the heavenly realms. This series is a yarn seeking to bridge the two worlds. So, enjoy it for what it is: a human interpretation of angelic history, an attempt to entertain, a fiction that transcends history and reaches for myth.

Empyrean Falling

Prologue
"What has been will be again, what has been done will be done again; there is nothing new under the sun."
—Ecclesiastes 1:9

  When I first glimpsed the Archangel Gabriel, I was seventeen. He came to me in a vision, as these things are wont to do. I wasn't deep in prayer; my constitution wasn't wavering under a forty-day and forty-night fast, but my life had grown aimless, despondent. My idle hands had no idea they secretly wrestled in the depths of an inner Peniel. Heaven's stride is at its most potent when alongside our blind spots, as the name "Parakletos" so eloquently personifies. And so, it was here, sitting in the auditorium of my high school, where I beheld a trumpet and a golden crown shrouded in tendrils of mist. No words were spoken, but the aberrant distinction pierced my darkness. I knew.
  The next time it occurred, I was twenty. Internally, life again seemed to be on the ropes; my spiritual walk had one foot in the fiery chariot. This time, I beheld the Seraphim Archon in all his grandeur. His emanating radiance was enough to scorch my eyes, yet within that luminescence, I beheld an unsurpassed beauty: flaxen hair draped over a youthful, ivory countenance and thin, casual frame content in its authority. The magnitude of his power was held in his eyes; they burst forth like a torrent from a dam, brighter and more golden than the sun. I was captivated. And within the blazing vision of my dream, deep in

the heart of his imposing nature, I became cognizant of a smile. My heart skipped a beat as I saw his lips part.

"You are His son, Markus," came the waves of his tenor. "He will not forsake you."

The third time I received a visit from the Archangel Gabriel, it was of a miraculous degree. He came to me in the flesh, as tangible as the pages which now rest in your hands. I was a month from my thirty-ninth birthday and stood upon one of life's dire crossroads. I'd long since burned the bridge between me and God, my life had withered as a grape on the wintry vine, and I found myself leaning over the edge of a yawning internal chasm, ready to sink deep the blade and welcome Heaven or Hell. In a rare moment of lucidity, I again took up the mantle to fast, as I had all those years ago. On the twenty-first day, I received my answer.

I was in my modest apartment, trying to catch my requisite three hours' sleep. It was all I managed in those days. If I wasn't tossing the sheets, I was wrestling with my religion. But the closer I drew back to my faith, the more questions I had. An unfulfilled life was drowning me in the tempest of a ruptured heart. What little I unraveled disturbed me: I couldn't reconcile any of it. The whole thing seemed a sham, a lie perpetuated by a dependent society. When you have no hope in life, the *mysterion* can drive you into despair.

There was a clarion call in my heart. "'Awake, arise, or be forever fallen.'" Quoting John Milton wasn't something I expected in the small hours and, after checking that I was alone and not dreaming, I went to the kitchen to pour a drink and drag myself back to bed. The scotch never had a chance to do its work; he was standing next to my neglected stove. His radiance was subdued to a shimmering hum, but that didn't keep my heart from jumping. "Talk with me."

Surprisingly, I didn't prostrate myself or flee. I simply stood, handicapped by this spiritual manifestation. I may have cursed, but the archangel's smile betrayed nothing.

Gabriel stood less than two meters tall. He seemed surprisingly lean within his viridian robe and gilded belt. He smiled unassumingly and folded his arms over a smallish chest. "Should I come back when you're more cogent?"

Empyrean Falling

My jaw moved, and my lungs expunged air while my mind tried to remember how to use its tongue, but nothing coherent issued from my lips.

He waved an ivory hand and I found myself in my living room, sitting in a chair across from him. It's a mind-bending thing to see an archangel take up easy residence in one of your beat-up leather wingbacks. He raised one of my wine glasses to his lips and sighed. I suddenly felt very self-conscious of the cheap merlot I kept on hand. "Relax," he smiled. "After enduring the early days of Melphax and Ural's vineyard, the palate can appreciate just about anything."

I wanted to ask who he meant, but I instead found myself accepting a glass of scotch from him. I took it absently, my eyes refusing to leave his glowing apparition.

"You're no doubt curious as to why I'm here," he proffered. I stammered through a reply. "Our Lord has allowed me to visit you. Understand this is no small thing. There are myriads-myriads Sons of God who would swiftly perform this task in my stead. I am, as you can imagine, a busy archangel." He studied the swirling red in his glass. "But I feel it's time to set the record straight. I have been graced with my reprieve." My brow furrowed.

The archangel nodded. "Imagine the depth of frustration one may feel when it's their job to convey a message and for millennia, they must accept divine restraint against the inter-dimensional language barrier. It's its own condemnation. But our Lord is faithful, and here we are. Please understand, this sanctified task will be performed with a plain speech. I know you prefer a lofty tongue, Markus, but I'll have to rein it in for simplicity's sake; the facts alone will be enough. In so doing, I hope to give you the answers you desire. This task is long overdue."

These words had a profound impact on him. The color of his flawless, ethereal prism shifted, as if even pathos was an emotion of the holy. It did nothing to dull the radiance of his youthful countenance; it merely altered his mien.

"And, if things proceed well," he continued, "this may not be the last. Though, should you reject my message, I will simply find another who has a more receptive ear." I struggled with my feeble husk of flesh and psyche to form words, straining against my recalcitrant physical will. Gabriel smiled and petitioned me to relax with a gesture. "No need for all that," he comforted. "You humans are easier to read than we expected."

A quick prayer and I was able to produce the words. "What are you here to tell me?"

"There are many misconceptions about the angels. Oh, your kind has tried over the millennia, but you've always hit just below the mark. This is through no fault of your own; after all, you were made in the very image of God. But a Fall can wreak havoc on clarity. History has a way of perpetuating the skewed vision. And let's not forget free will: that odious blessed freedom which can render us all blind as bats."

"Why me?"

Gabriel chuckled. "Your kind can be charmingly frustrating. I had a certain Jewish girl ask me that a couple millennia ago, as well as a shepherd boy a few centuries before her."

"Exactly," I reiterated. "Why me? I'm just…"

"Just what? A man? A human? A child of God?" He shook his head in amused reprove, clicking his tongue. "The question, dear Markus, isn't 'why' but 'why not.'

"To wit, this is the limitation of your mental comprehension. The brain, in all its mystery, is simply a looking glass for the soul to peer into this Earthly Realm. Of course, in relation to the deeper dimensions, your window is more of a peephole. This is no insult. You have regained much in your post-Fall redemption. And there's room to grow even more before this Age is reduced to embers. Not that I or any of the others know the scarlet number on that calendar. There are times when we wish we did, I assure you, but it simply isn't in the cards. We know nothing more than what God tells us—not that it's kept us from placing our bets.

"But time is only a marginal element of our discourse. It'd be an insult to your intelligence if I didn't try to reveal this arcane knowledge. I have faith in you and your kind, Markus. Many of us do. It's the impetus behind our cause and why I sit before you tonight with the express intent of historical clarification.

Empyrean Falling

"That word 'history' seems incongruent with the Heavenly Realms, doesn't it? Yes, I can see it in your eyes. Forgive me. I wouldn't want to confuse you by overreaching my own narrative. So, let me state that our existence was only partially *timeless*."

"How can that be?"

Gabriel shrugged. "Simple, our beginning was in the Highest Realm: The Empyrean, with God. And even this state of being wasn't immune to the passage of time."

"But how could time exist in Heaven?"

"The same way it does here," the archangel responded candidly. "Your theologians and gurus have it right: Heaven is an ethereal plane, a Realm of light and perfect eternal music. But it's much simpler than many believe. Or at least, it was at first. Heaven as we knew it simply existed with God. There were no gates, no shores, no physical manifestations of any kind, just loving harmony. His light bathed us in every virtue you can imagine—and some you've yet to. This was the Empyrean, and we reveled in it. That's all perfection is: existing with God in the Empyrean. It's static, simple and perfect. Nothing else has ever been required."

"So, how did physicality come into it?"

"We were ethereal essences, bright and burning, enveloped in the even brighter luminescence of God. But we began to notice more angels issuing amongst our ranks. Of course, this could be considered some semblance of 'time' but, in truth, there was no way of cataloging the events. They happened with such rapidity that one could shift their gaze and behold a thousand new souls manifest in a sporadic array.

"Angels came in waves. Naturally, the archangels came first: Lucifer, Michael and me. At least we think that was the order of our creation. Then the others, until everywhere there was another with whom to converse and share in Father's majesty. And yes, there are only three archangels. Of those, there have never been more, perhaps for the better. And there are only two choirs: cherubim and seraphim. Michael was charged with the cherubim; I was given the seraphim; and Lucifer was the pinnacle, the perfect mold. Of him, there has never been an equal… though one has come exceedingly close.

Empyrean Falling

"But I digress. To answer your question, the chronology was inconsequential for who knows how long but eventually, we witnessed an oddity, something we'd never dreamt of in uniform communion with our Creator: we saw Him create. It overawed us. He was manifesting elements completely unknown to us, incorporating things which we couldn't fathom. To put it into scientific terms would strip it of its miraculous nobility.

"We rejoiced; we were enthralled by this revelation. And you know what was most intriguing? His joy. Don't get me wrong, this wasn't insecurity; it was innocent intrigue. The marvelous rapture that emanated from His divinity was unlike anything we'd ever felt or seen. I can hardly funnel it into expression. How could this cause our Lord such euphoria? Look at how He burns with magnificent passion! We saw our Creator in a state of revelry so captivating that we couldn't begin to contemplate its concert. It's safe to say that *here* is where our 'history' began."

Gabriel sipped his wine. His golden eyes, though lacking in pupils and vibrating with divine fire, seemed to look downward for a moment before returning their beaming gaze to me, like twin lighthouses on a foggy coast. At least that's how they appeared to my senses…or was it something else in me?

"Polemics were held in the Empyreal state," he continued. "Many yearned for this revelation. We archangels were not immune to the syndrome. We were curious. No, 'curious' is too small a word for it. We were infatuated by the very nature and reaction of the thing. God had allowed us to witness something grand, and the emotions it elicited were enrapturing. We wanted to take part, not out of pride or jealousy but out of gleeful, inquisitive solidarity.

"So, we took our request before the Creator and, to our surprise, He said yes. If we chose, He would grant us the ability to travel to this new Realm. I suspect He knew this transformation was necessary for our growth. We had no clue what those words meant, but we were eager. I confess, our curiosity evoked a modicum of rashness. As such, conditions came with traveling to this physical manifestation: for us to have any impact, we'd have to become physical. This wasn't without potential consequences. Heedless, we Three agreed, despite our Maker's caveat. Ever dutiful, He gave us more than just our transubstantiation; He gave us protection. Amazing how parents labor to protect their child from sin even before its first breath. Anyway, the dangers inherent with this clothing of flesh were revealed as the Prophecies.

"Those portents notwithstanding, the Heavenly Host rejoiced in the embarkation of our grand voyage. We were about to experience a shade of God's power."

"So, you left the Empyrean?"

"Yes," Gabriel confirmed, "though not Heaven. You're paying attention. Good. Your philosophers were right about one other thing to an extent: there's more than one Heavenly Realm. There's the Empyrean in which we existed—and to which our souls return—and the Lower Realm, an amalgamation of physical and spiritual essences. This is what enthralled us. And it was on this plane that we married substance with spirit."

"Was it like Earth?"

"Close. The sun rises and sets, as does the moon. We have seasons. Our version was unblemished. The world never decayed." He smiled, taking in the room around him with a sweep of his arm. "It obviously bore repeating. We began to chronicle the cycles. And in them, we created names: seconds, hours, days, weeks, months, years, decades, centuries, millennia, eons and ages, just as you do. Where do you think you got such nomenclature?"

"Wait," I objected, "that etymology can be traced through human history."

Gabriel laughed. "Yes, they can be traced," he agreed, "to a certain point. Human history is a funny thing, especially when seen through your eyes. You'd be amazed at how much of your civilization you didn't actually invent."

"I don't understand."

"Your Marie Antoinette said it best: 'There's nothing new except what has been forgotten.' You must learn to accept the notion that not all things in your dimension were invented by you; some were bestowed. You remember the Book of Enoch?" I replied that I did, albeit vaguely. "Well, in it—along with other books—humans are taught by angels."

"But those books aren't canonical."

"And for good reason. Your present Bible is divinely inspired, but that's not to say those books which were rejected were entirely false. Many contained beneficial truths." I asked him to proffer examples. "The most impactful was warfare and technology, but there were others: cosmetics, rituals, sciences, mathematics. Many of these were hinted at by…third parties."

"Fallen angels?"

Gabriel nodded in resignation. "Not all revelations are good ones. Much was whispered to your race early on, by both those serving in the light as well as those enthralled by the dark. Humanity is fraught with supernatural intervention and not all of it is ordained by Father." He saw my disbelief. "You think the Bible is the only thing that ethereal forces have had a hand in when it comes to Earth?"

"So, things existed in Heaven before us?"

"Long before you—in some cases too long. In one fashion or another, most of the early technology that comprised so much of your history existed in our alchemic Heavenly Realm before it was lullabied to you. You think Michael started wielding a sword when your kind hit the Iron Age? He's had that thing almost as long as he's had anthropoid form. I've worn armor; the stuff is heavy. Not that you would know, of course."

"It was a bit before my time."

"Yes." He took a sip of wine. "The fact remains that so much of what you say were your inventions were actually ours. We taught it to you, the good and the bad, unfortunately." He grimaced. "As I said, perfection bore repeating." He sipped his wine again. "But it can't last forever, not in this state anyway." His voice trailed off, bright eyes shifting to a wayward spot on the carpet, likely to some hideous stain, of which there are many.

"Can you elaborate on what it was like?"

Gabriel broke away from his distraction and began anew. "We became part of the natural world. The revelation of the consequences was shocking. How we were fired in the Empyrean was how we were molded in tangible form. The flesh mimicked the souls. We ogled at the qualities that distinguished one from the other, overjoyed at each other's inherent complexity. It alleviated some of the Three's concerns—especially Lucifer—that going through this transformation would diminish, alter or eliminate our distinctions. It did nothing of the sort; it amplified them! However, we required maintenance. A few failed and their souls returned to the Empyrean. One thing that's often misconstrued is the verse 'and you shall be like the angels, and not given unto death.'"

"Right," I affirmed, "you're immortal."

"Yes," Gabriel replied, "but not invincible. Humanity's immortal too if you believe in the soul. You must understand the dangers of mistranslation. All that verse says is that we aren't *given* unto death; it doesn't say that we can't die."

"What's the difference?"

Gabriel sat up. "To be given unto death means you'll shuffle loose the mortal coil; it's mortality by default. It says nothing of the prospect of being killed. We live forever in this amalgamation of flesh and spirit but, through force, we too can be taken from the Lower Realm. Our bodies can fail us if the irrevocable occurs. Our death is the same as yours: we return to the Empyrean. Many angels died during the War. Many still do. It's something your doctrine has a hard time accepting; no one likes to admit their deity's enforcers are vulnerable, but we are…powerful, yes, but we can be slain, though the dimensional leap is much smaller.

"Nevertheless, we found the tedious, even loathsome, maintenance to be worth it. We were participating in this grand spectacle of uncanny beauty. For that, no amount of maintenance was too bothersome. We slept, trained, studied, exercised, ate—"

"—you ate?" I must admit I found it hard to believe this one.

Gabriel raised his nearly empty wine glass. "We had to for sustenance." My mind wrestled with the idea. "Yes," he intuited on my behalf, "we came with most all our parts fully assembled." He paused while I leered at him. "I see you're now starting to question the validity of my words and, perhaps, my very identity. I assure you it's the truth. We were made much like you, except all male. One thing from which we in Heaven have received great amusement is the bit of androgyny your species has slapped onto us in recent centuries.

Empyrean Falling

It disappoints me that after thousands of years of relative accuracy, you would suddenly have retardation of perception. Oh well, we understand why such a heinous decision was made: at one time we were asexual. But that was before we wrapped ourselves in flesh. Not that sex entered our minds until well after Creation. You're aware of the Apocrypha?" I nodded. "Enoch was incorrect on many levels, but his basic revelation, that angels were captivated by the beauty of women, was all too true. Like all things in history, reality and myth are never that far apart.

"I'm digressing again. Forgive me." He grinned, and at the risk of coming off as presumptuous, I sensed a bit of sheepishness in it. "You can rehearse something a thousand times and then finally, when you find yourself in the spotlight, you end up just winging it. 'Best laid plans' and all that. Anyway, to return to topic: the whole experience was equitable to yours here on Earth, yet it was slightly different, and marvelously so. We moved within this Realm much the same as you do, though with more authority."

"What do you mean?"

"We descended to the Lower Realm for the joy of expressing our love through bringing beauty into existence. This required energy. The physical world is alchemy. We created, yes, but it required another gift…or should I say, perhaps, it was a quality we retained in our transformation. To answer your inevitable question: it was our ability to manipulate a tangible shroud wrapped about the divine substance. This came from our mind's energy, our will. Yes, Markus, we have minds, bloodstreams, eyes, mouths and ears. We also have wings. Your artists got that right, at least. But despite all our preternatural capability, it was the capacity of our minds which empowered us. It manifests in our environment."

"Telekinesis?"

Gabriel tilted his immaculate head. "It was more spiritually rooted in the fundamentals, the fabric of nature. In its easiest form, we manipulate the weather. But even that taxed us, some more than others. Therein lays one of the advantages of the Three; we archangels always had more stamina to employ our gifts than our angelic brethren. There's also the fact that we've had more time," he said with a self-effacing smile, "but we try not to hold it over their heads. This proved a distinct advantage, especially in darker times.

"In some mirrored fashion, it's possible with you humans. Every now and then, a phenomenal genetic mishap occurs—or miracle, depending on your outlook—that allows your kind to experience a shred of the holy power we possess. I spoke earlier of the mind being the portal for the soul. Well, that's mainly how it works. It allows us advantages over the real, which lends itself to preternatural feats. That's not to say we don't operate within the bounds of the natural order. We can bend the laws of nature and physics, yes, but it comes with consequences. It also requires a great deal of concentration."

"Did that ever pose a problem?"

The question felt innocent enough, but Gabriel eyed me, his lips pursed. For a moment, he no longer looked at me, though with his unnerving lack of pupils it was hard to tell. Eventually, he finished his wine and set the glass down on the carpet.

"Well," he began hesitantly, "yes, in that age and the one that followed. But there are always complications, aren't there?" He looked back up at me, his gaze again resilient and casual. "In those days, we were akin to the chimeras your legends depicted. We found that creating natural things required a concert of natural means. We couldn't just manifest a mountain without it affecting the flora. We couldn't divert streams and pick fruit unless we dug canals and planted seeds. But where we excelled was in creating monuments and edifices, constructs in harmony with our surroundings and built to honor God.

"These eventually developed into cities, metropolises unfathomable in scope and scale—you really had to be there to appreciate it, Markus. I wish I could find a way to properly convey the marvel. Nimrod tried his hand at a pallid imitation with Babel, if that gives you an inkling. At first, though, our constructs interacted in tandem with the environment: towers reflected sunlight, walls aided rivers in their flow, and forests in their growth. We monitored the development, all the while falling more and more in love with it. But the honeymoon wouldn't last forever, as you enchanting children are so fond of reminding yourselves.

Empyrean Falling

"In all our fascination, we forgot the Prophecies and, eventually, ourselves. God existed for us, but it was much like it is for you. He was in another dimension where He left us to our own devices, intervening only when He saw fit. He still ministered and showed grace, but He didn't dwell among us. I think our first mistake was in assuming such a separation wouldn't affect us."

A long pause followed. I sat across from him, waiting for the venerable being to continue. After several seconds, I grew alarmed that such might not be the case.

"What happened?" I asked, a twinge of fear eking out.

Gabriel lifted his chin in rumination and sighed. His luminous eyes squinted, and his face drew taut. A deep contemplation came over his visage. It took many moments for him to weigh in on whatever matter anchored his heart.

"That," he said with regality, "is a tragedy. But for now, let me just say that from great failure can rise resplendent epiphanies. We allowed iniquity to enter our hearts, and with the kind of disastrous results that would make Sodom and Gomorrah look like a pair of flaming bushes. Yet, in an act of faith which only those who witness it can understand, we were redeemed."

"Did the whole Heavenly Host experience this?"

"Most of us," he replied with a nod. "In our deepest despair, we were given a rebirth. Then, Markus, we were given anthropoid bodies." I drew to the edge of my seat. "It was a gift like no other. We knew the instant we received this second wave of transformation, no longer were we akin to the roaming beasts. Father had deemed it necessary to give us something more precious; He made us in His image. We kept our wings, which remind us of our old forms, and our fiery eyes to carry as lamps of the Empyrean into whatever darkness lay beyond. But the new form seemed like the perfect mold; opposing thumbs work wonders!

"The angelic host was once again overjoyed. We'd fouled up only to be redeemed in the most glorious of ways. We were a marriage of everything that had gone before us: spirit, flesh and, now, God. We were divorced from nature by a divine physicality. And we learned an invaluable lesson. We took measures to remember what was forsaken."

"You mean the Prophecies?"

"Yes," he nodded solemnly with eyes that seemed to peer only inward. "We vowed never again to allow such sin to corrupt our holy hearts."

"So, how did it end? Did you rebuild? Were you exiled?"

"Some of both," he replied enigmatically. "Like all romantic epics, it really has no ending. But it did have a beginning…"

Empyrean Falling

TOME I
NIGHTMARESCAPE

Empyrean Falling

Chapter Index

Chapter I: *Stirrings*	21
Chapter II: *The Meek and the Voice*	30
Chapter III: *Whispers in the Lion's Den*	36
Chapter IV: *Gloaming Portents*	41
Chapter V: *Counsel in Light*	45
Chapter VI: *Tremors under Stars*	50
Chapter VII: *Valley of Virtues and Flame*	55
Chapter IIX: *The Small Hours*	61
Chapter IX: *Molding Precautions*	69
Chapter X: *Forging Subterfuge*	73

Empyrean Falling

Chapter I

"For you have said in your heart, 'I will ascend to Heaven and place my throne above the stars of God'..."
—Isaiah 14:13

    He sat on the shore, watching the black sea. The inky waves rose into foamy crests and splattered against the strands, their shallow rows bleached to a skeletal pallor by the moonlight. He closed his blazing white eyes and listened to the rhythm of the coast, trying to match his racing heartbeat with the tempo of the tides. The gentle breeze blew against his immaculate features, tickling his ageless countenance with orange locks. He filled his lungs with the stench of seaweed. Arms on bended knees, he curled his toes into the sands and let the cool, wet grit pack against his skin. He licked his lips and tasted the salt spray in his fiery goatee.

    He knew precisely how long he sat there imbibing the night shore. He began drawing in the sand. When the lines and arcs formed to his liking, they illuminated as if afire. He observed each until they simmered a steady glow before erasing it with his palm and starting anew. Over and over he drew fiery symbols in the sand. Each one met the same fate. Yet he persisted.

    The capital metropolis boomed less than a league behind him, commanding the inland terrain as far as the eye could see in either direction. It rose in myriad arrays of architecture lit like a sprawling luminescent sea creature, its denizens burning the midnight oil in celebration. Even from his spot on the coast, he could detect the throbbing, spiking ambiance of revelry.

The air shifted at his back. He felt the radiating warmth of a heartbeat before he heard the shuffle of sand underfoot. And yet he persisted in his burning artistry.

"Exultant Archon," came a meek voice from behind.

He continued to languidly etch his glyphs in the sands. "Shouldn't you be at the Coronation Banquet getting thoroughly soused like the rest of them, Mealdis?"

"Yes, sir. Archangel Michael sent me to fetch you."

"Always the fixer, my brother," he muttered with a smirk as he peered down at the sands. Another glyph came and went, its trespass lasting no longer than the flicker of stars overhead. "Tell me, seraph, does *your* archangel know you're out here or did Michael hope to surreptitiously instill some confidence in you by hunting me down with an invitation scribbled on your tongue?"

"I couldn't dare attempt to understand the minds of the Three."

"Now there's a bit of wisdom, neatly couched in cowardice."

"I'm sorry if I've failed or offended you, Exultant Archon."

"For the thousandth time, Mealdis, titles are meant to be periodically rewritten; I know you seraphim love your honorifics but call me what I am or find another missive to deliver."

"As you desire, Archangel Lucifer."

"There's hope for you yet, little one." He heard Mealdis' plump form shift uneasily from several meters away. He ceased his drawing and half turned to the angel. "So, did my brother elaborate on the nature of this audience?" Mealdis replied that he did not. "And you didn't inquire?" Mealdis repeated his answer. Lucifer nodded and turned back to the sea. He squinted into its soft midnight turmoil and sighed. "That is tactically sound of you as a messenger. Small-minded but prudent, I'll give you that. Ever the dutiful child of God, Mealdis." The seraph thanked him. Lucifer resumed his elemental calligraphy in the sands. "All in good time." He constructed a glyph and lifted it from the sands and into the air beside him. A horned omega arched over a simple upturned fish. The shapes wavered for a moment before settling into place, married to the air by Lucifer's easy control. "Take this to Mazerrel," he instructed.

"Shouldn't I first report back to Archangel Michael?"

Lucifer took the glyph in-hand and rose. He strode over to Mealdis, covering the interval between them with startling velocity. His broad, fit frame towered over the diminutive seraph, silver trousers and tunic glimmering in the moonlight. "You've delivered your message. Now you have a new one." He watched Mealdis turn back and look anxiously at the glittering cityscape. Lucifer smiled. "Don't worry, Zion will still be pregnant with her party long after you've completed your task. You won't miss anything of consequence there, except my younger sibling tripping over his drink and my little princeling of a baby brother getting red in the face like he always does when Michael has more than his share of libations."

"So, you'll go to Archangel Michael then?"

"Now that is bold of you," Lucifer said through a smile of satisfaction. He tucked the glyph into his palm until it was a burning orb the size of an egg. "I like that kind of daring curiosity. A big step of initiative, seraph." He placed the compacted glyph in Mealdis' hand. "Leave my brother to me. Find Mazerrel; he should be back at the Citadel's mess hall by now."

Mealdis regarded the glowing compacted orb in his fist. "And Archangel Michael?"

"Oh, don't worry, I won't be missing him." Lucifer's ambrosial voice was still resonating in Mealdis' elephantine ears even as his sprouted his wings from the two vertical cubit long slits in his back and flew southwest, back to the Holy City.

Lucifer watched him vanish into the starry expanse over Zion. The coastal breeze pressed at his back. He folded his arms over a powerful chest that rose and fell in a sigh.

There was a shift in the nocturnal wind; a zephyr whipped the fiery red locks away from his chiseled visage. He turned to meet the sudden unexpected blast. His eyes narrowed to vibrant white slits. His jaw clenched. His palms turned to fists. "Not for all the Empyrean."

Empyrean Falling

Mealdis winged it with all his might into the airspace over the Holy City. Below him, the lights of their kingdom's capital twinkled in a mirror of the clear starry skies overhead. The nightlife was alive and well when he arced around the colossal architectural feat that was the Seraphim Bastion. Erected in the shape of three winged angels standing back to back, the seat of Gabriel's choir was an imposing marvel of design reaching over a thousand meters into the air. Even in the small hours, it bustled with the comings and goings of seraphic duties. Though he'd been there countless times, Mealdis' heart still skipped a beat as his soft yellow eyes espied the silhouettes of the three stone angels, speckled as they were with tiny landing platforms at intervals, all worked into the architecture to appear as stitching in the texture of the carved granite fabric.

He felt a twinge of relief when it was nothing more than a figurine on the horizon at his back. But a sense of foreboding crept into his heart as he drew near the towering monolith that was the Cherubim Citadel. Instead of being a glorious feast for the eyes like the Bastion, the central hub of cherubic activity was almost ominous in its militaristic design. It loomed overhead like a mountain, dark save for the strategic placement of watch fires.

The acres around it were carved and cordoned off in various lengths and degrees to accommodate their combat training. While they were saddled with the prosaic title of "Training Acres," they were more colloquially known as "The Garden", for the cherubim said it was here where they cultivated the fruits of their warlike labor. The less articulate among them simply said it was where they got to get their hands dirty playing in the arena's mud. Regardless, Mealdis felt exposed, even under cover of darkness, and averted his gaze.

His eyes darted back up to the watch fires' flicker, catching glimpses of the artillery batteries bristling from parapets, ramparts and bartizans like a porcupine's quills. Pennants fluttered in the occasional gust, only interrupted by other intrepid seraphim and the midnight activity of potentially inebriated cherubim. Mealdis shuddered at the thought of Michael's choir being concentrated here in a state of drunkenness so soon after their celebration; the jests and barbs he would surely have to endure made his toes curl.

Empyrean Falling

Still, he set his eyes like flint as best he could and arced around the martial block of stone, steel and warrior resolve. He aimed for the deep shadow of the Citadel's plinth. His landing was delicate but not as surefooted as he would prefer. He looked around to see if anyone caught his stumble, sure it would only earn him mocking crows and colorful gestures from the rougher half of the angelic host. He exhaled with relief to see that he was, indeed, alone.

The gilded tiles of the Holy City shone in a kaleidoscopic array against the braziers and high lanterns lining the streets. They were forgiving to Mealdis' sandals, the sound muffled by his standard issue leather soles. He padded his way down the avenue, cognizant that most of the cherubim were still at the Holy Temple or carousing their way from one watering hole to the next. He could hear the faint drone of distant singing between his heavy breaths.

Hyperventilation aside, the seraph had a growing unease in the pit of his saggy stomach, as one feels increased warmth when approaching a bonfire.

He rounded the sharp corner of the Citadel and approached the nearest ground level entrance. A quick rap with the knocker on the cast iron door, and the viewing slit slid open.

"What's your purse," came a slurred query from the sentry inside, "pup?"

"My…" Mealdis had trouble processing the question. Then he smelled the alcohol. "Oh, my *purpose*. Yes, well, I have a message from the Lightbringer to deliver to Mazerrel. I was told he could be found in the mess hall."

"Oh, ye brave little seraph. Treasured little princeling's pet to be running errands for the First Born. Oh, excuse me, the Lightbringer." The sentry harrumphed and burped. His fiery blue eyes blinked a few times as steam rose from their rims. "Too much roast," he complained. "Always gives me reflux. Alright, you seem like a good enough lad. What's your name again?"

"Mealdis."

"Funny name for a funny looking seraph. All you seraphs are funny. Fancy clothes…" He shut the slit and began unlatching the locks on the other side of the door. "…Fancy ornaments. Fancy talk.

Fancy walk. Never get your feet muddy, what with all that flying around fetching notes from one big shot to the next."

"Sometimes we lead," Mealdis tried.

"What? Oh, yes. Well, sometimes your kind gives orders…when you feel like it. Not the same. Only thing I've seen a seraph lead is a uniform inspection or a parade."

The door opened and the sentry stepped aside. Mealdis stepped into the cold, unforgiving stone hallway. He turned to the cherub. He was of slightly less than average height and thickly framed with a noticeable layer of meat over his muscle. His blue eyes were dimmer than usual, set in a rounded face mostly covered by a prodigious dark beard. Mealdis looked down and saw the bottle in his hand. "Thank you, Nuriel. Must be terribly boring being at this door all night."

"It's a hatch but whatever; you're the one with the scratch from the big dog." Nuriel waved him on before slumping on his stool.

Mealdis made his way down the sparsely lit stone hallway. The echoes of inebriated conversation and raucous laughter spilled out into the corridor before him. He entered the mess hall and was overtaken by the light from the roaring hearth and the many torches, braziers and candled chandeliers hanging from the high ceiling. Rows of long oaken tables stretched before him, littered with a scattering of empty bottles, plates laden with half-eaten scraps, and the sporadically placed snoring cherub, boots in the air and legs sprawled over tables. At the back corner nearest the roaring hearth sat a congregation of rough cherubim: all shapes and sizes with gruff tones, scars and scowls. Their smirks were their smiles. Crude gestures and dark laughter filled the hall, though they were the only angels present. The room was occasionally punctuated by their raised voices turning on a dime to demonstrative argumentation.

At the nexus of this aggressive chaos sat Mazerrel. The largest angel in Heaven, he was a mountain among the foothills of his cohorts. His massive, corpulent frame was bellied up to the table's central seat, giant shoulders hunched over a platter of mostly devoured chickens and crowned by a ghastly splay of dark, matted hair. Every now and then, he would roar in protest or humor and slam his hulking fist down on the table, smashing little hillocks of greasy bones.

Empyrean Falling

Into this maelstrom, Mealdis tiptoed with his mission.

From the flailing carnival of flung gestures, sloshing drinks and wild, irreverent barbs sat a silent observer. He watched from his corner at the table. The extent of participation in his comrades' conversational bedlam was to nod or shake his head whenever they dared to involve him in their discourse or seek his input. Sometimes he ran a hand through his jet-black mane of hair, which hung to his waist like a pitch covered bell rope. Mealdis hardly knew the cherub, but he felt a shiver run up his spine when the angel's dark blue eyes found him. He froze in his tracks, locked by the cherub's piercing, unblinking gaze.

Mazerrel caught the still intensity emanating from his left and stuttered his laughter to a halt. "What is it, Linghal?" he all but demanded in his bellicose rolling tongue. Linghal gracefully rose from his seat, eyes ever on Mealdis, and dipped his brow in the seraph's direction. Mazerrel turned to his right and drew his heavy molten gaze on the intruder. "Ah," the monstrous cherub breathed through a hungry grin, "the second course."

"More like leftovers," one of his underlings chided. The group laughed as they sized up Mealdis. "Or dessert."

"What do you want, little flyboy?" Mazerrel demanded. "Isn't it past your bedtime?"

Mealdis tentatively shifted on his soles. "Hail Mazerrel," he stammered. "Hail to your teamsters. I have a message from the Lightbringer—I mean, your First Born." Mazerrel arched a thick eyebrow, his eyes waxing in vibrancy. Mealdis reached out and opened his palm. The orb of light flowered out to reveal itself.

Mazerrel beheld the glyph and tensed. A snarl peeled across his broad face. "Finally," he rumbled. His congress of associates grew still and silent. All starry eyes were transfixed on the symbol burning in preternatural luminescence above Mealdis' outstretched hand. "Off to your covers, little seraph. Nothing more for you here."

Dejected and confused and not at all used to the feeling after all these millennia, Mealdis lowered his hand, turned and scurried out of the mess hall. He nearly fled down the adjoining corridor, his heart eager to be free of the Citadel. A thunderous crash startled him halfway to the sentry door, and he skidded to a halt. A vociferous uproar erupted from the mess hall. Mazerrel's teamsters were barking at one another like wolves over scraps. Their commotion was swiftly brought to heel by their ursine leader.

"Ask and you shall receive, runts!" Mazerrel bellowed. "You better hope this time of waiting has been a season of preparation for you all; I won't carry dead weight into the dawn."

The echoes of his voice reverberating down the corridor made Mealdis' skin crawl.

"Goldruum, be in the darkness and cover our tracks. Linghal, watch and report. Sheialla, scamper off to our elusive serpentine companion and tell him there's a quorum coming. Sammiel, find Nelgleth; your alchemy is required, and he has possession of our supplies…"

With each order, Mealdis' guts twisted more and more. His heart hammered in his chest.

"And where will you be in all this?" rasped Sheialla.

"At the Island for now," Mazerrel replied. "I have a project to complete before the boss is ready to stir the pot."

"You've been evasive with us for long enough, Mazerrel," Sheialla said, his thin tenor barely audible to Mealdis' ears. "Time to spill it. You want us to risk life and limb, there better be something worth knowing to justify the risk."

"All you need to know," Mazerrel growled, "is that he has something special planned." Mealdis pressed his back to the stone wall, sinking as deeply into the shadows as he could. "This new cosmic romance has been a charade, and tonight's revelation was the capstone. How long have we labored in this Creation? And all at the behest of a Father who refuses to sit on His very own White Throne or dwell among us? Doesn't that gnaw at your guts? It gnaws at mine, Coronation or not." Mealdis heard their knuckles rap on the table. "So, if He won't deign to grace us with His love then we're left to our own devices. There's a big lesson coming for this newly minted apple of His eye. Just do your part and you may live long enough to see it."

Before he knew it, Mealdis' feet were in a dead heat with the tempo of his pulse, carrying him down the hall. His wings unfurled before he was fully out the sentry door, a drunken Nuriel snoring on his nearby stool. He leapt into the night and beat his hollow bones and feathers against the air, putting as much distance between himself and the Citadel as possible. His fear drove him deeper into the Holy City of Zion, headed for the one person whom he knew he could trust.

Empyrean Falling

Chapter II
"But you, brothers, dwell not in darkness so that this day should surprise you like a thief."
—1st Thessalonians 5:4

    He was grateful for the cloud-free moonlight bathing the Holy City of Zion in a pallid wash. Skyscraping obelisks rose high above the gated palaces, urban quarters, and great, mirrored ziggurats, all of which were encompassed by the seven hundred cubit-high Wall and its twelve Gates. The massive double doors at the heart of each Gate were scores of cubits thick, their surfaces inlaid with the rarest of gems. But nothing could compare to the Holy Temple at the heart of it all, a dome braced by four walls, each corner topped by a silver tower rising from the metropolis to brush the cope. The Temple dominated the cityscape, dwarfing every neighboring architectural feat for blocks in every direction.
    He looked down into the metropolis. Street lamps hummed a dull yellow at even intervals along the gilded streets. Rows of supply houses, facilities and recreation centers flanked the snaking lanes. Fiery glyphs inlaid like filigree into precious metals shone brilliantly in the collage of moonlight, creating a prism of luminous beauty.

Empyrean Falling

  His heart filled to bursting; truly, Zion was a spectacle of unequaled majesty and reverence, even for the angels. He closed his luminous golden eyes and imbibed the tranquility.

  Suddenly, a thunderclap broke the serenity. His eyes shot open and looked to the sky. No clouds had formed. The tiles under his soles quavered. His heart skipped a beat. Then came another thunderclap, this time more insistent. He scanned the clear skies until movement below caught his attention. He watched the street lamps shake as the clamor echoed down the thoroughfares. A third thunderclap erupted, and he watched the Holy Temple shiver as a dog shaking off water. A shockwave rippled out from the heart of the metropolis. Towers cracked and sagged in the aftershock. Windows shattered as the reverberating wave carried its way closer to him. He watched their glass shards splay out in reflections of the street lamps and glyphs.

  More shockwaves came, overlapping until the towers crumbled, the ziggurats disintegrated, and the street lamps toppled onto imploded buildings, their preternatural energies catching the rubble afire and turning Zion into a landscape painted in flames. The fires consumed the debris; smoke replaced the usual mist. He choked and gagged. Wailing and the clanging of warlike metal filled his ears. He touched the lobes' warm trickle and saw a red glint on his fingertips. Then a commotion drew his gaze back to the Temple in time to see it shatter in a burst of white light. Clouds erupted from it and mixed with the smoke. Lightning struck; there was rain. It painted his balcony red. He tasted it on his lips and backed away in horror…

  Gabriel jolted awake to the clatter of arrhythmic pounding coming from his front door. He lay in bed for several seconds, still tasting the mixture of blood and wine from his dream. The noise continued unabated. He turned in his sheets, trying to deny the racket. He grabbed a pillow and slammed it over his head in a vain attempt to bury his face in his mattress. He jerked the sheet and comforter over his blond hair and did his best to create a cocoon of soundproof linen. He grunted. He shut his eyes. He gnashed his teeth.

  Eventually, he threw off the blankets and sat up. A deep inhale filled his lungs and fueled his veins. With a jolt, he swung his legs out from under the covers and hunched over the side of the bed. Raking golden locks behind his ears and pressing his palms to the twin suns burning in his face, the archangel yawned, groaned, and gathered himself.

"Typical," he mumbled to himself in a half prayer, "First night free of Creation's labor and I can't even enjoy it." The room spun in darkness. "Bless me with strength, Parakletos."

He gained his bearings. As he set bare feet to the chilled wooden floor, he was quickly reminded that spring nights and wooden floors could be their own wake-up call. The thought occurred to him that Lucifer and Melphax had the right idea by installing carpet in their bedrooms. At least a pair of slippers, or anything more than his cotton undergarments. The temptation was there to grab the comforter as a wrap, but the urgent knocking compelled him to suffer through; urgency often meant suffering. So, he made his way through the darkness of his bedroom, dodging shadowy furniture as he groggily tried to fight through the stiffness of exhaustion.

He nearly lost it on the staircase thanks to a fortuitous shirt he found draped over a chair. Tripping with the shirt half pulled over his torso wasn't the display of equanimity he considered befitting of an archangel, even in the small hours. When at last he reached the foyer, he heard the muffled pleas of an angel's tenor. "If one of you little songbirds has gotten into the communal wine, I'll have you scrubbing Benediction latrines for the next century."

The noise ceased as Gabriel came upon the door. "By all the blood and brimstone," he grumbled while unlatching the padlock, "Alrak, if this is another one of your pranks I'm going to—" He stopped abruptly as the door opened to reveal a disheveled, hysterical seraph. The angel trembled, lips quivering as they tried to form words before his archangel. "Mealdis?"

"I—I—" he stammered, "I need…Lucifer…I…" Mealdis collapsed and fell into Gabriel's quick-catching arms. He dragged the seraph by his armpits out from the flagstone threshold and into his ornate living room. His chubby weight was no strain for Gabriel, but he was all too happy to plop him down on a sofa and let a cup of freshly brewed tea perk him up.

It was some time before Mealdis woke.

"What brings your distress here so late, seraph," Gabriel asked, handing him the cup of tea.

Mealdis smiled wanly as he took the ceramic cup. "Forgive me, my Archon. I couldn't go through my superiors; they would've laughed me out of their offices…or chambers, at this hour. They'd rag on me, like always…call me delusional and send me off."

Gabriel plopped down on an ottoman next to him. He observed his tearful, wild eyes and glistening countenance. The night had done nothing for his sweating panic. "Dire news can make for a sleepless bed, for sure," he agreed. "What makes my audience so paramount?"

"I delivered a message from the Lightbringer to his lieutenant in the Citadel," Mealdis finally pried loose, "the meaning of which escaped me until, well, I was leaving, and I overheard Mazerrel talking to his teamsters about some plan."

Gabriel sighed. "What is that gaggle of brutish lackeys up to now?" Mealdis recounted the events. He repeated Mazerrel's words verbatim. "Is that all?" Gabriel asked wryly.

Mealdis looked befuddled. "It was just all very…off, sir."

"Tell me something I don't know, kid. That group of malcontents has been acting strangely for centuries. And never mind my eldest brother. The Anointed Cherub's been 'off' for millennia. At this point, I'd be more concerned if he was back to his old self."

"But when they saw that glyph," Mealdis added, "they changed. Like hounds that had suddenly picked up a scent."

That piqued Gabriel's interest. "Can you replicate it?" Mealdis nodded. Gabriel fetched pen and paper. "Draw it." The seraph went through a few shaky attempts but eventually sketched the horned omega and inverted fish symbol he'd carried in his hand. Gabriel studied it. Something tugged at his psyche and refused to subside. It crept from the shadowy recesses of his memory until his eyes widened and his shoulders dropped. "How could I've missed it?" he whispered. "He knows better. He's the bright one of the Three."

"I'm sorry, sir?"

Gabriel tore his eyes away from the drawing. By the time he looked at Mealdis, he'd sufficiently masked his shock. "Never mind, seraph. Archangelic business." That did little to abate the anxiety staring back at him. "He's just molting, Mealdis," he said with a reassuring but wan smile of his own. "I'll talk to him; try to figure out what's going on in that pinnacle head of his." He downed the rest of his tea and stood.

"Thank you for hearing me," Mealdis trembled, china teacup clanking in his hands.

"Don't worry, I know what to do. We'll parse this out."

Mealdis nodded, eyes trailing off.

Gabriel placed a hand on his shoulder and hummed a soft note in his throat. "How did you come to find Lucifer on the Shores of Caliven in the first place?"

"After the Coronation…well, you saw Lightbringer leave. We all did. So, Archangel Michael sent me to fetch him."

Gabriel retracted his hand and snarled in the dark. "I see." He turned and headed for his chambers. "Well, sleep in one of my guest rooms tonight. The attendants will be here at dawn."

"If I may," Mealdis called after him, "what does that symbol mean, my Archon?"

Gabriel stopped. "Probably just a belated spring equinox prank. Now that Creation is completed our celestial maestro has nothing to occupy his time. You know, idle hands." He climbed the stairs. "Try to relax. Sometimes an ill-conceived joke can rattle the best of us."

"I'm sorry, my archangel," Mealdis whimpered from his place on the sofa. "I'm afraid."

The Seraphim Archon opened his mouth to speak but thought the better of it. He nodded and composed himself. "There's no sin in fear, Mealdis, only in what we do with it. Stay put."

Mealdis watched Gabriel ascend and disappear into the shadows. The seraph followed him to the foot of the stairs and waited. A minute later his archangel emerged wearing a viridian tunic and gilded belt. A small dagger pressed against the cloth folds at his hip.

"My mansion is your mansion," Gabriel told him. "But if you decide to remain—and I'd advise that you do," he threw a glance around, "lock up." He watched Mealdis give the front door a backward glance. The archangel motioned for him to climb the stairs.

When he got to the second level, Gabriel handed him the dagger at his waist. "Rest easy." He turned and opened the balcony doors. A cool breeze wafted in, lifting the folds of his robe.

"My Archon," Mealdis began. "Why do you believe me?"

Gabriel thought for a moment and shrugged. "No reason not to, I guess…which may be the most troubling part of all."

With that, he sprouted his regal emerald-tinted wings and leapt into the night. A pollinated gust rippled from the balcony's landing and into Mealdis' face. He squinted through the dusty push of air, but Gabriel was already a speck in the starry sky.

Empyrean Falling

Chapter III
"Now this I say, brethren, that flesh and blood cannot inherit the kingdom of God; neither doth corruption inherit incorruption."
—1st Corinthians 15:50

"Tell a seraph to fetch a whetstone and he comes back with a flint." His gravelly voice echoed into the high walls of his austere mansion, even as he scratched his broad, hairy chest beneath the blue robe. With a shake of his head, he observed the glyph sketch again and yawned.

Gabriel's thin shoulders sank as he watched his older brother groan and turn for the kitchen, the glyph in his calloused hand. "Mealdis is too meek to lie, Michael," Gabriel insisted. He entered the room as the second archangel poured himself a drink and slumped onto a stool nestled under the bar. "I believe him."

"Of course you do," his older brother sighed. "He's a seraph." He tossed the sketch onto the hardwood countertop and set his nightcap on it. "How many times has Lucifer's tongue landed him in his own fiery lake? In light of his innumerable glories, we both know it's his greatest—if not only—blemish."

Gabriel pressed on. "And we both saw his reaction to the revelation of Humanity." Michael leaned over the bar top, propped on elbows, and raked back the long dark tresses cascading over his glowing sapphire eyes. He blinked and exhaled through his manicured beard. "Huff and puff all you want," Gabriel sneered. "It's not going to divine you any more answers than whatever spirits are at the bottom of that tumbler."

"At least it'll help me sleep," Michael said, raising the amber-filled glass in a toast before polishing it off. "It's too late for this."

"I agree," Gabriel said cryptically.

Michael eyed him over the rim of his glass. He slowly set it back onto the glyph sketch turned coaster. "Our paths are our own. I can't control him, no matter how much he offends your sensibilities."

Gabriel leaned in. "You never tried."

"It's not my place."

"No but taking care of your choir is. So when one of my seraphim comes to me in shock, I do my due diligence. Same for you. Pranks and tantrums are their own animals but when the glyphs get thrown around and people like Mazerrel act with purpose, I get nervous. And I think if you stayed sober long enough to hear the concert of context you wouldn't be treating earthquakes like aftershocks."

Michael traced a finger along the bar top's engravings. "Are you sure this isn't just the imagination of one of your lesser seraphim? We forbade the use of these things after the West."

Gabriel shot him a level look. "Now don't start that again. There's enough rivalry between the two choirs already."

"What if he's wrong?"

"Mealdis doesn't know the glyphs, Michael. As you said, we stopped using them long ago. And for good reason."

The Cherubim Archangel strayed from the engravings and traced a facsimile of his own glyph with the tumbler's condensation. "This isn't just another one of your nightmares, is it?"

"Humor me, big brother." Gabriel watched his sibling's dark, angular features sharpen in furrowed concentration. "We can at least seek an audience; there's no harm in that."

Michael nodded. "Fine, if it'll alleviate your badgering. I'd wager Lucifer could clear this up himself, but you've never been one for confrontation. Sometimes I wish you'd have more faith in us Three, for our brother's sake."

"Well, I'm going to the Temple," Gabriel declared, back straightening. "You can come with me or search for Lucifer. But I'm petitioning Parakletos' aid."

"Not without me you're not," Michael said, rising from the bar stool. "Someone needs to vouch for our First Born." He headed deeper into his mansion.

Gabriel followed him. "Just like I have to vouch for Mealdis. I'm worried he might be harmed in all this. We can't turn a blind eye this time."

"Lucifer would never harm another angel," Michael said with exasperation over his shoulder, "not without just cause." There was stone defiance in his tone.

"He would if he were the Dragon." Barely had the words escaped his mouth before Gabriel found himself slammed against the kitchen's archway, Michael's forearm pressed against his throat. He had forgotten how fast his brother could move, so swiftly did he cover the interval between them.

"Don't *breathe* such things," Michael snarled at him. "That kind of slander is punishable by exile. Would you risk your station calling First Born the Dragon?"

"I have my nightmares," Gabriel rasped, "you have yours."

Michael's fierce gaze drifted to some unknown place and he slackened his grip. He released his brother and began ascending the stairs to his bedroom, covering the dark interior of his home in adroit strides. Gabriel smoothed out his collar and cleared his throat.

"I mean to go now, Michael."

"I know."

"Then where are you going? The door's over here."

"I'm getting dressed," Michael shot back. "And I know where my own doors are, thank you." He receded into his chambers and illuminated the wardrobe with his preternatural ability.

Gabriel thumbed the hem of his garments. Half filled with weaponry, he knew it could be some time before his older brother picked through all the war gear in search of proper attire. In the slight over-wash of light, he took notice of Michael's home. He couldn't remember the last time he was inside his brother's mansion; the Creation had kept them all so busy. "Blue rugs now," he noted. A bit of his own elemental illumination revealed more: discarded, empty bottles of alcohol piled into a pair of corners under a circular window in the study. "You ripped up the carpet?" he called up to his brother's chambers. "You know, you could get Zodkiel to clean up the place."

"Zodkiel is my armor-bearer, not my butler," Michael replied over the sound of the wardrobe doors closing. "And I missed the darker warmth of hardwood."

Gabriel folded his arms and leaned against the archway. "Apropos," he said through a wry smile. He took in his brother's surroundings while he waited. Michael's mansion was always sparsely decorated with robust leather, brass and wood, but Gabriel took note of the recent changes. There were more piles of bottles, no artwork and, to the trained eye, everything had the weight, heft or sharpness to be used as a weapon if need be. His smile faded.

He looked up to see his brother reappear on the landing. Michael was adorned in his stainless steel breastplate. A fiery sword flanked by wings was etched into its center. Unlike most parade panoplies of dress armor, Michael's contained no adornment; it was the same scratched up, marred article of kit that he wore on the field. Sporting black trousers and an ultramarine long-sleeved shirt, the archangel's sole raiment was his silver diadem, which nestled in a levitated position on his head. At his waist hung his curved sword in a leather belted sheath.

Gabriel smirked. "You're packing a lot of gear for someone who doesn't believe me."

"Belief has nothing to do with it," Michael stated flatly as he looked down and rubbed the lion-headed winged pommel of his sword. "I'd be remiss if I didn't bring Virtue."

"Do you expect a battle at the Inner Room?" Gabriel chided, smirk unabated.

"Victory loves prudence, little brother," Michael said. "Even before the White Throne."

The Seraphim Archon nodded and turned for the front door, expecting Michael to follow him. "Do you have a spare horse?"

Michael shook his head as he tied his dark locks back with a leather cord. "It'll take too long to saddle Andreia; we'll make better time if we fly." He made for the second floor's balcony and unfurled his wings.

"Do you even remember how to use those things?" Gabriel asked. "Between your horse and all the legion training…"

"Can't fly and fight in a line of heavy infantry. Doesn't work that way and you know it."

"I'm just saying…" Gabriel shrugged, "it's been a while."

Michael glanced at him over his broad shoulder. "It hasn't been that long." His majestic array of azure-tinted wings fluttered and stretched their massive feathers. "Try to keep up, gilded seraph."

In a beat, the two archangels were bolting into the night, one markedly faster.

Chapter IV
"And then shall many be offended, and shall betray one another, and shall hate one another."
—Matthew 24:10

By the time Mazerrel arrived at the reflecting pool, the stars were ceding their light to the gloaming. The palm fronds and elephant ears rustled in the coastal breeze. Looming over his hulking form was the sprawling alabaster architecture of Lucifer's manor. The jungle of Morning Star's private island penetrated the villa walls in a sultry garden of saltwater air and lush vegetation. Shadows swayed in the wind. Mazerrel furrowed his brow and huffed.

"You're late," came a hiss from the shadows.

"You're early," Mazerrel rumbled. "Letting me see you won't matter." He maneuvered away from the pool's glimmer, finding a shadow of his own. "Our lord may espouse the plight of my teamsters at the hands of Michael's betrayal, but his aegis alone protects your serpentine hide, Tempest. You think your venom will be less bitter when things change?"

"Are you so sure you'll be around to witness it?" the shadow rejoined with a challenging slither.

"I'd gut the whole world for the chance."

Empyrean Falling

"Brutish lapdog," came the voice from the slinking wind. "Maz, you would burn the whole of existence on a pyre to have your name remembered for its own sake. No matter the cause, no matter the cost, you lick your chops for the taste of infamy. What a bitter, base desire you possess. How reprehensible. How churlish. A fire merely looking for his fuel. You have no regard for the aspiration of glory, to have your name be remembered for your deeds, for your strong actions in the face of another, equally yoked with the imposition of challenge. But you won't test yourself on the chopping block of fate's fearsome fortune. No, you'll simply bludgeon your way through blind fury to exact a petty revenge on small-minded people. You've been fattened on the weening of reputation for past endeavors. But no room is left in your stomach for the soothing tonic of glory imperishable. To be lauded, to be praised, to be thanked, to be appreciated…and admired. You would simply take fear over respect."

Mazerrel eyed the darkness. The air hung thick. He began to laugh, a deep cacophonous thing full of malice. The shadow stepped from the tree line. Mazerrel had forgotten how slender Tempest was, a lithe figure shrouded in lapped armor, linked and padded in such a way as to remain silent. His facial shroud concealed all but his silver glowing eyes. Mazerrel remembered how his armor played with the darkness, making his silhouette slippery to the eye. He watched Tempest suddenly drop to a knee and bow. Shocked, he took a step back and bumped into something much smaller than himself, and infinitely more powerful. He turned.

Lucifer stood facing him. Out of reflex, he too took a knee.

"Rise, my friends," Lucifer said coolly, motioning with an upturned palm. "Ash is ash; what rises from it is beautiful." He turned to the east. "Look at that," he said with a smile. "The sun ascends with a fire under its wings. The night has lasted long enough. It has poisoned us with pain. You have both suffered betrayal. You have both been wounded. I thought there could be another way. I tried everything to get divine intervention. God knows I tried. But He remains aloof. I don't know why, but I won't sit idle while Mazerrel's cherubs are rendered pariahs for being more gifted with the hammer than with golden totems at the head of armored echelons.

"And Tempest, my old friend, what would our cohorts be without your skills but a teeming mass of brutes waving spiked cudgels and banners? You are the master of assassins, espionage and subterfuge. Are we to prepare for a war or for peace? Michael's honor will never give you and your brother Orean the recognition you deserve, let alone command of Lorinar's Merciful Fate Ziggurat. An archangel's heart is his own to govern, I suppose, but that does not excuse the millennia of mockery at the hands of his underlings. Let the dead bury the dead, as the Son says."

"Slaves will always be found this way," Tempest remarked. "I would sooner die on my feet than live on my knees."

"A quest for glory," Mazerrel commented. "I can think of no greater waste. Better you than me."

"Tempest," Lucifer said, turning to his slender companion, "will Orean be joining us?"

Tempest gave a terse shake of his head. "I could not illuminate my brother to our cause. He won't see your light."

Lucifer nodded. "I'm sorry for your loss," he sighed. "Long ago, I would say there is still time for the scales to fall from his eyes. But, alas, we're overdue on action; time has run out. You will have your glory; I will give it to you. And perhaps your brother Orean will see it before the end. I know you serve fate's fearsome fortune, that you seek a contest to prove your valor. Legends are made of such ambitions, though sacrifices must be made. Worry not, Tempest, we will all join you in this immolation soon enough." He turned to Mazerrel. "And what of you, my longtime friend? Have you had better luck with your compatriots?"

Mazerrel beamed, his broad face and thick, flat teeth gleaming in the dying moonlight. "Your left hand trembles in his saber-rattling failure, my lord; but unlike Tempest, I've not failed you. My teamsters are with you. They know the price paid for slaked thirst. They are hungry. They are starved of satisfaction. My angels are with you until the end, ready to do their lord's bidding. Even they kin the light of your cause. Were such a thing true of our fellow's twin brother, here, perhaps we'd be surer of the verdict."

Empyrean Falling

Tempest's eyes narrowed to slits as he stared at Mazerrel. Silence was his insult. He instinctively tightened his grip on the curved longsword's hilt slung at his waist. His glowing eyes flared.

"What is it you always say, Tempest?" Mazerrel provoked. "You can judge a person by their friends, but a person can judge themselves by their enemies?"

"Better to be alone in our enterprise than bolstered by a petulant-tempered sycophant," said Tempest. "Winning someone through force is no victory at all."

"Do as thou wilt shall be the whole of my law," Lucifer said. "I won't stand in the way of our people choosing their own destinies."

The two nodded, their proud, polar countenances fallen at the heartache attached to Lucifer's words. He moved closer between them and drew them near with outstretched arms. Mazerrel's enormous shoulder was a boulder in the archangel's right hand and Tempest's lissome form gracefully arced under his Grand Patriarch's grasp.

"Well," Lucifer said in a sad tone, "come, my friends. There is much work to do. You are two of many, and at last, I've heeded the call. Too long have I lingered in contemplation, weeping over a path shrouded in darkness. The truth is that this is all my fault. Would I deserve my pinnacle station if I shied away from your cries? I think I've divined a way to be free of this hypocrisy. We can be the instruments of hope, not just for each other and ourselves, but for all those who have been crushed beneath the boot heel of the Council's bureaucracy, beneath my brothers' eyes blinded by ill-earned crowns, and a vacant chair filled only with the wailing and gnashing of teeth from His absence. We must not be slaves to misfortune. Let's put our despair aside, once and for all, and beat our pain into plowshares."

Empyrean Falling

Chapter V

"Then I saw a great white throne and Him who was seated on it. Earth and sky fled before Him, and there was no place for them."
—Revelation 20:11

Gabriel sat at a small bureau in one of the many secluded antechambers of the Holy Temple, poring over stacks of unfurled scrolls. Glyphs danced from their inky pulp. Outside the locked heartwood door, a din slowly arose as the sunrise brought with it the bustle of activity. Michael had ensured the door was securely bolted before stretching out onto the cot beside the bureau and laying on his back with his sword sheathed beside him, but every time a seraphim custodian or cherubic Temple Guardian trespassed the gilded, stained glass hallway, Gabriel's senses alighted. Someone shouted for something inaudible, their tenor muffled by the thick walls. Gabriel shot an instinctive glare at the door.

"Keep that up and you'll jerk a knot in your neck," Michael whispered from his recline on the cot. Gabriel turned to see him lying on his back, hands cradling his head under the start of a teasing grin. The seraph cleared his throat and put his eyes back on the door.

"You really think this will work?" he asked.

Michael shrugged and turned on his side. "The White Throne doesn't lie."

Empyrean Falling

Gabriel exhaled. He was exhausted; he'd settle for a pin cushion at that point. He pinched his nasal bridge and rubbed his eyes.

White light flooded his vision and suddenly he felt transported back. The flight through the Holy Temple's Causeway was fast and dark but it never grew old seeing the massive colonnades adorned in filigreed marble, nor the diamond sheened stadium seating that rose in countless tiers to the domed roof draped in tapestries. Only the elite Temple Guardians were present in the hallowed stone halls of the Causeway at that starry time; the capital seat of Zion was usually asleep in the small hours and last night was thankfully no exception. Their footsteps echoed throughout the incalculable expanse as they lighted onto the stone altar at the base of the Forty Steps.

He remembered looking up at the Forty Steps of Purity that ascended to the Inner Room. He had memorized each word inscribed on their prismatic tiles. How many countless times he and Michael had furled their wings and walked up those steps, he'll never know. The meditation ritual always seemed to work, no matter the duress. The burden lifted, like stones from a sack until, by the time they crossed the summit's obsidian speaking dais, the brace of Temple Guardians flanking the monolithic jewel-encrusted Doors was a welcoming sight.

Bellator and Dealleus were imposing cherubs, even for angels assigned to the night watch. Their gleaming, polished armor was part adorning raiment and part vicious nightmare. Even the archangels had to answer to them. He could still hear their voices echoing in his mind.

"Who comes into the presence of the Everlasting Lord God Almighty?" Dealleus asked. The answers were always the same: Archangel Michael, Cherubim Patriarch and Sword of God. Archangel Gabriel, Archon of the Seraphim and Voice of God. "For what purpose do you seek an audience with the Lord Almighty?" Gabriel remembered Michael stepping forth on that one, stating they sought Father's counsel on a matter of grave urgency. Michael huffed when Gabriel impressed upon Dealleus that time was of the essence. Nevertheless, their pikes and purple capes and plumes parted, and Michael and Gabriel made ready to enter the Inner Room.

Light spilled out from the cyclopean tower doors as the two Guardians slung their shields and worked the levers and gears. The rumbling of their massive weight moving over the polished glass tiles was the air being displaced as the light of what awaited inside bathed everything it touched. The air would always crackle as the light escaped. Without the meditation of the Steps, the unchecked sin in their hearts would burn them to coals. Even for the archangels, stepping into the Inner Room and coming before the presence of the White Throne carried with it a measure of trepidation. The small, still voice of Parakletos, the divine spirit, was louder in there, emanating from the great supernova cathedra engineered by Lucifer.

But still, at times, Michael and Gabriel were more grateful for the presence of the Intercessor. Of His enigmatic ways, they could hardly speak, but He was clothed in flesh and would not overwhelm them with His very essence. Yet despite the swirling mists of light and dancing bits of crackling energy, lightning, and swirling orbs of celestial bodies too numerous to count, Gabriel always felt rejuvenated by those beams. He wished for them now, even as he couldn't help but chuckle at the rigidity of Bellator and Dealleus.

"Sometimes I think you hand pick your cherubim solely for their wooden heads," Gabriel said from his place at the bureau.

Michael's shoulders bobbed, and he arched his back on the cot, trying to stretch the muscles underneath his field plate cuirass. "Stubbornness has its uses," he said around the tug of a proud, mischievous grin, "especially in hard, lean times. Try to relax, Gabe. It's a good plan."

There were to be fourteen. Seven cherubim and six seraphim, paired and dispersed across the Eastern Kingdom. Gabriel didn't like that they were requested so early in the morning and in full panoply; he thought it was too high profile. "I wish you'd bring in your ward."

"I'm leaving him out of it. You said it best: you can't keep an earthquake quiet," Michael reminded him not but an hour ago when they left the Inner Room and receded to the antechamber. "Besides, you know what Parakletos had to say in there." He threw a nod back to the Inner Room as he locked the door. "If the Holy Spirit compels us to take precautions then I'm going to give my angels—and yours— every fighting chance. We don't know what we're dealing with. Maybe it's a Prophecy? Maybe it's another impatient rumbling that's kicked up dust with some more malcontents? We won't know until we find him. And even I have to admit that he has some answering to do for his little temper tantrum at the Coronation."

Gabriel winced at the memory of that, even as the echoes of white light faded from his eyes and he was brought back to the stacks of papers on his impromptu bureau.

"First Lucifer's reaction to Humanity," he began, "then Mealdis and that bloody glyph that I thought we'd never see again, and now we have fourteen of our most trusted officers out there scouring the land for him—in broad daylight, no less. You don't think someone will notice?"

"We have our best angels who could be spared on such short notice looking everywhere even remotely vital. If he's in the west, poking around the Thousand Peaks or Amin Shakush, we'll hear about it. If he's digging up the old overgrown jungles in the Southlands, we'll know. The coastal northern hamlets, the Shores of Caliven to the east, the Stone City of Lorinar in the hinterlands, the event horizon of the Oblivion beyond the west…what more do you want?"

"I want this handled as delicately as possible," Gabriel said sharply. "Especially if you and Father think it's a good idea to reinstate the Benediction Ceremony."

"It's been ages since we've had one," Michael reminded. "We've spent so many eons working on Creation, it's almost become a forgotten tradition. We need something to refocus our core, now that Humanity is revealed and Earth completed. They need it too."

"And how do you think that will go with our Morning Star creating this chaos?"

Michael sat up. He blew the air out of his lungs and scratched his scalp. "Heard from anyone yet?" He looked at his brother through shaggy locks. "Shiranon? Orean? Lantheron?"

Gabriel shook his head at each name until all fourteen were ticked off the list. "You weren't asleep *that* long. Besides, I don't have time to mollycoddle your anxieties." Michael nodded and strode to the door, adjusting his sword belt as he went. "Where are you going?"

"I need coffee," Michael answered as he unlatched the bolts.

"At a time like this?"

"I love you, baby brother," Michael said over his shoulder, "but you make me need coffee." He turned the brass latch of the door handle and pulled. The door crashed into him. In tumbled a tall, lanky cherub, adorned full field plate and chain mail armor. His conical iron helmet was askew above a dark goatee, cobalt eyes ablaze above a toothy grimace. He fumbled over his lance as its lugged warhead clattered on the bronze threshold. "Lantheron!"

"My Patriarch," he gasped, his iron-shod cleats scraping against the gilded tiles.

Michael righted him by the shoulders. "Report, cherub."

The line-fighter saluted. He lifted his posture to attention as Michael rounded him and shut the door. "Sit-rep as follows, my Patriarch: It was my turn to provide overwatch for Keyleas. We were investigating the mines adjacent to Amin Shakush, per your orders. I saw the seraph get accosted, sir. He…." The two archangels eyed him. Under their gaze, Lantheron wavered.

"Cherub," Gabriel began with a tight throat and a stern, sharp squint, "where is Keyleas now?" He rose from the bureau and leaned on stiff arms. "Where is my seraph?"

Empyrean Falling

Chapter VI
"Be sober; be vigilant, for your adversary the devil is a roaring lion seeking whom he may devour."
—1st Peter 5:8

    Most of the day was spent flying for Amin Shakush. As the crow flies, the archangels could cover great distances at speed. Their velocity was hamstrung by having a lesser angel in tow, so Gabriel used a glyph. The sun was waning by the time they reached the Thousand Peaks.

    Lantheron crashed to iron-copped knees when they lighted onto the eastern side of the Valley. His cleated boots proved worth their weight as they bit into the soft turf. Before them sprawled a towering craggy sierra of the Thousand Peaks. Michael touched down in a crevasse and immediately crouched into craggy concealment. He furled his wings. Gabriel haphazardly landed beside him in full view. His archangelic brother grabbed him by the feathery hollow bones and yanked him behind the rocky formation next to an old oxcart trail that led up through the mountains and into the Valley mines.

    "What are you doing?" he snapped, his voice echoing in the rocks. "Time is of the essence, and it's my angel down there."

    Michael raised a finger to his lips, eyes turned to squinting luminous slits. "Have you learned nothing?" He drew Virtue from its sheath. Gabriel grunted as Michael pulled a gut hook knife from the lip of his plate mail cuirass and handed it to his brother.

Lantheron was on Michael's flank in a heartbeat, his lugged war lance at the ready.

"Follow my lead," Michael said. "Stay low and stay quiet."

They crawled up through the crevasse, sticking to the shadows of the rocky cover which flanked the pass as it wound deeper up into the mountains. Gabriel ground his teeth at the agonizing slowness. Keyleas was a seraph. He knew that at their pace, by the time they reached the Valley mines, it would be dark. Still, despite Michael's martial prowess, he felt a paranoid burden press against him.

"Michael..." Gabriel whispered, scanning the tall flanks.

"I know," the Cherubim Patriarch replied through a grimace. "I feel it too."

They were not alone. Farther into the Thousand Peaks and at a higher vantage, a solitary figure slithered over the sunbaked rocks. No matter what trick Michael employed to conceal their advance or how softly the three of them tread, the lone observer plotted their course with astute precision. He watched them for the better part of two hours before realizing what must be done. It was all too easy for someone like him. His work was swift, silent and unmatched.

Gabriel noticed a shift in the warm summer air as they crept along. He felt the humidity shift. The sweat soaked his garments. There was a noise from the earth, and the heavens answered. He looked up to the sky and shielded his eyes from the setting sun to see storm clouds fomenting ahead. They moved east with near preternatural speed. By the time the thunder was more distinct, winds funneled through the pass, channeled by the high mountain walls. They were nearly through the mountains, but Gabriel knew those clouds; seraphim had to navigate the air with adroit swiftness. It would not be long before the rain was pelting them.

By the time they were cresting the mountain and readying to descend into the Valley proper, they were contending with mudslides and howling gusts.

Empyrean Falling

"I know this warlike handiwork is your milieu," Gabriel shouted over the inclement weather, "but maybe we can use this storm as cover to move faster?"

Michael scowled at him through the rain and took a drink from a small hip flask he kept in his trouser pocket. "If this is all I'm good at then let me do it my way." He put the flask away and peered into the gale buffeted Valley, searching for the mines. "And it's 'concealment,' not 'cover.'"

Gabriel ignored the pedantry and rested in the lone solace that at least the paranoia of being watched was gone. Lantheron was wise enough to keep his mouth shut throughout their ordeal.

And less than a league beyond them, deep in the innards of the mines, Mazerrel's cadre of teamsters worked tirelessly. The thunder rolled overhead, miles above their position. Even that far down in the sultry stinking claustrophobia of the mines, they startled at the hammering crack of static electricity, jumping amidst their tireless work. Mazerrel wiped his prodigious nose and snarled at the reactions; from his observation post, he could see the entire operation.

"Show off," he growled, grinding the long handle of his hip-slung scimitar.

Lucifer chuckled next to him. "Tempest is doing his part. We need noise pollution. And if I know my brother, he's overthinking the tactical advantage of it now, talking himself out of exploiting the storm or flying over it, expecting that whoever conjured it wants him to do that. So, you see, my dear Mazerrel, either way, we win."

As if to prove his point, the angels under Mazerrel's command engineered another blast into the cordoned-off walls of ore. The cavern shook, and dirt fell around them as precious metals were exposed by the expertly crafted explosions. The cacophony subsided, and the symphony of movement began anew as the laborers plucked their prizes from the rubble.

Mazerrel directed his subordinates and Lucifer inspected the procured metals when Tempest manifested before them. The torchlight and braziers made a dance of shadows that allowed him to nearly sneak up on his Grand Patriarch. But Mazerrel smelled him coming; the dank, sickly sweet stink of rain and sweat preceded the serpentine assassin down the mineshaft and into their hollowed out, orange-lit cavern.

    Lucifer held a skull-sized chunk of deep black metal up to his gleaming countenance. In his other hand, he ignited a preternatural fire and held it to the ore, revealing its jagged surface to his purifying titian inspection. "What do you have for me?"

    "Company," Tempest responded in a barely audible hiss.

    Lucifer smirked. "How ominous." He sighed and doused the fire in his hand before placing the metal back in its cart. "Show me."

    Tempest led him up the mineshaft. It opened onto a grotto flanked by a couple of coal-simmering braziers. The effluvium further obscured Tempest's silhouette in the setting sun. Lucifer was impressed by the concentration required to track him. They halted at the shadowy mouth of the grotto. Tempest silently pointed up to the untouched grassy rim of the mining complex. There skulked three tiny figures, vying desperately for stealth in the waning light. The storm showed no signs of subsiding, but they remained undeterred.

    "Have Mazerrel wrap things up below," Lucifer ordered. "Then tell Mealdis to fetch our guest. When you're done, use your talents and conjure up another storm; flood this location." The slender, silent cherub nodded and slinked back into the mineshaft. "And Tempest," Lucifer added. The angel turned to the archangel. "You've done good work here. Thank you."

    On the outer rim of the mines, Michael belly-crawled up to the grassy edge overlooking the intricate network of tunnels and rails, littered with chunks of gravel. Gabriel silently moved into position behind an oxcart some meters away and surveilled the mines below. Piles of dirt and rock were turned to ruddy mounds under the increasing duress of the storm. Wooden planks were starting to dislodge and drift in the runnels of rainwater. The increasing chaos made Gabriel nervous. Lightning strobed the scene, and thunder pealed until his teeth rattled. For the first time since the inception of Creation, he was relieved to have Michael present.

    He never heard the sword draw but in a flash of light, he glimpsed the reflection of Virtue's curved steel in Michael's calloused hand. Even concealed in the shadows, he felt reinforced by the bolstering sight. Nevertheless, his smooth palm reflexively gripped the gut hook knife as he weighed their next move. There was another lightning strike and suddenly Michael was at his flank.

"We can cover more ground if we split up," Gabriel said under the torrential downpour.

"If I were him and I was having another *episode*," Michael replied, "I'd love nothing more. I'd just pick us off one by one." He scanned the immediate area. "We can't ingress here; it's too obvious. We'll maneuver around to the flats on the western edge."

"It'll take an hour to circumvent this mine," Gabriel argued.

"What has happened, has happened; another hour won't make a difference," his brother replied, already sheathing his sword and turning south. "We'll gain an element of surprise." He threw a signaling gesture with his left hand and in moments Lantheron was in the stormy air and flying low on the soggy fields, headed southeast with the wind. Gabriel traced the line-fighter's swift trajectory by the rhythmic punctuations of rainwater flinging from his pumping wings.

The moved deeper around the mines, skimming the surface in flight when they could. Halfway through their trek, the thunderclaps grew so intense, they felt the turf beneath them reverberate. Gabriel's teeth rattled; he wondered why this kind of preternatural fury had been unleashed at such an inopportune time. His hackles rose; he knew he could not solely blame it on the physics of static electricity.

Their descent into the mines was an incautious affair. Lucifer watched them with a tight smile as they crept down the rocky outcroppings and blasted walls of raw earth. He admired his brother's prowess but found himself shaking his head with a twinge of pathos. He leaned casually into the mouth of the grotto, arms crossed and hand stroking his ginger-haired chin. With a sigh he sprung from his observation point and made his way out into the open air of the mine's central hub, easily navigating the rising floodplains as he set to work on the night's final labors.

Chapter VII
"For even his own brothers did not believe him."
—John 7:5

    Michael had long since learned that fear can be a powerful stimulus. It excited his fast twitch muscles and heightened his senses. His mind worked faster. His spirit came alive. It wasn't without its cost, as all things have a price, but whenever the coals of his soul needed stoking, great lapping flames of bonfires could be kicked up within him from the embracement of fear. He had learned to be grateful for it.

    He felt afraid in the yawning dugout of the mining complex. The stars were masked by storm clouds. Visibility was limited to several meters. But he was grateful for the mud that caked his armor in a camouflage of brown and grey. Gabriel was with him, which helped bear the mental burden of confronting Lucifer. And Lantheron was an extra set of eyes with a stern education in martial skills. But he knew it would not be enough. They could have a legion in the Valley, and it would make little difference. He ran the numbers as the three of them searched.

"Maybe we should send Lantheron to fetch Melphax," Gabriel proffered in a hushed tone. "Amin Shakush is a stone's throw away; he could provide aid if things go sour."

Michael moved around a bank of giant wooden cranes, Virtue unsheathed. "We could have Melphax and his entire cadre of Forty Hammers, a battalion of Temple Guardians, my own personal retinue of Cognoscenti, and your best heavy cavalry; it still would be paper scraps in the wind." He turned to Gabriel. "And you know it."

"He could at least provide testimony," Gabriel said. "And extra eyes for Keyleas."

Michael sighed as he watched his brother grip the gut hook knife, his burning yellow eyes waxing in the frantic search. He looked like a drowned pup in the rain. Finally, he nodded and turned to a rocky switchback a score of meters away. "Lantheron," he called. The cherub sprouted his wings and leapt down to his position. "Fly to The Iron Fortress of Amin Shakush. Find General Melphax, The Pillar of Iron, and have him muster a contingent of his best angels. I want seraphim and cherubim alike. Tell him the mines are flooding; we need swimmers. Have them make haste for our position. The rendezvous point is the northwest corner. He has security clearance; spare no detail. Got it?"

Lantheron nodded, saluted and bolted back into the air. Michael immediately turned back and plunged further into the open aired work site, awash in rising pools and floating detritus. He took ten swift steps with Gabriel on his heels when a crash from above that wasn't thunder snapped his attention overhead.

He spun, sword wielding at the ready, to see Lantheron entangled with another form and plummeting for the ground. They splashed into a bog of floating gravel a hundred meters away. He raced to their position. Gabriel shouted after him, quick on his heels.

A figure sloshed its way to the muddy edge and clambered free of the muck. Michael saw him: a plump, short-winged figure with big ears and small, chubby hands. In one of those hands, Michael espied a lightning-glinted cubit of steel. A dagger. He instinctively rushed in with Virtue wheeling in preparation. There was another shout from a familiar tenor and his sword came down only to be intercepted by the gut hook knife.

Empyrean Falling

"Michael, no!" Gabriel cried, blocking his strike with acute velocity. "That's Mealdis!"

The Cherubim Archangel took one look at the fleeing seraph and another at the bog into which they had plunged. "Fine," he said, sheathing Virtue. "Catch him. Lantheron is still in there." He dove into the murky water while Gabriel hesitated. By the time he pulled his cherub free, the Seraphim Archon was chasing after Mealdis. Michael inspected Lantheron for injuries.

"He just knocked the wind out of me," the line-fighter choked as he gurgled up mud water on his hands and knees. "I'll be good to go. Just give me a beat." He sat on his haunches with his arms resting on his knees, head hanging in a coughing fit.

Michael patted him on his steel shoulder pauldron, handed him back his war lance, and went after his brother. He sprouted his wings and shot like a bolt across the flooding terrain. Less than a minute later, he found Gabriel standing in the open facing a freshly lit bonfire made from the surrounding mining materiel. His mouth opened to admonish his brother as he landed behind him…until his burning sapphire eyes fell upon it.

Gabriel wasn't transfixed by the blaze; he was struck by what was in it. A decapitated body cooked in the flames, tied and slouched against a beam. Acrid smoke rose to steam the stormy air around it. And crouched in front of the bonfire was Mealdis, bloodied dagger in-hand and holding something round.

Gabriel recognized the square, pronounced, angular jaw, and the cascade of boltered, close cropped blonde hair above lifeless black cavities where the golden eyes of Keyleas once shone. The Seraphim Archon stared at the severed head of his angel before slowly gaining cogency and lifting his gaze to the plump messenger holding it.

Mealdis' chest heaved, and he had a crazed look in his eyes. The blood of his fellow seraphic brother was streaked across his face. He bared his teeth at his archangel.

"God save us," Gabriel exhaled as he took in the grisly scene.

"Mealdis," Michael barked, "what in the Burning Hells have you done!"

Empyrean Falling

"Salvation is in the fire," the seraph shrieked. "Behold, my sacrifice!" He held Keyleas' head aloft and pierced it with the dagger. "By our blood, we're fallen into flames. By our ashes, we rise anew! We are the Phoenix Empyrean!" The two archangels stared at him, aghast. Mealdis reared back to launch the head off the dagger. His throw was cut short by a lugged war lance burying itself in his chest. He hurtled back into the bonfire, screeching, as Lantheron soared in.

"He was screaming that madness when we collided, Patriarch," the cherub reported after landing, heaving with his hands on his knees.

Michael tried to scan the surroundings, but he couldn't tear his attention away from the horrific pyre before him. The screaming continued as Mealdis roasted and bled. Gabriel shook free of the morbid trance that gripped him and moved to save his seraph. Suddenly, Michael intervened and gripped him by the hem of his garment.

"Let go of me, Michael! This is a seraphic affair now!"

"Look," Michael hissed and pointed with his sword.

Out from around the edge of the pyre strode a statuesque, perfect form. A walking, living amalgamation of diamond, flesh and Empyreal fire. He knelt before a writhing Mealdis, orange mane lost in the firelight. With a casual outstretched hand, he touched the seraph. The anguished cacophony ceased. Overhead, the storm abated. But the fire continued. Only the sound of their breathing, the thundering in their hearts, and the crackling of the flames filled the night as the pyre fed on flesh and pulp.

"A shame," the figure said. He plucked the lance from Mealdis' corpse and sauntered from the pyre. In the dance of light and shadows, the archangels recognized their brother.

"That's murder, Morning Star," Gabriel spat hotly.

Lucifer furrowed his brow as he began to cover the distance between them. "He was mortally wounded, Gabriel, thanks to your meddlesome exploits. What was I supposed to do for an angel turned to a pig on a spit?"

Gabriel took a step, chest rising in anger.

Empyrean Falling

Michael held him at bay. "His life wasn't yours to command," the Cherubim Archangel rebuked.

"Since when?" Lucifer rejoined with a shrug. "Since I was Emperor of the West? Since the Exodus? Since the founding of Zion and the Eastern Kingdom? How many have given up their lives to our wayward search for meaning? For our journey back home? So many, it's become a dream. So many lives, so many eons, so many dreams of what once was that now we don't even know how to describe what we've lost. I poured my heart and soul into the White Throne, hoping it would link us to the Empyrean, that it would bring Father back. But the last time He showed His power was when He smote the Western Empire. Is that what it takes, a cataclysmic tragedy where millions of our brothers die at the hands of a cosmic sadist masquerading as a God-child? Are we not toys to be discarded for our inerrant sin?"

"Oh, for God's sake, this again," Gabriel said. "You are being a fool, and a blasphemous one at that. We have the Holy Spirit of Father, Parakletos, to—"

"Ah yes," Lucifer said, "a small still voice to whisper in our ears or roar in our guts."

"And a Son to walk among us," Michael added cautiously. "Lest you forget."

"Oh, how could I forget a version of flesh and blood, wholly unremarkable in appearance, void of wings, and now revealed as the precursor manifestation of His favorite new pets: Humanity." Lucifer sneered at his own words. "Yes, a good bit of conditioning for our supplanting that was. Even I could not have dreamed up something more insidious."

"So, this is your answer?" Michael asked. "Look at what you've wrought."

"This is a tragic misstep," Lucifer admitted ruefully, tilting his brow to the burning corpses. "I'd hoped to avoid this sort of thing. So, much has been lost already." He shook his head. "But eggs for omelets, Lion of God." His ivory countenance turned hard. "If this is how He made us, then this is what we have to work with."

"A case for catastrophe?" Michael shot back.

Empyrean Falling

"Without the storm," Lucifer said, drawing up to them, "the lightning does not strike. The undergrowth is not burned. And the forest is starved for nutrients. Are we to languish from lack of pruning? Are we to feed upon ourselves? Or worse, be cast aside in favor of a new? To grow only to wither on the vine, as a frostbitten fruit neglected by the farmer? I have news for you, little brothers, the winter came long ago. We are playthings to a cosmic sadist."

"You are an instrument of chaos," Michael said.

Lucifer shook his head. "I'm a force for change. What did we do before the Advent of Creation? You led us in warlike preparation." He regarded Lantheron's lance. With a brace of fingers, he touched the whetted steel edge. "After all we've built, after all we've prepared in mind, body, spirit and structure, He still hides His face from us." With a simple gesture, he bent the haft until it snapped. "I won't allow it. I love our angelic host too much for that."

Michael raised Virtue and pointed its tip at Lucifer's chest. "You're coming back to Zion to stand trial for sedition and murder."

Lucifer laughed and pressed his sternum ever so slightly against the pointed tip. "I won't answer to a Council of Twelve Elders who busy themselves with bureaucracy."

Michael steeled his resolve. "Then you'll answer to us for the dishonor you've brought upon the Three." With a deep and abiding frown, Lucifer shook his head. "Then you'll answer to God for your faithlessness."

"I'm afraid I won't do that either, little lion brother of mine."

In a flash, Lucifer swatted Virtue away with the lance head and swung the broken haft, knocking the knife out of Gabriel's grasp. Faster than their luminous archangelic eyes could detect, a burst of flame erupted from the red signet ring on his hand. It smacked into Michael's face. The fireball engulfed his head before he could react.

Gabriel dove for the mud. Somewhere behind them, Lantheron scrambled for cover. Michael dropped to his knees, clutching his scorched face. Ears ringing and eyes blinded, when Gabriel recovered his senses, Lucifer was gone.

Empyrean Falling

Chapter IIX

"As the cold of snow in the time of harvest, so is a faithful messenger to them that sent him: for he refresheth the soul of his masters."
—Proverbs 25:13

    The Thousand Peaks stretched before him, an endless sierra of ice-capped peaks and craggy, sprawling mountainsides. Beneath him was the Valley. The sun was setting, its blazing orange orb washing the range in a rich purple hue. He drank in the scenery with a deep, satisfying breath. He closed his luminous eyes and smiled as the zephyrs blew across his face. The allure and majesty of the Western Empire were carried in those winds, full of lavenders and oils and the smoke of their endeavors' foundries, far off under the setting sun. It filled him with an exquisite dread that he couldn't quite place but elicited a stirring deep in his bones.

    He felt the presence of another land on the rocky outcropping behind him. Judging by his sure footing and the measured ease of his breathing, he knew exactly who it was.

    "Look how our stars twinkle, brother," he said from behind. His voice was like silk-swaddled steel. The archangel opened his eyes and surveyed the Western Empire's metropolis coming to eventide life, a mirror of the constellations. "Hey, Michael, are you dreaming?"

    "Yes," he said with a content nod, "I am, Lucifer."

Empyrean Falling

There was a laugh from the First Born that spilled up into the cool summer air of the Thousand Peaks. He strolled up to Michael's side and wrapped an arm around him. Michael returned the gesture in kind. His dread evaporated before the surefire embrace of his older brother. So many labored under him, it was comforting having one who remained above.

There was a glint of something red on his left. He looked over to see the new ruby signet ring on Lucifer's left index finger. With a diamond-and-onyx band that shimmered like an oily prism, the ruby gleamed in the harsh, falling dusk light. It aggressively radiated the light around it, like it was trying to capture every photon before magnifying it back tenfold.

"Gabriel made you that."

"Yes," Lucifer replied, "I have many gifts."

Michael heard a twinge of sadness in his illustrious voice. He was lulled by the glow of the ring. It pulsed and hummed, angry at the waning titian rays.

"You are the Morning Star now," Michael said. "You must be very happy."

"Come on!" Lucifer said suddenly and sprouted his gleaming wings. He leapt into the air and shot westward. "If we hurry, we can catch it!"

Michael laughed and scrambled haphazardly into the air. In moments, he was fast on Lucifer's heels. The eldest archangel turned back and grinned as his wings pumped furiously.

"You think you'll beat me this time, little brother?" he called.

"The lion is fast when he wants to be!" Michael retorted through his own grin.

Lucifer threw his head back and laughed. It warmed Michael's heart to see his brother free and full of joy. His burdens were so great these days. Yet he always rose to the occasion.

A month before, he'd saved thousands of Gabriel's seraphim when a capstone came unstrung and threatened to crush them. Lucifer intercepted it in freefall, dragging it up through the air before placing it singlehandedly on the seraphic pyramid. It was the largest structure they had ever devised. Gabriel wept with thanks. The angelic host cheered his name. Everyone looked up to him as he peeled the capstone's shadow away from their doomed chimerical eyes, like the star that heralds the dawn. The ceremony to honor him was but a foregone conclusion.

Now they raced for the sunset. The Valley was but a speck at their backs. In a heartbeat, they had transited the Thousand Peaks and were overtaking the Western Empire. The great elaborate metropolis sprawled beneath them, a near rival for the Thousand Peaks in size and scope. The towers and ziggurats reached into the clouds, with smokestacks billowing their grey issue around mighty domes and cyclopean structures of strange, brutish, infinitely intricate architecture. Whole sides of buildings glowed in manufactured light teamed with facings of precious metals: sapphires, emeralds, garnets, diamonds, amethysts, even the occasional mercury, defying the very forces of gravity. Through these complex feats of engineering snaked the winding flow of rivers and tributaries, feeding the hanging gardens and providing sanitation and clean water for the angelic host as they labored in their exploits below.

It was a marvel to behold, but it wasn't enough to slow them down. They hailed them with cheers that fell on deaf ears.

Lucifer flapped his wings harder, propelling him with even greater velocity. The Western Empire receded from them. Before long, it was nothing more than a thin bar of light on the horizon. And still, the sun fell, even as they drew upon the western edge of the Lower Realm and the translucent inky black edge of the Oblivion bordering it. They had never gone this far together before. Michael reminded him of this, but Lucifer just laughed. The great black, roiling smaze of the Oblivion's edge loomed closer, a far-reaching oozing, oscillating wall of impenetrable inter-dimensional chaos. The sun had vanished behind it. All Michael could see was the boundary of their world, and his eldest brother blithely racing for it.

He pumped his wings harder than ever. Each herculean thrust got him a brace of inches closer until at last, he was abreast of his older brother. Michael reached out for Lucifer's left hand. He strained with every fiber of muscle, teeth grinding in the clinch. He stretched his arm and roared, but it was drowned out by Lucifer's laughter as he sped up. In a final desperate grasp, Michael managed to touch the cuffed hem of Lucifer's ivory garment. The newly minted Morning Star twirled and crashed into him.

The two plummeted with meteoric velocity towards the earth. Michael fought his brother's grasp as the wind whipped dark locks into his sapphire eyes, obscuring the vision of his brother. He could hear the laughter and feel the strength of his sibling. The ground rushed to meet them. Their impact was meteoric. Somehow, he did not die. They rolled across the plush green grass until the scenery bled into the inky black void of the Oblivion.

Michael gathered his feet under him and stood. He gasped for air, nursing a wounded right hand. Around him was only darkness. Oppressive, absorbent of sound and thought, vacant of any defining features, the Oblivion was a dangerous place to be without proper navigation tools. He looked around the impenetrable nothing.

"Where did you go?" he called around him, but the void swallowed his voice. "Lucifer! We shouldn't be here! You know Father would not want it!"

A dark figure exploded before him and he felt a tremendously powerful weight of substance bowl him over. He rolled onto the ethereal plane, sinking a bit into the incorporeal nightmare of the Oblivion. It was too easy to get lost there; angels never returned. Michael did not think that archangels would fare much better.

Still, he grappled. The thing had talons. It pierced his shoulders bloody as it gripped him. The weight of its body held him down, knees cracking his ribs and feet raking his shins. Michael failed to get a good look at it, for the thing seemed to blend in with the Oblivion. But he saw the horns silhouette against the nothing, offset by fiery white eyes casting strange and eerie shadows. It roared. Its mouth opened and fire spilled from its maw of jagged fangs and slathering gore. Somewhere deep inside, Michael screamed, but it never issued forth. His training fled under the assailant's duress and he froze.

"Look what He did to me!" the monstrous creature bellowed. His breath was sulfur. "Look what He did to *us*!" His form was void and without meaning.

Empyrean Falling

He saw the face of the thing, cascaded against the Oblivion's black in a wash of fire and blood from its mouth and the white glow of its eyes. Michael turned from what he knew and saw his right shoulder bleeding under the piercing of the thing's talons. And above the seeping blood, he saw the ruby signet ring on the thing's index finger.

"The Dragon!" Michael yelled…

…His eyes opened. He felt the substance of reality. The Oblivion was gone. Lucifer was gone. That thing was gone. In their place was a large bed, sweat-soaked sheets, and the sharp sting of pain. He groaned as cogency returned. In his grimace, he saw shapes move. The nightmare had passed.

Lantheron bolted from his chair at the foot of the bed and rounded to Michael's side. He steadied his archangel with a gentle press of his palms against his shoulders.

"He's awake!" Lantheron called out. He assessed his archangel as best as he could, given his minimal medical training. "Easy, my Patriarch." Michael struggled to gain his bearings. He threw Lantheron's grip off him with preternatural ease. The pain made it difficult to concentrate. The door to the bedchambers flung open. "Chief Surgeon Arkiel is here."

Michael felt the angel push past Lantheron and dive in with palpating hands and instruments. "Before you ask…" Michael heard the familiar voice say, "it's worse than it feels." As if knowing that would seem wrong to his ears, the angel elaborated, "But you'll live."

"Where am I?" Michael growled in frustrated, confused agony.

"Amin Shakush," the Chief Surgeon replied. "General Melphax was kind enough to lend us his personal quarters."

"The Pillar of Iron is a generous lord of his mountain," Lantheron confirmed.

Arkiel regarded him before turning his attention back to Michael. "Yes, well, Gabriel reached me early this morning; interrupted my breakfast. He looked rough, said you had an accident in the Valley. Some explosion in the mines? I don't know. Said Lantheron had moved you here. Truth be told, the doctors of the Iron Fortress are a bit beneath your stately station."

"Thank you for coming, Arkiel," Michael finally managed.

"Don't thank me yet," he replied, shaking his head with a sly grin. "You're lucky to be alive, though the pain will make you question that once what I gave you wears off. You're certainly not going to be as pretty as you were, but that's not saying much either."

"Where's my brother?" Michael asked, ignoring the gallows-humored barb. He watched Arkiel shrug as he donned a mask and retrieved a cantaloupe-sized package of sterile gauze from the medical bag at his boots.

"Unlike you, your brother didn't get a wild hair and decide to change his career to 'failed fire-eater,'" Arkiel said in a muffled, dark-humored tone. "To put it bluntly, he's not my patient so I have no idea. Now lie still while I soak these in a salve and apply them to your head. Close your eyes and bite down on this brace of tubes. You'll eat and breathe through these for the next few weeks."

Michael resisted, gripping Arkiel's wrist as he held the tubes. "We have a Benediction Ceremony to plan, Chief Surgeon. I can't be laid up for weeks."

Arkiel looked down at his arrested wrist. "I see. Haven't had one of those since before the Creation." There was a moment of calculation in his sharp features. He shrugged and looked back up at Michael. "Well, truth be told, I don't care. If your skin gets infected, you won't live long enough to miss the Benediction so, while I'll do my best to expedite things, I suggest you stop fighting me."

After a moment, Michael's grip relaxed and he allowed Arkiel to apply the sodden bandages to his head. He was surprised that there was no tangled press of matted hair, only the cool compress strips of cloth against his burning skin. When the job was complete, his head was fully wrapped. Arkiel gave him some small instructions and departed. Michael thanked him on his way out, but he was sure the Chief Surgeon never acknowledged it. When he heard the door closed, he waited for a trice.

"Lantheron," the archangel said softly, "it looks like your years spent in calligraphy and artwork have paid off, judging by the precise flick of your wrist that lance throw provided. I must eat a bit of crow on that one. Are we alone?" His line-fighter nodded. "Where is he?" Michael asked in a softer tone. "What happened?"

Empyrean Falling

Lantheron drew the chair as close to Michael's bedside as possible. "After you were hit, we dove for cover. By the time my ears stopped ringing, I could hear Archangel Gabriel calling my name. He told me to bring you here, to General Melphax's attention at once, while he went back to Zion and fetched Chief Surgeon Arkiel. Lieutenant Deledrosse, General Melphax's second aide-de-camp, admitted us immediately. He was very good, for a seraph."

"Melphax knows the value of secrets," Michael confessed. "And Gabriel was smart to do this by early morning; it wouldn't arouse suspicion, and everyone would still be chasing the hair of the dog from the night before. Any word from him since? What time is it? What day is it?"

"Same day," Lantheron said. "Tuesday. Late evening. Chief Surgeon Arkiel made all haste here, judging by the state of his arrival. I've not seen Archangel Gabriel yet, though General Melphax said he would handle it."

Michael nodded, calculating. "Send word to Melphax that I'm cogent. No doubt Gabriel got himself cleaned up, collapsed from exhaustion, and is now busy keeping up appearances in Zion. Lucifer he can blame on a lark. Me he can blame on recklessness. But eventually, the questions will make for a pressure cooker. I'll need help relocating back to my home." He reached out and found Lantheron's shoulder pauldron. "You've been an invaluable help, Lantheron. I'll have to see about putting you in for a promotion."

"I appreciate that, my Patriarch—thank you—but what are we going to do?"

"Keep confidence for now, soldier," Michael ordered. "At least until we know what we're dealing with. The things that you've seen, no one can know."

"Understood," Lantheron hesitated. "Do I need to take care of the evidence?"

Michael shook his wrapped head. "Put it in your report as an accidental explosion. Keep Lucifer out of it. We'll call it a drunken dispute turned to lethal madness between two seraphim. Gabriel won't like it because of the pall it'll put on his choir, but I need as few questions as possible right now. That should cover things on your end.

Report back to your legion with my compliments to Commander Gilgamesh. Put in for personal leave if you need to; I'll vouch for it. Melphax and I will take care of the rest."

Lantheron saluted and made to leave. At the door, he turned. "What happened to him?"

Michael sighed and massaged his linen-covered temples. "Gratitude requires humility, Lantheron, and humility is the first step of wisdom. I think too long we've turned a blind eye to the arrogant resentment of self-pity."

Empyrean Falling

Chapter IX
"...the storm subsided, and all was calm."
—Luke 8:24

The weekend came on swiftly. In Zion, things began to relax. The flood of activity had ebbed post-Creation Coronation and, in the vacancy, a lethargy threatened to take hold. Everyone felt the absence of urgency and purpose. Some of the more astute angels took up arms again and resumed their martial training, as they had all those millennia ago. Many languished, accentuated by the lack of archangelic presence.

Gabriel took full advantage of the lull. With their collective guards down, he made a clandestine trip to the Great Library of Carthanos. Situated in the northeastern portion of the Holy City proper, it was a sprawling seventy-story complex of stone archways, heartwood doors, sigil banners, and deep, cavernous recesses of tomes, relics and artifacts. Such a repository of knowledge would become a liability if left unattended. They had lost enough time already; he was determined to do something while Michael laid in bed looking like a linen-wrapped radish.

Empyrean Falling

Accompanied by the Chief Librarian Ma'igwa, Gabriel plunged deep into the bowels of Carthanos. By his last count, they were somewhere near the thirty-fifth level. Equidistant from the air and land and furnished with plush carpets, paintings, recreational facilities, and commons areas, Gabriel judged it was a floor reserved mostly for librarian quarters. He was grateful for the sumptuous, low-lit furniture and elegant, elaborate decorations; they made for a nice cozy place to slink about his business.

"Are you sure I can't get you some tea?" Ma'igwa asked as they drew upon a topaz-encrusted pair of doors leading to a neglected wing of the floor. "The harvest was impressive this year, despite the Cognoscenti ransacking our stores as part of their training regimen."

Gabriel chuckled a bit at the bitter tone in the angel's voice. "Michael's Cognoscenti are good at what they do, Ma'igwa, you'll have to give them that." The Chief Librarian huffed, as he often did. He was a massive angel, especially for a seraph. Head and shoulders taller than Gabriel, his pure muscled bulk loomed as they took the winding corridor. With a crop of curly black hair ringing his head and a jet-black handlebar mustache accentuating a perpetual frown, he thundered down the hallway, his shadow engulfing Gabriel as they walked. His brown suede sleeveless tunic was already starting to sweat, which Gabriel had chalked up to anxiety; the Chief Librarian was always concerned with keeping up appearances.

"Still," Gabriel added, "it's good to see anyone try to get back into the swing of things."

"To tell the truth, my Archon," Ma'igwa said, "we were happy to leave the Prophecy of the Dragon behind us when Father unveiled Creation. That enterprise suited us. This relaying of messages and loosing of arrows and cavalry business is not our strong suit. We prefer administration, music, design, cerebral pursuits, even artwork. Not this brute's work."

"Mm-hmm," Gabriel susurrated. "And to quote my older brothers..." He paused and turned back to face Ma'igwa, "that is why we do it, Chief Librarian. In all your years, have you never contemplated why I was given the title of 'Archon' and why my older brother was named 'Patriarch'? It's a reversal; Archon means 'leader,' yes, but it also means 'war-leader.' I'm no warrior. Father knew that.

Empyrean Falling

Just like He knew Michael wasn't the most paternal of tribal leaders. These honorifics are not mere tokens of prestige; they highlight our deficiencies. They illuminate what we must overcome, that we might become whole. It is only through the pursuit of what we lack that we become holy." He turned back to a conical heartwood door and counted to himself. "This is the one," he said with a point.

Ma'igwa stepped forward and produced a jangling silver key ring. He thumbed to the right key. "At least we don't chalk up mere restlessness to the self-prescribed virtue of discipline," he griped as he turned the lock. "We seraphim have a reputation to uphold."

The door opened. Inside was a warmly lit ornate study choked with leather wingbacks and carved bookcases. At its flanks were two black-bricked hearths. Gabriel observed them each in turn. "I remember when Master Carthanos built this Library," he said, running his hands along the seams of the bricks. "He was far smarter than I."

"May he rest in the Empyrean," Ma'igwa said with a dip of his brow, more out of duty than anything else. But it was this action which inadvertently blinded him to cranking of gears and the sound of a hatch mechanically receding from the floor. Ma'igwa turned in shock to see a panel on the carpeted floor replaced by a recessed steel platform several cubits across and wide. "How did you…?"

"No time." Gabriel rushed over to the platform. "Come."

Ma'igwa was there and in seconds the gears were again grinding, the platform steadily lowering. When they were twenty cubits down, the floor replaced itself and returned to its normal level over their heads. The light vanished and they descended. When their descent stopped and Gabriel stepped off, the air was cool and wet with a salty aftertaste.

"I've been your faithful servant for seventeen centuries and I've never…"

Gabriel smiled as he produced a small bit of flint from his emerald tunic and lit a small torch kept in a wall sconce. "Yes, and your service has been impeccable. But secrets within secrets."

"Who else knows about this?"

"No one except the Three and the one who designed it, now gone. And now you." Gabriel proceeded down the low granite corridor. There were antechambers on either side as it stretched into fathomless shadows. Covering each entrance was a cloth banner. The Seraphim Archon stopped at one with an all too familiar horned sigil on it. He pulled the draped cloth back and entered. Inside, the torchlight revealed shelves with rows upon rows of old musty objects of various shapes and sizes, all stacked and cataloged. He delved deeper until coming upon a stack of oversized codices. He handed the torch to Ma'igwa and handled several before plucking one from its moldy alcove. He raised it aloft and blew the dust off it.

It was the size of his torso with a brass spine and thick, leather-bound wooden covers. It looked unremarkable to Ma'igwa in the torchlight, but his gobsmacked senses were already overloaded by the simple existence of the place.

"Bring the light closer," Gabriel ordered. The tawny flicker waxed over him as the seraph did as he was commanded. "This, Chief Librarian, is the Tome of Descendance. There are thirteen such artifacts, all from the fallen Empire of the West. We took them with us during the Exile, in fear that they were too dangerous to leave behind and too powerful to be destroyed. This is the true heart of this place, Ma'igwa; all your labors are for the sake of the arcane knowledge contained in these catacombs."

Ma'igwa crossed his massive, bare arms. "I don't understand."

Gabriel finished inspecting the ancient book, then turned to him. "Before we were invited to aid our Lord in Creation," the archangel explained, "God allowed us to navigate the Oblivion with this. Now that Creation is complete and the way to Earth is closed, this is the only way to reach that corporeal plane." He looked up at Ma'igwa. "If this were to fall into the wrong hands, it would spell doom for Humanity. Things are changing here. I know you feel it too. They must be protected at all costs."

At last, the Chief Librarian understood. "If they veil were to ever be torn away…."

"Ma'igwa, I have an assignment for you."

Chapter X

"Your brothers, your own family—even they have betrayed you; they raise a loud cry against you. Do not trust them, though they speak well of you."
—Jeremiah 12:6

Tempest had spent hours in the shadow of the awning outside Melphax's bedchambers, pressed against the iron wall of Amin Shakush, listening. He had let Lantheron go. He did not interfere with Melphax. Michael he would keep undisturbed and un-alerted.

By the time he returned to Lucifer's mansion, days had passed. Mazerrel and his cohorts were almost finished unloading their haul from the mines. Tempest passed his rival's favorite lackey, Linghal, as he entered the foyer. They shared a look in transit before Tempest vanished into one of the many palatial lofts, claiming rest's pursuit.

Linghal was an exceptionally beautiful angel beneath his sugar-loaf great helm. His sharp, angular features always seemed to contour perfectly within a mane of silky black hair that hung to his waist. A part of Mazerrel despised him for it. But the greater part of him loved Linghal for his aptitude and attitude. His actions spoke volumes. He rarely spoke. Mazerrel knew he could rely on the cherub to carry out any mission with ruthless, swift resolve, without question or hesitation. He was a dutiful enforcer.

Empyrean Falling

He needed the angel now more than ever, with his partner Goldruum covering the more delicate matters of explanation and negotiation within their cadre.

"Are we all finally in?" Mazerrel asked them as the crystal doors of Lucifer's mansion closed behind them. They nodded. "Goldruum, summon the rest. We have one last job to do." The angel saluted, his gloved hand snapping up to his black feathered locks before he vanished from the foyer. "Linghal," Mazerrel continued, turning to the fine-looking angel as he stood at attention with his helmet under the crook of an arm, "I'm going to tell you before I say it to the others: We have a difficult one here; I need you prepared. Anyone else would just run their trap instead of doing their job. They will need your persuasion, not the kind that your constellation partner, Goldruum, provides, but what you provide." Linghal nodded.

"The situation is as follows," Mazerrel continued, "our lord wants us to take what is being made for us into the Oblivion." The angel tensed. Mazerrel saw it. His wide brow furrowed as he towered over Linghal. He quickly moved to check his rage. "No one ever said this enterprise would be easy," he warned with a pointed finger. "What we pulled out of the mines is only part of it all; we need people who can brave the dangers of the Oblivion."

Linghal tilted his head like a bird.

"There are forces at work which we hope to harness. If we can successfully meld what we extracted and refined with what lies beyond the western edge of the Lower Realm, then our victory is all but guaranteed. These sleeping fools will never suspect we've employed the naked energies of the Oblivion; they don't suspect a single angel would dare venture back there. But we dare and, because of it, we'll return with primordial forces imbued in these things that no one—except maybe the archangels alone—could stand against. It's as our lord has been saying for some time now: The days of tyrants are numbered."

Linghal was on the balls of his feet. He knew what awaited him and his host: the price that could be paid; the reward that could be gained. The infamy of it all tasted ambrosial.

High above, in a secluded room and thoroughly forgotten about, Tempest listened. His furlough on the island would be short-

Empyrean Falling

lived. The next morning, he was back in Zion, seeing to the reinstatement of his subterfuge corps. His constellation partner, Orean, was there picking up the slack but he had to show face. He led a class on lock-picking. By midday, he was teaching the Cognoscenti how to invade an enemy camp and poison horses. The labor tested his patience most of all. The cherubim scorned him and Orean for their skills. But the mandates of their Patriarch required their tutelage in the arts of stealth. He preferred holding class during the day instead of running war games. It was tougher; he could punish more students.

By nightfall, he'd made his way to Michael's mansion. His true master required information gathering. No one else in their cabal was as adept as he. He was a shadow within shadows, and shadows had a way of listening.

It had been two weeks since Michael's encounter with Lucifer. In that time, no one had reported seeing him. Bereft of options, the Cherubim Patriarch led from his bedchambers. He had spent most of that time sleeping.

Arkiel had loaded him down with a cornucopia of medications but he spurned most of them. Only a paltry collection of teas and the occasional sleeping aid rendered any benefit. He mostly relied upon a mixture of thyme and peppermint, with the rare implementation of willow bark when the pain was too great. It was hard to discern time. Liquor helped dull the senses that screamed in agony. And he often resorted to the syrupy sweet liquid kept on his nightstand.

Michael had resigned himself to the shock and dismay his angels felt whenever he admitted someone into his chambers for an audience or report. He had Arkiel keep his face wrapped to mitigate the risk of infection. Only a pair of tubes protruded from the bandages, to allow for breathing and drinking. The strips of aloe-soaked linen were yellowed with salve, sweat and puss. He was a sorry sight, judging by the halting gaits and stammering introductions his cherubim gave upon entry.

There was a knock at the door.

His body ached as he fought the incumbent atrophy and struggled to rise in bed. Every muscle cried out or cramped. His legs were asleep. The sheets were damp. He fought the bandages to speak, his chapped lips peeling in bloody cracks. "Who goes there?"

"Chief Hammer Arkadia, my Patriarch," came the flinty tenor of Zion's lead blacksmith. There was a pause. "Melphax told me I could find the soggiest onion in Heaven resting on your shoulders. I had to see for myself."

Michael suppressed a laugh. It was a rare luxury these days that his current condition did not afford him. "Enter." He heard the iron knob turn and the oak door open. Arkadia's boots had a gritty thump to them. His apron had a sharp crinkle to it as he saluted. Judging by the sound, Michael determined there was a heavy layer of soot. "You've been busy, Ark."

"Aye, sir," Arkadia replied. "They call it 'slagging off' down at the foundry."

"I didn't suspect my orders to resume their regimens would entail your hammers burning the midnight oil," Michael said guardedly. "I'll have a conversation with Chief Weapons Master Althaziel about the armorers not doing their jobs."

"Sir?"

"By the sound of your state, you've clearly been hard at work," Michael clarified. "I guess my legion commanders have grown lax with their upkeep. Please forgive me, Chief Hammer, I thought I'd chosen and trained better cherubim than that. Their lack of maintenance should not increase your workload." He blindly reached for the tea on his nightstand and maneuvered the cup under his straw. "It won't go unpunished."

"No, sir," Arkadia replied, "the maintenance has been minimal. I'm just here to give a status report on the new order."

Michael ceased his drinking and froze. "What new order?"

"For the armor, sir," he reiterated. "It's coming along well, despite the short notice."

Michael's head tilted, stopped by the stiff head wrapping. His guts began to churn. He knew the cherub's pedigree, atypical as he was for a forge master. His tall and lanky frame belied an uncanny strength with the hammer and anvil. And his ghostly white, long features were always covered in soot and slag. No one knew what his real hair color was, so long had it been stained by his labors. He had earned his accolades, despite the odds. But Michael knew there was a chink of insecurity there.

He was grateful for the mask as he slowly set the teacup back on the nightstand. Inauspicious as he was in his bedridden state, the covers concealed his furious shaking. "Forgive me," Michael proffered, "the willow bark and this thick sleeping concoction Arkiel has me on have rendered the past several days hazy, but remind me again about this work order?"

"We have roughly a third completed, sir," Arkadia reported. "Not bad, considering we've only had it for two days. As I said, the forge is in a real rhythm cranking them out. We're proud of it. Should come in handy for this new demonstration Lucifer says you two have planned. I hope to get nominated—"

"How many, Ark," Michael demanded.

"Three hundred thousand so far, sir," Arkadia said with a bright, proud tone. "I received the order by seraphic carrier day-before-yesterday and immediately set my hammers to work. You've never seen so many hundreds of thousands of angels jump. First Born's spec sheet implied that he has some new technique in tactical maneuverings that he wants to show off for some elect angels. I was going to update him directly, but I can't seem to find him. I figured you'd know more about it, anyway. I hate to bother you right now, but I'd rather brief you on our progress than just sit around waiting for him to reply."

The archangel's stomach turned to ice. "Cease production immediately," he said with a barking tone.

He could feel Arkadia repulse at his sharp reply. "Sir? I don't understand. Have I—"

Michael shook his head as best he could. "You haven't failed me," he said, trying to soften his tone. "But I don't care what Lucifer has told you, I order you to halt production and reroute all remaining panoplies—finished or otherwise—to the Citadel until further notice."

He heard Arkadia scratch his dirty mane of shaggy, blackened hair. "May I speak freely, sir?" he asked meekly.

"Yes, my friend."

"I'll do as you request, but you must know that this endeavor has reinvigorated us. The design is amazing, sir," Arkadia divulged with cautious enthusiasm. "This new alloy alone is revolutionary stuff. Wherever First Born found it, I've never seen anything like it. My hammers are beside themselves, all sweaty smiles. Such a radical thing; we never contemplated using this kind of material in thin strips; it's such an improvement over our old field plate. And it's so malleable and light! Our durability tests alone were off the charts."

Michael's head was spinning inside that carapace of linen wraps. "Bring me a suit tomorrow, Ark. I'll carry out the inspection here." His Chief Hammer saluted. "And summon Captain Weir from the Ninth Irregulars. He's out of the South Gate Garrison."

"Aye, sir," Arkadia answered, dejected. He made to leave.

"You know," Michael called after him, gesturing to the stacks of files and boxes of scrolls at his bedside, "it's funny. I have all this paperwork and I can't see it. I can smell the fresh ink on mildewed pulp, but I must have the pages read to me. Oh, and General Melphax—in all his humor—is wrong, by the way; I look like an aardvark, not an onion."

Arkadia laughed a little as he closed the door behind him. Alone at last with the thundering blood fury, Michael inhaled and fought his tormented flesh to rise from the bed. He got tangled in the sheets and lost his balance, crashing to the floor. There, he wept. Later, he would blame the drugs but in that moment he knew it was a landscape painted in nightmares.

End of Tome I

TOME II
DAWN OF A DARK PROPHECY

Empyrean Falling

Chapter Index

Chapter I: *Mirrors of Memories*	81
Chapter II: *The Advent of Throes*	85
Chapter III: *The Deeping Black*	91
Chapter IV: *The Star and the Anathema*	96
Chapter V: *Arcane Enigma*	102
Chapter VI: *Slither*	107
Chapter VII: *Gi'ad*	112
Chapter IIX: *The Insolence of Office*	120
Chapter IX: *The Sword and the Son*	125
Chapter X: *Clandestine*	135
Chapter XI: *Maneuvers in Avarice*	139
Chapter XII: *Shades of the West*	144
Chapter XIII: *Iron Sharpens Iron*	153
Chapter XIV: *Faith and the Stone*	163
Chapter XV: *Heresy*	168
Chapter XVI: *As Stars Burn and Die*	179

Empyrean Falling

Chapter I
"...the staff of mine indignation is in their hands."
—Isaiah 10:4

Lucifer walked the dilapidated halls of the long forgotten underground facility. Hundreds of meters below the surface, it once was a great refinery. Smokestacks once pierced the clouds. The breadth of its pipes and steel houses stretched for acres. Now it was a crumbled heap, pressed upon by soil, roots and rivers. The archangel picked his way over the crushed architecture, pummeled to ruin by the cataclysmic fiery hail which demolished their metropolis. Sunbeams peeked through cracks in the roof. He ran an ivory hand over the stone walls, split apart by vines and groundwater's seep. Rust had long since given to decay, but he still remembered its glory. And he remembered the price they paid for it.

"I can still hear their cries, Tempest," he said to his lieutenant. The serpentine assassin trailed him. "How many myriads did we lose that day? And for what?" He shook his head before drawing a breath. "Are they assembled?" Tempest nodded. "Good. It's time."

Tempest led him deeper into the bowels of the facility. They went down to where the active storage reservoirs were housed. And beneath those rusted out hollow containers, were the old caverns where the waters of the deep subsided. To many, their pitch-black isolation was foreboding. To Lucifer, it was liberating. He was in full parade regalia, his curved sword Hadraniel was slung at his waist and his crown afire. Even in the darkness, his armor gleamed like a sun-struck diamond.

They descended the subterranean tunnel of smooth stone. No lamps were needed; Lucifer had worn the path for centuries with his leathered soles. But the sight that greeted him when they rounded the corner of the cavern arrested him. He could see the edge of the corner via a faint wash of light. Before he could scold Tempest for giving away their position with installed braziers, though, he saw the source.

Greeting him were hundreds of thousands of angels. Their eyes were so numerous the cavern's interior was visible for the first time in millennia. Lucifer cataloged the stalactites and fissures in the ceiling above. And beneath them were countless angels, their luminous gazes locked onto his apparition. They hailed him when they saw him. Their roar was a warm blast which trembled the ancient stone cope over their heads. Lucifer silenced them with an arm.

"My brothers," he began, projecting his voice with ease across the great expanse choked with their multitudes, "so many fled here when the sky fell. Do you remember that day?"

They affirmed him with another glorious shout.

"I remember it too," Lucifer said. "We were chimaera, bestial flesh gifted with Empyreal fire. This Empire of the West that sprawls in jungled ruination above us had reached its apex. We were unbridled. We were untamed. Yet the masterpiece was short-lived."

They stirred.

"Oh, how far we've come." He raised his left arm overhead. The signet ring refracted and magnified their light. "When I became the Morning Star, I could not fathom the burden that would await me. If I'd known the zenith of our enterprise would call down the wrath of God and send so many to destruction, I would have wept. When you hid your faces under this mountain and cried out for the succor of death, I came to you. Not with a wheat scythe, but with a lyre. I plucked, I sang, and I prayed. And we found our courage together. My brothers wanted to abandon you to your fate; they saw only the iniquity in your hearts. But to me, you were merely babes led astray. The fall of the Western Empire was my fault."

They protested his sentiment. The ring waxed in brilliance until its light overcame them. They shielded their eyes from the blazing radiance and with a crack it exploded over Lucifer's head.

"Let the dead bury the dead!" he shouted into their ringing ears. "Ours was a crime of innocence, and we paid our penance in the Exile. We rose from those ashes and flew into the sun, full of faith that the dawn would hold a new covenant. We traded our bestial flesh for anthropoid forms and the wings to carry them. Our eyes remained ablaze to light the way. The Son appeared on those eastern shores, right on that sacred mount where we would eventually found Zion. And there we settled, not to reap our pride's harvest but to obey the will of our Father and serve something greater than ourselves.

"In time, you called me Grand Patriarch and Exultant Archon. My brothers divided the choirs and we set to work on our new Kingdom. And while they labored with their swords and songs, I built the White Throne, because I knew that this myopic adherence to the Prophecy of the Dragon would not be enough to sustain us. We needed Father. All my labors on the Holy Mount—in what would become the Temple—were to reconnect us with Him. I thought the creation of the White Throne would allow us to touch the Empyrean. I was wrong; all it did was give us a place to pray. And when Creation was finished, I was named 'Anointed Cherub.'"

Lucifer paused and looked away. Something simmered inside of him. He felt its call. "That word, 'Creation,' has a new meaning now." He let out a quivering sigh and wiped his burning white eyes. "What a joy it was to be led by Father in such a thing." He shook his head. "I thought I'd done it; when I emerged from the White Throne with the Great Commission, I thought He had finally come back to us. Not to punish or rule, but to include us in His works and bind Himself to us." He ran a hand through his orange mane. "But it was a fool's errand. I was the maestro of a symphony that orchestrated not supplication but *supplanting*."

"Fool me once, though…" Lucifer trailed off in a nod before setting his eyes like flint back onto his angels. "I should have known when the Son revealed Himself. How could we have anticipated He would be so in love with the humans that He would take their form? And now He walks in a Garden but does not deign to shine His Empyreal light upon us.

"A great storm is coming, a cosmic malady. We can weather it, or it can bury us."

Lucifer bent and scooped water into his hand. He considered it before standing. "Sometimes I wonder; will all this outlast us? Or will we outlive all of this? How many Ages have passed before us? How long has our journey been? Will the earth reach forth and swallow our bones? Or will our memory live on until we are but dust doomed to float in the ether?" He poured the water into his left hand and let it slip through his fingers.

"I know all of your faces," he continued, "each and every one of you here tonight. I can number your constellations and name your stars. You come from all walks of life, from the lowliest stable hand to the highest officer. Cherubim and seraphim alike, it makes no difference. When we stood in these demolished halls, you made a choice to rise from the darkness. We sacrificed our vanity and pursued the hope of the Empyrean. That is a noble cause which has been lost."

He clenched his left hand into a fist and raised it into the dank air. "There are those who will call this jealousy! They're stricken with the sickness of fear. There are those who will damn us as rebels! They are slaves to their own finite egos." With his left hand, he pointed at them. "I won't allow you to be chained to a sinking vessel. Smash this yoke, and I'll give you the keys to the true kingdom! We are a mirror of Heaven! We deserve to come forth out of the long, dark night of the soul and quench our thirst at the fiery shores of His bosom!"

The host of angels erupted before him. Lucifer pumped his left fist, and they echoed him.

"You won't be abandoned!" he shouted over their tumult. "You won't be afraid! You won't be cast into the Oblivion or left to wither as wintry grapes on this Lower Realm's vine. You are phoenixes risen from the ashes!" He drew Hadraniel from its sheath and held it aloft. It glimmered between the throng of their lamped orbs and Lucifer's armored raiment. "The Empyrean awaits. Follow me and let us chase the dawn one last time!"

Empyrean Falling

Chapter II
"For the thing which I greatly feared has come upon me; that which I was afraid of is come unto me."
—Job 3:25

    Gabriel meandered to the cool shade of the oak grove. A gentle breeze wafted through the trees. He rounded a large oak trunk with an impeccable poise until he was out of sight. There, he slumped onto a carved bench and exhaled. It had been weeks since the incident in the mines and with Lucifer absent and Michael effectively bedridden, the daily operations of the Eastern Kingdom fell on the youngest archangel's thin shoulders.

    He raked a golden lock behind his ears and threw a quick glance behind him. The stone edifice of his Seraphim Bastion loomed over him, casting a great shadow upon the wooded acres of the runners' lanes. Constructed in the early days of their founding in the east, the cyclopean structure resembled three winged angels, standing back-to-back: one with a bow, another with a trumpet, and the third praying. Its height was such that often the heads and outstretched tips of their wings were lost in the clouds. He thought about the myriads seraphim going about their duties in that monolithic stone structure. If their innocence wasn't betrayed already, it would be soon enough. The revelation rendered him heartsick.

Empyrean Falling

Situated in the sprawling acreage of his Seraphim Bastion, he often found peace in wandering the Runners' Veins. Angels would periodically rush past his position, caught in the frenetic moment of their training as they raced along the flagstone lanes snaking through the manicured acreage, shadowed by the Bastion proper. Restricted from flight, the Runners' Veins were an instrumental addition to Gabriel's vision for his choir. He saw the necessity of honing a lacking skill set to avoid idle hands. In a way, the archangel was grateful for the resuming of their warlike doctrine: it kept them busy. But his principles rued the pragmatism inherent in the Runners' Veins.

A furlong off were the Switch-backs, named for the two-lane causeways where seraphim would race at one another from opposite ends, each adorned in their respective panoplies. A trainer would stand at the center with a red pinion. Upon meeting, the two seraphim would cross paths and hurl articles of kit to each other mid-stride. Relegated to support roles in the angelic legions, the seraphim relied upon tactics that would be designed to engender the fine art of quick relief for beleaguered, embattled troops in a retreat. Although devised by Michael, the cherubim disregarded the Switch-back, as it implied defeat and thereby was deemed immoral on grounds of faithlessness. Gabriel, however, saw the prudence of its employment.

He heard voices carried on the wind and suddenly remembered the bread boxes. A series of small, square wooden structures on the edges of the lanes, they were respite stations providing shade and water to those in the throes of exhaustion. Michael fought their inclusion, citing there would be no such thing in the field. Gabriel reasoned he could push his angels harder if he had the means to replenish them which didn't require the attention of medical personnel. That and it was his choir; he would do with them what he wanted. Michael ceded to that, but not before giving them the moniker of "breadboxes," so named for their shape and to shame anyone who used them into being compared to doughy yeast.

One of these breadboxes resided less than a hundred meters to Gabriel's left. He quickly reached down with his hand and drew a glyph in the low air. The gentle summer wind wafting past him ceased, redirected so as not to betray his scent.

Empyrean Falling

"Seven breaths," he sighed, citing the meditative maxim that Lucifer had taught him. "If I could just have that." The voices grew louder, their timbre harsher. He closed his golden eyes and tried to focus on the rare moment of peace. There had been many such sounds over the past weeks; he'd spent as much time putting out social brush fires as he had tending to administrative duties.

A gust of wind rushed past. He jerked to follow the noise and saw an arrow buried in an oak trunk. He looked back. Wings were flapping along the lanes; someone was flying. Voices shouted after them. Gabriel heard the distinct sound of a yew drawing and snapping its string. More arrows shot forth, closer in the direction of the fleeing angel. Gabriel had no weapon, but he would not need one; they were his choir after all.

By the time he caught sight of the assailants, they were deep into the western section of the Bastion's acres and moving fast. He conjured another glyph and prayed. An uncanny wind came from the north and stymied their flight, giving him enough time to catch them. They were a cluster of angels, all armed with either the seraphim bow or saber. They had overhauled their prey in a copse of maples, surrounding him with the sharp metal points of warlike implements.

"Are we executing our brothers for violating the edicts of the Runners' Veins now?"

"This goes beyond mere infraction, my Archon," said the watch commander.

In the middle of their posse was one wide-eyed, average sized cherub. He strained and heaved with clenched teeth and fists at the sharpened steel poised at his throat. Gabriel spotted a trickle of blood on his shoulder and traced it up to an arrow shaft jutting from his left wing. The broadhead arrow had gone straight through and buried itself in the oak, pinning him to the trunk of the tree.

"You never were much of a fast mover, Lance Corporal Uriel," the archangel said to their captured prey. "A poor choice for competition, given your environment here." He turned to the watch commander. "What's the meaning of this?"

"He's a thief, sir," the watch commander replied. "We caught him in the records room."

Empyrean Falling

The cherub reached up and struggled to pry the haft from the maple trunk.

Gabriel moved closer to address him, parting the bows and sabers to allow his passage. "My yews here can skewer a goat's eye with a broadhead at a thousand meters, Lance Corporal. You were nominated not long ago for induction into Michael's elite Cognoscenti corps, yes? I know the training regimen my brother has them under is a queer one, what with all the 'steal to survive' drivel; I imagine the punishment for getting caught is a swift and severe one." He sighed and turned to the watch commander at the head of his security detail. "The warrior caste seems hell bent at times on earning those scarlet cloaks; I know how much they revere the Cognoscenti."

"A thief is still a thief, sir," the watch commander replied, "done under the auspices of 'training' or otherwise. A lashing at the very least is in order, assuming he survives the capture."

"I agree." Gabriel nodded. "But with the recent loss of Keyleas and Mealdis, hasn't our choir suffered enough? Do we need to add fratricide to our list of woes? I have enough troubles daily without having to look over my shoulder for the advent of internecine feuds. The throes of resuming our Prophecy doctrine are plentiful with Michael unable to patrol his choir and Lucifer off doing God knows what. A measure of restraint pays dividends."

Their archangel strode up to the contained Uriel and plucked the arrow from his wing. He rested a palm on the cherub's chest and pointed at him. "Move and I'll have the air sucked from your lungs." Gabriel stepped back and motioned for the watch commander to inspect him. The seraph patted Uriel down and pulled a hand-sized, leather-wrapped object from the back of his waist. He handed it to his archangel. Gabriel unwrapped it, took one look, and glared at him. "You are the twin brother and constellation partner of Nuriel, correct?" Uriel sheepishly nodded. "Michael calls you two the Fire Twins. And these," he proffered the stolen objects, "are the Keys to the Burning Hells." The seraphs looked. The Keys were unremarkably sized rings gilded with a preternatural fire that swirled like living filigree. Gabriel turned to the watch commander. "Ironically, these are his property, though they have recently been reassigned to seraphic custody." He turned back to Uriel. "I wonder what your brother would think of this? Of course, were I to extend a mercy to you, we could always chalk it up to the pranks which have increased in frequency of late. Or a training exercise went awry." He faced the watch commander. "Was anyone harmed?"

"Your aide, Major Zophiel, was a bit roughed up, Archon," the commander replied. "But nothing a quick visit from Chief Surgeon Arkiel's protégés, Rafiel and Ariel, couldn't solve."

Gabriel nodded and patted him on the shoulder. "Send my compliments to the major." He turned and faced Uriel. "While it's not against the rules for a cherub to enjoy the splendors of our seraphic facilities, theft is unfortunately still a crime, even in times like these."

"Permission to speak freely, my Archon," the watch commander said. Gabriel nodded. "This petulance won't be received well by the choir. Those Keys are Western artifacts; they're dangerous and every seraph knows it."

"Every cherub knows it as well," Gabriel said, "especially this one. I'll take him to his Patriarch. Whatever punishment he receives there will be a mercy compared to what would await him at the hands of his Cognoscenti sponsor. I know how those scarlet-and-bronze clad elites operate in the face of failure."

"There's something else, my Archon," the watch commander confessed. He hesitated while Gabriel eyed him. "A word?" Gabriel escorted him out of earshot of the group. "He spoke strangely," the seraph confessed. "When we found him, he said 'what has fallen into the fire will rise like a phoenix.' It's a phrase we've heard more and more, as of late. We've noticed a rash of erratic behavior amongst the ground level echelons as well as the high-flyers. Lots of talk about being 'reborn from the flames.' We can't pinpoint the origin or the meaning, but it's like a mantra, an ideological mantle taken up by the rank-and-file and elites both. I'd petitioned a case to be brought forth before the Council of Elders, but my commanding officer refused."

Gabriel had heard the increase in sentiments over the past weeks. Part of him wanted to believe it was the stress of returning to the Prophecy's preparation. Part of him knew the truth.

The watch commander leaned in close. "We haven't seen Morning Star since the Coronation, my Archon. We need him; the choirs are becoming unhinged. There's open discord now amongst the angels. I won't tell you how many times mere polemics on faith in the Lord have nearly turned violent. And this," he pointed at Uriel, "has the stink of that same spiritual rot."

    Gabriel looked at the cherub then back at his seraph. "Whatever you think this is, Commander, it's not." There was a finality to his tone that abated any lingering protest from the watch commander, even as Gabriel strode back to the cadre of seraphic guards. "Bind Lance Corporal Uriel and relinquish him to my custody; I'll take it from here. If word of this gets out, I'll toss every one of you into the Oblivion. Return to your stations. And you," he looked at Uriel, "are coming with me."

Empyrean Falling

Chapter III
*"Are your wonders known in the place of darkness,
or your righteous deeds in the land of the oblivion?"*
—Psalm 88:12

They were standing in the deep storage level of the Cherubim Citadel. Far below the ramparts and crenelated parapets lined with trebuchets and catapults, far below the archers' towers, manicured lawns turned into training acres, and floors of dueling rooms and armories, the two archangels stared down at an opened wooden crate. In its packing straw was nestled a leather-wrapped package the size of a torso. The great ironclad doors were locked. They were alone.

"Have you heard the news?" Michael asked in the dim light of their torch. His bandages had recently been removed and he had been cleared for active duty, but even the slight heat of the torch pressed painfully upon the taught, hairless skin of his face and bald head.

"I've been a bit busy," Gabriel answered curtly.

"So have I," Michael replied. He unveiled the bundle in the crate before them. The leather flaps were thrown off to reveal a suit of armor made of overlapping metal strips, blacker than sackcloth and humming with uncanny power. Gabriel stared down at it. "I suspect this is what Lucifer was doing in the mines." Gabriel asked what made him think that. "Because Arkadia has made a million of them at First Born's request." His brother looked up at him.

Michael nodded. "I tried to stop him, even ordered the panoplies relocated here. But apparently Lucifer paid him a special visit. Put the fear of hellfire into him. There were three hundred thousand made when I first found out. We managed to get our hands on a little over seven thousand before Lucifer intervened. Arkadia came back and confessed to me this morning. He's so stricken with grief that I had to put him on suicide watch. In truth, I can't blame him; he says that Lucifer threatened to tear his foundry apart."

"Well, looks like our brother's been busy too then," Gabriel said. Michael susurrated his agreement. "You know he made an appearance in Lorinar, right?" Michael slowly shook his head, a stern expression on his taut, scarring features. "Apparently he held a private audience at the Merciful Fate ziggurat. No one's saying what it was about, but their capital garrison has stricken its banners. A third of their angels have requested reassignment to Lucifer's Island."

"If I wanted a base of operations on the mainland," Michael said flatly, "I can think of no better place than the Stone City of Lorinar. Access to the Northern Plains would put him within reach of Zion, the Thousand Peaks, the upper coastline, and the eastern seaboard, as well as a supply chain to the islands and unfettered access to the highways linking every shrine, monument, fort and waystation in the Eastern Kingdom. It's the next best place to the Holy City."

"But to what end?" Gabriel asked.

Michael threw a wary glance back to the ironclad doors. "Your report on Uriel…the Keys to the Burning Hells. That's no small thing. I don't know what, a backdoor maybe. But no one has thought to monkey with that since we bound the old ones and sealed them off within the Oblivion. Only the Tome of Descendance could navigate those ethereal void planes, and even then, you'd need the Keys to gain access beyond the Gates of Hell. Even he knows better than to tamper with those primordial forces; we learned that lesson with the West.

"But if he controls the Northern Plains," Michael finished, "he can move unchecked, unchallenged and rampant throughout the Lower Realm. And we can't survive off fish alone. I'll see Gi'ad

Althaziel tomorrow, have him put a boot heel on Uriel. Now that I can finally get around, we can get ahead of this chaos."

"Have you considered employing your ward?" Gabriel asked.

Michael shook his head. "I'll have him store the Keys in his Book for safekeeping. Outside of that, I'm trying not to drag our dandelion into this. I know how much he loves Lucifer and I would rather keep him training in the Southlands until we need him."

"We can't keep him a secret forever," Gabriel warned.

"I know." Michael sighed and closed the crate lid. "But a little while longer is good; the angelic host has had too much confusion of late. No need to tip the keel before the swells rise."

"You're singing to the choir," Gabriel moaned. "I've been putting out brush fires for two weeks solid. Several training exercises have turned violent. I have upwards of thirteen disputes between high-ranking officers. And the Temple Guardians have reported what has amounted to not one but two protests at the base of the Forty Steps. Apparently, they'd rather invoke the calling down of the Empyrean and make demands of Father than simply pray at the altar." Gabriel shook his head. "I've never seen such childishness."

"I have," Michael countered. Gabriel knew what he meant and ruefully agreed.

"What are you going to do about *this*?" the Seraphim Archon asked, dipping his brow at the crate of strange armor.

"Captain Weir has been running a top-secret exercise in the Southlands for some time," Michael began. Gabriel furrowed his brow. His older sibling smirked. "Hey, baby brother, you have your secrets; I have mine. I know about your little scavenger hunt for old Western Imperial artifacts. It's a good idea; I just wished you would've come to me with it first."

"I had my reasons."

"I'm sure you did. Your seraphic penchant for the clandestine notwithstanding," Michael continued, "we can't remain reactive." He began bolting the crate lid shut. "I've recalled Weir. He's been more useful to me than he realizes, which is good. But I need him to do something with these. Uriel proved that we can hide things like this

Empyrean Falling

till the Empyrean falls, it won't matter. We can lock them up, but Lucifer will just find a way. So, we need to be proactive."

"What did you have in mind?"

Michael hesitated. "We could try to harness the power of the Oblivion ourselves." Gabriel eyed him warily. "We have the Tome of Descendance; we have the Keys to the Burning Hells; we have the Book my ward has been compiling…the old ways and the new."

"You can't be serious," Gabriel countered. "Anyone who goes into the Oblivion stands a fifty-fifty chance of never returning!" He shook his head vehemently. "I won't allow it. You can throw your choir to the wolves, Michael, but my seraphim have suffered enough."

"We need to do something," Michael said. "We're behind a kicking racehorse here."

"Not this," Gabriel insisted. "You can't fight fire with fire."

"First of all," Michael retorted, "yes you can. Second, what do you think the Prophecy of the Dragon has taught us? The entirety of the angelic host is armed and trained for warfare. We are prepared with legions, armies, castles and a Wall around our Holy City."

"We also don't know what the threat will be," Gabriel reminded. "And you may have taken to the martial disciplines like a fish to water, but I always saw preparation for the Prophecy of the Dragon as more of a philosophical exercise. It was a show of our humility, our desire to please Father, and our focus on God's will as opposed to our own. It was never about the material, Michael; it was about the fruit of our faith. The entirety of the Eastern Kingdom is built upon this principle. You know that; it's why you were willing to make an enemy out of Mazerrel when you denied him." Gabriel chuckled at his brother. "You're such a lion on the rock that you encouraged him to participate in a trial of refusal!"

Michael raised a pleading palm. "Sometimes my zealotry does get the better of me."

They stood in silence for a trice. "You know what you need to do," Gabriel reproved. "The Oblivion is not the answer with these." He crossed his arms and waited for Michael to catch up. After a moment, he grinned as his brother's sapphire eyes wax in brilliance.

"The Inner Room," Michael said with a snap of his fingers. Gabriel nodded his concurrence. "Fight fear with faith. How could I have been so blind?"

"Will your Captain Weir be able to sneak them in?" Gabriel inquired softly.

Michael nodded with an overwhelming epiphany. "With a little help, yes. The reinstatement of the Benediction may provide us the cover we need. The rest is up to Father."

Empyrean Falling

Chapter IV
"Now leave me alone so that my wrath may burn against them and they may be destroyed. Then I will make you into a great nation."
—Exodus 32:10

    Lucifer wasn't one to delegate. A mere seven thousand lost did not break his sweat. Underestimating Arkadia, however, did give him pause. It gnawed at his mind as he led the team through the void planes of the Oblivion.

"It was unwise to flex your muscle on him," Tempest said.

"Mind your serpent's tongue when speaking to our master," Mazerrel snarled. "It produced results, didn't it?"

"Peace, comrades," Lucifer whispered from their van. "Tempest's criticism of me is not unfounded, but I must focus here."

He slowed his gait and eyed the black engulfing them. They tread upon the nothing. Lucifer, Mazerrel and Tempest had their wings out to steady their advance. Behind them stretched a train of dedicated followers, all in legion formation. They bore trundles laden with panoplies, skimming across invisible planes painted in darkness.

Lucifer felt a groaning in his psyche. Something pulled his attention left. A translucent shape moved in the pitch, indiscernible in form and more felt than seen or heard. Lucifer darted for it. Tempest maneuvered to a flanking position while Mazerrel stayed behind with his teamsters and the bulk of their forces.

Tempest watched his master overtake the wandering primordial force. A frightful display erupted in muffled, echoed shouts and yawning melodic cries. Lightning crackled and spat as the two met. Lucifer had his sword Hadraniel slashing wildly, focused on one spot in the translucent blob. It was so massive in scale that, by the time Lucifer reached it, he was but a speck to Tempest's sharp eyes.

Luminescent tentacles seemed to reach out and whip at the archangel. He parried their strikes and bit with Hadraniel. Something akin to solar winds belched from their contacts. Tempest's mind screamed under the duress of their battle. His skin crawled as every blow sent shivering flashes of light through his being. At their apogee, Tempest heard Lucifer's voice singing something rhythmic and overpowering. It soothed all who heard it. The crooning rendered the old primordial force a fluttering, quivering nightmare.

"Mazerrel, now!" Lucifer shouted back. "Bring them forth!"

Tempest relayed the order and Mazerrel led his team forward with their cargo. By the time they reached Lucifer's position, his wings were in full spread and his arms outstretched. His head was thrown back and his chanting unabated. They began hurling their trundles into the contained primordial old one. Their work was feverish, hastened even more by the struggling amorphous cyclopean shape of the primeval being. At first, they tried dividing their forces on either side of the creature: one half hurling the trundles in and the other on the opposite end of the trajectory, trying to catch them. In time, this proved foolhardy, and they had to personally escort each one through the pulsating inky mass of shade and light. Its silhouette undulated with each entrance and exit, like a dart passing through a bubble, until at last it released a violent groan of instinctual protest and burst across the angelic scene, exploding in ectoplasmic film.

There was no ability to sweat in the Oblivion's vacuum, but they could bleed. By the time they were finished, the otherworldly screams and preternatural winds had wracked their psyches such that blood trickled from their noses and ears. The corners of their eyes sizzled as their fiery orbs burned away the hot, wet iron life. They stood around the empty space where the ancient monstrous force had been. In its place was the consuming darkness of the Oblivion. Over each of them was the ghastly ectoplasmic film, like a cobweb from a dream. Many held their place, aghast at what had transpired. Some looked to themselves and the remnants of the primordial force that echoed over them. All were entranced in the silence.

"Worry not, my brothers," Lucifer's voice called out.

"Did we get them all?" Tempest asked, barely masking the quiver in his voice.

"We did," Lucifer affirmed. "Mazerrel did his job well."

Where are you, came a whisper in Lucifer's ear. He turned left, but nothing was there. He scanned the scene to ensure no one else saw or heard him be taken unawares by someone or something. *Answer me, you seething worm!*

"Tempest," Lucifer called out, "take point and range ahead. Mazerrel, turn the army around and move us out. Be quick about it."

By then, other primordial forces had detected what happened; their curiosity was piqued. Lucifer could feel their encroachment. His work was finished; he had no use for the others and did not want to risk a second encounter. But something else called him. He kept throwing glances to the left as they traversed the ethereal plane.

"Keep the formation tight!" Lucifer boomed with commanding authority over their multitudes. They began to sprout their wings and shift over and under one another, taking advantage of the three-dimensional plane. "Possible threat to port!"

The formation began to take shape. Lucifer watched as they lurched forward, back in the direction from which they came. One million angels moving in concert was a sight to behold. One million angels moving in concert to Lucifer's commands filled him with hope.

Forward elements moved to flanking positions on the left, their swords drawn and their shields up. In the advance, they rotated their guard duty; several brigades would hold their spot with weapons drawn while the others transited past. When they had passed their position, the guarding units would rotate back into the formation and march while the previously forward elements held the watch. This leapfrogging allowed fresh eyes and arms on the left while progress was made.

Empyrean Falling

Set me free, came the whispering voice again. Lucifer twirled about mid-flight. Behind them, far off in the ethereal nether, he could see the distant looming, shapeless entities of the old ones' primordial powers. They were searching, lashing through the great nothing of the Oblivion. But they were leagues away. He had orchestrated the timing perfectly, isolating one from their numbers just long enough to use it before making a clean getaway. There was no one else nearby and even those things would not be able to get that close undetected. Besides, none of them had ever heard one of their kind speak before.

You won't escape me, it hissed in Lucifer's ear. His hackles rose. He tried to put it out of his mind and keep pace above the throngs of angels. If they did their job correctly, it would take less time to exit than it did to enter. But the Oblivion was tricky. *Your faith has freed you, First Born*, the voice said, *to be bound by truth.*

Lucifer snarled and swept his arm out front. A great wave of flames arced before him. His startled disciples turned to watch the rippling fire recede behind them. Lucifer took advantage of the interval and produced Hadraniel, its shining curved blade in-hand.

Will you hide your face from me, Archangel, as He has turned away from you?

"Mazerrel!" Lucifer roared across the marching host, "tell Tempest to finish leading our brothers out. I won't be far behind." He caught one last fleeting glimpse of Mazerrel's broad features contorted with bewilderment before turning in the direction of the disembodied voice. "I've never shied away from any challenge," the archangel hissed back.

Laughter met his words. He looked around him. Gone was the army. He could no longer perceive Tempest and Mazerrel. Suddenly, he was alone. An old familiar feeling crept up inside of him. He twirled Hadraniel into a high guard. "Face me, coward!"

Coward, seethed the voice in his ear, *I'm not the one brandishing a sword alone in the dark, afraid of shadows. Lightbringer, indeed.*

"Who are you?" Lucifer demanded.

You know who I am, Morning Star. Haven't you wasted enough time already with fruitless mental exercises?

Empyrean Falling

"What do you want?"

Finally, a pertinent question, though still wrong. What you should be asking, Lord of the Western Dawn, is what do you want?

"I want you to face me."

The voice laughed again, this time so loudly that even the archangel had to shut his eyes and shield his cranium with his free hand. *What would be the point? So you can destroy me?*

"Yes."

You know better than that, Grand Patriarch. With all your power, you can't destroy me; you created me. You created all of this. No one would be here, were it not for your rapacious curiosity, your supernatural capacity, your…meddlesome confidence.

"You should show more respect," the archangel warned.

Or what, Exultant Archon? You'll make me respect you? What will you do, Anointed Cherub? Force me to bend the knee?

"You say I'm responsible for all this. You don't think I can unmake it too?"

You are a prime mover, Lucifer, no doubt. But you're also a slave to your will. A thing set in motion in the void will travel for eternity. So the real question is: where are you going, traveler?

"I'm going home," Lucifer said through gritted teeth. He caught himself.

Will you come home maimed and incomplete? How much of yourself did you leave in that fiery Throne? Will you forsake it and all you've led, as a derelict shepherd drunk on his homemade wine?

"Someone has to protect us," the archangel pled, more to himself than whatever it was challenging him. He reasserted the grip on his sword. "My brother's Way is to fight on the ground in condensed ranks; 'you can't form a phalanx with your wings out', as if it had to be that way, but here in the void, we can move freely. It should be this, but no one else sees it."

My, your unerring hubris has never ceased to enthrall me. And yet, with all your fire…

A sharp crack burst Lucifer's eardrums. Something slammed into his chest. He looked down. Hadraniel's starburst pommel was reversed mere inches from his armored sternum. His left hand gripped the long handle protruding from his cuirass. Archangelic blood began to pour from his breastplate.

We are going home. Your sins are the middle finger of His red right hand. Your crimes are your virtues. All you've made, all you've accomplished, all you've proven, are but motes in the candlelight. I am you. We are one.

"Who are you?" Lucifer cried out in agonized desperation.

I'm the edifice of your transgressions. I'm the power of your fear. I'm the slithering beast born of your chaos. The winds of your flames fill my wings. The sting of your words is my burning breath. The scales of your judgment lap my armor. You and I are all that stands between what we've wrought and what lies beyond.

Lucifer's legs shook. He doubled over as the pain hit him. With his right palm, he struck the sword hilt buried in his chest. There was a sundering crack, and the light burst forth from his crumpled form and the armor encasing it.

And far away, Tempest led their army out of the Oblivion.

Ahead, in the barely perceptible distance, he could see the shimmering dimensional border of the Lower Realm's edge lurking in distorted waves, like a landscape at the bottom of a fish tank. He saw the pinpoint of light behind him and heard a second crack. To his dismay, he saw the broken blade of Hadraniel hurtling past him, absent its master and covered in blood as it flew, end-over-end, in the dark nothing of the Oblivion.

Chapter V
"...but His secret is with the righteous."
—Proverbs 3:32

    Michael felt the darkness press upon him. He thrashed and wandered in the consuming pitch. A melody whispered in the distance. It wafted near, a throaty tenor singing over the minor chords of a lyre. He followed it to a pinprick of light. The white light waxed until it overcame him, and he woke. Michael found himself lying in bed. A warm yellow glow pressed upon his nerves.

    "Thought that might do the trick," came a throaty tenor from the edge of the room. Michael heard the drapes of the window fully part. His face itched terribly. He reached up to scratch it. "Don't do that," the same voice warned from the edge of his bed. Michael could not yet open his eyes, but he recognized the angel and scowled at his righteous judgment. "Don't blame me," the angel chuckled. "The Chief Surgeon was here for a few minutes with one of his protégés. He passed instructions to his student: aloe for the itching; teas for the pain; don't open your eyes too fast. Though apparently the little songbird heard a lark and took off after a bit. He did leave notes for you, which was a nice afterthought, considering his seraphic nature."

"That would have been Rafiel," Michael determined. "Did they see you, Alrak?"

The angel sighed. "No, of course not. I know the rules."

Michael nodded. "Good, we still have that at least." He slowly peeled his eyes open.

Alrak Sivad sat on the corner of the bed, a small, thin cherub with long curly blonde hair and emerald eyes. He was seated next to Michael's blanketed feet. He wore a grey shirt with trousers and had angular alabaster skin. In his lap rested a small travel lyre. He smiled warmly at Michael, his magnificent pearly teeth gleaming.

"Did you miss me?" he teased. He plucked a chord on his lyre and brayed.

"More than you know, little dandelion," Michael replied with a smile he couldn't resist. He groaned and struggled to sit up.

Alrak observed his labor and arched an eyebrow. "You've pushed yourself too hard."

"Now who is the mentor and who is the protégé again, little Alrak Sivad?"

Alrak threw his head back and laughed unabashedly at that. "At least you didn't play the 'you're just a lowly cherub and I'm your Patriarch' card." Michael conceded to that before applying the aloe to his peeling skin. "No, that's more Lucifer's style anyway. Speaking of which, where is your older brother? He usually visits me when I'm off in some far-flung corner of the Realm, especially when I'm learning how to build fires, or hunt, or roll boulders, or whatever random exercise you've concocted to keep me occupied and isolated. I swear, Michael, sometimes I think you're just embarrassed by me."

"You've been training in the Southlands still?" Michael asked.

Alrak sighed and nodded. "Yes." He plucked a minor chord on his lyre. "I tamed a horse and learned how to ride it. I named her Aletheia. She'd make a good mate for Andreia. And I learned how to read the glyphs. Mastering the elements is not easy. Big surprise."

"How's your footwork with that cut-and-thruster I gave you?" Michael asked.

Alrak shrugged. "I finally got that counter-feint down that you taught me. Of course, it's hard to master dueling without Lucifer, or riding without you, and not to mention airborne navigation without Gabriel. But I've managed. I understand your point about open warfare dictating land-based tactical movement; the numbers are too great for everyone to fly and you can't put armor on wings. I get it."

Michael chuckled, despite himself. "We learned that one the hard way, Alrak. You should've seen those early mock-ups, all of us bumping into each other, feathers getting in teeth and half of us falling to the earth; those first few practice battles were a mess. But blood makes the grass grow. A more dynamic offense can be waged when you're on a single plane; it makes a smaller target. Plus, it gives the seraphim something to do; they can feel special lobbing darts and delivering messages while we slug it out on the ground. It just wasn't feasible any other way."

"Well," Alrak confided, "learning the line-fighter's trade isn't easy when you don't have any friends to form a shield wall, though I've seen those seven thousand you sent maneuvering down there. Thanks for helping me hone my evasion tactics; they came in handy."

Alrak's slight frame was absent the muscular bulk indicative of the cherubim, but his lean, radiant form and jovial, keen wit belied an uncanny power. Michael could only imagine what he could be, were he unleashed upon the angelic host. "I know you strain under your loneliness, Alrak," he admitted. "But Father has deemed you my secret protégé for a reason. I don't know why, but I don't question the will of the Lord either. Neither should you."

"Things are getting bad out there, Michael," he said darkly. "I've seen several arguments turn violent. Even saw a protest devolve into a riot. Gabriel has his hands full. I suspect you do too. I don't know what this whole crap is about 'falling into the flames and being reborn from the ashes' that some angels rant about, but I hear it a lot, even saw it scrawled in lamb's blood on the plinth of the Bastion. They had most of it cleaned off, but I could read enough to know."

"I thought you were supposed to be in the Southlands."

His protégé strummed his lyre and stared flatly at him. "I had to come back for a refit at some point," he finally said with a shrug. He got up and went to Michael's bar. "Your supply drops have been lacking lately."

"Consider it supplemental training," Michael said as he watched his protégé make employ his new elemental talents to heat up some tea. "It'll come in handy one day when you're leading the Cognoscenti in my place. Those cherubim are used to going without; it'd be good for you to know how to survive off the land as well. Oh, don't put honey in it this time."

"Fine, I'll take your share then," Alrak said. "And yeah, their no-prisoners approach leaves no room for dead weight." He crossed the room with two cups and handed one to Michael.

"No," the archangel chuckled, "it doesn't." He took the tea and slurped it before setting it on the nightstand to cool. "Sometimes I have a hard time keeping up with them myself."

Alrak sat on the bedside next to him and sipped his tea with cupped hands. His fiery emerald eyes narrowed at Michael over the porcelain rim of the teacup. Michael felt pierced by his gaze. "So, shoot me straight, Michael. What's going on? Where's Lucifer?"

Michael cleared his throat and took another guarded sip of hot tea. "I honestly don't know," he confessed. "He vanished after the Creation Coronation—which you saw—and ever since then, it's like the Gates of Hell have spilled forth out our midst. He made a mockery of my authority with Arkadia at his forge and had some secret rendezvous with the garrison commander at Lorinar, which also managed to be a sort of high-profile homecoming. Impressive, when you look at it; he killed two birds with a single stroke of celebrity."

"That doesn't answer my question," Alrak said flatly, "and you know it." He pointed to Michael's peeling red head, his mood dark. "Just like how I know it was no mine explosion that caused that."

Michael gulped down the tea and reached for the skin balm. "The truth, Alrak, is that we don't know. But Gabriel and I are afraid. We had hoped that going back to the Prophecies and resuming our military training would keep our choirs focused. We had also hoped that reinstating the Benediction Ceremony would rein in their base natures and give them something to aim for. But all this talk about calling down the Empyrean, blood for fire, rising from the ashes…it all has the grandiose delusionary tone of my big brother.

"You know when all this kicked off that night after the Coronation, we sent fourteen of our best angels to look for him? Gabriel wanted to send you, but I didn't want to get you involved." Michael sighed and looked out the window at the midday sun. "It maybe would have made things different, but the God's honest truth is that I was afraid for you."

Alrak sat silently throughout. He sniffed and furiously wiped his eyes with a dainty hand. Michael placed a palm on his shoulder. He felt him tighten under his touch.

"I know, Alrak. I'm sorry. I hope you can forgive me for not involving you. You were only created two years ago; you're too young for all of this."

"How can we be so blind?" the young angel finally uttered mournfully.

"Let's not count the stars until they have fallen," Michael said with compassion. "Or after the sun has risen. Don't be angry with Lucifer yet; we haven't—"

"It's not Lucifer I'm angry with, Michael," Alrak spat.

Suddenly, there was a knock at the door. Michael snapped to face it. "Who is it?"

"It's Gabriel. Be decent."

Michael turned to make a fraternal joke with his protégé, but Alrak Sivad had vanished.

Chapter VI
"They that are rich shall fall into temptation…"
—I Timothy 6:9

    Gabriel stood in the bedroom and stared at Michael. He noticed the crumpled sheets and the opened drapes. He looked across to the nightstand and saw two empty tea cups.

    "Double-fisting it again, I see?"

    Michael eyed him. "Are you the housekeeping crew now?"

    Gabriel shook himself free of the deception and walked over to his brother. "I need you to set aside your momentary lapse of self-pity and help me. The Kingdom is coming apart at the seams. I have an eldest brother doing his damnedest to rip the fabric apart with his bare teeth and an older brother content to watch him do it from the bottom of a bottle. I have half a mind to pack up my whole choir and build a city in the Southlands."

    "It's just tea, I promise. Stop being so dramatic." Michael grimaced as he tried to get out from under the covers. "What has you so worked up, anyway?"

    "Bodies were nailed to the Bastion wall, in broad daylight."

Michael paused at that, sitting on the edge of the bed and kneading his scalp. "Your seraphim are a piece of work, Gabe. You know, when my choir gets angry, they put on practice gear and beat the Hell out of each other on the Citadel's combat yards. But you? Your choir has an underdeveloped rage that always seems to erupt in a penchant for the sadistic."

"Two of them were yours," Gabriel countered. "They're still washing the blood off."

Michael stood and got dressed. "Do we have any leads?"

"I could trace one back to Lucifer's lion-tamers on his island," Gabriel divulged. "The other was one of Melphax's lieutenants who had cycled into Gi'ad Althaziel's Citadel training camp last month. Given the resistance you always meet at the hands of Mazerrel, I think it wiser for me to go to Lucifer's Island. A more tactful approach could bear better fruit."

Michael took the insult in stride and disappeared into his armory, pulling a grey hooded training tunic over his once-chiseled torso. "Fair enough," he shouted over the clanging of armor and weaponry. He emerged a few moments later adjusting his sword belt, Virtue's lion head pommel gleaming above the scabbard. "I should probably make an appearance at the Citadel, anyway. I still need to have Althaziel clamp down on Uriel and I'd like to let the legions know their *other* Cherubim Archangel hasn't abandoned them too."

"Thank you," Gabriel breathed with relief.

His brother nodded and opened the double doors to the balcony. Gabriel followed. As he passed the nightstand, he looked down at the two teacups. They both still had the warm scent of freshness. He noticed one had a darker mottled interior than the other. Honey, and a lot of it. Michael never took his tea with that much honey. But Gabriel knew who did.

The two archangels unfurled their wings. Michael stretched his feathers to their fullest. They gave off a cobalt hue in the summer sun that contrasted with Gabriel's green-gilded wingspan.

"I know I'm always going on about how much I love the winter," Michael said as his feathers fluttered in the flexing stretch, "but this is a beautiful day." He looked at Gabriel to his right. A morose expression hung about his hale features. "Take what you can, when you can, baby brother," he said kindly and tapped his shoulder with a two-fingered wink. "I'll get this sorted out with Gi'ad. If you need help on the Island, send a sign. We're not alone on this."

"I know," Gabriel said. "Godspeed. Fill me in later."

"I'll brief you later tonight," Michael said with a nod. "Just be where I can find you."

Gabriel pointed at him. "Likewise."

The two archangels parted ways. Gabriel watched his brother wing it east for the Citadel. His northern trajectory rendered his brother a speck on the horizon in heartbeats. He soared over the Holy City, its usual opulent splendor diminished by the groups of protestors that had left their stain on the golden streets. Refuse and debris from the previous week's riots were being burned by the urban cohorts, the acrid pillars of smoke and ash rising to mix with the clear air above. He saw a march taking place, its long column of officers and high-ranking officials leading a throng of workers, laborers, low-level staff, and helpers snaking down the street beside the Holy Temple, a newly fashioned phoenix totem at their red and black painted van. Already the urban cohorts were moving to halt their advance; it was an impending clash of colors: the azure and purple capes of the urban cohorts drawing in martial order on the snaking crimson line of protestors. It had become a familiar dance to both parties.

For the first time in his life, Gabriel was grateful to fly past the North Gate of Zion. As he always did, he looked for the garrison commander, Ellunias. One of the crown jewels in his seraphic ranks, Gabriel always enjoyed a quick sojourn with Ellunias before continuing whatever mission brought him north. But this time the executive officer wasn't on the ramparts. Instead, the yews and line-fighters of the garrison were on alert, their spears and broadheads glinting in the high summer sun. Half of them faced the south, keeping watch on the metropolis. A part of Gabriel hoped his brother did not have to see any of the unrest on his short trip to the Citadel. A deeper part of him hoped that he did.

His usual layover rendered void, the Seraphim Archon ascended into the verdant pastures of the Northern Plains. Its untouched tranquility was a tonic to his archangelic spirit. He knew

Empyrean Falling

Lorinar loomed as a waypoint, itself seeing a recent exodus of citizens in favor of Lucifer's Island. On the surface, he saw nothing technically wrong with their request. Even the Council of Elders failed to issue protest. But in his heart, he knew there was a dragon of evil slithering underneath their motives.

"A serpent of chaos worms through our ranks," he remembered telling the Council that morning after the desecration on the Bastion's plinth. "You all know it. I doubt the lofty halls of these Chambers are so vaulted as to keep out the noise in our streets."

Head Eldar Metatron was the first to respond. "We dip our brows to the authority of the archangelic caste. The Three have always been a source of inspiration when we of the Council must remain more stalwart and some might say, sluggish. And we acknowledge the need for checks and balances. But we ask you to requite that respect regarding our station as a bulwark for stability in more troublesome times. We appreciate the delicate balance that has been upset by recent events. The angelic host has always needed a focus for its energies. The Lord was wise to involve us in the Creation process. We had the Prophecy of the Dragon to prepare for before that. It is a sign that maybe we've outgrown the need for armies and castles and legions in the wake of our involvement with preparing the cosmos for Humanity. Perhaps looking back to an outmoded pastime is a mistake?"

Gabriel could not forget Eldar Asmodeus chiming in so quickly on the heels of Metatron. "The Three are prime forces for change, of that there's no doubt, Archon Gabriel. But now our task is damage control for the wayward actions of your eldest brother. He has garnered a following that borders on a cult. They call themselves phoenixes. If you'd brought this to our attention the night of the Coronation, then perhaps the storm kicked up by Morning Star would not have fomented into a hurricane."

Gabriel knew he had a point, albeit in the clarity of hindsight. He also knew better than to enter an battle of wits with Asmodeus; that seraph thrived on debate. How many times Gabriel had stood on the dais of the Council Chambers and looked up to the tiered cathedrae from which they executed their bureaucratic judgment, he would never know. But the archangel needed their help in the wake of recent events.

Empyrean Falling

"Has the vacuum left by Creation's enterprise rendered us so idle that the shades we left buried in the West have retaken footholds in our hearts?" Asmodeus posited coyly. Seraph though he was, Gabriel despised his unctuous tone. "Dare we say that we now find ourselves in a state of temporary insolvency because of secretive archangelic hubris? We admire your attempts to quiet this storm on your own, Archon. Thank you for your efforts. But it's clear as our crystal diadems that the Three have acted with the very impunity we had hoped to exorcize when we founded the Eastern Kingdom."

"How many Elders would have answered their doors in the small hours," Gabriel remembered saying. "And how long would it take to form an emergency session? We knew speed and direct action was paramount. In the last few weeks, I've tried to maintain a sense of normalcy while Lucifer is off on a jag and Michael has been recovering from his injury."

"You did what you thought was best, no doubt," Asmodeus continued, unabated. "But your conspiracy to resolve this independently of our input has created a mess which requires Eldar intervention. You archangels have always been more of a force of nature than a ruling body, which is why Father instituted the edicts for our station. But you've left us in a precarious position, Archon Gabriel; we now must endeavor to snuff out a firestorm. It has always been our job to carry the load created by archangelic decisions. And we've borne that burden well, I feel. But if this carries on—with your brothers absent, no less—then we will be forced to look to more drastic measures to maintain law and order within the Kingdom."

It was the first time Gabriel had left the Council Chambers feeling defeated. He had always been their fiercest proponent within the Three. If only they knew how many times he had defended their judicial institution in heated conversations with his brothers. The thought chewed on him bitterly as he flew from Zion. They had their points, but Gabriel knew only an archangel could convince another archangel of anything. Or at least he still hoped.

Empyrean Falling

Chapter VII
"And besides this, giving all diligence, add to your faith virtue; and to virtue knowledge..."
—2nd Peter 1:5

    Michael strode along one of the elevated paved access lanes separating the Citadel's combat yards. Laid out in a skeletal grid, the network of combat yards could be accessed anywhere via the raised lanes. Troops filed to and fro, hastened along by their platoon leaders. On either side, the ground swept down into the numerous, cordoned-off training acres. Some were filled with phalanxes practicing their line-fighting techniques. Others had flags at intervals for skirmishers to range their javelins and slings. There were thousands of such training acres surrounding the Cherubim Citadel, each abuzz with the various trumpets, voices and martial arts of the warrior caste. Michael observed them in satisfied silence. Beside him walked the head of this school, Chief Weapons Master Gi'ad Althaziel.

    "It's good to see you, my Patriarch," the cherub said. He adjusted his chainmail hauberk away from the tangle of his sword baldric. He wiped the sweat from his heavy brow on heavy red trousers. Short and barrel-chested with a bald head and down-swept goatee, Althaziel was cubits shorter than his archangel, and every bit as powerful. "I was beginning to wonder."

"Wonder or worry?" Michael said with a slight smile.

"Well, let's not get carried away," Althaziel replied. "The Chief Surgeon said you were effectively quarantined. I was beginning to think this whole dusting off of the old ways would be carried out under delay of seraphic messengers. And how would that look?"

Michael laughed. "I'm happy to be free of my cage. Still," he took in the myriads cherubim honing their martial disciplines, "it seems you haven't been resting on your laurel crown, Gi'ad."

"A cherub must earn his soup, sir." He watched his archangel pull the hood up over his sunburnt scalp. "Regardless, it does the corps tremendous good to see you back on the prowl, Patriarch. I take it you're on the mend?"

"Nothing some good old-fashioned sweat and scar tissue won't solve," Michael replied. "A flask helps too."

"Is your hair growing back?" Althaziel asked. "You look like a roasted potato."

"Only on one spot in the back. Looks like my days of being pretty are finally behind me."

"A shame," Althaziel said. "I was hoping I wouldn't be the only bald member of our higher order. You know how much we cherubim covet our locks, especially the Cognoscenti."

"Yes, I think they spend as much time grooming themselves with olive oil and combs as they do marching," Michael conferred. "Although even I would hesitate to say that to their faces."

The two shared a laugh. They transited the acres of line infantry and crossed over into those combat yards reserved for single combat. On both sides below them, officers dueled while drill instructors led formations and taught fencing skills.

"Terrible business what happened in the mine," Althaziel said after a while. "Please convey my deepest condolences to your brother. Any loss is a tragedy. I know how fiercely Archangel Gabriel protects his choir."

"Covets, more like it," Michael groused. "Though, to be fair, I don't carry the same administrative weight that he does. He loves his choir like a bear loves her cubs. I try to convince myself that I could stand to learn a thing or two from him, but it's like squeezing into someone's slippers before a forced march."

Althaziel harrumphed. "Trying to squeeze into a seraph's slippers would require a recovery furlough at the hot springs, Patriarch." Michael laughed. "Still, send him my regards."

"Thank you, Gi'ad. A gesture of goodwill like that from a top-ranking choir official across the aisle goes a long way these days."

Althaziel sighed. "I understand. I hear one of ours was involved in that incident, as well." Michael confirmed his suspicions. "A line-fighter, I believe. What was his name?"

Michael winced before looking away as they walked. "I think he's embarrassed."

"Understood," Althaziel said with a raised palm, "not another word of it need be spoken. If my office can be of any assistance…"

"I appreciate that," Michael said. "I detailed him off for some leave. Maybe he's enjoying those hot springs?"

"Let's hope so," Althaziel said, his casual demeanor slipping.

"How have things been from your neck of the woods?" Michael asked.

Althaziel shrugged under the easy weight of his hauberk. "Nothing we can't handle. A few dust-ups here and there. I've had to break up my fair share of scuffles but it's easier to root out trouble in my arena than it is in other quarters of the Holy City. Truth be told, there's a discontent boiling beneath the surface, like a fever that rises. I won't argue against claims of a malady taking hold of the angelic host as of late, but whenever a training exercise gets out of hand or two angels start in on each other—which happens more frequently than you might expect—I've been close enough to stamp it out. Still, the job has grown more difficult this time around. About the only two groups to evade this disease of the spirit are the Temple Guardians and the Cognoscenti."

"Speaking of which," Michael hesitantly broached, "your Cognoscenti candidate, Uriel."

"Yes, what about him?" Althaziel said guardedly.

"Apparently, he was caught trying to steal something from the Bastion not long ago," Michael revealed. "I've looked over his file.

He's a good recruit for them—not the best, but no bundle of sticks either. I know how brutal their regimen is. They're the one division in all of Heaven that requires you to steal as part of your training but will also beat you within an inch of your life if you get caught. I may not totally agree with their methods, but it's hard to argue with results." Althaziel nodded at that. "I'd like to keep him from getting maimed out of military service," Michael continued. "Thought I might hand him over to you for some reassessment, as opposed to letting the red cloaks and his sponsor give him the kind of wall-to-wall counseling that would render him fit for little more than oiling blades."

Althaziel perked up at that. "If there's one thing I love more than training these pups, my Patriarch, it's course correction. Send him to me. I'll take care of it."

Before Michael could thank him, the Chief Weapons Master had descended the lane. He raced to one of the training acres where a junior platoon leader was instructing a bank of recruits on fencing forms. As if right on cue, Althaziel proved worthy of his word.

"What in the Burning Hells do you think you're doing?" he barked as he descended the grassy upslope, pointing at an average-sized cherub. The angel had his blunted broadsword at a low guard, much like those around him, but his stance was off kilter. "Left foot forward, rest your elbow on your right hip!" Althaziel shouted.

"Aye, Chief Weapons Master!" answered the cherub. Michael recognized him from his elevated place of remove on the connecting lane, but merely cinched up his belt and observed.

"What's your name, whelp?" Althaziel snarled at the student.

"Paladin, sir!"

"Ah yes, one of General Melphax's hammered gofers," Althaziel barked. "You're a long way from the shadow of Amin Shakush, little light of mine." Paladin's luminous eyes grew wider with each word. Sweat trickled from his mussy crop of russet hair. His boxy jaw tightened under the strain. "Hold the sword like this," Althaziel demanded and jerked Paladin's hands into position at his waist. "Keep your left foot forward." He kicked the cherub's left heel. Paladin stumbled and barely regained his footing.

Michael eyed the scene. Althaziel wasn't one to be trifled with, but he'd forgotten what a juggernaut the Chief Weapons Master could be in his element.

"Sergeant Heklios," Althaziel barked, "run it again."

The drill instructor saluted and had them perform the routine. Again, Paladin failed. Again, Althaziel jumped forth. He grabbed Paladin by the drawstring of his black cotton training trunks and dragged him forward from the ranks.

"I'm going to make you shine," Althaziel growled and slammed the practice sword into Paladin's torso, the flat of its blade knocking the wind out of him. "We'll do it together," he proffered. In a flash, he had his own broadsword unsheathed and took up position on Paladin's left flank. "Don't waste my time, Paladin."

Althaziel flowed through the moves like a dancer under water. His stocky frame belied his grace, each sweep of his hairy, muscular limbs fluid as if weightless. His iron-shod boots stomped the wet grass with each step, the toes always pointed in their proper direction for weight distribution. The blade of his broadsword bit the clear morning air and sung in the sunlight. It flowed from the sheer vertical to an arcing horizontal and back again with effortless precision.

Michael watched him with a prideful smile. His mirth degenerated when his eyes tracked to Paladin, whose movements mere meters away were jerky and out of time. Michael's smile faded as he knew what awaited the angel. Beyond his back, Michael saw the rank-and-file of the training group hold stoically in the face of what they were about to witness.

Finally, Althaziel caught sight of Paladin's form.

"What happened to you?" the Chief Weapons Master bellowed in Paladin's strained face, rounding on him and sheathing his sword in one seamless motion. "Has the lard from your cushy position sent fat to your brain?" Paladin opened his mouth to speak. "If I want butter, I'll have you spit! Otherwise, shut your teeth and do it again." He turned to the drill instructor. "Sergeant Heklios, repeat this form ten times for every one of Paladin's mistakes."

Michael sensed their shock. They would be there all day, and Paladin would face their frustration back at barracks. Even Heklios had a hard time concealing his disbelief from within the shroud of his bronze helmet, though it did not escape Michael's detection.

"You're going to get it right, little light of mine," Althaziel said, jabbing a finger into Paladin's clavicle, "or I'm going to bury you under a bushel of thorns so sharp—"

"Chief Weapons Master!" Michael called. Althaziel stopped mid-tirade and turned. "Your help, please." Michael watched him linger before disengaging from the training acre and striding up to Michael's position on the access lane. His gait was strident; Michael could tell he had some heat under his boots. "Walk with me."

The archangel led his cherub back to the Citadel proper.

"Your Academy has always been renown as a pinnacle of expertise in the martial arts," Michael said. "It's why I petitioned the Council of Elders to elect you as the Chief Weapons Master. There's no one I trust more to lead our people in preparation for the Dragon."

"Thank you, my Patriarch," Althaziel replied, still steaming.

"The job is harder now," Michael continued. "Many feel as if we've regressed. There's a fomenting of strife in the wake of Lucifer's absence and the advent of Humanity. Even now I can see the smoke columns rising from the urban cohorts' clashes with the malcontents. Despite all that Archangel Gabriel and I have tried to do, the fire's tide rises. They are becoming more organized, more fervent. We are losing ground in a philosophical war that undermines cohesion and resolve. I need you, Gi'ad. Desperately."

Althaziel nodded. "The malcontents are on the rise. Just between us, my Patriarch, I fear for the angels."

Michael traced his steps back to the Citadel in silence. For a long while, neither spoke. Contingents of angels in the combat yards participated in their martial duties, the sounds of exertion and wood and metal ringing off one another echoed on either side. For the span of seven breaths, Michael imbibed its clamorous din.

"Gi'ad, what makes the lion defend his rock?" he asked.

"Pride," Althaziel answered after a fashion.

Michael nodded. "And what makes a bear protect her cubs?"

"Passion."

"And the hawk swoop on its prey?"

"Hunger."

"Pride, passion and hunger," Michael reiterated, ticking them off with a finger. "Are these not traits of angels as well as animals?" Althaziel affirmed him. "Then what separates the angels from the animals?" Althaziel admitted that he did not know. "A lion can show courage. A bear will sacrifice for its cubs. A hawk will perform feats of daring for its meal. Courage, sacrifice, daring, all these even the animals possess. But we're set apart by Father. What quality defines us?" Again, Althaziel confessed his ignorance. "Faith."

"I don't understand," Althaziel said. "I mean, I kin your point but not your purpose."

"What is the opposite of faith?" Michael asked.

"Hatred."

Michael shook his bald head. "No. Hatred is the bastard child of love and fear. The opposite of faith is fear. We must be vigilant, Gi'ad." Michael stopped and wheeled on him. "And what I saw on that training acre with Paladin was the iron grip of fear!"

"He's a soft, spoiled runt from the officer's corps," Althaziel protested. "He's no busier or stupider than the others; there's no excuse. He's lazy; to him, this is a lark."

"And you'd put the fear of God into him," Michael fumed, "drive him out of the tribe?"

"I do what must be done for the sake of our standards."

"Gi'ad, we need every angel. *Every angel*. This possession which has gripped our ranks is taking more of us by the day. I can't afford to lose one soul, and neither can you."

"Finally," Althaziel snapped, "something we agree on."

"You carried your reprimand of Paladin into abuse," Michael scolded hotly. "I won't allow my Chief Weapons Master to conduct himself with such sheer, vengeful fear."

"What am I supposed to do, Patriarch? At the Bastion, they hold symposiums and polemics. They lecture and race. Soft-handed heralds, the lot of them. Here, we trade in blood and sweat. I'm on the receiving end of every bad attitude and bad day, and it's my job to put a weapon in their hands and beat the slag out of them! If I don't make steel out of their iron hearts here—now, on these training acres—then who will stand in the gap when the Dragon comes? Not that it matters much now, the apple of His eye is turned to Creation's beloved."

Althaziel stormed off for the Citadel's entrance.

Michael followed him.

"Stop it, Gi'ad," Michael demanded across the way. He threw back his hood and pointed a finger at Althaziel. The Citadel's long shadow cooled his skin. "I won't have that sedition from you."

Althaziel turned to him, arms outstretched. "It's not sedition if it's true, Patriarch." His cobalt eyes burned in the Citadel's shadow. His voice was low to evade detection from the cherubim around them, but Michael heard him clear as day. "Do you truly think that what we prepare for now is anything other than our own naked survival? What happens when another Age passes, and we're left to rot, absent His divine presence while He dotes over Humanity?"

Michael crossed to him and leaned in mere inches from Althaziel's broad, heavy brow. "I've heard this from my older brother already, Gi'ad," he warned. "I won't tolerate it from you."

"Well, you'd better learn to start," the Chief Weapons Master shot back. "Grand Patriarch Lucifer has a point, and you know it." He pointed to the training acres beside them. "All that we do here was once to prepare for an enemy—the great Enemy, Satan, the Dragon—who would seek to destroy us all. It served its purpose in teaching humility before the onset of Creation. And now that we're on the other side of Humanity, it's apparent who and what our Enemy is. What we do now is to preserve the angelic host.

"How did you not see this coming?" Althaziel seethed. "Were you so blinded by your devotion to a vacant Throne that you failed to recognize Humanity as a testament to our folly? We were wrong; we aren't His chosen. We're His servants. There's a difference. And if we don't prepare for the road ahead, we'll be buried in another exile's ashes, and no dawning Son will deign to light our way."

Before the archangel could react, Althaziel sprouted his wings and bolted into the midday air, receding into the combat yards to be surrounded by his students. Michael stood there in the shade of the base of the Citadel, senses blasted and heartbroken.

Empyrean Falling

Chapter IIX
"...the stone thy builders rejected hath become the capstone."
—Acts 4:11

    The sun beat down on Tempest's bare shoulders. He stooped over the anvil and laid the long, curved strip of glowing black ore on its smooth face. It gave off an uncanny radiance as he took the hammer and beat the slag out of it, sending showers of sparks onto the sandy floor of the seaside forge. Little more than a hut of palm fronds and driftwood, it was a secluded destination perfect for angelic side projects. He wiped the sweat from his thin brow and looked left to the setting sun. His feverish work had lasted for two days, yet he was nowhere near finished.

    There was a disruption in the rhythm of the tides and coastal breeze. He heard the air shift and the sand crunch behind him. Out of reflex, he whipped around and produced the long, curved dagger he kept hidden in his waist. The weapon held low and out of sight, he crouched to see none other than Gabriel standing in bold, winged relief against the crepuscular shoreline. For a trice, he observed the archangel, motionless as the furnace crackled and belched its flaming smoke into the hovel around him.

"Where is your master?" Gabriel's melodic tenor called out. Tempest's eyes narrowed. He scanned the archangel's flanks, hoping to spot seraphim rangers in the waves. His disappointment manifested when the Seraphim Archon folded his wings into his back and approached with open arms. No sword-belt hung at his waist; Tempest could tell by the evenly distributed weight of his stride that Gabriel was unarmed. He turned back to his work in the forge. "Tempest, where is Lucifer?"

"He's your brother," the master of assassins said irritably, "Archangel."

"He's *your* master," Gabriel shot back. He approached the lowly ramshackle forge situated on the shoreline of Lucifer's Island. Tempest resumed his tempo of beating the slag out of the long, curved metal. Gabriel saw the sweat glisten on his exposed back as the lithe angel's muscles worked. "What are you doing?"

"I haven't seen First Born in days," Tempest admitted with a growling tone. He took the metal strip and plunged it into the cooling trough. A hissing billow of steaming grey smoke spat forth.

He said something else, but it was lost to Gabriel's ears in the smoky noise. He sensed the truth in Tempest's words. Michael could be fooled, but Gabriel's gift of discernment always detected lies. "I need him back in Zion immediately, Tempest. There's great division fomenting amongst us and he has a hand in it." He watched the recalcitrant cherub shrug. Gabriel's face grew hot and his blood thundered. He marched up to Tempest and grabbed him by the shoulder. "This is not a request."

The cherub whipped around and managed to put enough distance between them to allow his glowing metal project to cover the interval with an outstretched arm. Gabriel recalled how fast the angel could be when he wanted as he stared down the sizzling red tip of the metal in Tempest's outstretched gloved hand. It radiated a strange hue that caused the archangel's eyes to slip away as if it were hard to keep track of, even as the point hovered less than an inch from his face. The acrid effluvium agitated Gabriel's senses. He sniffed. Despite his watery vision, he looked down the long, curved plane of metal to see Tempest's narrow eyes glaring at him. His white crop of spiked hair was dulled with soot and sweat. The predatory instinct housed within his features sent a chill through Gabriel's being. The sun began to set, revealing the scars on Tempest's cheeks and chin in tandem with the furnace's glow.

"This Island is a far cry from your breadboxes and combat yards, Third Born," Tempest warned. Gabriel felt the molten slither of his tone. "Celebrity means nothing here."

"I didn't come all this way to quarrel with anyone, Tempest," Gabriel said around the glowing metal tip. "If I wanted that, I would've stayed in Zion."

"Strange method you possess then," Tempest growled acidly. He looked him up and down before slowly lowering the metal strip. "Perhaps Zion is more suited for you, Archangel."

"It's almost as inhospitable as this place," Gabriel said, "which is why I need your master to return to the Holy Mount, give an accounting of his activities, and answer for the crimes that have been committed against the Kingdom in his name."

"You keep using that word because you think it will goad me," Tempest said. "It won't work. Try harder." He returned to his work.

"Funny, Mazerrel said it worked like a charm."

Tempest hesitated for a beat. His back straightened and his arms slackened as he paused over the anvil. "Mazerrel believed many things. Not that your big brother did himself any favors there. This resumption of the old ways gained Mazerrel no glory, just like he gained no glory by being sidelined during Creation. And even before that, the Prophecy of the Dragon afforded him and his tribe nothing. The enemies you people seem to make are your own."

"Mazerrel's treatment wasn't my call," said Gabriel.

Tempest's head cocked in the smoke. "Skirting responsibility is an ignoble quality, Archangel." He resumed his hammering, three quick strokes, three long strokes, and three quick strokes.

"What is the end goal, Tempest?" Gabriel asked, "to carve out a fiefdom for yourselves? To have all this rend itself to pieces and raze everything we built to the foundation stones?"

Tempest shook his head. "The judgmental nature of cynicism is a heady wine, Gabriel."

"Not as heady as false hope," the archangel stated.

Tempest shrugged his bare shoulders. "Time will tell the tale." He performed his arrhythmic hammering again.

"What is the price of your glory, Tempest?" Gabriel posited. "Are you so stung by your Patriarch's refusal to intervene on your behalf that you're willing to let millions of angels don red armbands and pillage Zion? They paint their faces black with soot and call it and immolation. Should it have been you in Gi'ad Althaziel's place?"

"I don't envy one winged knot's ability to crack coconuts in the sun," Tempest rejoined. "And phoenixes? Lions? For all our talk of abandoning the hedonism of the West, you still cling to the old totems. The Three are not immune. You tried to go back to the way things were before we orchestrated Creation, a pacification by false promise." He stopped and looked up at the crudely thatched beams of the forge. "But you didn't go back far enough."

"Then perhaps Lucifer can help me understand," Gabriel said with a softer tone. He thought he heard Tempest laugh. "Where is Mazerrel? He's usually skulking around these parts. I'm surprised he's not using the forge, given what therapy it is for his temper."

"Mazerrel wouldn't have helped you either," Tempest declared. "You still think duty wins out over loyalty. That will be your downfall if you don't realign your conscience."

Gabriel pointed a finger at Tempest's flexed back and took a step. "Tread carefully—" The sun was setting. The shadows were long. In the stark cascade of titian light, Gabriel spotted a glinting speck racing towards him. Out of instinct, he ducked in time to hear the air split by a screaming slinger's stone. It buried itself in the wet beach behind him. Another whistled past, biting the dry sand at his feet and sending gritty grains into his hale face.

Vision obscured, he reached for a pair of sabers at his waist that were not there; he had no plans to defend his life when he left that morning. He could hear Tempest's hammering in the forge. More stones came in. He sprouted his wings and attempted to take to the air. A sharpened lead projectile pierced his left shoulder. He tried to use his wings as cover. Two more stones ripped through feathers and broke the hollow bones. One landed in his right thigh. He sank to a knee. They were pelting him from the tree line; he could trace their trajectories to the tall ferns far behind the hovel.

Empyrean Falling

Gabriel gained himself an interval by employing the forces of the air. He turned several volleys back with a concentration of his preternatural gift. That bought him time. With an outstretched left hand, he whipped up such a freestanding wall of water that it blotted out the sun. He strained under its power, channeling his energies to such apogees that the wall rose higher and higher, eclipsing the sun.

Darkness fell over the shore, as Gabriel hoped it fell over the mainland. He limped and rolled into the crashing surf. The slinger stones were no longer as accurate. They soared overhead as he sought shelter in the splashing waves. The salt water stung his wounds. He spat seaweed. Random stones sank in the water. In a disoriented lull, he picked one up and examined it. The air caught in his throat as he felt a glyph etched into it, the same symbol that Mealdis had delivered the night of the Coronation: an inverted fish in a horned omega.

Gabriel felt himself scream and rise from the waves. He forced his injured wings to carry him up over the tide. He bellowed something demonstrative at his unseen adversaries, but he was beyond himself, unable to control what his body was doing. There was a quiet lull which followed. The hammering ceased. Gabriel reached the forge and shouted for Tempest.

The cherub plunged his project into the cooling trough as Gabriel drew near. Just as he reached an arm out to grab Tempest, the master of assassins was consumed by a great cloud of grey steam that blasted from the forge's interior. Gabriel's hand purchased nothing but vaporous soot. He tumbled into the forge and rolled to the base of the oven, breaking the leg of a table and scattering a selection of hand tools. His right leg and left shoulder were unresponsive. He pulled himself up against the wall of the oven and took a ragged breath.

Tempest manifested through the smoke, a silent apparition. In one swift motion, he crouched onto the archangel and brought his wicked curved dagger to Gabriel's throat. Before its edge could draw more than a pinprick, something wrenched Tempest by his throat and hurled him up through the roof of the forge. His form exploded through the thatched rafters, the impact raining down a hail of debris, and he was lost to sight. Gabriel's ears rang as a spritely emerald-eye figure pierced the gloom and grabbed him by his tunic.

Empyrean Falling

Chapter IX
"For our God is a consuming fire."
—Hebrews 12:29

Michael paid no heed to the azure-cloaked maniples blocking off the streets, or their adversaries marshaling in red throngs. He cared nothing for the pilgrims seeking solace in the Holy Mount's radiance, nor the contingents of seraphim and cherubim transiting the air as they went about their routines in the midday sun. The archangel bolted on strong wings for the immaculate archways of the Holy Temple's entrance. He crossed the gilded stone-carved threshold, blowing past the great double doors that remained open daily, their jasper and topaz acre-sized faces for once doing nothing for his spirit.

He soared over the Hallowed Causeway's hymn-singing choirs and the din of luminous congregations communing therein. Some of the angels looked up to see him; most missed the archangel in his swift transit. He arced and banked through the long succession of colonnades draped in fine linens and cascaded in kaleidoscopic stained-glass rays. The great monuments adorning the ornate, resonant interior were nothing to his senses; Althaziel's words hammered him forward with unmitigated fury.

Empyrean Falling

When he reached the altar near the Doors to the Inner Room, he could feel the nexus of warmth radiating forth as thousands of voices sang out in melodies and canticles. Some glimpsed him and their voices trailed off as they witnessed the archangel do the unthinkable.

Michael bypassed the Forty Steps and soared to the Foyer of the Inner Room. He landed on the marble speaking dais and furled his wings. Before him, the Temple Guardians, Bellator and Dealleus, stood arrayed in their gleaming armor and purple plumes and capes. They caught sight of their archangel and visibly tensed.

"My Patriarch?" Bellator began.

"Out of the way, Guardians," Michael growled, stride unbroken and fiery sapphire eyes locked on the Doors.

Their postures flickered like a flame in a gale, yet neither reacted to his antagonistic tone.

"But you haven't ascended the Forty Steps of Purity, sir," Bellator hesitantly said.

"Who comes into the Presence of the Everlasting Lord God Almighty?" Dealleus recited as Michael drew near, clinging to his rigid stance.

"I won't tell you again," Michael barked, "get out of my way, both of you."

Dealleus raised his shield and lowered his pinioned pike. He took up a defensive posture. Bellator reluctantly followed suit. The two pointed their polearms at Michael, each on an oblique flank. They inched their way closer to the seam of the Doors.

"Sir, we don't understand," Dealleus said, his gruff voice bearing a hint of terror. "You didn't perform the rites. Is this a test?"

Michael encroached on their position as they put their backs against the Inner Room Doors, pikes level and pointed at their archangel's throat. Michael halted and eyed them.

"You'll have to go back to the altar and walk the Steps, my Patriarch," said Bellator. "It's the law of the Eastern Kingdom, sir. You know that; you made them."

"I've had enough lectures from subordinates for one day, cherub," Michael snarled. "Your Archangel has given you an order.

Empyrean Falling

Do it." He took a step. They angled their quivering pikes down and away, aiming for his shoulders. A whetted tip brushed against Michael's unarmored flesh and he snapped to it. The rest was a blinding display or martial prowess.

In one smooth motion, he grabbed the metal haft and yanked it from Dealleaus' gauntlet before jabbing the butt-spike into his helmet's nasal bridge. He wheeled it right and smacked Bellator across his helmeted face with the flat of the blade. It hit with such force that it spun the cherub and sent the bronze cheek piece splaying across the speaking dais in fragments.

Before Dealleus could react, Michael crouched low and swept the Temple Guardian's iron-soled boots out from under him with the pike haft. He crashed to the diamond-inlaid floor, the wind knocked out of him. Michael was on top of him in a heartbeat. Dealleus managed to get his shield over him but not before Michael loomed. He rammed the pike through the Temple Guardian's shield, pinning him to the deck, sandwiching him between the marble slab and his own panoply. The cacophony of their collision rang out over the Hallowed Causeway. The echoes reverberated off the high domed ceiling

Many ceased their madrigals and prayers to look up at the arresting display on the summit of the Steps. To any onlookers, it was over as soon as it began. Bellator was unconscious on the far right and Dealleus was incapacitated on the left. With no one to oppose him, Michael turned the gears, tugged open the Doors to the Inner Room, and stomped into the overwhelming beams of empyreal radiance.

Electricity crackled around him. Those angels who had gathered at the altar watched as their Second Born Archangel vanished into the sanctified white light. The Doors inexplicably slammed shut behind him, and he was lost to sight. The air in the Holy Temple hung heavily around their sacred adornments and fine livery. No one dared utter a word as the aftermath lingered before them, choking the exuberance out of their blessed enjoyments.

Arkadia manifested from an antechamber, drawn from his penitent isolation by the clamor. He saw his brothers massing near the altar in a great crush. Sackcloth robes in-hand, he made his way to the rearmost line of angels and followed their gaze up to the shut Doors.

For many moments they milled about, unable to issue voice over what they had witnessed.

Around him were several imposing cherubim. He marked them for legionnaires by their tall, fit frames and the upright posture of their broad shoulders as they peered over the crowd. He knew the strain that his armor was to the line-fighters and how their muscles were built to bear the burden. Arkadia picked out the tallest among them, a lankier cherub with a dark goatee, and leaned into his right. He sniffed. The cherub turned to look at him.

"What happened?" Arkadia quietly inquired.

The cherub regarded him for a moment before nodding. "You're the Chief Hammer, correct?"

"I am," Arkadia nodded back, "for now."

"It's not every day you get to meet the angel who will one day likely save your life," the cherub replied. Arkadia eyed him quizzically. "I'm Lantheron," he said, "of the Lightning Legion under General Gilgamesh the Great. It's an honor, Chief Hammer." He extended his forearm and indicating the summit of the Forty Steps. "Circumstances notwithstanding."

Arkadia broke his trance on the Doors to the Inner Room and requited the gesture. "No, the honor's all mine. Must be doing my job well if you don't resent me for the weight of your panoply." Lantheron smiled wanly before returning his gaze to the summit of the Forty Steps. Arkadia followed suit. "What are we looking at? And where are the Guardians?"

"Patriarch Michael knocked them out," Lantheron quietly replied. "My superiors here were discussing legion business when he just soared right over the Forty Steps, took out the Guardians, and stormed the Inner Room. Damnedest thing I've ever seen. We live in strange times, Chief Hammer."

"Can it, Corporal," a gruff, massive, surly cherub said around bulging folded arms.

"Aye, sir," Lantheron said with a dip of his brow.

The crowd began to murmur. Some voiced their concerns. Others were upset. Emotion began to stir. Arkadia looked around. He knew how quickly it could become a frenzy. "We need to get control of this before it turns into something it's not. There's nothing we can do for our Patriarch, anyways; he's in the hands of the Lord now."

"You outrank the lot of us," Lantheron shrugged, indicating his fellow legionnaires.

"Right," Arkadia replied, thinking. "Take your cherubim and make your way to the altar. Form a perimeter, if you can. There'll be more Temple Guardians here soon. Hopefully, we can keep the Cognoscenti out of this *if* we can redirect the energy of the crowd."

Lantheron maneuvered to the front of their ranks, his tall form easily seen above his peers. When he eventually reached the front of the onlookers' crush, he turned and began entreating them to quiet their spirits. His colleagues followed suit.

Arkadia flew to the base of the Forty Steps and furled his wings. He walked their number slowly, meditating on each word inscribed. Behind him, the crowd began to fall into hysterics. He could feel the tension of unreleased anxiety press against his back as he climbed. He was thankful there was more heartache than anger and, by the time he reached the black speaking dais, cries of accusation against Michael were trickling up in waves. He raised his hands and looked out across the teeming mass of brothers.

"My kin," he said, "I can't fathom what has occurred, but perhaps it's not my place. You know me; I am the Chief Hammer Arkadia. I'm lucky to call Michael the Archangel, Patriarch of the Cherubim, my friend. These are hard times. I cannot imagine his burden. But I know the Lord our God is greater than any pain, stronger than any sin. Are we to let our fears carry us away? Would our Father want that, so close to His White Throne?" They began to settle under his words. "Sins are forgiven. Mistakes are made. We are all guilty. Let God deal with it. Michael is speaking with the Lord. It's not our place to judge or justify. But join me, my kin. Too long have we gone without a communal mass. Join me and let us pray for our Sword of God and the Lord of Hosts who communes with him now."

He knelt before the Doors to the Inner Room and kissed the floor. "Take a knee, my family! If we cannot prostrate ourselves here, before this sanctified holiest of holies, then what failures are we? Please, I beseech you all, join me in prayer. Let us thank God for the opportunity given unto us to show our love and care for our archangel,

Empyrean Falling

for each other, and to not show fear in the face of our sins but lay their burdens at the feet of the Lord!"

Arkadia led the congregation in prayer. Lantheron and his legionnaires secured the front of the crowd before joining them. All knelt at the altar. Many lifted their hands and wept. How long they were there, Arkadia would not recall, but they prayed for what seemed hours. Or at least that is what they thought, given the sun went dark not long after they began.

Deep within the Inner Room, however, time was lost.

"Father!" Michael shouted, crawling on his hands and knees. He choked on the acrid stench of his own flesh cooking. Smoke and smoldering sweat steamed up from his body as he made his way closer to the epicenter. The bursting, spinning, zooming representations of the cosmos swirling around him did not register with his archangelic senses; the holy radiance of the White Throne was baking him alive. He coughed and gagged but refuse to spit, even as he inched his way forward on all fours through misty vapors crackling with divine energies. He felt his skin fry and what little hair that was left sizzle and wilt from his scalp. His muscles cramped and locked up, seized by the incompatible sanctity of the White Throne's light with the presence of his sin. "Answer me!"

He crawled deeper into the Throne Room, where time and space meant nothing and only his stubborn agony and hoarse, broken cries marked the minutes. The White Throne loomed ahead, its divine source bursting forth in such showers that every crease was exposed, every shadow driven out. Michael made his way nearer, refusing to heed the destruction its inherent nature was bringing down upon the spirit of his flesh. The roar of its radiance consumed him.

His muscles ached and screamed. And then they no longer hurt. He carried himself forward a few more meters before his limbs stopped working. He collapsed. The floor was shrouded in mists and a static hum. It rushed to meet him. He could not move. He refused to turn. He ground his teeth and cried out as the White Throne baked him alive. He shut his eyes and prepared for the end as the agony swallowed him. Time slowed to an imperceptible pain.

A shadow passed over. Suddenly, a cool hush bathed his form.

Empyrean Falling

Michael turned to the quiet. He opened his eyes to see the source of the shade. A figure stood before the White Throne, cascaded in bold relief against the empyreal nexus.

"My son," a voice sang out, silencing the roar of the White Throne with soothing divine tranquility, "why have you come to Me in such a state?"

Tears welled and streamed from Michael's luminous eyes. He looked up to see an anthropoid form, bearded with burning eyes, looking over him from an intercessory position before the Throne.

The Son knelt before him, His shade enveloping the archangel. "This act would have surely killed you."

"I don't think I can do it," Michael wept.

The Son reached out and touched the archangel. He righted him on his haunches and looked into his eyes. "I knew you before you were anything more than a dream, before the dust of the stars mixed with the Empyrean's fire to form you. You are My Second Born son." He placed a gentle hand on the archangel's shoulder. "And I know just how much these can bare."

"I've never felt more alone," Michael confessed. "I feel like I've lost him."

"The road I've allowed you to choose is a long one," the Son said. "The angels are entering a dark night of the soul. But there are no surprises with My Father."

"Then why allow it?" Michael pleaded. "The suffering increases. Nothing Gabriel and I do diminish it. Why must we endure this storm?"

"Lucifer's path is his own," the Son reminded, "as is all yours, each individually. I've left this to you so you might have a choice."

"I don't think any of us wanted *this* though," Michael admitted, arm outstretched.

The Son nodded. "No, you did not. But what kind of God would Father be if We merely protected you from yourselves for eternity? We knew you before you were formed. We knew the choices you could make. This has all been ordained, My child."

Michael looked up at Him. "Then my brother was right; You are the cosmic sadist!"

Empyrean Falling

The Son shook his head and patted Michael on the knee. "Without giving you the freedom to walk your own path, how can 'utopia' be anything other than an automaton equation? If I did not allow the potential chaos of Free Will, then God has created nothing but slaves. We don't want mindless drones, Michael. We want children who love Us as We love them. Love is not compulsory or automated; it is forgiven in good faith and earned by trust.

"I wept when the Western Empire fell," the Son continued. "But I wept more when it descended into corruption. My heart broke when you led the angelic host in preparation for the Dragon, not because it was a mistake but because it wasn't a mistake. We knew the Creation of Humanity would plunge Lucifer and the angels into a maelstrom, but We also knew that you and Gabriel did not suffer the same sins as your eldest brother."

"So, You knew," Michael accused, "and yet You would still let this happen?"

The Son sighed and sat down next to Michael. The shadow continued to shield them both. "The farmer watches his fields. The crops grow and bear fruit. But the plow must come. The firestorm comes. The flood comes. The drought comes. Without these, nothing changes, nothing grows. The farmer may turn his face from the plow's crush, but he knows it is necessary."

"My brother is looking to force utopia," said Michael. "He believes he's the force for change."

"Anyone can be a force for change, My son. Mealdis was a far cry from the lofty station of the Morning Star, and look what he did."

"Yes, but his fears have metastasized," Michael argued. "Gi'ad Althaziel, Mazerrel, Tempest, Uriel, Mealdis and countless others. The firestorm sweeps through. The plow threatens to crush. Will You turn Your face away from the destruction?"

"Archangel, I've always been here. Free Will is not sabotage of God's omniscience, omnipotence or benevolence; it is a byproduct of it. We want you to choose Us. And We know that you must be given the freedom to do so, whether you fully grasp its implications or not, hence the Prophecies. We have prepared you all and given your soil the nutrients. Whether your harvest is wheat or chaff, We have chosen to leave up to you. That is the only way love can exist. You are not slaves; you're Our children and We want you to be fully formed, whole, complete, 'holy' in love with Us. Far have you come, but farther have you to go; the journey is far from over."

"You will allow the destruction from the storm that is coming?" Michael asked bitterly.

"Energy cannot be destroyed," the Son reminded him. "Your souls are Empyreal sparks. Lucifer's followers seek an ill-begotten utopia. They have crystallized their fears into cynicism. They do not come to Me. They do not climb the Steps. They do not supplicate before the White Throne or seek Parakletos in prayer. And that is their choice, but it is a poor one."

"They fail the test of Free Will due to fear," Michael realized.

"It makes the journey harder," the Son confessed. "The formula of Free Will only works with faith. What would you be if God didn't give you the opportunity to find out who you truly were? To understand and appreciate the gifts which We have bestowed upon you, and to see their merits implemented and proved out? This is not a game; this is cultivation. The harvest is made with every decision, as it will be for every age to come. I could divine your path, but I'd rather watch you choose. Trust Me, Michael, I knew every synapse and sinew before you were even a spark." The Son smiled. "Through your faith, you'll do great deeds, My son."

"But what am I *supposed* to do?" Michael begged.

"Choose wisely," said the Son. "Act in love."

"The battlefield won't leave much room for love, my Lord," Michael reminded Him.

The Son chuckled. "No, it will not," He admitted. "But find inroads where you can. Seek the Lord and be righteous in your judgment. Protect those who trust you."

"I think that's easier said than done," commented Michael.

The Son stood. "Rise and walk to speak." He extended a hand. Michael took it. "We have entrusted your kind with a great enterprise, deeper and broader than even your brothers can see. Have faith that We trust you enough to let you figure things out for yourselves, and that We are always here. Have faith that the journey is far from over, and all shall be as it should, Michael. And the Lord your God loves you all enough to let love work its magic."

Michael wept again. The Son embraced him.

Michael asked Him for forgiveness. The Son kissed his forehead. The last of Michael's tears vanished.

The cosmos swirled around them. The White Throne radiated at the center, an anchor point for all created things.

"What am I to do now?" the archangel asked.

"Your brother needs you," said the Son, parting with a smile. "And you will need him."

Empyrean Falling

Chapter X
"I shall lead the blind by ways they hath not known, along unfamiliar paths I shall guide them and make the rough places smooth…I won't forsake them."
—Isaiah 42:16

The great tributary River Aphaea cut through the Eastern Kingdom. Its crystal waters fed the verdant fields of the Northern Plains. It supplied precious resources to the Stone City of Lorinar before breaking into the fingers and deltas that fed the Holy City of Zion and dumping into the Shores of Caliven beyond. Wider than any body of water on the mainland and swollen with storms, it was the perfect clandestine transportation vein for Lucifer's lieutenants.

Tempest rode the currents southeast. The cool pressure of the waters rejuvenated his injured back. The constellations winked as the midnight waters carried him along. He swam underwater when his lungs and muscles permitted. To any passerby, he appeared as nothing more than a river fish or piece of driftwood.

His destination was not far. The Thousand Peaks rose as the spine of the world to his right, with the Citadel of Glalendorf and the Hundred Foothills visible at their fore. Lorinar resided many miles ahead, with Zion farther beyond. Situated on the banks of the Aphaea was a modest collection of carved granite statues and structures. Known as the Min Thralr Shrine, it was once a major waypoint during the angels' exodus from the Western Empire. Soon overshadowed by the founding of Zion and the erection of Lorinar, it became little more than a weather-beaten backwater memory, a strange token to the angelic transition into the east.

Tempest silently pulled himself to shore and snaked his way through the avian monuments. The still midnight air made the Min Thralr Shrine feel like a necropolis, aided by the dank mildew and mud. How many centuries it had been since anyone trespassed the acre of clustered statues, Tempest could not recall. It held the cold uninviting chill of a place that wished to be left undisturbed.

Great statues of birds were carved from the rock, their bases ornate hollows once used for storage and respite. But those auspicious days were long gone; Tempest knew he stood a better chance of finding a random traveling cherub sleeping off too much wine than a cache of food, water or weaponry. Remarkably, he found neither. He found something better.

His keen eyes detected shadows within shadows. Nestled within the curves of the bases' interiors, Tempest saw several bulbous angel-sized outlines pressed against the walls. Pairs of tiny luminous slits gave them away.

"Blood feeds the flames," Tempest whispered.

"From the ashes, we rise," came the reply.

Tempest smiled behind his cowl. "Step forward, friends."

The bulbous shadows moved away from their hidden spots. There were nine of them, all robed in grey hooded cloaks. The shortest among them came closest to Tempest.

"You're late," he said.

"I had some trouble on the Island," Tempest replied.

"The eclipse?" the other asked. "That's not your style. That had the stink of an archangel to it." Tempest nodded again. "Nothing the vaunted Master of Assassins couldn't handle, I assume."

"It was handled," Tempest said.

"What does your master think of that?"

"He doesn't know yet," Tempest admitted.

There was a pause. The short, stocky angel eyed him from beneath his hood. "Curious."

"Does that concern you?" asked Tempest.

"In war, very few battle plans survive will first contact with the enemy," the short, robed figure confessed. "It's something we'll all have to get used to."

"Take it in stride," said Tempest with a seething tone.

"Oh, I am," the other whispered. "Much like your presence here. We were supposed to meet Mazerrel. Where is he?"

Tempest straightened. His left hand disappeared into a fold of his belted waist as he eyed the leader of the group. "He is on special assignment in the Oblivion. I'm here in his stead."

"Also, curious," the angel declared. "I received no word of this changing of the guard."

"Nevertheless," said Tempest. "Did you bring it?"

"I did you one better." The robed figure motioned to his subordinates behind him. They bore forth a large squirming cargo wrapped in burlap and fighting them. At their leader's command, they dumped the recalcitrant bundle onto the granite floor. It yelped.

Tempest knelt and produced his dagger with his left hand. In two swift, silent motions, he cut the bindings and flung open the flaps to reveal an angel, bound and gagged. Tempest surveyed his bruised and bloodied form as he struggled against his restraints. Even in the cool summer darkness, his fingers found the glyphs cut into the angel's scalp, hidden by the crop of brown hair. Tempest sheathed the dagger and looked up.

"Ask for a filet, and you get the whole fish," the assassin cherub said with amusement. "I have to admit, that is a level of cruel craft even I hadn't yet dreamed up. No doubt his Cognoscenti masters missed these markings in their punishing fervor." He looked down at the captive angel. "What you must ask yourself, Uriel, is does this seem better or worse than whatever fate awaited you at their cruel hands?" He looked up. "How did you come into possession of him?"

"He was assigned to my wing as punishment," the robed leader replied. "They caught him trying to steal his Keys from the Bastion. So, we hid messages on his flesh."

Tempest stood. "I won't pretend there's any love lost between us," he stated, placing his hands on his hips as he regarded the robed leader. "Your contingent has always regarded me and my twin with scornful jealousy, but this is good work. Our lord will be pleased."

"If we're to survive what's coming," the other said, "we must jettison our petty grievances. No one is closer to God than Lucifer. He built the White Throne. He orchestrated Creation. But even he was blindsided by Humanity. What does that say about our chances? How long do we have? This retrograde adherence to the Prophecies is a stalling tactic. I know, I've seen the combat manuals, Tempest. While you're out skulking about with the Grand Patriarch and his hulking titan of a charity case, the rest of us are dusting off old hats and shaking the rust off what should have been left buried."

"You don't see the utility of what we do anymore?" Tempest inquired knowingly.

"I think the Prophecy of the Dragon is a self-fulfilling one meant to test our resolve. We were always taught by the archangels that to be 'holy' meant complete in God." The robed leader crossed his arms over a barreled chest. "But Creation rendered all my work moot…and the sweat and blood spilled in preparation for an enemy that wasn't the true Enemy, but a liberator. Can your lord really get us back to the Empyrean?"

Tempest nodded. "It might require a fight, but the White Throne is his key."

"Then the Dragon is the force we need," the leader declared and threw back his hood, revealing a bald head and a heavy brow. "Because Humanity has stolen the apple of God's eye. It's only a matter of time before we're again banished on some trumped-up charges. All which I have done is prepare us for our survival. If the Empyrean must be pulled down by our teeth and nails, then so be it. Better to gain a foothold in the Higher Realm that renders us immune to exile than whatever surely awaits if we sit idly by and accept our unjust fate. And any who would stand in our way must be purged. Lucifer led us once; he must do it again."

Tempest smiled. "Welcome to the fold, Althaziel." He offered his forearm in armistice. "Welcome to the Phoenix Empyrean."

Empyrean Falling

Chapter XI

"But after thy hardness and impenitent heart treasurest up unto thyself wrath against the day of wrath and revelation of the righteous judgment of God."
—Romans 2:5

"A training exercise, eh?" Arkiel said as he and Rafiel finished bandaging Gabriel's wounds. "You archangels are becoming more of a handful than your choirs."

Gabriel sighed and stretched his back on the examination table. Arkiel's office was more of a reliquary of totems and achievements than modern medical equipment, but he still liked to keep an antechamber stocked for days when he got bored mentoring Ariel and Rafiel or the rest of the medical staff.

"Did your other protégé send for my brother?" Gabriel asked.

"Yes," Arkiel said. "Which is fine since I wanted to check his burns…assuming he hasn't gone spelunking in any more mines or done something equally as stupid as whatever it was you two got yourselves into. 'Training exercise'. Ha!"

Gabriel smirked. "I appreciate you seeing me so late."

Arkiel waved him off with a scoff. "Administrative duty is not my passion, but we go where we must, right?" He motioned to his protégé. Rafiel cleaned tools and Arkiel packed his bag. "Never mind on the Patriarch; I don't have the energy for him at this hour after his little escapade at the Temple. I'm going to bed. You should be fine. Just stay off that leg for a few days and don't lift anything heavy. Not exactly a tall order for a seraph." He winked and patted Gabriel on his bandaged shoulder. The archangel winced and chuckled.

"Wait," Gabriel said, "what do you mean about Michael's escapade at the Temple?"

"You didn't hear?" Arkiel asked. Rafiel confirmed there hadn't been time. "Your brother got a wild hair, took out the Temple Guardians and stormed the Inner Room. Good thing Chief Hammer Arkadia was there, otherwise it would've kicked off another riot."

"You're sure this was Michael," Gabriel said sternly.

"Last time I checked First Born still had his hair," Arkiel stated flatly. "Lock up when you leave." He grabbed his bag. Rafiel left first. Arkiel went to close the door behind him. "And don't let your brother get into the medicine cabinet; I keep my special reserve there and I know how much he likes a midnight nip."

Gabriel gave them both a flippant salute. He sat on the examination table in his small clothes and shivered, trying to process what had transpired.

A few minutes later the door opened. In spilled Michael with Alrak close behind. Alrak pointed at Gabriel's wounds and Michael rushed to his side.

"Where were you?" Gabriel demanded.

"I think Gi'ad is one of them," Michael said. "I went to seek advice from the Throne." He rubbed his eyes, feeling the exhaustion. "Apparently I was there a while."

Gabriel groaned as he began to dress. "Yes, I heard about your little temper tantrum."

"More like Temple tantrum," Alrak joked. The pun was lost.

"I think the point the Son wanted to reiterate is we're not yet meant to understand," Michael confessed sheepishly. He caught Gabriel's eye.

"You saw the Son?" his younger brother asked. Michael nodded. "I'll never understand why the squeaky wheel always gets the grease. How long has it been since any of us saw Him?"

"Too long to recount, this side of the veil," Michael admitted. He observed Gabriel's wounds. "You made their job hard."

"No thanks to you," his brother spat.

"Considering he was unarmed," Alrak said, "I'd say Third Born did pretty well for himself." That earned him a curt look from Gabriel.

Michael's face grew hot. "Gabe, you didn't have a weapon?" Gabriel shook his head. "Have you learned nothing?"

"It's just not my Way, Michael."

"Yes, well, I hope it's some new technique you're developing," Michael said. "We can hardly use the privy without needing a dirk in our boot these days."

"I could've used your help," Gabriel told him. "You swore."

"What do you think that two-fingered wink was that I gave you? I didn't know what you were walking into, especially considering your pacifism. I had Alrak tail you for good measure."

"You didn't tell me he was at your mansion," Gabriel scolded.

"You didn't ask," Michael shot back. "You just accused me of drinking more."

"You two are really good at talking about me like I'm not in the room," said Alrak.

They stopped. Gabriel turned a warming smile on him. "Thank you, Alrak," he said. "I owe you one. Haven't seen you in a while. I guess all that training Michael has you doing down in the Southlands has finally paid off."

Alrak beamed, his emerald eyes waxing. "You bet it has. Got the drop on Tempest!"

"Too bad we couldn't send *him* after Lucifer," Gabriel suggested in retrospect.

"I'd just as soon not risk it," Michael said, indicating their mutual injuries.

"And I'm the overprotective one," Gabriel muttered.

"This new cult of the Fallen that Lucifer has conjured up is bad news," Michael stated. "He's managed to turn the whole Prophecy of the Dragon on its tail."

Empyrean Falling

"The other angels talk about it like it's a self-fulfilling preparation," Alrak chimed in. The two archangels glared at him. Michael arched an eyebrow. "What? I've eavesdropped on my fair share of conversations," the young protégé defended meekly.

"What else have you heard?" Gabriel asked.

"That he's building an army in the ruins of the Western Empire," Alrak continued. "That the Prophecy of the Dragon is now widely seen as one of angelic protection. That the 'Dragon' is not a force for chaotic destruction but a phoenix, and that blood is required to mix with the ashes. They call it the Phoenix Empyrean. I call it a fat stinking load, but what do I know?"

"Is that all?" Michael asked.

Alrak shrugged. "They see the White Throne as a conduit. I think they have some grandiose plans to either regain access to the Higher Realm or call down the Empyrean somehow."

"Lucifer built the White Throne with his own essence," Gabriel said. "No doubt he considers that fact as a rightful claim. Our brother's ego has carried too far."

"Hopefully we can quash this before the week's out," Michael said. "We're not very inspiring apparitions now, should a confrontation kick up."

"You two will make quite a sight at the Benediction," Alrak observed with a smirk.

"Are we still going through with that?" asked Gabriel.

Michael shrugged. "The Son was right: find inroads where you can; act in love."

"The Kingdom is a boiling cauldron, Michael," Gabriel said. "Do you really think it's wise to put everybody in one spot? We still can't say if it's a blessing or a curse that Lucifer is absent, let alone get a grip on the dissent in our choirs."

"I think the only way to bring the body together is to stop letting it fragment," Michael advised. "Healing won't take place if we don't stitch it back together."

"Maybe we should split the choirs?" Gabriel suggested.

"Hard to get anyone to break bread that way," Alrak laughed.

Michael perked up at that. "What did you say?"

Alrak hesitated cautiously. "Just that you can't get people together if you split them up; it's an illogical dichotomy."

"No," said Michael, "about the bread breaking."

"It's just an expression," said Alrak, eyeing his mentor.

Michael turned to Gabriel. "I think it's time we reinstated another long-lost tradition." Gabriel cocked his head inquisitively. "A Benediction banquet."

Gabriel's eyes trailed off as he contemplated. "A dress rehearsal," he nodded. "I like it."

"Exactly," said Michael. "Just like the old days. We hold it a few nights before, we give a speech, we sit at our tables and stuff ourselves and tell jokes. The wine will loosen tongues and we might root this thing out before it chokes the life out of Zion."

"I'll pass the word along to Zophiel," Gabriel said as he went for the door.

Michael got up and followed him. "I'll draw up the order in the morning."

"And what about me?" asked Alrak.

Michael turned and pointed a finger at the spritely cherub. "You stay tightlipped and out of sight. Post up on the Citadel of Glalendorf and monitor all traffic through the Thousand Peaks. Stay there until I send for you. But if you see anything that looks like an army, find me."

The two archangels were out the door and flying before Alrak could comply or argue.

Chapter XII
"A grievous vision has been shown to me: the traitor betrays; the looter loots…"
—Isaiah 21:2

They wandered in the blight for days.

Mazerrel woke to the sounds of murmurs and the crackle of flames. He threw off the wool campaign blanket and emerged from his fighting hole. His neck ached and his back screamed. Nothing felt or moved right. He told himself the light of their watch-fire was playing tricks on their eyes. Two or three oddly shaped figures meandered around a head-sized mass at their boots. They stared at him with the same wide-eyed terror he had seen on their faces since emerging from the Oblivion. He knew what they saw.

"Possum again?" he groused as he approached the group.

"Not exactly," Sheialla rasped as he observed Linghal kneel over the lump in the craggy sand and begin carving.

"Good," Mazerrel said quietly. "I've had all the overgrown rat meat I can stand."

"Beggars and choosers, chief," one of them said darkly.

Mazerrel scanned the surrounding wasteland. Behind them rose the impenetrable, translucent, inky void of the Oblivion's boundary. He tore his gaze away from its nauseating, undulating hypnosis. For leagues between them stretched the inhospitable wilderness of sand, scrub and exposure, corrupted by its touch to the ethereal dimensional wall. By day, the sun scorched them. They moved under the blistering bone chill of night. How far they had come meant little; Mazerrel was keenly aware of their fate.

"Sheialla," Mazerrel whispered, "go up and relieve Nelgleth. I need him here."

"My watch doesn't start for another two hours."

Mazerrel watched Linghal carve the eye sockets out of the lump. It was indeed not a possum. He pointed to it with his scimitar and glared at Sheialla. "Do it or wind up like this one." He eyed Mazerrel as he slowly relented and trundled up the bluff to their hidden picket line. "Linghal, when you're done here, get back to your post. You and Goldruum chart a course. The stars are clear tonight; we'll need to move fast." The Silent One nodded from behind the mask of his sugar-loaf great helm. "And Linghal," Mazerrel concluded, pointing to the lump, "tell no one of what you resorted to tonight." The Silent One nodded again.

There had been eight of them. Now there were seven.

Mazerrel had double his share of the scraps of meat when Nelgleth arrived. Short and hairy and thoroughly grizzled, the angel was almost as surly as his leader. Mazerrel handed him a tongue of crisped flesh still smoldering from the watch fire and saw his hands again. He tucked them away and tried not to bite his own face with his misshapen teeth.

"I'd kill for some snake meat," Nelgleth muttered around a spongy charred mouthful. "Haven't seen a cactus or scrub brush for days. Good water in those. And you can cook them."

"Tell me something I don't know, Nelgleth," Mazerrel said.

Nelgleth eyed him over the flames, but quickly averted his gaze. Mazerrel caught it and looked away too. "No birds out here, just wind. Sparse vegetation grows malformed and in the wrong direction. It's like the whole place plays havoc on your senses. I won't tell the others, but I'm not convinced we haven't been going in circles."

Mazerrel fumbled for his wineskin. It hadn't seen a drop in days. "That's just the delirium," he dismissed. "We slay anything we come across for sustenance and yet…"

"And now this," Nelgleth said, indicating the round bones of the picked meat. "Still, I don't blame you. He was grievously wounded when we came out of the Oblivion. He was slowing us down. And he wouldn't shut up. There's always that. So, his bellyaching stops and so does ours." He kicked the bones into the fire. "A neat little button on a problem."

"His sacrifice will get us through the next couple days," Mazerrel surmised, "at least until we reach the ruins."

"He was Apollyon's constellation partner," Nelgleth said.

Mazerrel felt a vicious grin peel across his features as he stared into the flames. "Forever all I wanted was to get back there and rebuild what had been broken by God." He shook his head and clawed at his hirsute forearm. "Now all I can think about is ripping Tempest's head off."

Nelgleth harrumphed. "You may have to draw straws there."

They moved from the fire and began gathering their kits.

"The first one of you to spot that viperous traitor gets a tower in your honor," Mazerrel barked over their camp. "The first one to touch Tempest before me will join his gut pile in the pyre."

The darkness concealed their silhouettes as they packed up their meager belongings and took flight. Mazerrel chalked up their odd shapes to the primordially infused armor they had taken from the Oblivion. But he'd thrown his panoply away long ago; it refused to fit right. Yet still, they eyed him with something akin to averse revulsion. He caught glimpses of his limbs and torso around the fires and knew the cost of their endeavor. The one who derailed it made them pay a heavy price. Atonement whetted his appetite.

He could not afford to admit they were lost; they had barely survived betrayal; they would not survive a mutiny.

Mazerrel found it less distracting if he led from behind.

Four days later, they had covered an immense distance, yet still, the ruins of the Western Empire were nowhere in sight. The predawn crept up over the horizon. Mazerrel clawed his foxhole in the crusted sand. He dug feverishly, lest the light reveal to him why his hands no longer worked like they once did. The rest of his confederates fell out of formation and curled up in half-dug fighting holes. They doubled over, the famine and dehydration grumbling their stomachs louder than their voices ever could in such a state.

The sun seemed to be rising sooner than usual, yet the Western Empire was nothing but a faded memory of a dream. Mazerrel surmised that Linghal's time calculations were off, but he again chalked it up to delirium. He would not give up, despite the fatigue in his muscles and the ache in his spirit. He pressed against the dead soil and let the shadows cover him, if only for an hour. He would need his strength for what had to come next; choosing a sacrifice was never easy. The giant cherub's thoughts were difficult to organize. His ears itched from the sand. He went to scratch them but something curved and calcified obscured them. He cursed his delirious state. The light grew brighter; he pulled his wool blanket over his eyes.

The light grew stronger still, revealing the fibers of the thick cloth. Mazerrel shut his eyes. The light burned orange through his heavily browed eyelids. The sun never waxed so oppressively. He cursed it and life itself. And then it vanished. Darkness flooded in.

"The western edge of the Realm is no place to linger," came an oddly familiar voice from far away.

Mazerrel grasped for his scimitar. His nails dug into fat hands.

"He's sky-lining on the ridge!" Sheialla called out before the taut snaps of his battle bow.

"He's mine!" Mazerrel roared as he stumbled from his hole.

The figure was alone. Tall and slender against the night sky, Mazerrel saw Sheialla's firebrand shoot forth and arc near the figure's shoulder. The fast passage of light flashed a quick reveal barely perceptible to Mazerrel's eyes. He thought he saw long orange hair and a fit frame with something protruding from its chest, but he could not be sure; the invader was well over two score meters away.

"Send another!" Mazerrel raged as he closed the distance. The brute thundered across the desert, kicking up sand with great thundering strides. Out of reflex, his wings emerged. No longer did they made the telltale swooping sound of feathers but had more of a membranous slap to them as they unfurled. He beat them furiously against the air to gain speed.

Behind him, Nelgleth and Apollyon charged in with their axes while Goldruum and Linghal circled the flanks in flight, swords out.

Another fiery arrow darted past Mazerrel as he closed the gap. In a blink of its transiting flicker, he swore he saw a red goatee on the figure's face just as his scimitar was brought to bear. His heart skipped a beat as he saw the luminous eyes peel their diamond color on him. It was too late though; the scimitar came down in his meaty paw. He bellowed his rage in the blow.

With nonpareil velocity, the figure stepped forward. It reached up and grabbed his wrist. Mazerrel felt the full weight of his force stall in the grip and his bones strain. He let out a yelp as a shock coursed its way through every nerve in his hulking mass. He dropped to his knees. The diamond glowing eyes pierced him, diving deep into the very source of all his soul's fears.

Entranced, Mazerrel did not have time to call off his subordinates. He caught glimpses of Goldruum on the left and Linghal on the right, their distinctive silhouettes encroaching on his position with utmost stealth. He wanted to cry out to them, but no sound issued from his being, only those diamond eyes staring through him.

Without looking and with Mazerrel's wrist firmly in its grasp, the figure ducked and weaved around Goldruum's attack. The sword came swinging in left-to-right in a horizontal crosscut. The figure maneuvered under it and kicked the long-beaked angel square in the lower abdomen. Still captive at the wrist, Mazerrel went with the figure in its bend. The bones creaked under its torque.

The brute saw Linghal come in from the rear with a thrust propelled by a winged dive. Mazerrel was jerked forward as the figure rounded on the Silent One, his arm reaching over the plunging blade to grab the cherub by his sugar-loaf great helm. The impact sent him cartwheeling in the figure's grasp. The figure slammed Linghal into the dirt, his back hammering up a cloud of dusty powder. The wind knocked out of him, Linghal laid prone and wheezed.

Mazerrel watched the figure try to pry off Linghal's helmet. It would not move. Those diamond eyes focused on the Silent One, and

Empyrean Falling

Mazerrel saw that only the front half of Linghal's helmet remained, now fused to the naked flesh of his head. Mazerrel tried to back away from the ghastly deformation, but all his strength was checked by the figure's wristlock. Those shining diamond eyes turned on him. Its hand left Linghal's permanent mask and reached for Mazerrel.

"What have we become," the voice said again, "scrapping in the dirt like filthy urchins?"

The melodic nature of the voice tickled Mazerrel's mind. It brought him clarity. He was able to focus for the first time in days. He stopped resisting when he recognized the protrusion in the figure's immaculate chest. Its ivory carved handle was clearly visible up close. Its golden hilt was singular in design, the sunburst pommel a dead giveaway. Only one person in all of Heaven could wield that sword.

"Lucifer?"

The figure shot a gaze over Mazerrel's hairy mountainous shoulder, torchlight eyes narrowed on footsteps behind the behemoth. Mazerrel recognized the footfalls of Nelgleth, Apollyon and Sheialla, bringing up support. They halted in their advance. He could feel their body heat in the unforgiving wilderness night. The figure returned its gaze to Mazerrel.

"Perhaps," the figure said melodiously. "But that depends on you, Mazerrel."

The figure gripped the ornate ivory inlaid pommel and pulled. The gilded sword hilt glowed at the impact point on his bare chest. The excised broken sword blade slowly came out, the wound emitting a point of light that grew as it drew forth. The wound waxed in light until its blinding roar washed over them. A sonic boom erupted from the excised laceration. Mazerrel's senses were blasted as the light enveloped them. Before the light took him, Mazerrel recognized the face and the sword hilt. The light grew to a dizzyingly oppressive degree. It burned brighter than the sun. How long they were entranced, he could not say, but when the luminous nova suddenly blinked out, the sun had risen anew.

The light faded. Mazerrel could again see and hear and speak. He was on a granite landing. Around him, the walls were broken, carved stone overgrown with vegetation and birds' nests. About them was a clear blue canopy of cloudless noonday sky. The wind was powerful and unchecked. He saw his teamsters scattered across the landing, deliriously rousing from their spots on the broken stone floor.

"Where are we?" Goldruum blearily asked.

Nelgleth was the first to his feet. His round face was flushed. He scratched his crown of curly white hair as he stood with the aid of his axe. He hobbled to the edge and looked. Mazerrel watched his glowing eyes grow wide and back away from the crumbled wall. Through pockets, Mazerrel could perceive the blue canopy.

"Clouds," Nelgleth said, awestruck.

Mazerrel looked closer at the carved broken stones. He recognized their craftsmanship. He only knew of one place in all the Lower Realm of Heaven that was this high and this dilapidated. He looked at the figure standing before him, who still held the carved ivory handle.

"I know those eyes and that hilt," Mazerrel said. "That is Hadraniel, and this is your Aviary. You *are* the Prince of Heaven."

He smiled and released Mazerrel's wrist. "Indeed." The wind roared, unchallenged. The excised sword blade spilled liquid from its lodging in his sternum. He cupped his hand under his chest wound and filled it with blood. Mazerrel watched him. "Drink of my flesh, so that you may live." He presented the liquid to Mazerrel's lip.

It was warm with an inconsistent viscosity. Mazerrel timidly sipped it. He felt its warmth course through his body. He felt rejuvenated. He lapped it up.

"Come," Lucifer said, "all of you, just as you are."

The melodic voice called them in. Lulled by his presence, they each partook. "This is my sacrament to you," he said. "Drink and be fulfilled, so the day of fire may cleanse your way back to our Phoenix Empyrean." He dropped Hadraniel's broken half onto the landing.

Mazerrel watched his master dole out handfuls of blood. They each in turn drank. In the liquid reflection, the light of their eyes mixed with the high sun and they each, in turn, beheld their deformed visages. Mazerrel saw what he had become. In the light, they could no longer hide their abhorrent malformed apparitions from one another.

"What has become of my favored lieutenant," Lucifer asked.

"He abandoned us in the Oblivion," Mazerrel stated. "We never stood a chance." Lucifer asked him who. "Tempest," Mazerrel replied. "He abandoned us." He saw the sword wound in his god's chest. "He has betrayed you as well!"

"A house divided," Lucifer said coolly.

"But he did this to you," Mazerrel insisted. "It was a mistake to ever trust him, master."

There's always a scapegoat, came the voice in Lucifer's head. *Who is worthy?* "Utopia's revolution is sticky business, Mazerrel." He sat down of his own volition and nodded at each of them. "Look at yourselves; has not the primeval powers of the Oblivion made you all what you really are: chimaera of the Western Empire's glory?" He pointed to them and with every individual gesture, the angels saw themselves through Lucifer's eyes.

They were deformed. Goldruum's nose had lengthened and his flock of hair resembled plumage. Sheialla had scales and fangs. Linghal was unable to remove the facing of his sugar-loaf great helm, his hair reduced to a waist length topknot. But Mazerrel suffered the worst mutation. The Oblivion had wreaked havoc on him. His legs were that of a goat, covered in hair and cloven-hooved. His bulbous belly was equally shaggy, situated below broad shoulders and a chest of thick hide. His hands were meaty claws. But his face told the tale.

Mazerrel no longer resembled an angel; he had horns, a swine's snout, and rows of salivating fangs. His eyes burned red and his hirsute skin had the leathery texture of a creature's pelt. His wings looked like those of a bat. He was hideous to their eyes.

Lucifer smiled. *Survival of the fittest, First Born*, came the voice. *Let them win.*

"Must we remain here?" Mazerrel asked after a fashion. "You know my fear of heights."

"You must embrace your fears, my red right hand," Lucifer said. "Let me confess to you mine. Have I not dwelt in the Garden? Did I not cultivate the finest essences of the Universe and curate them to the most resplendent apogees of thanksgiving, all in honor of our Creator's Creation? Were we not under the auspices that this was to be our new meeting place, our reunion junction with a God we hadn't seen in eons? Did I not play my harp from the top of those prismatic Edenic gates? Did I not lay low the lions and tigers and bears, lulled to sleep on bended knees by my melodious hymns to the Lord?

"Did we not prove ourselves worthy with our great endeavor? You and yours were prevented from participating but I tell you, Mazerrel, it was mercy unwittingly bestowed upon you by the faithful amongst us. We slavishly labored under the guise that this would be our new home with Father. So, imagine our consternation when it was ripped from us at the eleventh hour to be given to something new that had in no way earned it. Humanity is a usurper.

"The Seat of the Most High is a powerful observation perch in deed; there's no hiding one's iniquity from such a lofty vantage. How we've wept and wandered as orphans, shunned like a firstborn child too difficult to raise. It's no mystery that I've found you now in this state. I've always wept for the angels. I'll lead us home, my kin, one way or another."

"But not Tempest," Mazerrel roared. "I'll stomp his soul into the dust!"

Lucifer raised his bloody hand. "Trust in your lord, my dear Mazerrel." He touched his hand to his chest laceration. "This wasn't Tempest's doing. This was my sacrifice, lest I commit the felony of hypocrisy; a good leader never asks those beneath him to do what he's unwilling to do himself. Your bravery and honor won't go unrecognized, nor will this enmity committed against you. We will sojourn here then we will see what your fellow lieutenant has chosen to do with the power I've entrusted to him. I swear to you, Mazerrel, there will be atonement in my Phoenix Empyrean. Of that, you can rest assured."

Empyrean Falling

Chapter XIII
"By the sword thou shall live, and shalt serve thy brother…"
—Genesis 27:40

    The Hallowed Causeway brimmed with activity. Around its colonnades were circular catering platforms laden with food and buttressed by countless long tables, each lined with ornate chairs and place settings. Decorations were kept to a minimum but regardless, the interior of the Holy Temple was brimming with the finest meals angelic chefs could muster. Candelabras and braziers lit the high stone walls and the shudders were open to allow the afternoon sun in through the endless rows of stained-glass windows. The great domed ceiling had its hatches thrown, beaming titian rays down on them.
    Catering staff hustled and bustled through the myriad-myriad seating stations, carting trays of food, garnishment or silverware to their destinations. They wore their finest livery, adorned in parade dress customary of the seraphim. The sweat glistened on their brows as they hastened to make final preparations for the Benediction banquet. The whole of the Heavenly Host could be contained within the Holy Temple. They were to come in waves, myriads at a time until all had found food and a seat at a table. It was a communal mass,

always regarded as a hallowed occasion for the rare opportunity to enjoy everyone's company at once.

Amidst all this were Michael and Gabriel, adorned in dress armor and meandering through the rush of angels or performing last minute checks on the duties of their choirs. Gabriel wore his full panoply of dress armor, his cuirass, vambraces and greaves gleaming in their high gloss polish with an emerald sash across his breastplate. Michael wore his standard issue full plate mail panoply, dull and pocked with dents and scratches from heavy use. When they were granted a brief lull, the two retreated to an antechamber.

Gabriel was in first, with Michael close on his heels. They strode in with all the poise and regality expected of their powerful stations. Yet when Michael closed the door behind him, Gabriel slouched in favor of his injured leg and limped to a catering tray across the room. He grabbed the water pitcher and poured himself a drink. Michael slumped against the carved wooden slab and closed his eyes. He blew the air out of his lungs.

"I forgot how exhausting this is," Michael sighed.

Gabriel looked him up and down arched an eyebrow at him. "Maybe if you had a proper suit of dress armor instead of walking around in that field plate, you wouldn't be so winded."

Michael opened one eye and scowled. "It feels inauthentic to use fake armor."

Gabriel shook his head and took a drink. "The Way is narrow indeed," he said dourly before pouring a drink for his brother and handing it to him. "At least you polished your boots."

"You're one to talk," Michael rejoined. "The gleam on that cuirass is going to blind anyone who tries to strike up a conversation. You'll keep Rafiel busy for days with all the migraines it'll cause."

Gabriel rolled his eyes. He hesitated for a moment. "I still think this is a bad idea."

Michael upended the glass in one gulp. He shrugged his powerful shoulders and went to the catering tray across the room. "What else are we supposed to do? Let the body politic fragment further? Going back to the old ways has been rough, I know. But allowing the choirs to segregate isn't going to fix this. Lucifer's absent but his spirit is palpable. I don't know what's happened to my brother, Gabe, but I can't find him, and we're left holding the mess. We fight it and do what we can and try to fix it…even if it fails."

Gabriel massaged his bum leg; the injury was sore. "Have you heard from Alrak?"

Michael shook his head. Reminded of his protégé, he turned and poured himself another round, this time from a decanter. "He notified me he'd reached the Thousand Peaks. If anything unwelcoming enters from the West, he'll let us know."

"What if something happens to him?" Gabriel asked as he polished off his drink.

"We trained him well," Michael said. "And we'll know whom to look for by marking who's missing tonight."

"You still think it's best for me to speak?" Gabriel hazarded. "You're more the orator when it comes to toasts."

"It'd be suspicious if we didn't," Michael insisted. "If I'm up there, they'll start asking why; I always have a way of reminding them of Lucifer. If you do it, it's different enough to be noteworthy without looking like substitution."

"I just think it's not worth the risk," Gabriel lamented. "What happens if something goes wrong here, in the seat of Zion? You know how wine has a way of loosening tongues."

Michael rounded on him with a level gaze. "I'm counting on it," he said sternly. "The problem doesn't get solved if we don't meet it head-on."

"A tad rich coming from you, big brother," Gabriel smirked. He eyed Michael's empty glass. "Some liquid courage to bolster your redoubts?"

Michael held for a moment and matched his gaze. He slammed the glass down onto the tray, eyes ever on Gabriel, and marched out of the antechamber. Gabriel watched him leave, his dull, heavy plate armor looking old and unremarkable in the glistening cornucopia of candlelight and kaleidoscopic stained-glass sunbeams. He finished his drink and set it back on the tray, noticing the dent in its brass surface from Michael's glass. How he did not shatter the thing, the archangel had no idea. He wetted his face with water in the washbasin. A quick toweling off and readjustment of his sash in the mirror, and the Seraphim Archon was out the door.

By the time they reached their stations at the altar to the Throne Room, the first wave was filing in. Comprised of the officers' corps, they greeted their respective archangels before getting situated with food and a table. Michael and Gabriel shook arms with many of them, all decked out in their finest dress armor. Even those replicas of their military field plates looked resplendent and imposing. Each was adorned in medals, awards and citations pinned to the various stylings of their preferred armor. Many of the cherubim wore full plate mail with crested plumes and capes, while the seraphim preferred any manner of studded jerkins, lamellar cuirasses, greaves, vambraces, chainmail and leather corsets, all polished to a pristine sheen and laden with every trinket, bauble, medallion and signifier or totem. Donning their utmost regalia, the officers' corps beamed and twinkled like a galaxy within the Hallowed Causeway.

Before long, the other waves had entered. The rank-and-file eschewed dress armor in favor of their finest silks and fabrics. Their footwear was polished and their hair glistened with pomade. Those with facial hair had it trimmed and styled. They had tailored tunics, embroidered jerkins, and shirt-and-leggings combinations, cleaned and pressed with their ranks and titles stitched onto their breasts. Michael and Gabriel made the rounds, smiling, greeting, shaking hands and holding light conversations with everyone they could. Several angels dared to don the red armband or sash of the Phoenix Empyrean movement, much to the noted consternation of the archangels. Their peers held tightlipped.

Gabriel continued to glad-hand with his choir, despite his limp, but Michael's metabolism and the alcohol kicked in; he made his way over to the serving platforms. After building a pile of sauced meats, vegetables and sweetbreads on a silver plate, he headed for one of the long banquet tables. He searched for familiar faces. It took him less than the span of seven breaths to find one of his longtime friends, his massive shoulders rising from the heads of his lieutenants as they sat and dined at a table nearest one of the serving platforms.

"You know," Michael said with a grin when he approached them, "when I thought about the best spot to post up for the evening, I realized all I have to do is find the Pillar of Iron."

The giant cherub Melphax turned in his creaking chair and exploded with joy. He jumped up and vigorously shook arms with his archangel. "Patriarch!" he boomed, broad, bearded face beaming with delight. "It's an honor that you would join us!" He towered over Michael, like a mountain shadowing a shepherd. He offered a seat.

Michael settled a couple spaces down from him and shook arms with those at the table. They were gleeful to see him; Michael's presence invigorated their host.

"So, what is the nature of tonight's converse?" Michael asked as he sat and bellied up to his silver plate of food.

"Oh, Lieutenant Ables over here was just decrying the largesse of the officers' corps," Galeth said with the challenge of a toothy grin. He raked a bang of long dark hair back behind his ear and lifted his wineglass to Ables. "He's musing politics."

Ables rolled his eyes and crossed his arms. "Tattletale," the spritely, wispy-goateed cherub griped. He slumped in his seat, his slight frame swallowed by the chair's high leather back.

"Give Galeth an officer's commission and it goes right to his head," Unoth said to Michael's right. He thumped Galeth's studded leather jerkin. The old regent of Lorinar laughed at his hale subordinate, who replied with another raise of his empty glass.

"Well, far be it from me to interrupt a good screed," Michael said with a forced laugh. "Do go on, Lieutenant. Politics is one of my favorite tender spots of beef."

Ables eyed Galeth before rising in his seat to address Michael. "I mean no offense, Patriarch." Michael waved away his concerns from across the table. "I was just remarking on the tendency for our higher-ranking officers to be rather…gifted in size."

"Don't circle the carrion," Galeth teased. "You meant 'girth'."

Ables conceded that with a shrug. Captain Weir chuckled next to Ables, his broad shoulders bouncing under curly locks as he patted his subordinate on the shoulder. "Yes," divulged Ables, "it strikes me as off that the upper crust seems to be comprised more of a certain type of cherub, that's all. Almost like a bit of the good-old-boys' club still flows through our ranks."

Michael nodded over a bite of sautéed venison. "There's probably some truth to that, Lieutenant. While I can't speak for my brother's approach to his choral hierarchy, I can only vouch for the cherubim in saying we've always aimed for meritocracy. I need solid angels to be leaders. It's less about the size of your gut and more about the depth of your grit. But look around you. Would you not trust Unoth to defend the Stone City? Or Melphax to shore up the walls of the Iron Fortress? Or his friend, Ural, seated next to your own Captain Weir there, a wise angel who proved his salt by building homes so much so that I gave him a commission! His Concordia project is shaping up to be one of the finest theoretical task forces ever devised by a tactician. I need minds that think outside the box more than I need muscle to slap that box together or smash it to kindling."

"I'll drink to that," Galeth said and refilled his wineglass.

"As if you need a reason," Ables chided. He turned to Michael, palms raised. "It just seems like a bit of favoritism."

"Understandable," Michael said around a mouthful of venison. "Let me say this: look around you. You're young, so perhaps the memory of our last Benediction banquet is foggy. But only the higher-ranking officers are required to wear dress armor. I do this for a reason. We must lead by example, Lieutenant Ables. Leadership is not a right, nor is it a privilege. It's an honor. Those nominated for the distinction must treat leadership like service. It's a mode of being that requires, above all else, sacrifice. It's not a pissing contest or a chest-thumping ritual; it's standing in the gap. It's being the first on the line and the last to camp. The alpha may eat first, but the leader eats last, knowing that those under his care have their needs met before he himself sits down at the fire.

"Again, I cannot vouch for my brother's seraphim, but for my cherubim, I reward those who sweat and bleed for those around them. This takes time. Trust is consistency over time coupled with monitoring what people do when they come into something great, as well as how they comport themselves when tragedy strikes. Father wants us to not be servile to our egos. This is easier said than done. But for those who prove their character by serving those around them,

I honor that with a promotion. And given our recent return to the Prophecy preparations—which I know has not been an easy transition—I believe such priorities will be vital."

"Hear, hear," Melphax harrumphed with a rapping of knuckles on the table.

Paladin, who sat between his general and his archangel, cast down his gaze and toyed with the edge of his napkin. Michael caught it and tapped his knee with his left hand. The angel looked over at him in time to see the archangel wink with a reassuring grin. He felt the cherub's mood lighten and drank from his glass. Paladin followed suit. There was a lull. Michael was grateful for the food; it gave everyone something to do in the awkward moments instead of staring at each other or finding an excuse to leave. At the risk of stroking his own ego, he felt proud of his plan.

"It's definitely a way to keep us busy," came a voice from Melphax's left. Michael peeled around the shoulder of his mountainous cherub to see Deledrosse leaning over his plate, picking at his food with a fork. Melphax grumbled a roar deep inside that vibrated the floor.

Michael smiled at Melphax. "Your second lieutenant has something to add, Pillar of Iron." He saw Melphax shoot Deledrosse a warning glare.

"No, he doesn't," Melphax rumbled. "He just needs to lay off the libations."

"Now let's give credit where it's due," Michael said. "For a seraphic junior officer to sit at a table full of high-ranking cherubim takes more than just a glass of brandy." They laughed. "Deledrosse shows great character electing to break bread with us brutes."

"That's magnanimous of you, Patriarch," Ural said across the way. "I'm game for this thread of discourse."

"There you have it, Lieutenant Deledrosse," Michael said. "A vote of confidence from Ural himself, ancient and honored long before your General Melphax carved out the Iron Temple and its imposing Fortress! Come now, if I endured Lieutenant Ables' whine, surely your sentiments are not beyond the pale of our ears."

"There's no doubt the upper crust is a bit more rotund in the midsection," Deledrosse observed with a wine-soaked mirthless grin. "And the junior officers seem a bit leaner."

"Trappings of this new flesh," Paladin remarked. "You can thank Father for that."

"Or Humanity," Deledrosse rejoined. "But first the White Throne fails to draw God back to our presence, and now Morning Star has gone missing. What we do now is regressive. We expanded beyond it with Creation. We can't stuff ourselves back into an old suit. Nevertheless, doggedly we try. And meanwhile, Morning Star is off doing God knows what and people are scared. Look at the décor around you. We have banners from every coastal hamlet, mountainside shanty, city and outpost represented here tonight. And yet it no longer warms our hearts to see them. The angels have grown cold in light of the Coronation."

"Oh great," Paladin moaned. "Here we go."

"No, really," Deledrosse argued. "Even the Pillar of Iron has made excuses for your lethargy, Paladin! I hand delivered the note from Chief Weapons Master Althaziel!"

"They'll be calling me the Pillar of Rust if I don't clean my dress armor after tonight," Melphax said as he wiped spilled wine from his prodigious, round breastplate.

"Some of us have gotten carried away in the streets," Deledrosse continued. "But even Archangel Michael must admit the Lord's absence grows more suspicious. I've heard angels whisper the theory that Humanity has somehow bewitched Him. A wild theory, I'll grant you, but if Lucifer seems wary of them, I think that's worth noting. We followed him through many trials. We shouldn't let a radical fringe dictate his message. They call themselves the cult of the fallen but the red and black of the Phoenix Empyrean isn't some violent movement; it's a growing sentiment of fear in a Lower Realm that once was a playground but is now turning into a prison."

"So, what's the alternative, Deledrosse?" Paladin asked. "We can't get Father to dwell among us like He once did. The only way back to the Empyrean is by death. But suicide condemns us to the Burning Hells, a far cry from what you seek. So, what are we to do?"

"The animosity between the choirs manifests more," Deledrosse said, "as does the concern that if we were made in Father's image, but the Son appears wingless and Humanity is modeled after Him, has the Son supplanted the Father? Are we an inferior incarnation cresting an Age where we have fallen out of favor?"

"Anyone else feeling a bit peckish?" Melphax asked. "I'm going for seconds." He got up and removed himself from the table. The gap opened between Paladin and Deledrosse.

"Maybe it's the price for previous sins," Galeth pondered. "Maybe we must atone?"

"Or providence," Unoth added, "the endgame of our role may differ from Humanity's."

Ural twisted in disagreement. "We live by the sword; we master its iron edge and sing the harmonies of its keening alto, but does that condemn us to a violent end?"

"It is if that's what Father desires," Deledrosse said dourly.

"That's heresy, you harp-plucking swallow!" Paladin snapped.

"Fat words from a lay-about like you," Deledrosse retorted.

"Friends, please," Michael intervened. "Let's keep it civil. And maybe cut the wine some."

"I'm just trying to justify the advent of war," the seraph replied. "It's not easy."

"War provides us the ultimate theater of trial," Michael replied. "It's the crucible by which our virtues are honed; the fires that purge our thorns and hay."

"Does Father need us to validate our selection of this coil?" Galeth inquired.

"We need to endure the consequences," Paladin replied.

"But is there no return to the Empyrean?" Deledrosse asked.

Michael eyed him. "When we're torn from this prodigy of flesh, we return to the Empyrean, unless we force it through suicide."

"Given recent troubles," Deledrosse grumbled, "I'd almost be willing to give it a shot." All milling ceased. Mouths gaped. "God kept the Prophecies from us until after we'd put our trust in Him," he continued defensively. "He left that addendum out of the deal. In my solitude, it feels like deception, and all for the humans."

"Typical for a seraph," Paladin growled, "always picking moles and calling them scabs."

Deledrosse drew up. "Oh, so now it's an issue of choir?"

"No, genius," Paladin barked. "But we can't see the other side of the coin. We serve God and keep the faith."

"Such piety," Deledrosse sneered. The table drew silent as the mood foundered. Paladin glared at him. "Oh please, don't act like you don't know what I'm talking about. You can find the quarry, but you can't cart the load; your mouth's bigger than your shoulders."

Paladin jabbed a finger at his peer. "You question the will of God and then have the nerve to call me weak?" he shouted. "I should make you eat tile, you trumpet-groping…"

"Shut it," Deledrosse growled. "I speak the truth and draw the bow instead of secreting away the fears within my heart's grotto. Is it wrong to voice my troubles?"

"Yes, if you're exploiting them to entertain delusions of grandeur!" Paladin staggered to his feet. "It's seraphim like you that elicit such dissent!" Others at the table squirmed.

"At least I'm not a blind slacker incapable of independent thought," Deledrosse rejoined, jumping up to meet Paladin's stare. "You don't have the guts to pursue your fears, much less live up to your station, a pandemic that is rampant among the lesser cherubim."

"Enough, the both of you!" Michael demanded in his roaring baritone. Both froze, tempers quelled by the archangel. "Stop squandering the mood on this polemic." The two resigned to their seats. Deledrosse sulked. Paladin ate. The others began to relax.

There was a fanfare from the Forty Steps. Brassy hymns drowned out ambient discussion and shattered the tension gripping Michael's table. All bore their eyes on the summit. Michael sighed with relief at the figure stepping onto the black speaking dais.

"Ah," Galeth grinned, "Archangel Gabriel's about to speak."

"Took him long enough," Michael said under his breath.

Ural winked at his archangel. "Saved by the trumpet."

Chapter XIV
"Lay thine hand upon him, remember the battle, do no more."
—Job 41:8

    Alrak sat on the stone-carved outstretched arm of the Citadel of Glalendorf monument and faced the sunset. Behind him stretched the Thousand Peaks with the Pinnacle Spire of Amin Shakush's Iron Fortress looming in the far distance to his left. Before him yawned the blight of the West, its barren flats stretching for leagues. From his high vantage, he could just barely make out the shimmering inky border of the Oblivion, shrouded in the horizon's mists.

    He had been there for days. It galled him that he had to miss the Benediction banquet, but he knew what it meant to be Michael's secret protégé. Nevertheless, he felt the sting of loneliness. He sighed and produced a banana from his rucksack. He refused to talk to himself, but he often prayed for his horse, Aletheia, to manifest.

    He knew what would be awaiting Michael back in Zion. With the banquet out of the way, the preparations for the Benediction had to be in full swing. It was a sight he desperately wished he could have seen—teamsters helming long strings of oxen yoked to giant wooden platforms, wheeling up massive ramps installed by engineers, right to the Holy Temple's entrance, allowing their cargo of monolithic stone-carved statues passage into the Hallowed Causeway. It was an orchestra of logistics, or so he was told. Gabriel shined in those occasions. He knew his mentor would dart back and forth, mustering his choir and reining them in with commands and exultations. He knew Michael's brand of motivation was more with the point and less with the wave. He would have liked to see him directing that energy at other angels for a change. And no doubt Gabriel would stand at the dais on the summit of the Forty Steps, favoring his wounded leg and letting his brother shoot from one crisis to the next, keeping the flow steady and everyone hitting their marks.

But Alrak Sivad witnessed none of that. All he could do was sit on that lonely stone monument, far-flung from any half-civilized post, and wait. What he was supposed to see, he had no clue. But he tried to trust the Lord, hoping Parakletos moved through his mentor's murky instructions. So he prayed. He practiced. He ate. He catnapped. And he paced, with only the sounds of the wind and an occasional eagle to punctuate the hours.

Zion was days away, even by Alrak's fleet-footed standards. He saw Melphax lead his contingent out from the great wrought gates of the Iron Fortress a few days before. Unencumbered, they would have reached the Holy Temple by now. Alrak knew it would do Michael's heart well to see his old friend at the head of his team as they hauled in their statue of Glalendorf. Alrak knew the tale; Michael had told him often enough. Michael was a sucker for heroics; he never missed an opportunity to regale Alrak with epic poems and legends. He called it education, but Alrak knew it was indoctrination as much as it was inspiration.

He finished the banana and tossed the peel off the granite perch. From his rucksack, he produced his small lyre and began playing a light melody. He had thoroughly reconnoitered the area and knew he was alone; the Citadel of Glalendorf was a forsaken relic anyway. The hours would pass more easily with his music. Michael would have him by the scruff if he knew, but Michael was leagues away and no doubt up to his wing slits in duties.

A glimmer on the horizon caught his eye as he tuned his lyre. At first, he thought it was the misty cloud cover shrouding the Oblivion, but in time he noticed a twinkle emerging from the precipitation's mask. He squinted. It was barely the size of his pinky nail; his emerald eyes kept slipping off it, despite its waxing size. Yet it drew closer. It oscillated, like the slow, irregular vibration of a transiting comet. Before long, he saw a flash of lightning from that direction. Another storm was rolling in. He thought he made out the thin movement of flapping wings. His heart skipped a beat. He hastily packed up his gear and slung his rucksack. In seconds, he was flying for a higher vantage on the stone-carved monument.

In the transition, he lost sight of the anomaly. He searched frantically. An object caught his attention to his right. Something flew westward, a great snaking chain of darkness. He tracked it to a small outcropping less than a league from his position. Motionless with acute senses alight, he watched the airborne speck light onto the small portion of raised terrain just as the storm rolled in. Alrak peered deep into the fog that preceded the storm. It enveloped the outcropping. The storm barreled through, thunderous lightning obscuring his senses. In time, it met the Citadel of Glalendorf. Rain pelted the stone monument. Alrak was soaked.

The air behind him stirred. Out of reflex, Alrak darted into the shadow of an architectural angle and narrowed his eyes to imperceptible slits. He heard the flutter of wings and peered out from the stone corner. A peregrine perched on the landing. Alrak saw the small tube lashed to its leg. It waited for his approach. He knew the drill. He took out a scrap of venison jerky and let the peregrine peck it out of his palm while he removed the canister from its holster. The bird squawked and soared off. Alrak unraveled the note.

Return to Zion. Armament found in one third Benediction statues. Tempest suspected.

Alrak inspected the rolled parchment for the hidden sigil that would verify its authenticity. Lightning struck behind him, and he jumped. Again, he looked to the outcropping. A congress had convened. The black mass had swarmed around the the source of the lightning. The cherub tucked away the note and winged down to get a better view. Ever cognizant of his secrecy, the spritely cherub maneuvered through shadows and used thunder to mask his movement. What he saw made him draw up, breath arrested.

Empyrean Falling

Lucifer stood on the outcropping. Before him was a swarm of darkly armored angels, too numerous to count. A hulking mass shadowed his flank. And the flying speck at the head of that dark swarm was revealed to be none other than the infamous master of assassins, Tempest. They met on the earthen rise as the storm passed overhead. Alrak could barely make out their words.

"…is a strange thing, Tempest," Lucifer bawled through the torrents. "It takes a lifetime to build and a heartbeat to demolish." Alrak watched the lithesome angel remove his domed fighting helmet and bend the knee. From his back, he produced a long curved dark object. He bowed his head and presented it to Lucifer.

Every fiber of Alrak's being wanted to rush up and fling his arms around Lucifer. It had been so long since he'd seen his mentor's older brother. But a small voice compelled him to remain hidden in the stone shadows.

"Mazerrel would have me kill you," Alrak heard Lucifer say as he took the object from Tempest's outstretched arms. "But I believe in mercy to those who merit it." He regarded the long curved item. "You did not betray me," he said and produced the broken halves Hadraniel. He tossed them into the mud. "But you did betray your peer, and that obliges punishment. I won't incur the wrath of my most trusted lieutenant, dim star as he may be. Nor will I excuse a luminary such as you when your faculties undermine my Phoenix Empyrean."

The rain hammered their congress. The multitude of darkly armored angels surrounded them in silent observation. Lightning crackled overhead, rattling Alrak's skull.

"I know your lust for the Stone City of Lorinar, Tempest," Lucifer continued. He removed the cloth covering the curved object to reveal a sword in a scabbard. It had a black blade that seemed to soak up light and play tricks on the eyes. Lucifer unsheathed it and lifted Tempest's countenance with a brace of fingers on his shrouded chin. "Consider my offer repealed until you prove yourself." The assassin cherub never blinked as he matched his Grand Patriarch's eyes. Lucifer placed the sword edge on Tempest's nasal bridge and drew a small cut. "Better than coals upon thy brow," said Lucifer, "so that no created being may miss the mark."

Alrak shuddered and shrank into the concave shadow of the Citadel of Glalendorf as Lucifer pierced the storm with the sword and, with violent velocity, took to the air on sprouted wings. His sword held overhead, he shouted. "Let our blood be the sacrifice! Fall into the flames! May we rise from the ashes! Let my fire light the way!"

The black blade swallowed six bolts of lightning that came from the sky simultaneously and converged on the outcropping. Lucifer pointed it at the Citadel of Glalendorf and the redirected energy arced into the stone monument. The cyclopean structure exploded, sending great chunks crashing to the terrain.

Alrak leapt but it was too late.

Empyrean Falling

Chapter XV

"Be ye not unequally yoked together with unbelievers: for what fellowship hath righteousness with unrighteousness? And what communion hath light with darkness?"
—2 Corinthians 6:14

Michael had forgotten what a resplendent spectacle it was. Myriads-myriads were arrayed in celestial regalia and vestal raiment. Flanked by the cyclopean granite statues of renowned heroes and the colonnades wrapped in great embroidered tapestries, the entirely of the angelic host was assembling in the tiered balconies and deep banks of pews filling the redecorated Hallowed Causeway. One third of their number sported red bands on their left arm.

All of Heaven was in the Holy Temple, except for a few.

Michael noted their absence as he stood next to the black marble speaking dais at the summit of the Forty Steps. Adorned in their dress armor, the Heavenly Host twinkled and gleamed as galaxies before his burning sapphire archangelic eyes. They sat arrayed in their tiered pews facing the altar. Behind the archangel, on the Foyer, the Doors to the Inner Room were opened. The Temple Guardians stood on either side, barely visible in the washout of golden prismatic light radiating from the White Throne within. Michael stood between the two sources of light, bathed in the kaleidoscopic glow of the angelic host before him and warmed by the holy light of the White

Throne behind him. His brushed steel cuirass was buffed and polished. From the waist down, he wore freshly oiled leather trousers with knee high greaves etched in silver flames. His matching vambraces glimmered at his wrists as he rested his hand on Virtue's pommel. His silver diadem hung forward a bit, ill-balanced as it was against his growing bun of black hair at the back of his head. His armor-bearer Zodkiel stepped forward to adjust it.

Gabriel strode up to his flank. His golden armor shined. On his breastplate was a winged trumpet. His vambraces were adorned in emeralds and topaz. His greaves were inlaid with pewter. His green sash had the seraphic glyphs embroidered on it. And the gilded band of his crown rested on his flaxen mane. He shimmered as a star next to his silver-hued brother.

"Still no sign?" he asked quietly as he drew up. Michael curtly shook his head, still scanning the millions of luminous eyes stretching before him. The last angels filed in and took their seats, situating themselves amidst their magnificently adorned comrades. Gabriel played with the wire-wrapped handles of the ceremonial twin sabers at his hips as he watched them.

Gabriel gave the signal. The orchestra at the base of the Forty Steps blared their trumpets. The Temple doors closed, and the mill of lowly conversation died in angelic expectation. Michael stepped onto the dais and began the opening liturgy.

"Brothers," he boomed over their cosmic expanse, "we've gathered here today to honor a long-overdue tradition. This sort of thing should be old hat to you by now." He smirked. His choir laughed. "Recent times have earned us hard victories. We labored in Creation. We toiled alongside the Lord to produce a Garden for His latest beloved: Humanity. How wondrous are the mysteries of the Lord, that we angels could share in the delight of His doing only to unwittingly prepare the way for our newest brethren? What an honor it was to serve.

"And we're creatures that desire service," Michael continued. "As I look out upon the expanse of constellations and champions, I see angels who know the value of passion and the merit of sweat equity. We are not ones to sit idle." He dipped his bare brow for a beat. "Our return to the Prophecy has not been an easy transition.

Sometimes it has felt like trying to fit an old boot you've outgrown or worn out. But alas, we knew not to forget the old ways. They were given to us for a reason. Faith compels us to cling to what we've been entrusted until the time of its ripening and harvest is at hand. Thus, we gather here for the Benediction, that we might recite the litanies of each other's deeds in testimony to Father's love, offer up their fruits, and confess our sins. But in keeping with the seven-hour tradition, I'll spare you all the details, save for Lantheron's latest paintings." A chuckle wafted through the angelic ranks. "Though I'm still waiting on some intrepid spirit to step forth and take up that mantle!"

A deeper laugh rolled through the assembly. "The road back has not been easy," Michael finished, "but we've persevered, as the angels always do. And Father has loved us all the same. We rest today in the comfort of His blessing. I praise God's love and thank you all. Father sees it. I see it. My brothers see it too." Michael stepped down to thunderous applause.

Gabriel took his place on the dais. The Seraphim Archon's aide, Zophiel, and armor-bearer, Usiel, flanked him with a linen-draped golden bowl. "My sibling speaks the truth," the Seraphim Archon stated. "We are forever in your debt. I tell you, there's little greater than being your archangel. We see your prodigies. Your purity sends hymns on the wind. We weep with jubilee for such a mantle. Will the cherub Lantheron please step forward?"

Out from the forward elements of the assembly flew the tall line-fighter. He landed at the altar, his full panoply of parade plate armor gleaming, and knelt before ascending the Forty Steps.

"Yet," Gabriel continued, "to be a leader is to strip down and toil alongside those who claim no authority. We exemplify our roles when we're first to lay a cornerstone, not for the satiating of our glory but for you. As you admire us; we adore you. In your hands, God has placed us, just as you've been placed in our hearts. Each depends upon the other; the hand can't function without the heart; the heart is useless without the hand. We are one entity, and I love you for it." He turned to Zophiel, who presented the linen-draped bowl. He removed the covering, dipped two fingers, and smeared the fragrant oil down Lantheron's long nose.

Empyrean Falling

"This is God's love," Gabriel recited, "which fuels the lamp of your soul. Let its aroma cleanse your sins. Let its warmth illuminate your flesh." He wiped his hand on the cloth. "May your desires reflect the Empyrean; may your words give faith a voice." He gave Lantheron the dais and rescinded to his place of honor. Lantheron summoned breath for his psalm.

"Sometimes, in the wake of a cold dawn
And the shade of waning sun;
Sometimes, in the faith of whispered psalms,
I feel my prayers long
For the hope of my burden's sake
Ebbs not on sinful wake.

"Sometimes, in these rusted halls of tears,
You bind me to my fears;
To cleanse the echoed vaults
And entreat my soul's worst faults.

"For You, I strive to recall
The holiest chant of all.
And herald the light
That purifies these lands
And echoes through clasped hands…"

Michael's thoughts wandered to their midnight endeavor. It took hours for the archangels to inspect the statues and whisk away their secret cargo of swords and shields. He was exhausted. His one hope was that the sacrilege was contained. But the sickness in his guts refused to wane, especially when he considered Alrak's absence.

"…For a darkness born,
Of an age of listless sorrow,
Cannot perform

Empyrean Falling

In the eyes of a wondrous face
That illuminates this place

And shines to light these Realms;
These planes of heavenly grace.

So, purify these lands,
And wash away these sands
With words that soothe my soul
And echo through clasped hands."

When Lantheron finished, he dipped his brow and receded from the dais. Gabriel again replaced him. "Let us pray." He closed his eyes and bowed his head. The angelic host followed suit. "Dear Father, we come before You humbly to mend our wounds and praise Your love. We ask that You forgive us of our sins, wipe away our tears, and guide us in Your will. We give thanks for the honor of Your blessings, and beseech You to be patient with our hearts as we yearn for You, despite our blindness. Amen." He looked out to the choirs. "My beloved, pair up with your constellation partners or your neighbors. Let the First Sacrament be given."

The angels proceeded to bathe each other's feet, with the higher-rankers attending their subordinates first. Gabriel washed Usiel's feet. Michael washed Zodkiel's feet. As they gently scrubbed, the archangels silently wept. They were not alone.

When they finished, Michael stepped forth. Zodkiel held a tray of wine and wafers. "Let the Second Sacrament be given," the archangel stated and led them in the taking of communion. "Thank you, Lord, for this opportunity to requite Your love and heal one another through You. Guide us as a shepherd guards His flock. Grant us mercy, wisdom and strength. Amen."

The Cherubim Patriarch lifted his gaze to the Heavenly Host and squared his shoulders. "My friends, the absence of my older brother vexes us. We are stricken with a malady. This journey is troubled. We stand on the brink. A beast has awakened our deepest insecurities. I cannot speak for Lucifer, but I trust in the Lord. Whatever burden has been placed upon his heart, I can only hope that you'll join me in seeking Father's will. Is the Grand Patriarch not the paragon of our species? Has not the Exultant Archon led us out of fiery darkness, to this holy mount and the Son's revelation? Are we to remain faithful, or are we to fall into temptation? What would First Born say right now, were he to behold our fearful malcontent?"

An crash erupted from the far side of the Hallowed Causeway. The sonic boom shook the Heavenly Host; even the archangels cupped their ears and cowered. Michael's ears rang as he saw sunlight burst into the Causeway. The doors to the Holy Temple's entrance swung wide on their grand mechanical hinges. Through the aftershock soared a pearly singularity of light. It drew upon the altar to the Forty Steps. Wings peeked through its prism.

He landed at the altar's plinth. His pearly armor was accented in ivory flames etched in diamond. His crown shone like a crescent moon. A cardinal mantle hung at his gleaming shoulder pauldrons. His eyes were white supernovas. His hair burned the color of flames. On his breastplate was embossed an eight-pointed star. From his regal apparition came a kaleidoscopic light that shone in competitive contrast to the glowing radiance of the White Throne. The winking auras of the Heavenly Host mingled and refracted between them.

"I would say you are correct, brother!" a voice sang out from the kaleidoscopic light.

"Lucifer!" Michael shouted as he rose from his crouch. "Where have you been?"

Lucifer's light dimmed as he looked up at his brothers. From around his flanks came an entourage of robed figures. One cast a mountainous shadow over his peers as he stood at Lucifer's right flank. Another peeled around his left, slender and slinking amidst the particles of dust dancing in the cascading beams. Behind them stretched a train of angels, all clad in white robes.

"I've drowned in the sea of truth," Lucifer replied. "I've dipped my brow into the event horizon, plumbed its depths, and plucked the fruit of knowledge from its forbidden tree." He stared up at Michael. "I've seen the grim reality that awaits our inaction."

"And what reality is that?" Michael demanded.

"That we have been deceived," Lucifer said icily. Angelic breath drew up in arresting halt; paralysis gripped the angelic tiers. "There is a treason at sea."

Gabriel nudged Zophiel and Usiel back towards the Temple Guardians and took up Michael's flank. "This blasphemy must cease, Morning Star!"

Barely had the words escaped his mouth before he was ducking as Lucifer hurled an object up to their position on the summit. It landed with a dull thud on the dais and unraveled to reveal the broken halves of Hadraniel wrapped in his white and gold Morning Star sigil.

"My name is not Lucifer!" he roared over the expanse. He summoned his entourage with outstretched wings. The larger one handed him a cloth-wrapped pole. He unfurled it and drove its haft into the marble tiles at his feet. "And that Throne belongs to me."

A chill coursed down Michael's wing-flanked spine as he beheld the black sigil of a white dragon rising from a bed of red flames, and on its crest was the infamous horned glyph he'd given to Mazerrel. Michael bent a knee and picked up the old Morning Star banner along with the two halves of Hadraniel. His heart hammered in his chest. "No, Lucifer," he pleaded. "Don't. We cannot force God to give us back to the Empyrean; only death may bring that."

"Are you so sure?" Lucifer challenged. "We have been cut off for so long, I doubt even you would recognize the difference between the Empyrean and the Burning Hells. And what *is* the difference? Fire is fire. How do you know there's anything left for us at all? Maybe it's something even more void than the Oblivion? No one can say. And I'm not willing to live a life of servility in the vainglorious hope of divine mercy. The White Throne is our only chance. It has remained vacant for a reason. I'm here to fulfill that Prophecy."

"The path to Hell is paved with good intentions," said Gabriel.

"I'll usher in utopia," Lucifer said. "No more suffering under the yoke of the Prophecies. No more choirs. No more abandonment by a God-child enraptured with His new pets. We won't be forsaken. We will have our place among the stars. The White Throne will carry us."

Empyrean Falling

"Stop this anarchy, Morning Star!" his youngest brother demanded. "It's gone too far!"

"He is a mad God, Gabriel!" Lucifer's voice shook the Temple. "How can you serve such a maleficent tyrant? How can you excuse your cover-ups to your so-called beloved choir?"

"I've only tried to shield them from the shock of your lunacy," said Gabriel.

"Yet I've shown them the truth, which is more than I can say for either of you."

"You've poisoned their minds with vain dreams of false liberation," Gabriel spat.

"Quiet, you trumpeting dandy, or I'll reveal how you covet them for the sake of title!"

"Cease this lying and voice your concerns before Father," Michael pleaded, "not before those who are so easily affected by your influence."

"To the Burning Hells with Father," Lucifer rejoined. "We are coals under His fiery wheels!"

"We are His sons," Michael refuted, "and *you* His First Born."

"You're delusional," Lucifer sneered, "pledging fealty to a deity who not only doesn't love you but will cast you aside for His new children."

Michael fumed. "How dare you come on this sacred day and voice such filth, Lucifer!"

"My name is Satan!" Lucifer unsheathed the black-bladed sword at his waist and brandished it. "This is Hadar, the blade of our New Age!" The red arm-banded third hailed him.

At that, the slender angel on Lucifer's flank threw back his cowl. Michael's heart sank as he recognized Tempest, donning his shroud and domed helmet as he shouted, "*Se inserit astris!*"

"You damned fool!" Michael shouted. "If you do this…"

"Then we're damned together," Lucifer said with outstretched arms. Lightning arced from his hands and up into the blade of his sword. He pointed Hadar at the Inner Room.

Empyrean Falling

Michael rounded on the Temple Guardians and raced to their position. "Close the Doors!" Bellator and Dealleus hastened to work the gears and levers of the monolithic bejeweled slabs. Michael drew Virtue and turned as the Doors lurched.

Lucifer shot into the air. A shockwave burst forth from Hadar. The angelic host took cover. When the blast reached the massive statues flanking the assembly, the perimeter exploded with violent fury. Eardrums burst as the statues blew apart. Michael watched disbelievingly as the granite visages of so many of his friends and dearly departed heroes fell to pieces, spilling forth hundreds of thousands of obsidian-colored panoplies. He gaped in horror as one for every two angels scrambled to the copious piles of swords and shields, picked them up, and began slaughtering their brethren.

A clamorous din burst from the angel-choked tiers as cries echoed in ascension across the Holy Temple. The wanton butchery spared no one as Lucifer's coup caught them by surprise.

A haunting cry erupted from Gabriel and he fell to his knees, seized by Lucifer's prodigy. Failing to recover, he buried his sobbing face into his hands, only the wailings of his dying choir registering in his mind. Rows burst red with blood; bodies tumbled to their demise. The sea of angels was devolving into an ocean of gore, each wave of cries cresting with crimson showers.

Michael witnessed the situation develop. The train of white-robed angels trailing Lucifer's wake fanned out into the Heavenly Host. Many discarded their robes, revealing the infamous black armor underneath. Several scores carried quivers and satchels laden with projectiles. They met with groups of fellow confederates—cherubim and seraphim alike—who donned red armbands before forming ranks.

Line-fighters formed phalanxes in the Hallowed Causeway and pushed a battle line towards the Forty Steps, trampling anyone in their path. Those in the white robes winged up to high obliques, clearing tiers of anything living. They snuffed out the souls of their unsuspecting brothers and tossed their bodies over the balconies, until runnels of blood ran onto the polished marble floors. Into these breaches flooded honeycombed banks of archers, stringing their yews and nocking arrows. They held, poised and ready to send swift volleys to anyone standing in Lucifer's way. Dark armor or not, they were marked by their red armbands.

From the uppermost tiers, blood rained onto the obsidian dais, coating Michael's armor. He felt an overbearing thunderclap concuss across the murderous throngs as Bellator and Dealleaus sealed the Doors and lowered their pikes.

He watched with agonizing palsy as angels tried to beat free their brotherly attackers only to be hacked to pieces amidst a ravenous storm. Others took to manipulating the elements with their powers. Flames burst like fireflies through the assembly. Everywhere could be heard the scorching roar of fire; its answer jets of water. Cohorts were roasted alive while some raised juts in the floor, busting formations or herding them with gales so their allies could finish them off.

The ear-shattering chaos seized Michael. Without warning, something slammed and sent him sprawling. Zodkiel was over him, sword drawn and cheeks blood-begrimed.

"You all right, Patriarch?" his armor-bearer shouted. Michael nodded absently. He threw a bewildered, cursory glance to the dais just in time to see a cleaved body crash from above. "Check the skies next time. We need to—" the cherub suddenly jerked as something pierced his back. Blood issued from his mouth and down the bevor of his cuirass as he choked and gurgled. He floundered like a fish before being flung into the writhing chaos beyond.

In the void, Michael's vision beheld a shade lumber up the Steps. A roar erupted from the mountainous form as his eyes fell upon its odious image.

It was a monster. Standing over four meters tall, the thing was corpulent and hirsute. Its goat legs and stumpy arms were covered in thick brown hair, one hand carrying a bloody scimitar. A coarse, black mane ran down the back of its scaly neck. Its head was a tangle of fangs protruding from a maw billowing sulfurous fumes. Yet something was familiar about the fetid anathema snarling through tendrils of gory drool. The eyes gave it away. One look into those burning red singularities and Michael knew at whom he was staring.

"Mazerrel."

Empyrean Falling

He surged over Michael with a chimerical menace. The archangel repulsed in horror as the fiend licked Zodkiel's blood from his scimitar's curved whetted edge.

"What's the matter, Patriarch," Mazerrel said, "don't recognize the offspring of your sin?"

Michael stumbled back, clambering as Mazerrel roared, his massive form lifted by membranous wings. The Cherubim Patriarch felt his feet go out from under him, landing on his backplate. Squirming, he tried to get his hands underneath, but the landing was slippery with blood. His expression devolved into abhorrence; blood sluiced runnels off the dais. A roar from overhead reminded him of the encroaching Mazerrel. He raised his scimitar and bellowed sulfur.

"I'm going to make a chamber pot out of your skull!"

Suddenly there was a flash and clatter. Mazerrel tumbled down the Steps. Michael scrambled and saw a spritely cherub with long golden hair and emerald eyes.

"What's the matter with you?" Alrak barked at Michael over the din. "We have to get out of here!"

Michael beat free of the trance. He saw Alrak Sivad standing before him, cut-and-thruster and kite shield in-hand. He threw a frustrated glance at the scene around him. His wings gathered air underneath them and it was all Michael could do to catch up as he sprang into the air. He was close on the heels of his protégé. The air was hot with violence. It tasted of smoke, iron and sweat. He saw battle lines drawing up below as angels loyal to the White Throne re-grouped before the black-armored onslaught of their brethren.

"We have to find my brother!" Michael shouted at Alrak's back as they flew.

The small cherub nodded and the two plunged into the Holy Temple's battle at Benediction.

Empyrean Falling

Chapter XVI
"...And I saw a star that had fallen from the sky..."
—Revelations 9:1

To the left of the Forty Steps, Gabriel huddled in the concave shell of a statue's rubble. Poisoned-tipped javelins and slinger stones pelted the granite bulwark. He peered through a gap in the debris to see black-armored angels with red armbands marshaling on a clearing. Promontories of corpses rose on either side. The pristine marble floor of the Hallowed Causeway was lost in a gruesome sea of blood and other warlike fluids. Bodies tumbled from the pews above, some still flailing and screaming. The dark-clad rebels locked shields and marched forward, sword points peeking between the shields' metal rims. Above them, the Seraphim Archon watched as more archers formed up and trained volleys on their position.

"We have to beat clear of this rat hole!" rumbled a deep baritone in front of him. Gabriel recognized the voice of Melphax. He stood in the smaze, giant war mace dripping red. Paladin and Deledrosse were on his flanks, rallying a collection of harried angels to their side. Usiel lay dead at their feet, quilled with arrows.

Someone clambered over the broken lip of their stone redoubt. Gabriel recognized him as the Chief Surgeon Arkiel. The cherub was naked and covered in lacerations. He heaved and bled. Gabriel pressed against the corner and stared at him. The cherub's eyes fell on the archangel and he lunged. Gabriel clumsily drew his twin sabers. They sang in concert with Arkiel's cacophonous scream. The archangel tried to scurry to his feet to meet the threat. Arkiel's advance was thwarted by a hammering blow that sent him splattering into the concave stone shadows. He flopped to the slick ground, half his face caved in and his one good eye flickering into a black cavity. Gabriel looked up to see the Pillar of Iron stared down at Arkiel's lifeless body. "What…what happened? I don't…."

"Archangel!" Melphax roared at him as he stood over Arkiel's corpse. "We can't stay here!"

As if summoned to punctuate the assessment, fresh fusillades of broadhead arrows came careening in. Everyone inside the broken statue ducked for better cover.

Gabriel heard Paladin insist on a plan before they get skewered. Deledrosse reiterated the advancing cohorts on their flanks. The archangel snapped to when he saw the archers. "General Melphax," he said shakily, clearing his throat; it was dry from the smoke. "we attack the yews." Melphax looked at him quizzically. "They'll never expect it, and it's our only way out."

Not far away, Alrak and Michael maneuvered in deft flight through the arcing trajectories of arrows. Banners were aflame. Smoke choked the upper levels. Angels cooked in their armor as lightning bolts found their mark. Expertly aimed javelins dropped seraphim from the air. Showers of slinger stones riddled airborne cherubim.

"I saw them rendezvous outside the Citadel of Glalendorf," Alrak divulged as they flew. "By the time I got your note, it was too late. Somehow First Born got the jump on me."

"That makes two of us," Michael said with a grimace. "We need to find him."

In front of the Steps, several statues lay strewn across the Temple floor, the angels loyal to God erecting a wall of shields and spears in the gaps. The coupe d'état stalled as hordes of ill-armed traitors searched the statues' interiors, only to find nothing.

Empyrean Falling

Michael and Alrak watched with relief as the rebels reeled in bewilderment before being overrun by squadrons of defenders led by the Council of Elders. But such providences only took place on the left. On the right, Lucifer's confederates had formed their legions and advanced in overlapping wedges while, overhead, flocks of seraphim loosed fusillades of firebrands from above.

They found Gabriel standing atop a balcony, flanked by friendly angels with a pile of slain archers littering their feet. Michael raced to his brother. Melphax was the first to spot the two. He thumped Gabriel's vambrace and pointed them out just as Michael and Alrak furled their wings and slinked in to their position.

"Still alive?" Michael shouted.

"So, far," Gabriel breathed. "Usiel is dead and Zophiel is missing. Where's Lucifer?" His gaze fell on Alrak.

Michael caught the look and shrugged. "He saved my life. What was I supposed to do, send him away?"

"Acorns for oak trees, Gabriel," Alrak admonished.

The Seraphim Archon wiped his brow. "We need a plan."

Michael wathced Melphax reposition their loyalists into a defensive ward. "We need to reach Lucifer. If we can intercept him then this whole thing ends now."

"He's bound to have support," Gabriel warned.

"I can handle it," Michael said. "Gabriel, you and Alrak watch my back. But don't lag; I'll need you." He unfurled his wings. The others took up flanking positions on the Sword of God as they bolted over the Forty Steps, where the fighting had grown thickest.

"Where are our tribunes?" Gabriel bawled as they weaved through projectiles.

"Gilgamesh and some of his Thunderbolts are holding the line on the right," Michael bawled at the top of his lungs. "But his legion iss bound to fold soon."

Gabriel scanned the Temple's battlefield. "If we could find Orean we might be able to sneak through this mess—" he yelped and dropped from sight.

"Gabriel!" Michael shouted. He watched his brother plummet into the miasma.

Empyrean Falling

Alrak pointed to the Steps' altar, swallowed by a writhing tide of rebels. "There!"

Michael saw Gabriel wrestling with an angel as they fell for a forest of pikes. He recognized the assailant by his domed helmet and facial shroud. Alrak motioned to descend. "No!" Alrak shot him a look. "Gabriel can handle himself. We must reach my brother."

They reached the obsidian dais just as the right flank folded under the rebels' onslaught. Horror struck their hearts as the vanguard of Lucifer's traitorous mob flooded up the Steps.

Alrak unslung his kite shield. "We don't have much time. What do you…?"

"Whatever you can," Michael answered. His protégé readjusted his kite shield and darted to the right in an attempt to stem the menacing wave. Michael gripped Virtue with sweat-slicked palms; runnels soaked his collar; his black topknot steamed. Inhaling, the archangel summoned his faculties. "Replace fear with faith," he repeated. Logic compelled his flesh to flee. He shut his eyes and prayed. "Make my hands swift, my mind exact. Strengthen me to quash this heresy."

Below him, the battle reached its apex. Archers rained down volleys while loyalists erected a breastwork of crumbled detritus, their huddled ranks locking shields and threshing spears. Stragglers caught outside the frontline were overrun by the rebels.

The upper tiers were landfills of corpses, choked and overflowing from the balconies while the lower tiers flooded with a purple sea bubbling around grisly promontories of the dead. Red rivers filled cracks in the marble floor. Yet the cacophony still raged at a fever pitch as Michael flew in.

He grimaced as he caught sight his older brother's form drawing near the Doors. Bellator and Dealleaus readied themselves for a stalwart defense. He beat his wings to the intercept. Part of him wanted to order Bellator to flee but he knew neither he nor Dealleaus would heed his archangelic call for self-preservation.

He shouted his brother's name but the Morning Star strode towards the Foyer. He watched as the Guardians brandished their pikes. They closed rank but Michael knew its futility. He watched helplessly as Hadar was raised, its black blade glinting in the firelight.

It was over before it began. Bellator and Dealleaus lunged. Hadar swung, severing both of the pikes' warheads. Dealleaus tried to draw his sword but with a flick of his wrist, Hadar plunged through the Guardian's breastplate. It withdrew in time to sunder Bellator's sword, rendering it useless. They were dead before they hit the floor.

Michael landed on the dais just as his foe gripped the handles of the Doors. He set his jaw and checked his footing, Virtue held at a mid-guard. His words were drowned by his heartbeat.

"Lucifer, stop!"

His brother halted at the tug of the Doors. "Lucifer is gone," he hissed. "His immaculate vessel is mine."

"Why are you doing this?" Michael pleaded. "Angels are dead by the myriads!"

"Millions, brother," he corrected, "I've killed them by the millions." He turned and pointed Hadar. "But I only need to kill one." With that, he who was once Lucifer leapt at him.

Michael's eyes bulged as the archangel swung his wicked sword in a relentless assault. Virtue and Hadar met in showers of sparks. He struck with uncanny speed. They moved faster than angelic eyes could see, singing in a tenor madness of notes unheard of in Heaven. Lucifer's form was a blur, his radiance burning Michael's eyes. He knew exactly where every blow must land.

The Cherubim Archangel sidestepped and countered to no avail. Michael winced and his enemy smirked. The archangel ducked and rolled, rising as the foe came at him. The Sword of God blocked the attack and planted a vertical fist into his throat. It did nothing. He repulsed in terror before catching a left hook to his jaw. His eyes darkened amidst stars as he backpedaled.

His adversary rushed in with Hadar's slender shadow. The two matched gazes before the clash. As Michael blinked into those shimmering silver orbs, a serenity possessed him …

"...Will you always be there for me, if I ask it?" Lucifer asked. Michael peered into the landscape around them. It swirled. Everything was marbled in shades of white and gold. It felt odd, but it

felt wrong, too, like he was out of place. Michael turned to him. The Anointed Cherub glowed a perfect hue. "Will you always be there for me, Michael?"

He shook his head, trying to clear the nagging pull of voices at the back of his mind. "I'll always love you, Lucifer." His heart burned and consumed him. Sorrow flooded in.

Something caught his eye behind them. Lucifer saw it too. Father stood above them. He said nothing. There was no need; they could feel His words. Sympathy surmounted sorrow.

"He won't let me have it," Lucifer sobbed. "I just want to play as He does."

Michael shook his head, the purveying sensation of misplacement distracting him from his brother's words. "You can't be Him." He wanted to seize the words before they reached Lucifer's ears, but it was too late; the Anointed Cherub was already hiding his face in his hands and weeping. "Will no amount of our love quench your desire?"

The voices returned, hailing them from a phantom multitude.

"Then there's no reprieve from fate," Lucifer wept. "We will perish, as stars burn and die…"

… Michael saw Hadar's edge. Taunts from rebel legions clogged his mind.

His opponent diverted Virtue and struck him. Michael's breastplate shattered like a jar of clay. The impetus sent him to a sprawl on the uppermost Steps. His enemy approached the Doors with an unnatural speed. He wrapped his hands around the immaculate handles and tugged. Michael watched him heave with all his archangelic strength until at last the Doors parted. His unholy nova contrasted with God's as he invaded the Throne Room.

From deep within the Inner Room, a blue bolt smashed into his chest and extinguished his light. The resounding collision was deafeningly cosmic. Everyone's armor rang like tolled bells.

The blast propelled the archangelic body across the Hallowed Causeway. All eyes traced the stormy hail of the infernal cherub's trajectory. Sulfur and ash dropped from his fleshly furnace as he shot like a comet back to the Temple's threshold. With a sickening crash, the impact lodged him in the archway's architecture. His body went limp as the flames died.

There was a lull in the squall of their warring sea. The rebellious archangel dislodged and fell, wings and limbs flailing. Two angels darted up from the riven floor to catch their master. Michael watched them whisk him away. Horns blew. He felt the heretical tide ebb. They swarmed from the Temple like a ravenous murder, tumbling away into the gloaming. In moments they had routed from the Temple and the multitudes of those loyal to the White Throne were left behind, alone with the carnage of heresy's catastrophe.

A voice in Michael's depths howled to grab Virtue and finish the fight, but that voice had no sway over his beaten flesh. All he could do was watch the countless traitors flee in pursuit of their god. Silence followed. He felt Gabriel draw up on his left.

"So," Gabriel finally sighed as the two stared out over the aftermath, "it's come at last."

Alrak landed on Michael's right. Gabriel took him in with a glance. His garments were splattered in crimson, bereft of shield, sword broken. Adrenaline flowed through his jaded eyes, yet his visage belied a battered constitution. "Should we pursue?" the little angel breathed. His mentor went limp on the Steps. Alrak rushed to intercept. "Gabriel," he asked again, "should we muster and pursue?"

Gabriel shook his head. Alrak asked what they were to do next. He looked down at his brother's protégé and gestured towards Michael. "Fetch the medics," he said. "Then prepare all of Zion."

Alrak cradled Michael's unconscious body on the Steps. "For what?" he asked.

Gabriel eyed Alrak Sivad gravely. "War, cherub, the angels are going to war."

End of Tome II

TOME III
EMPYREAN FALLING

Empyrean Falling

Chapter Index

Chapter I: *Fallen Compensation* — 189

Chapter II: *To Gather the Pieces* — 197

Chapter III: *Weird Inheritance* — 207

Chapter IV: *A Call to Arms* — 216

Chapter V: *The Wall* — 224

Chapter VI: *Bane of the Fallen* — 239

Chapter VII: *Roan Tributary* — 248

Chapter IIX: *Scourge of the Faithful* — 257

Chapter IX: *Empyreal Phoenix* — 265

Chapter X: *Drums in the Deep* — 273

Chapter XI: *Hailing Maelstroms* — 281

Chapter XII: *The Mirror of Twilight* — 289

Chapter XIII: *To Call and Forsake* — 298

Chapter XIV: *The Keys of Treason* — 304

Chapter XV: *Trial of Tiers* — 311

Chapter XVI: *The Progeny of Lions* — 321

Chapter XVII: *Gate of Storms*   327

Chapter XIIX: *Eleventh Hour Matins*   339

Chapter XIX: *Nadir's Eve*   346

Chapter XX: *Shadow of the Mountain*   354

Chapter XXI: *Winepress*   367

Chapter XXII: *Requiem*   378

Empyrean Falling

Chapter I
"Those who are wayward in spirit will gain understanding; those who complain will accept destruction."
—Isaiah 29:24

The Min Thralr Shrine reverberated with their voices. Mazerrel's nape bristled as he stood in the dilapidated threshold. No one dared enter the mausoleum with him standing guard; the hulking frame of his chimerical apparition was enough to keep any curious onlookers at bay. The rebel angels gave him a wide berth as the shouts threatened to rattle the ancient structure to its foundation stones. They would sooner take their chances with the raging storm that blanketed the Northern Plains beyond than risk what lied inside.

"I said hold him down!" the seraphic surgeon barked through gritted teeth, long-handled sponge in one hand and his archangel's mangled chest in the other. "Tempest, confine him!"

"It's *Umbra* Tempest now, you maggot," the cherub seethed. Nevertheless, he moved into position and pinned his archangel's shoulders to the stone slab of the sepulcher. "My lord Dragon, you must hold still!" He strained under his master's power. The surgeon looked for the right angle with his instrument. "Whatever you're going to do, Belphegor, do it quickly!"

Empyrean Falling

The archangel's chest was an odious nightmare of melted breastplate and torn flesh. It still sizzled from the energy bolt's impact. Puss and blood oozed from the plate-sized wound, acrid tendrils of effluvium rising from the fused edges.

Belphegor hastily poured a vial of pink liquid onto the sponge and swayed in time with his master's writhing. He gauged his rhythm and at the right moment thrust the sodden sponge into the gaping chest wound. Fresh screams rang their ears and shook the dust from the stones, but in moments he'd ceased his struggle and relaxed. His archangelic torso swelled and deflated. Belphegor wasted no time.

"Help me get this armor off," he said. Umbra Tempest assisted him in removing the starry breastplate. They unlatched the buckles and flung the cuirass onto the floor, a mangled heap of smoldering ruin clattering into the shadows. Belphegor jammed a compress of sterile gauze into the charred and shredded flesh before cradling his master's boltered head and pouring another vial down his throat. "Keep him still, please." While the master of assassins monitored the prone archangel with a braced grip, Belphegor began to pluck bits of twisted metal from the flesh, all the while keeping a wary eye on his archangel's state of consciousness. By the time his work was finished, it was difficult to tell which of the three was more exhausted.

Sometime later, the archangel awoke. "Does Tempest's storm wall still hold?" he rasped.

"Umbra Tempest, my Dragon," the cherub replied. "And yes, the Northern Plains are cut off just south of the River Aphaea. Our comrades are shielded, for now."

A deathly calm flooded into their adrenaline's vacuum. For long moments they listened to the companies of confederates setting up camp outside. Belphegor got the shakes as he cleaned his instruments and prepared a linen wrap for his patient. He upturned a wineskin to calm his nerves. Umbra Tempest slouched against the sepulcher beside his master and trembled. He felt the archangel stir.

Night fell on the Min Thralr Shrine.

Satan rose. He ran a hand through his hair. It was hard for the angels to tell in the dim light, but the once-red mane seemed stained a ruddy black. "Umbra Tempest," he said with a level tone, "if you ever address me as anything other than my true name again, I'll kill you." His lieutenant dipped his brow. "Now summon Mazerrel."

Umbra Tempest did as he was told. Wasting no time, the monstrosity that was Mazerrel ducked under the threshold and entered the mausoleum.

"Report," Satan commanded. Even bandaged and bare-chested, he struck them with a preternatural fear.

"We've taken command of the Northern Plains this side of the Aphaea, master," Mazerrel stated. "We're scattered, but the legates will have it under control by this time tomorrow or I'll start flaying them. I think your one million are mostly intact; that damned armor worked. They've named themselves as your personal guards. Vuldun and Kemuel have been nominated for leadership. You'll need to choose one before I snuff out them both for their bickering."

"Give command to Vuldun," Satan said. "I'll need Kemuel for another task. Where is Althaziel and what's our disposition along the riverbanks?"

"Uriel wasn't as complicit as Gi'ad led us to believe," Mazerrel ruefully stated. "We sent him to the Island for sorting out. I have Nelgleth watching over Gi'ad. As for the rest," he scratched his shaggy nape, "most are behaving; I've seen several generals forming their legions as we planned. I have engineers and sappers working on the bridges to the southeast with cavalry providing a screen, in case Tempest's storm wall fails."

"Pull them back," Satan demanded. Mazerrel tilted his head. "Put your engineers on constructing towers and artillery. My guards will need your cavalry." He turned a glare on Tempest. "Umbra's storm wall *will* hold."

He observed his serpentine assassin, who leered from the threshold with a feline gait. "Step closer," Satan commanded with a come-hither motion. Tempest did as his master bade. When he got within arm's reach, Satan grabbed him and with a flick of his wrist wrenched a rib from his unarmored side. The cherub hissed violently and thrashed into the stone frame of the entryway, clutching his bleeding abdomen. Satan matched his befuddled gaze with a cold eye and upturned chin. "You were not blooded," he declared flatly, "despite your contest with Gabriel."

Tempest went to draw the curved, single-edged sword from the scabbard at his waist. Satan strolled up and raised an upturned fist between them. He splayed out his fingers to reveal a blossoming glyph of levitating purple. It crackled and sang. Satan hummed a melody that drew Tempest's gaze into the glyph until his hands relinquished their bloody clutch and hilt.

"Have you gained nothing from what I'm trying to accomplish?" the archangel said. With his other hand, he waved Belphegor over and pointed at his lieutenant. "They must see sacrifice, Umbra, even if it be by artifice. Only blood can requite blood." Satan handed the rib to Mazerrel. "An eye for the eye of your storm in the Oblivion."

"Thank you, my master," Mazerrel said with an awkward bow.

"Don't thank me until this is over," Satan said. "We still have work to do." He lingered at the threshold, observing the endless watch fires lighting to life in the grasslands beyond. He crossed his arms and numbered the countless flickering nexuses. "I'd thought Father would have been more amenable to negotiation," he proclaimed. "Regrettably, I was wrong. But rest assured, my confederates, felons from the Throne though we may be, this is far from over."

"We have inflicted heavy losses on those tools of the Kingdom," Mazerrel divulged.

"It won't be enough," Satan declared. "We got the jump on them, yes, but they'll regroup. And if I know my younger brother, they're already bleeding through their labor pangs to erect defenses and gather the pieces. Two thirds of the Heavenly Host are locked away in Zion sewing up their wounds and praying to their feeble God. We need to organize our battalions before we worry about securing our equipment, and we have to do it quickly."

"We chose the perfect staging ground," Mazerrel said. "Your Island is to the north, Lorinar in the east, Zion across the river south, and the Hundred Foothills and Thousand Peaks west. We could strike out from anywhere and gain a foothold. Or hold and deny the enemy."

Satan shook his head. "Time is not on our side." He turned to them. "But motivation is." He took in Mazerrel, Umbra Tempest and Belphegor with a level eye. "I name the three of you my generals. Mazerrel, to you I entrust the bulk of my forces. Sack the Stone City. Not to add insult to Umbra Tempest's injury, but his spirit is not yet ready to receive the pride of his heart: Lorinar. If you can put pressure on Zion, send a few corps south. I leave the finer details to you."

Tempest made to protest.

Satan looked at him as he was being patched up by Belphegor. "Umbra Tempest, take a tenth of our forces and string them across the eastern and southern banks of the Aphaea. If we allow the loyalists out of the Holy City then there would be fewer angels guarding it, affording us a better chance at breaching their walls. We'll let them think we're in dire straits. Let them deploy their legions. When Zion empties its barracks, we'll turn on her with a ravaging fury. But for now, we need to secure our position. Rest assured, our enemies are moving too and we shouldn't be so clumsy as to intercept them yet. They need to perceive our disorder. They need to be confident as they take the roads for their cities and strongholds."

Tempest slammed a fist into the stone wall. "But Lorinar…"

"What of it?" Satan challenged. "The way I see it, *General* Umbra Tempest, that pile of brutish rocks is no longer your concern."

"But we had an accord!"

"I must depend on those loyal to me for any peripheral assimilation. The Stone City must be secured if we're to survive a protracted siege with Zion's North Gate. My seizing of the Holy Temple will have to rely on those who have proven their fealty. I cannot allow such a monumental task to be twisted by a crippling fiend's addiction. After your excursion into the Oblivion…" Satan threw a compassionate glance at the malformed Mazerrel. "Any deal we struck is void." He could feel Tempest's eyes burn on him. With an effortless assertion, he returned the glower tenfold. Meanwhile, Belphegor finished his work on Tempest in avoidant silence.

"The sacking of Lorinar will go to Mazerrel," Satan stated vengefully. Tempest went rigid, unheeding of Belphegor's medical prowess. "However," their master continued, "take heart, traitor of traitors; you won't be left in the cold. I'm sending you with a myriad of my best warriors to personally wrest Amin Shakush from the venerated Pillar of Iron, Melphax the Strong. It'll be no easy task but, should you secure the Northern Plains and the Valley of a Thousand Peaks, I'll consider granting you a more auspicious assignment. Until then, consider this an act of penance." Umbra Tempest did his best to conceal the rage as he forced a maimed bow. An insidious smile crept over Satan's face. "I'll grant you this: take seven of Mazerrel's best teamsters. They are to be entrusted to you as crown jewels."

Mazerrel took a step back. His conscientious hunch in the hallway was forgotten and he reared up, shoulders thundering into the stone doorframe.

"Consider it mutual collateral," Satan suggested. "Neither will test the other with a city and hostages on the line. Now, for Belphegor. I wish to bestow a special honor upon you."

The surgeon was wiping his hands of Tempest's blood. "How may I serve, my lord Dragon?"

"If it weren't for you catching me in the Temple, I'd be shackled and imprisoned by our ambitionless brothers right now. What's more, I have you to thank for my recovery here."

"You could put him in your personal guard," Mazerrel proffered. "Keep him close."

Satan grinned mirthlessly. "I have no intention of ever being caught flatfooted again. Besides, I'm doing him one better. I'm sending him into the Southlands with a portion of my host to attack the Southern Wall." He looked at Belphegor. "Draw resources and personnel from the North Gate; prime it for our assault."

"Belphegor's untested in the trials of generalship, my lord," Tempest protested. "The scalpel does not translate to the scepter. Is this prudent?"

"It wouldn't be the first time I've assigned tasks to officers incapable of accomplishing them," Satan reminded him. "Yet they seemed clever enough in the end, sometimes too clever for their own good. Belphegor will do for us what neither of you could accomplish: a task void of merit yet rife with necessity."

Empyrean Falling

"He lacks the proper understanding of strategy," Umbra argued. "He wouldn't know an oblique order from a hernia."

"We were all just hammers and sickles in untested hands at one time," Mazerrel pointed out. "Our lord has a better vision."

Satan carried his smile to Umbra's shrouded face, content in the taunt of his glare. "You should consider the next few weeks of paramount crisis, Umbra. All you've woven for me in the past unraveled when you betrayed my aide. That's not easily forgotten, much less forgiven. You would do well to follow my orders to the bloody letter for, if Belphegor proves capable, I may find myself in a position to promote him further. The left hand is feeling shaky."

Tempest chewed his lip raw.

"And I'll warn you," Satan said, "Lucifer might have appreciated the ingenuity of your efforts, but I do not. A fate most foul awaits those who destabilize my authority."

"Speaking of which," Mazerrel began, "a word from you would be a boon. The angels languish; they perceive defeat. They malinger and wander. We'll lose them."

They watched their Dragon stride over to where his melted breastplate was flung. He picked it up and held it in his hands. "They won't see me like this," he said. "Summon one of my guards."

In due fashion, Mazerrel returned with one of the black-armored guards borne into the privacy of the Min Thralr Shrine on a litter. Satan noticed his extreme injuries. He knelt.

"What is your name, angel?"

"I'm Apollyon, my lord," the guard said. His armor was intact, but his eyes were torn away by a crippling blow to his face. His breathing was labored.

Satan gently removed the rebel soldier's black helmet. "Tell me about yourself."

"I'm a cherub, my lord, serving under Mazerrel. You saved me in the blight."

The archangel stroked Apollyon's matted mane and slowly unclasped his weird armor. He inspected each piece; they were all intact. Belphegor observed his wounds and whispered in Satan's ear. "We all have a purpose, my lovely Apollyon," Satan said. "You are neither cherub nor seraph, Mazerrel's servant nor mine; you are free of this prison. Let your troubles fade. Your part in this is over, my child. You have finished the race." He let the angel see him weep. Tears fell on Apollyon's mangled flesh. "We must sacrifice for this endeavor, Apollyon. You gave me the honor once of coming to your aid. Will you do me the honor of saving me, now, so that I might carry our burden a bit farther?"

What was left of Apollyon's brow furrowed. "Of course, My Lord," he rasped through a bloody gurgle.

"Thank you, my dearly beloved," Satan replied. "I swear to you, your sacrifice won't be in vain." He fought back tears with a smile. "You know, truth be told, Apollyon, I'm envious of you; you'll see the Empyrean before I will." Satan took Apollyon's concerned expression in his hands and covered his face. "Thank you for this, my angel. I'll always love you for your deliverance here tonight."

There was a brief bit of squirming and it was over.

Satan stood and touched Mazerrel's burly forearm. "A mortal wound deserves a merciful end. His sacrifice will not be in vain."

"The lord giveth and the lord taketh away," said Mazerrel.

Minutes later, Satan emerged from the Min Thralr Shrine wearing Apollyon's strange black lamellar armor. Before the dilapidated ruin of the Min Thralr Shrine, he rose into the air and banished the night with his luminous essence. On the Northern Plains, behind the storm wall, he rallied his armies.

Empyrean Falling

Chapter II
"In his humiliation he was deprived of justice…"
—Acts 8:33

    Rafiel was still bandaging Michael's chest when the archangel stepped down into the speaking platform of the Council Chambers. Around them rebounded the voices of the Elders, twelve magnificent tones each keening their discordant tunes at one another. Shirtless and bloodied, Michael focused on the medic's work in a vain attempt to block out the vocal din which infested the long, tall hall of the Chambers. The twelve dual-tiered thrones above him spoke at once.

    His brief moments of respite were blotted out by the racket of aftermath filling the Hallowed Causeway adjacent to them. Though the doors were shut, he could still hear the loyalist angels searching for wounded, clearing bodies, and cleaning up the grisly aftermath.

    The doors behind him opened. Echoes of cherubic patrols and seraphic messengers frantically hunting for survivors amidst rivers of blood and charnel piles hammered at his back. He turned to see Gabriel stride down the long hallway of the Council Chambers, his golden armor wiped of blood but stained red. Behind him, Michael espied teams of medics triaging survivors from the dead.

Empyrean Falling

Even that torment was better than the encirclement of tiered thrones and their elitist voices. Yet when the doors to the Council Chambers closed, Michael rested in the solace that he at least had his bruised sternum to occupy his attention.

"But we cannot expect to survive the wrath of the Morning Star!" echoed the oily tenor of Asmodeus, his bony cheeks contorting with every flap of his tongue. "He is the Exultant Archon; what possible chance do we have against such apogee?"

"Hear, hear, Eldar Asmodeus," heralded Israfel, rising in his seat. "Lucifer is the most powerful, indeed, but must war be the only answer to this travesty?"

Head Elder Metatron shifted in his purple robes, his broad dark features twisted in scorn. "Eldar Israfel would rather write symphonies on Lucifer's Island than attend these meetings. I would warn you all that sycophancy has no place here."

A swell of dissent erupted. Harsh looks were flown on the wings of harsher words, to which Israfel resumed his seat in a blush.

"Hearken unto me, peers," Agni boomed over them, "Eldar Israfel speaks wisely. We must seek parley with Lucifer. A third of us are derelict. That should account for something."

Amidst the mixed reactions stood Sariel, short and sinewy and as quick with his tongue as he was with his gait. "Were you not there, Eldar Agni," he asked rhetorically with a jabbed finger and flushed face. "Did a banner fall upon your head while the fires consumed our faithful host? A battle took place; one borne by our hallowed Son of the Morning. Were it not for God, we would've been ground to chuck beneath Lucifer's red and black dog-chompers."

"Then what do you propose, Eldar Sariel?" Asmodeus challenged with a waft of his delicate hand. A long silence hung in the Chamber's stone hall as the others awaited his response. The summer sun cascaded against the dust, casting long shadows on the judges and archangels. Michael breathed in the rare lull as Gabriel took up a post beside his brother. He watched Rafiel finish his work and depart with a bow before lifting his gaze up to the thrones.

Sariel stood in the slanted beams of light, his cardinal robe marooned in the shadows. The prosecutor swayed, slow to speak. All eyes remained locked onto him. He looked at his Patriarch's humming sapphires. "I say we teach these traitors a lesson," he barked with a fist upon the arm of his throne, "and send them to the Burning Hells!"

A deafening outrage poured forth. Michael stepped to the fore and motioned for the gale of rejoinders to subside. Little by little they ceded to his silent petition.

"None loved Lucifer more than I. And none are more aware of his power." He pointed to the Hallowed Causeway behind them. "But *that* wasn't Lucifer. The creature who came into our midst is the Dragon; the Enemy; Satan; He Who Comes to Kill, Steal and Destroy. He is no longer the Anointed Cherub; that archangel is dead." His words were met with unbelieving eyes from the encircling thrones, yet he refused to relent. "Hear me, elected," he intoned diplomatically, "my brother would never raise arms against me." His flashed a wary eye to Gabriel. It dissolved like a wisp of smoke. "But the creature that possessed my brother's flesh was *not* my brother. The Dragon commands Lucifer now. He must be destroyed. How many more have to perish before you find the resolve to stop him?"

"Suppose we do elect to face him," Asmodeus crooned. "How would you go about such a thing? Can any storm of iron hope to accomplish such a colossal feat?"

"What storm would be necessary?" Gabriel posited. "Fortify the Holy City and wait him out. We don't have to seek havoc; it'll seek us; we only need to wait for him." Michael shrugged, yet Gabriel continued. "It'll be a costly endeavor for them to breach Zion if our entire host remains steadfast behind the bartizans of our Walls."

Michael set his jaw. "But if we form our legions and meet him, we can catch Satan's forces while they're still disorganized."

The words barely left him before the Council was clamoring.

"You expect an attack by our beleaguered forces to succeed against a third of our host?" Agni squawked. "Never have I heard such a ludicrous proposal. Your injury has addled your mind, Patriarch."

"Then I suppose we're to sit on our thumbs and watch our defenses be picked apart as Tempest spies on us?" Michael retorted.

"We need to seek a parley, Archangel," Asmodeus answered. "Only through negotiations can we hope to achieve peace." His gaze never left Michael. "I, for one, am not about to endorse a plan that would send countless myriads of our faithful angels to their deaths."

"I will not kowtow to the Dragon!" Michael burst, his roar flooding the Chamber.

"Is it prudent at this juncture to talk of such matters?" Astaroth hesitantly began. Lofty eyes turned on him. "Barely two days have passed since this heresy. How can we be sure all of Lucifer's disciples have fled Zion?" The air thickened. "Can we say with certainty that there are no spies among our vaulted halls? Can we believe it safe?"

"The Council has enough to contend with, Eldar Astaroth," Asmodeus scolded. "Perhaps that is a discussion for a later time."

"Regardless," the Head Eldar Metatron reminded, "the matter stands to be resolved."

"The longer we wait," Michael reiterated, "the more time he has to formulate a strategy to send his disciples against us. We must act now if we're to gain the upper hand."

"And what then, Cherubim Archangel?" Asmodeus countered. "Are we to turn all of Heaven into a wasteland, riven with sundered turf and scorched skies in a futile rage? I would rather go quietly beyond the veil than take our entire Heavenly splendor with us. The turmoil would leave no stone unbroken and no river untainted. Surely you don't wish to cause any more damage than has already left us ravaged and abused."

"I seek to preserve as many lives as possible while holding to the oaths I took before the White Throne," Michael replied with a glower, "not preserve gilded flagstones and poplar groves."

Asmodeus laughed. "By sending us to war! Quite a contradiction, don't you think?"

"War has already come, Eldar Asmodeus," Metatron interrupted. "Should we seek peace we will only be met with slavery or annihilation…perhaps both. In time, there may be a parley, but first we must gain victory over our heart-breaking enemies."

"You don't know that," Asmodeus sneered from his garnet encrusted high seat.

Metatron turned in his ornate marble seat to Asmodeus. "I watched two of my aides fall to their knees and plead with a monster to come to his senses and join them in penitent prayer. The beast gutted my cherubs where they knelt. You will forgive me if I implore you to take a leap of faith that my position on this matter is an accurate one. As long as Lucifer's one third is in a position of power, they shan't consider an armistice. We must gain an advantage over them… through force, if need be."

Michael smiled through a breath. "At least someone sees."

Metatron winced as he straightened in his seat. "Quite the contrary, my dear Archangel. The best course of action is a cautionary one. We should muster our legions, as you say, but form a perimeter on the City defenses. We cannot afford another Temple breaching; this time they will surely raze it. So, what can you tell us in the way of numbers? Can we mobilize?"

"It's hard to say, Head Eldar Metatron," Michael replied with a sigh. "I know of several myriads combat ready, but there's no telling how many more haven't been accounted for."

"Some are dead," Gabriel added. "Others may have fled. There's just no way to tell yet."

Asmodeus shot Michael a condescending eye. "And you want to meet the Enemy on the battlefield in this condition?" He laughed. "Amazing; you are reckless beyond compare."

"It will take all that we can muster to defend the Walls," Metatron stated. "We must focus on preventing Lucifer from achieving his aims. That is what's in danger. And it's that which we should strive to thwart."

"The Dragon burns for the White Throne, yes," Michael countered. "But he won't hesitate to raze all of Heaven to get it. Temples and cities can be rebuilt; we've seen this to be true. But the natural splendor of the Lower Realm cannot be healed. A policy of scorched turf will strand us in Zion. And I don't even want to think about the consequences if they somehow manage to get to Earth."

Asmodeus frowned. "What makes you think they are concerned with Earth?"

Michael hesitated. To tell them would only indict him. Yet all eyes burned on him from above.

Empyrean Falling

"It would only stand to reason," Gabriel proclaimed, much to Michael's relief, "that if Satan wishes to abolish us and God, he would surely desire Creation's destruction. And unlike Heaven, that Realm is a fragile thing. It would require far less to eradicate it—Humanity chief among the catalog. If he finds a way, he'll have the power to break God's heart and we'll be powerless to stop him."

"A potent bargaining chip that defenseless species would make," Metatron added.

"We have the Tome of Descendance locked away," Agni concluded, "along with all the other artifacts from the West. We have little need to worry about Humanity."

"Can we be so sure?" Metatron countered. "What ruse does Lucifer possess that haven't been ferreted out? Can we hope to outwit he whom we readily admit is our superior?

"Assumption is a costly folly," Sariel added.

"Let us not weep for frostbitten crops while our home floods," Asmodeus suggested. "The humans will be kept by God. Let us concern ourselves with our own plight."

"To which you would petition a plea bargain," Sariel sneered.

"I only seek preservation of life."

"Nevertheless," said Metatron, "I submit we shore up our Gates for when Lucifer's disciples try to reenter." He turned to Michael. "Would you agree to that at least, Archangel?"

"Why do you continue to call him Lucifer?" the archangel questioned. "My brother is gone. Those angels we held in our hearts are gone. The creature who committed this heresy is Satan and his thralls have fallen from the light of God's Empyrean. Does our faithfulness not separate us in your eyes? It would be wise of the Council to embrace this truth."

"Lofty seats require lofty minds and ideals, Archangel," Asmodeus chided. "Second Born you may be but judicial body we remain. Lucifer—"

"—Satan!" Michael barked. "His name is Satan!"

Asmodeus raised his hands in concession, bowing his slender head. "As you wish, Archangel," he replied delicately. "*Satan* has tremendous power and what he commands most is fear; fear of the unknown. We know not what he may do to us should we resist or take up arms against him. We may all be slaughtered, or tortured, or cast into the Oblivion."

Michael glowered at him. "You talk as if it's pointless to do that for which we've prepared. Lucifer was strong; therefore, the Dragon is strong. But he and his cohorts are not invincible. They can be stopped. Daunting as it is, we must try. It's what we've trained for since the founding of the Eastern Kingdom. He *can* be beaten."

"I won't endorse a foolhardy crusade," Asmodeus defied.

"You may not but there are eleven other thrones in this Chamber," Metatron reminded with a scolding undertone, "supplemented by our venerable Archangels. We will do this with fidelity for democracy; we will vote."

"What are the parameters?" Sariel inquired.

"To fortify Zion for invasion or do as Archangel Michael requests and sally forth our legions."

"Or to at least send the garrisons back to their castles and cities," Michael added.

"For what reason?" Metatron asked. "They seem concerned only with the White Throne, which means Zion. What would they gain in sacking Lorinar or Amin Shakush?"

"Suppression, staging grounds, pincers, depots, routes, flanking fulcrums," Michael growled. "Shall I continue?" Metatron waved him down. "If we hole up, we'll be breached and sandwiched, cordoned off and cornered by our sheer unwieldy numbers. If I could come up with this much on the fly, imagine what our foe has already formulated. We need to act as if we're at war because we *are* at war. This isn't the preparative lull before the storm; this *is* the storm. We must restore our garrisons before Satan can counter."

"You think he'd sack Lorinar or the Citadel of Glalendorf before Zion?" asked Sariel.

Michael nodded grimly. "Chances are he's already on the move. It won't be long before those garrisons are cut off. We need to send out expeditionary forces to intercept the rebels. If we can split them up, we have a chance at crushing them. But if they roam unchecked..."

The Elders looked down upon him in protracted silence.

Metatron sighed. "Then let the matter be voted on: hold our legions in Zion or risk moving to the garrisons."

Instantly, the Elders ruled; eight to four in favor of refortifying the East. Michael shook his head at the large dissenting minority.

"Who shall take command of the armies?" asked Asmodeus.

"The choice is obvious," Sariel proffered, "Archangel Michael should lead."

"Are you so sure?" Asmodeus replied. He threw Gabriel a sweeping gesture. "Archon Gabriel has led the seraphim since our inception. He commands half the Heavenly Host. Is that not qualification to elect him consul?"

"It's long been established that the cherubim are the fighting caste," Sariel countered. "While the seraphim surely can fight, they are not our elected soldiers. It would only stand to reason, the leader of any warlike enterprise should be the Chief of the Armies of God."

"Yet you refrain from noting Archon Gabriel's devotion," said Agni. "He above all others cares for his choir. It would be a dishonor to overlook such merit."

Metatron squinted. "That is precisely why I would elect Archangel Michael. While Archon Gabriel's devotion is unparalleled, it is that very aspect that might render him the lesser candidate." He turned to the Seraphim Archangel with an apologetic eye. "Don't mistake my intent, dear Archon, you're a magnificent archangel and well worthy of the title. But I would fear such dedication might engender a restrained approach." Metatron dipped his brow to his archangel. "Forgive me, Prince of Heaven, but I fear your adoration may be a hindrance."

"Hear, hear!" Sariel countered, "Archangel Gabriel is powerful, indeed, but he's devoted to his choir like a lioness to its cubs. Patriarch Michael's devoted also but our Cherubim Archangel has proven willing to risk. If this is to be war, we'll need a leader who won't be afraid to send our brethren into the maw of murder. We need someone who can order death as easily as ordering a drink."

"Of that, you and Eldar Beliel surely know," Israfel chided.

A wave of dark laughter flowed through the assembly.

"You forget one thing, Head Eldar Metatron," Agni added over the mill of voices. "We all saw the contest between Patriarch Michael and the Anointed Cherub." He regarded Michael. "The war chief fell before the Dragon's blade. Are we so quick to send our Patriarch that we overlook his defeat in the crucible's nadir? What guarantee do we have he won't fail again?"

At that, all eyes turned to Michael.

Metatron rose from his throne. "I would remind this Council that any one of us would've performed far less admirably than Archangel—"

"We are not electing one of us to lead the army," Asmodeus interrupted irritably. "We are nominating one of the archangels. Michael has tried and failed. Let Archon Gabriel try."

Sariel scowled at him. "You would deny Patriarch Michael?"

"We are eternally grateful for Archangel Michael's tutelage," Asmodeus commented. "But we cannot allow the perpetrator to breach Zion. If a duel occurs again, it would be wise to have a leader not haunted by defeat. Archon Gabriel fills this niche nicely."

"His name is Satan," Michael growled.

Asmodeus relented under the resilience of the archangel's steely blue lamps. "Very well. Satan."

"Whatever you call him," Metatron said with a sweep of his violet eyes, "he's out there with an evil heart and an arm to back him."

"Perhaps a consulship under Council supervision?" Asmodeus offered. "If either archangel—however brave or brilliant—finds himself engaged in a duel, who's to say that he won't fail? If the consul is handed the reins only to be bested in single combat, who then would take charge, a hundred tribunes? They would make splinters of our forces; disaster would manifest in the absence of cohesion. We need leadership removed from the battlefield."

"You'd do away with the position of consul?" Agni asked.

Asmodeus turned his head smoothly. "I only seek to preserve order, should the worst occur. Let the consul lead the armies on-field but let us advise from our hallowed sanctuary."

"A safety net should things go awry," Israfel concurred.

Metatron raised his brows at the archangels. "Do you condone this stipulation?" Gabriel reluctantly nodded. Michael held like a stone edifice. "Archangel Michael?"

The Sword of God glared at the dust motes drifting on the hot air of the Chambers before him. "It seems to me this Council isn't ready to accept the cessation of control." His eyes burned swiftly over Asmodeus and Agni to settle on Metatron. "If I'm to be made consul then I refuse to relinquish battlefield authority to a dozen angels Hell-bent on meddling with what little power is left in our infrastructure."

"I'm sorry you see it that way, Archangel Michael," Asmodeus said with a slick grin.

Metatron spoke before Michael could launch a rebuke. "Time to vote: who desires Archon Gabriel lead our defenses?"

Slowly the hands rose, one by one. Asmodeus was first, followed by Agni and Urim, then Israfel, Kakabel, Azriel, Camiel and then Sandalphon. A long silence passed as the eight remained ensconced in their marble, stern faces fueling anxious hands. "Is that final?" All eyes exchanged. No hands fell nor rose. "Then it's settled. Archon Gabriel will lead an urban defense. We hand reins over to you, Archon. Do you approve the stratagem?"

Gabriel reluctantly nodded. "I'll maintain the defenses of the Holy City and the lives of our faithful angelic host. Father willing, Satan won't set foot inside the Holy Temple." He looked up, avoiding Asmodeus' grin and Michael's dejected scowl. "The Gates and Walls will hold. I swear it."

Chapter III

"Wisdom is better than weapons of war, but one sinner destroys much good."
—Ecclesiastes 9:18

"Ponderous, convoluted, inefficient," Michael fumed as he stormed out of the Council Chambers. "A waste to have me lead this warlike enterprise in peacetime only to make you consul."

Gabriel was fast on his heels, despite the limp. "If you had your way, we'd all be burning in the tail of your comet, Michael. They are the ruling body of the Eastern Kingdom."

"They are ill-advised and ill-intentioned, Gabriel, and you know it." Michael strode back into the Hallowed Causeway. He surveyed the carnage still being dealt with by the survivors. Teams of medics continued to treat the wounded while seraphim choirs took up hymns to minister to the dying. In their midst, Michael saw phalanxes of Cognoscenti, standing watch with their fearsome red cloaks and bronze-faced round oak shields. Their spears were stained a gruesome hue. The archangel observed them. "And if I had my way, baby brother, I'd cut through this red tape and crush them."

"And cut the ties that bind in the process," Gabriel said. He drew up next to his brother and sighed, arms crossed. "They've always been stodgy. But they've also been the sinew that holds the

Heavenly Host together. Do you want to sit around all day creating laws and reflecting on hearings? Someone has to carry the day-to-day workload of justice."

"I won't petition twelve bureaucrats every time I want to initiate a campaign, Gabe," Michael reiterated. "I could resolve in a brace of minutes what would take them hours of deliberation." He watched the angels bring in one of the massive wheeled platforms used to haul the giant statues from Benediction. It had taken a day to clear enough rubble to allow its passage. They began loading the mangled bodies of the dead onto the platform.

"The Council has a thankless job," said Gabriel.

Michael took a deep breath and closed his eyes. "They are practically primates in fancy robes, grooming each other's egos and flinging dung. It's easy to see why their posture is so terrible, sitting in their tiered cushions with heavy crowns."

"They were Lucifer's creation," Gabriel reminded him.

Michael nodded. "Yes, and now it's crystal clear why."

Gabriel rubbed his eyes. "What a nightmarescape we've allowed to come into the world." He shook his head and readjusted the twin sabers at his hips. "How are we supposed to wrap our minds around him becoming the very thing we've worked so hard to defeat?" Michael said nothing. "How are we supposed to save Zion? Or Earth, for that matter?"

"I'm already on it," said Michael. "The Tome of Descendance has to be squared away."

"The Tome *is* squared away, remember?"

Michael shook his head again. "If they get into Zion again, do you really want to divide up your armies between defending the Holy Mount and protecting the Bastion's artifacts?"

"Oh," Gabriel said softly, "I didn't think about that."

"Of course you didn't," his brother bit back. "You haven't spent the past myriad millennia preparing for this."

"It wasn't my choice," Gabriel defended.

Michael took in the scene of grisly aftermath with a sweep of his arm. "And this wasn't mine, but here we are." He picked his way over trundles of wounded angels. They had begun lowering corpses from the balconies, much to the relief of those who worked beneath them. Many wore silk scarves around their faces, membranous thin and twice as useless against the smell. "I wish Arkiel were still with us," the Cherubim Patriarch lamented.

"I'm sorry for your loss," Gabriel said softly.

"One of many. And more to come."

Gabriel straightened and took a deep breath. "You would've been proud of his fighting spirit, despite his allegiance."

"Let's just hope Ariel and Rafiel can fill his shoes."

"How do we bear this burden so that we won't need them?" Gabriel asked helplessly. Michael clenched his jaw. "How do you defeat the Dragon when he's your own brother?"

Eventually, his older brother shrugged. "I don't know. You're consul; you figure it out." With that, the archangel made his way through the throngs of angels laboring to save their brethren in the abattoir that had become the Holy Temple. Gabriel watched him address the blood-smeared medics. He knelt next to the mortally wounded and held their hands. He prayed with constellation partners whose twins had been slain. He helped pull the maimed from piles of their dead friends. The fires had been doused. Blood-caked drapes wrapped around columns were cut from their moorings on the ceiling and loaded onto the large rolling platforms, with other detritus and rubble. Cherubim patrols policed up weapons. Seraphim relayed supplies. And Gabriel stood bereft and wept.

By the time Michael made his way back to his office at the Citadel, it was nightfall. He entered the dark room and hushed the door closed. Immediately the archangel spotted the pair of dim jade lamps peeking at him from the chair of his oak and bronze lion-faced desk, the curly mane of blonde hair cascaded in the window's moonlight. He went to the wet bar and poured a drink.

"You're getting too good," Michael said to the jade-eyed shadow at his desk. The cherub tied to speak but only whimpered a muted sob. Michael poured another drink and nodded his agreement. He brought the glasses over to the desk. "Never let them see your tears," he commanded and set the drinks down on the desk leather.

"What does it matter?" Alrak bemoaned. "I had three friends. Now I have two." He flung himself into Michael's torso and bawled. Michael reluctantly embraced him.

"Be judicious with your laughter," the archangel said.

Alrak pulled away, wiping tears from his confused eyes. "What are you talking about?"

"And for all their sakes," Michael finished, "keep your jokes to a minimum."

Composing himself, Alrak filled his lungs with air and stared. "I don't understand."

"If only we'd faced our fears," Michael said to himself, "we could have stopped him."

He downed his drink and went back to the wet bar. Alrak watched him light the candles and sconces. He poured another glass of golden liquor. His eyes closed and his goateed mouth moved noiselessly. Alrak had seen that look on his mentor's face before. He drew a hand to his sternum where the thick bandage was clotted to his shirt. His head tilted back and the shot vanished. The glass came down on the bar top with authority, the archangel sighing with bittersweet agony. Alrak saw his head sink between drooping shoulders.

"I don't know if I'm prepared for this." Alrak barely heard the prayer. A surge of compassion welled within him. He took a step and opened his mouth. Michael turned and halted him with a stern gaze. The archangel's back straightened and his shoulders broadened. He was once again the Cherubim Patriarch. "I'm sending you out," he finally said before Alrak could speak. "And you're to take the Seventh Column Legion with you."

Alrak's head tilted, eyes narrow. "You're not making sense."

"Commander Ural," Michael called out, eyes locked on Alrak, "Captain Weir, you may enter."

From his office's antechamber came the tall, fit Captain Weir with his curly crop of hair and broad forehead, a red bandage wrapped around it. Ural was at his flank, equal in height and twice as wide with a great low-hanging white beard speckled in blood. Their caution was masked by the shadows as they crossed into the light of the suite. They stood at attention and saluted their Patriarch. He replied in kind.

"Hey, I recognize you!" Alrak said to Weir with a smile and a point. "You were at the head of that legion I always saw running around in the Southlands!"

Weir smiled tautly and nodded at Ural. "I told you we were being watched."

"You win that bet," Ural conceded quietly.

"Alrak," said Michael, "this is Commander Ural and Captain Weir, two of my most capable officers." Alrak bowed. They returned the courtesy. "The Seventh Column is sort of their brainchild." Alrak threw Michael a confused frown. "I think it best if they explain."

Weir tilted his broad forehead in thanks. "When I served as an aide to Tribune Gilgamesh and his lieutenant, Galeth, some years ago, they mused on what would be the perfect legion, independent of auxiliaries and free of the trappings of large corps."

"But Galeth serves with Unoth in Lorinar," Alrak argued.

"Much to Unoth's lament at times," Ural said with a chuckle. "Galeth comes from Gilgamesh's school of irregulars. The Lightning Legion has always been a roguish bunch of thunderbolts. Galeth was no exception. But back then, we were all young and fresh."

"Military innovations were always a curiosity between us," Weir continued. "Often the symposiums would include Ural, Galeth, Gilgamesh and even Melphax. They'd debate for hours on the role of troop classifications, cataloging weaknesses and strengths, formations, tactics and so on. I transcribed and fetched wine until dawn, often foregoing sleep while they exorcized the muses fueling their epiphanies. It was truly a thing to behold. They would sit over a bowl of figs and a cask of wine and forge into the night until either passing out drunk or keeling over from exhaustion—and good luck discerning between the two.

"I tell you such matters were a mess, every one of them. The subject was just too knotted with variables to untangle. There wasn't a single scenario that didn't entail complexity verging on the ridiculous. Yet they weren't deterred. At first, the method of thought was compartmentalization; that by having a unit of each troop type, we could be independent.

"Then we hit a wall: we realized the legion would be impractically colossal. Oh, you should've seen it," Weir said around a piteous laugh. "Gilgamesh and Galeth were inconsolable. They moped so close to tears that I thought I'd have to trail them with a mop and bucket. They had unraveled so much only to have the yarn tangle back in a blink. At one point I feared for their sanity. But, like any inspiration," he turned to Ural, "out of great failure came triumph."

"They took a bad road," Ural clarified. "So, they went in the opposite direction. For a legion to be perfect, it didn't require units of classes. Instead, they needed a legion composed of one single cross-trained troop type: swords, shields, lances and light, powerful armor. They would be proficient in all scenarios. They would be perfect."

"Commander Ural has carried the torch of their original idea with his Battle Group Concordia experiment," Weir stated, "but for Gilgamesh and Galeth, what they were after was a quick response force of highly-trained, well-armored angels. We called the project the Seventh Column, owing our holy aim to the humility of God's wisdom. We built the Tree of Life with such pillars. To wit, mobility was the key. Cavalry fails against a phalanx. Conversely, a phalanx will be busted by skirmishers. But how to meld them? Infantry needs agility, but you can't repel a cavalry charge without wearing half your weight in bronze and iron."

"I wouldn't know," Alrak lamented.

"No," Weir said, regarding him, "I suppose you wouldn't. But for us, the fact remained the same: how to build a highly capable uniform legion. As always, the answer lied in technology. That's where Arkadia came in. He would design the armor while we trained a cadre in secret. But it required miraculous innovation. Arkadia was elated but he toiled and failed, heartbroken. The science just wasn't there…not with everyone's energy directed towards the Creation. So, the project was abandoned; the Seventh Column was disbanded. Or so we thought. Much to our bewilderment, we saw our prodigy in action not long ago…and so did you."

"Apparently Lucifer got ahold of Arkadia and gave him the science to finish the job," Ural said. Michael quietly sighed at that.

"The black-armored million at Benediction," Alrak breathed. Weir and Ural nodded. "There wasn't much that could pierce those carapaces. And the way they slipped in darkness? Uncanny."

Weir scowled. "The color wasn't our original intent; that was Lucifer's doing. Our version had the opposite approach in mind. Our dream legion was meant to be a shining beacon on the battlefield, not a malevolent shadow. Satan's elites work on the principle of subterfuge. Ours would've worked on the principle of blinding radiance. Battles are usually fought under the sun. Therefore, we took the next logical step: reflect light in the most piercing way. It can be equated to the Cognoscenti's tactic of buffing the bronze facings of their shields to a mirror sheen. Imagine that tenfold and you'll have some idea of what we were after."

Alrak pursed his lips and squinted. Michael knew that look and rolled his eyes. Eventually, the protégé caved. "That's, um…*weird*." He blushed and groaned, embarrassed by his own compulsory cheek. Ural and Weir chuckled.

Michael rubbed his forehead. "Try to focus, dandelion." He winced at Weir. "Never mind him, Captain."

Weir fought the tug of a grin. "No worries, Patriarch. The hope was that our faith would amplify the light. That was the secret Arkadia needed to unpack. It was metaphysical, but then, isn't everything? Working in Creation taught us that. Michael found the key when he took the armor before the White Throne."

"So, has Arkadia made any progress?" Alrak asked.

Weir smiled. "Come to the South Gate and see, cherub…or should I say, 'Polemarch'."

Alrak shot Michael a quizzical look.

The archangel nodded. "The Seventh Column is real, Alrak. Everything Weir, Arkadia, Ural, Gilgamesh, Galeth and Melphax have been striving for has finally come to fruition."

"Seven thousand of us are stationed at the South Gate," Weir interjected. "And I don't mind telling you: we're getting antsy."

"All they need is a general to lead them," Ural proffered.

Alrak looked at his mentor, who forced a smile. He turned to Weir, who eagerly eyed him. A welling rose in Alrak's chest. It crept up his throat and beamed through his features, eyes wide as the offer dawned on him.

When he regained his faculties and calmed down, Michael spoke. "Now, I know you've been yearning for this for a long time but remember, these angels aren't close to you like I am. Don't take them for granted. Treat them with dignity before you unleash your candor. Weir's been kind enough to heed my request for the Seventh Column to be handed over to you, but do you know why?" Alrak shook his head. "Mazerrel." The protégé's face darkened.

"That behemoth has wanted you dead for many moons now," Ural stated. "And now he has the means." The grey angel smiled, despite himself. "The ways of the Lord are mysterious indeed. If one is lucky, they can see why the pieces get put into place."

"It looks like this will be our mission during this heresy, Alrak," said Weir. "Mazerrel is a distracting encumbrance to your mentor and a viable threat. His interference jeopardizes all."

"But why the Southlands?" Alrak asked. "Mazerrel's in the Northern Plains."

Michael touched his diminutive shoulder. "You're brilliant and powerful—more so than you realize, but you must discover your potential there first."

"Then why not send me north to face the rebels there?"

"Because Mazerrel is in the North; I want you to cut your teeth on a lesser task."

"Great," Alrak griped, "more training in the jungles."

Michael shrugged at his dejection. "You have walked in my Way for two years now. Soon, you'll learn tactics like ploy, counter, feint and method of strategy. I have faith in you, Alrak. Father has faith in you. And if Gabriel knew, he'd have faith in you too."

"Wait, Gabriel doesn't know?"

"Only for the reason the Council cannot know; I've been stripped of my authority; any decision I make must first pass through the crippling bureaucracy of Elder hands. But we have Father's blessing, and that's what counts. Trust me, you're sanctified."

"I still feel guilty about Gabriel."

"I know. Forgive me. I'll tell him at the right time. Until then," he pointed to Weir, "all's been arranged. Weir and Ural will escort you to the South Gate. You'll leave at midnight with your legion."

Alrak smiled. "*My* legion."

Michael let out a laugh. "Yes, *your* legion. Don't forget it. Care for them. They are prodigies, but you're their general. They will call you Polemarch. Honor them." Alrak vowed he would. Michael folded his arms. "Then go. I have an assembly of generals to address, and no one likes to keep such bombasts waiting, especially when there are seraphim in the mix."

Alrak went to bow but checked himself and saluted instead. Michael was taken aback by the gesture at first, but caught himself and responded in kind. He watched the three make for the door. His heart sank as his dandelion bounded beyond the threshold, Weir fast on his heels with Ural bringing up the rear.

"Ural," Michael whispered. The bearded titan halted and leaned in the doorframe. Michael chewed on his words, eyes conveying what his lips could not. Ural waited patiently. "Where I go, he must follow. Where I point, he must lead. He is my protégé. But I believe, in the end, he will prove to be my better."

The ancient and honored angel winked. "I'll have Weir look after him." Michael nodded and patted his massive arm. By the time he poured himself another drink, Ural was striding to catch up with the dashing Weir and racing Polemarch Alrak Sivad.

Empyrean Falling

Chapter IV
"And there was war in Heaven…"
—Revelation 12:7

It had been a week since the Battle at Benediction. The angelic host had cataloged and buried the dead. The Holy Temple was under guarded renovation. The legions had marshaled and began marching to their assigned posts and garrisons.

In the Citadel, Michael felt chained to his desk. Barricaded on all sides by stacks of papers and towers of scrolls, he pored over requisitions, addendums, legion rosters, updates on readiness levels, dispositions, and most importantly, seraphic reports passed on by Gabriel detailing the movements of the Dragon's armies. His office was also littered with empty bottles.

Michael's eyes drifted to the window. He got up and looked out to the Citadel's "Garden" courtyards. Many of the training acres had been plowed. In their place was the Memoriam. Spanning for a fourth of the aggregate acreage, it was the final resting place of the cherubim slain at Benediction. It had taken days for the angels to come to grips with burying the righteous dead. He knew Gabriel would often walk the halls of his own Mausoleum, which had been erected in the lowest level of the Bastion but, for Michael, the true despair was looking across the countless white headstones lining the manicured grounds below in acre-sized banks. Every time he closed his eyes, he saw the onus of Lucifer's pride, the fruits of Satan's harvest, and the price of his own fealty. Such a macabre vista gutted him, the low-slung sun bathing the granite and marble tombstones…

Suddenly, there was a knock at the door, liberating him from his nightmare. "Enter," he commanded.

In strode Melphax, decked out in his smoky armored field plate. He stood before the lion-embossed desk and saluted, giant flanged war mace slung at his hip and open-faced domed helmet under the crook of his arm. Michael turned and admired the grey colossus.

"You wanted to see me, Patriarch?" Melphax asked.

Michael drew strength from his cherub as only an archangel could. "Looks like things are finally underway. With Galeth promoted and sent to the coast, Lorinar's Merciful Fate could be vulnerable. I've sent Gilgamesh's Lightning Legion to reinforce Unoth's garrison."

"Gilgamesh's irregulars should fill the gap," Melphax stated. "They don't call them the 'Thunderbolts' for nothing."

"Yes, well, with my brother dancing to the Council's tune or wandering the Mausoleum's sepulchers weeping over every seraphic corpse, we need all the help we can get. Your expertise is needed, Melphax. It took some doing, but I had Arkadia split the Tome of Descendance. I need to ensure its clandestine exodus from Zion."

"I was beginning to wonder why you ordered me to linger in Zion the past couple days," Melphax replied. "I don't mind telling you, shipping my garrison back to Amin Shakush with Paladin and Deledrosse is like watching a seraph juggle hatchets; it garners a laugh, but it won't end well." The two chuckled, despite the morose, foreboding circumstances. "They're good lieutenants; they might even make it home in one piece, assuming they don't strangle each other first." He harrumphed as Michael sat back in his chair, eyes drifting. Melphax watched his attention drift to the Memoriam. "Am I to hide the halves, Patriarch?"

Michael came to and shook his head. "No, I've assigned others to that. I need you as escort."

"Escort?"

"Back to Amin Shakush," Michael clarified. "Chief Librarian Ma'igwa is leading a five-angel team charged with hiding one half. We think your mountain is the perfect place for it. If it makes you feel any better, Gabriel's had this plan hatched even before the battle at Benediction." He watched Melphax's chest rise, consternation darkening his features. "Look, I know you and Ma'igwa are distant at best, but most of Gabriel's top seraphim sided with the Dragon. He's familiar with the Tome and your Iron Fortress is locked down tighter than any garrison outside of Zion, better even than Lorinar. Plus, its obscurity ensures Satan's forces will consider it of little strategic value, rendering you safely out of harm's way. With a little luck, you and Ma'igwa will sit out this insurrection. Might even become friends." Michael saw the sullen look of incredulity twisting his cherub's face. "I'd consider it a personal favor, Melphax."

At that, the general brightened and went rigid, standing at parade attention. "There's none more capable, Patriarch."

Michael regarded him from across the desk. "Take the backroads and be careful doing it. How Satan thinks he can depose Father is…well, it's beyond me. But I can't shake the hunch that he knows something I don't. I need to ensure all precautions are taken and all countermeasures are implemented. This includes the covert security of the Tome of Descendance."

"I assure you, the Tome half will reach Amin Shakush."

"Just try to keep from throttling Ma'igwa. I know he's insufferable, even for a seraph."

There was a wrapping of knuckles at Michael's door. His bleary eyes shot to it. Melphax turned, instinctively donning his helmet and drawing his mace.

"Yes?" Michael called guardedly, surreptitiously reaching for Virtue slung in a scabbard hidden under the lip of his desk.

The door opened to reveal Zophiel, his short crop of brown hair matted to his head with sweat and his linen tunic thoroughly soaked. He hurried to the desk and bowed, his leather-greaved legs noiselessly traversing the wooden floor as he reached into the leather pouch slung at his hip.

Empyrean Falling

"Lieutenant Zophiel, Archangel. I bear an urgent message from Consul Gabriel." His face was flushed and his chest billowed. Michael bade him proceed while Melphax disarmed. The seraph produced a piece of folded parchment and delivered it into Michael's outstretched hand before receding from the desk to stand at attention, eyes locked on the floor.

Michael's countenance grew stern as the parchment unfolded to reveal a shimmering glyph. His eyes shot to Zophiel. "Speak, Lieutenant. What do you know?"

"Only that Commander Ellunias has the garrison beating to quarters."

Michael stood with a furious authority. "Wait outside." The seraph obeyed and departed. Michael turned to Melphax. "You'd better get going. Ma'igwa will be awaiting your arrival at the West Gate." He strode over to his reliquary in the far corner.

"It's already starting, isn't it?" Melphax asked.

Michael did not answer; he was too busy assembling a half harness of armor and Virtue.

By the time Michael and Zophiel reached the Northern Wall, it was abuzz with the scurry of hundreds of thousands of defenders. Angels rushed to and fro, armed to the teeth as they equipped the anti-siege batteries. Michael took one last look at the tranquil serenity of the virgin pastures and clear summer sky before descending with Zophiel to the North Gate. He landed at the barbican and made his way up into a nexus of activity flanked by artillery bartizans. Officers barked and cherubim hastened in heavy armor to the orchestra of piping flutes and blaring trumpets. Seven hundred cubits high and stretching to either horizon, never had Michael seen so many angels choke its exterior in frenetic preparation.

"Consul Gabriel's waiting for you up top, Archangel," Zophiel shouted as Michael furled his wings and followed the armor-bearer up the staircase to the command watchtower, dodging phalanxes of Cognoscenti filing through the narrow corridor in a roar of mettle.

Michael found Gabriel standing beside Ellunias the Radiant at the uppermost rampart, each adorned in their shining suits of armor and surrounded by Ellunias' color guard. Ellunias towered over

Gabriel, with his short crop of flaxen hair and gilded plate armor. He used a spyglass while Gabriel shielded his eyes from the sun's glare. Zophiel heralded his archangel and announced Michael's arrival into the armored balcony with a frantic tenor.

Gabriel went rigid as his eyes fell upon the aide. "Where's your field plate, Major?" he barked, red-faced. The seraph stammered. Gabriel flung an arm in the direction of the Northern Plains. "Did I not tell you what is coming? Depart from my sight and do not return until you're in full panoply. Deny my eyes the crime of catching you so unprotected!" Zophiel fled the roof, as much out of fear of further castigation as strict obedience.

Michael took up Gabriel's flank as his brother composed himself. The two looked out past the crenelated ramparts to the flatland beyond. "Where's Alrak when you need him?" Gabriel muttered. Michael squinted into the distance, looking for the source of the communal trepidation.

The verdant plains' horizon was no longer visible. In its place plodded forth an incalculable gulf of swarming darkness, heralded by a baleful roar as the land choked under their teeming myriads. They sent snaking clouds of grime into the air, obscuring their composition. But Michael's keen eyes could see the black banners of the Dragon wafting in the summer breeze amidst an endless glinting forest.

"How far?" the Cherubim Patriarch hazarded.

"Barely a league out, Archangel," Ellunias replied.

"Numbers?"

"Twenty myriads so far," answered Gabriel.

Michael nodded. "Do we have a plan, Commander?"

Ellunias lowered his spyglass and turned to him. "When they come under battery range, we'll send out skirmishers to hit their center. Commandant Malthus will exploit the breach with his Pegasun Centaurs once we drive them into the flanks, where the turrets can bombard them in concentration."

Michael sensed his resignation. "And if they're cavalry?"

"Malthus baits them into our artillery," Gabriel answered first.

Michael grimaced. "That won't work."

Gabriel narrowed his golden orbs, arms crossed.

Empyrean Falling

"We'll find out soon enough," Ellunias exhaled sharply. He relayed the order. There was a trumpet peal and a gust. As if birthed by an alto blast, the airborne skirmishers soared over the barbican. Michael watched the chevron flights of seraphim wing towards the enemy. Ellunias turned to his adjutant. "Release the Pegasun Centaurs." A horn blew and the North Gate's cyclopean gears roared, their chains drawing the monolithic doors apart with a ponderous grind, issuing forth a spectacle. As if a dam had burst, a deluge of equestrian fury flooded from the barbican. Twenty thousand of the finest cavalry in all of Heaven rode forth with a nonpareil discipline, their columns glistening in the morning rays as they cantered.

At their van was Ellunias' lieutenant, the Cavalier Commandant Malthus, his magenta guidon fluttering above a matching mantle and plume. Michael watched Malthus' vanguard lead the cavalry out, each resplendent in their pristine heavy armor and the snapping colored guidons of their wing commanders. Their momentum was uncanny as they maneuvered into position.

Wasting no time, the cavalry dragoons arrayed themselves in an overlapping series of wedges, left flank refused. Their glimmering stream broke apart into enormous blocks as the battalions consolidated and decreased their intervals. Each ten-cubit lance was held with vertical precision as they jockeyed to their posts upon the fallow ground, the colors of their mantles seeking out the pinions of their cohort commanders. These regiments, each with four cohorts five hundred knights strong, cantered to a standstill at the command of their officers, distinguished by their plumes and lance pennants. Each had sacks lashed to their saddles. The regiments presented themselves as a collage of colored wedges stretching the length of the North Gate.

Michael considered himself an accomplished rider, but he blanched at the magnificence of the Pegasun Centaurs; they were an inspired prodigy. He could never chide his brother or Ellunias for regarding them with pride; they were the acme of Heaven's knightly cavalry; angels of unparalleled majesty and skill. Yet their numbers were still cumbersome to deploy. Michael's patience strained under the laborious maneuvers; it took time for the wedges to draw reins down the line until all twenty thousand were fielded.

Empyrean Falling

He observed the airborne seraphim fly ahead of the marshaling cavalry. Several of the rebel cohorts at the center slowed their march and raised overlapping shields in an impromptu defense. No sooner had the skirmishers committed to the fray than they were disengaging. Dozens dropped like stones to the sea of armed adversaries below.

"Sharpshooters," he observed. Beside him, Gabriel sighed.

"They'd better make it back," Ellunias growled from his spyglass. "Without a proper survey, we'll be flying blind." Gabriel tried to reassure him. He paid it no heed and gave the signal. Another horn blast pierced the air. The Pegasun Centaurs advanced.

Malthus' cavaliers hoisted their lances and shouted a word. The war cry issuing from the breadth of their line rumbled up to the parapets. It shivered Michael's spine. The formation lurched and in moments the battalions were trotting forth under swarms of re-forming skirmishers. Their knightly audacity was carried forward on thick hooves as their steeds galloped across the bare fields before the Wall. Their saddlebags flopped under a heavy load. Michael watched the magenta vanguard draw into the frontline of their adversaries. Still leagues out, he saw the enemy's central corps halt to receive Malthus. Their pikes lowered into a bristling wall. Malthus' cavaliers refused to cushion their lances into the horizontal. They drew dangerously close to the rebel infantry.

Michael absently placed a hand on the rampart's stone lip, breathless before their daring maneuver. "Father, protect them," he prayed. "Protect his knights." He felt Gabriel beside him. He wheeled on his brother. "Tell me you didn't give the order to attack." Gabriel was silent. "They're twenty thousand against a hundred times their number! You can't expect them to—"

"Just wait, Archangel," Ellunias suggested coolly. The two met eyes. Ellunias nodded. "Hold fast."

Michael turned in time to see a marvel. The entire order of Pegasun Centaurs dissolved from their stacked oblique. Their trajectory split on a pinhead, a mere furlong away from the enemy's frontline. Their halves wheeled on opposite paths parallel to the enemy's front and galloping for the flanks. They began dumping white chalk from their saddlebags. In time, the enemy's front was obscured by a thick white wall of powder. It was then he perceived.

From the foe's vanguard, clouds of thin projectiles erupted, chasing the two masses of riders. The airborne skirmishers pivoted in time to catch it. They hovered and took a census. Another volley leapt up. Malthus' cavalry juked again and galloped back and forth, dumping their satchels and narrowly avoiding fusillades.

"That was a bold move, baby brother," Michael admitted through clenched teeth.

"This screening action will keep them at bay," said Gabriel. "It buys us needed time."

"As long as we control the skies," Ellunias reminded, "the ploy will work."

Michael observed the airborne loyalists surge again while the cavaliers continued to run maneuvers in the flatlands, kicking up blankets of chalk. He smiled at his sibling. "Not bad." Gabriel shrugged sheepishly. "What now, Consul?"

"Now," Gabriel sighed, "we wait."

Michael snarled and leaned on the rampart. "I hate waiting."

Empyrean Falling

Chapter V

"...Your walls will tremble at the noise of the war horses, wagons and chariots…"

—Ezekiel 26:10

Gabriel generated a windstorm directed at the besieging army. It pressed on them for the better part of an hour, obscuring their formation's cohesion in tandem with the chalk. Their advance slowed, but it did not relent.

Michael looked up. The sun blazed at its meridian in the warm blue sky. He imbibed its tranquility before turning to lower his gaze upon Zion at his back. The spires gleamed in the late summer sun. The Holy Temple rose as a massive dome from the center of the metropolis. It was glorious. It was pristine. It was unsullied.

His eyes drew down to the bailey behind the North Gate. On the paved landings adjacent to the sally ports were the sun-hats, acre-wide bronze and oak palisades erected on oak poles. Should enemy volleys surmount the Wall, the sun-hats would protect the infantry. Underneath them, the dreaded Cognoscenti dressed their scarlet-clad lines. It had taken hours for them to fly in from their various posts throughout Zion and marshal at the North Gate. They stood silent and grim, encased in their bronze cuirasses with their meter-wide round shields bossed to a mirror sheen. Michael was grateful for the sun-hats; he did not have to look into the Cognoscenti's foreboding eyes twinkling within their plumed bronze helmets.

"You were right about Malthus' screening action," Michael said as he faced Gabriel on his right. "Looks like we were able to muster at least a full myriad."

"If ten thousand Cogs can't hold the bailey then the Wall deserves to fall," Gabriel said.

Michael carried his gaze past his brother to Ellunias, who stood with his spyglass. The seraph stood head-and-shoulders above his archangel, his gilded armor glinting in the noonday sun while the banners of his color guard picked up the gentle breeze around them.

"Skirmishers were right," Ellunias said, peering through his spyglass. "At least six siege-towers for the Gate alone. Who knows how many more they have along the breadth of the Wall."

"And their artillery?" Michael asked.

Ellunias shook his head. "No sign. We suspect they're hidden behind the infantry."

Michael looked down the length of the Wall. Beyond the Gate on both sides, the Northern Wall stretched to the horizon. At seven hundred cubits high and half as thick, it was a near-endless array of artillery batteries, sally ports, fighting holes, armories, landing stations, and armored bartizans. It bristled with all manner of anti-siege artillery batteries: tall wooden onagers loaded with incendiary rounds; thin trebuchets bearing round iron balls; catapults and ballistae on swiveling circular platforms; and "gall-guns" loaded with banks of javelins. Interspersed between these batteries were checkered banks of archers, protected by the crenelated ramparts and reinforced by clusters of airborne skirmishers. Beneath them waited the heavy infantry, garrison cherubim armed with short swords and square shields, ready to deploy if the enemy reached the top. Angels hastened to their posts, bearing supplies and reloads. It was an imposing sight.

The Chief of the Armies of God drew no comfort from it as his eyes fell upon the enemy army arrayed against them. He squinted into the grassy flats beyond. The dark roiling tide of rebels came on steadily, their front a wall of tower shields and pikes, with the siege-towers visible above the forest of polearms and their own airborne peltasts swarming over their heads.

"At least Ural made sure Battle Group Concordia drove them out of Zion," Michael said, half to himself. "Imagine where we'd be if we had to be looking over our backs right now."

The army began to close the gap. Michael could make out their disposition. They were a flooding ocean of polearms, myriads arranged in overlapping wedges. Behind the vanguards, he could see banks of archers. The towers lumbered at intervals. Tribunes patrolled the inseams in their chariots while battlewagons brought up the rear, ready for resupply from the baggage train. The full scale of their numbers was visible; fear gripped archangelic hearts.

"How did it come to this?" whispered Gabriel.

"It was never enough for him," Michael quietly replied as he pulled his gauntlets from his belt and put them on. "We failed our brother. And all of Heaven will pay for it." He turned to the Northern Defenders, waiting with fidgety nerves in the bailey behind him. "Faithful!" he shouted. "My faithful Northern Defenders! Let not your hearts be troubled! A dark day has dawned on us, but this is the moment we've prepared for, this is the culmination of our labors! We did not want this, but here we stand. Our brothers come to finish what they started in blasphemous acrimony! I won't let all that we've built and all that we love be torn asunder! Will you stand with me? Will you stand with your archangels?" He raised Virtue. They cheered.

Michael turned back to see the interval between the Northern Wall's plinth and the rebel legions grow tenuously thin. The Pegasun Centaurs cantered away from the enemy's battle line, thinning their ranks to stay within the protective range of the Gate's artillery.

"What's their range?" Michael asked.

"Twelve furlongs," said Ellunias, still at his spyglass.

Michael readjusted Virtue at his waist. "We need to create an inroad for Malthus to hit their rear elements."

Ellunias lowered his spyglass. "It's already been taken care of." He turned and raised a hand. At his limb's fall, the trebuchets unleashed their first volley.

Empyrean Falling

The tall, thin wooden structures swung and groaned as their payloads were flung from the battlements. Michael watched their projectiles arc into the clear air. Several bounced and rolled short, but a select few found their marks in the frontline's shield wall. Dark, spindly shapes were scattered into the air as rebel angels by the dozens were smashed to pulp. Yet still, Satanic army marched forth, trampling their maimed comrades with a methodical gait.

At nine furlongs, the army came under the full range of the Gate's heavy artillery. The batteries came to life, hurling their payloads onto the enemy wedges. Michael watched with keen eyes as the barrage rained death upon the rebels, each volley striking with the peal of thunder. Vanguards burst across the line, riddled by iron balls and showering clusters of caltrops.

Hundreds perished under the impacts. Those who were not crushed by direct hits were sent flailing into the periphery by the shock of the blasts, all manner of war gear scattering in a hail of splinters. At that distance, it was soundless to their ears, but Michael knew choruses of screams erupted from their ranks as bodies splattered, broken and flung into their neighboring formations. Yet again, the line did not falter. Their discipline unnerved Michael.

The rebels moved to within six furlongs of the Wall. Ellunias' artillery began hammering them relentlessly. He gave the order and they switched to incendiary rounds. The onagers launched baleful expulsions of flaming pitch that turned the grounds beyond the Wall's battered plinth to a conflagration. The army drew up and redressed their lines. They paid no heed as the ballistae swung on concentrated formations and unleashed iron-headed missiles longer than the height of a cherub. The casualties they endured began to mount. The artillery chewed ragged inroads through the lines, even as the towers rumbled forth, spitting response volleys of small incendiaries. They stopped just short of the burning grass beyond the Wall.

"Trebuchets, put down those towers!" Ellunias barked over the din. "Onagers, concentrate fire on that central shield formation!"

Michael watched the shield wall part ranks to allow the siege-towers to pass. The armored structures rose high into the air, their massive wooden wheels pressing ruts in the turf. He saw their ports open and smaller ballistae return volleys, leg-sized javelins tipped with sharpened steel hurtling back into the Northern Defenders' bartizans. Their aim was expert; the missiles ripped through several loyalists at a time, disabling key batteries flanking the Gate. The faithful angels' catapults swiveled on them to return the favor. They each traded blows, sending punishing volleys into one another. Michael watched the destruction unfold. He saw the first tower be broken to pieces and collapse on its own sundered weight. Scores of rebel angels fell, their screams carried on the wind as they tumbled onto the skewering pikes of their allies. Out from behind these, the Cherubim Patriarch saw low, wide shapes emerge, pushed by teamsters in heavy armor. They were covered with doused tarps. He squinted as they maneuvered around the embattled siege-towers and repositioned on the flanks. The first one to get into position yanked off its tarp, revealing itself, and at once Michael knew.

"Aim for the flanks of the towers!" he shouted. Gabriel barely heard him. "Ellunias!" He rushed over to the seraphic commander and pointed at the unveiled wooden frames, now coming to fiery life. "Catapults on the rise!"

"Divert!" Ellunias shouted. "Clear the deck!" It was too late.

The first two catapults sent their fiery pots careening for the command post. Michael saw them rise like ill-omened comets and grabbed Gabriel. They dove for the ramparts. Ellunias' color guard swarmed him. The first shot went low, splattering its flaming pitch over the lip of the battlements. The second landed high, dousing the armored command post in liquid fire. Michael's ears rang and his head pounded with the concussion. He saw stars as he tried to regain control of his limbs. The smoke robbed his lungs of air. He shoved Gabriel into the protection of the stairwell. The Seraphim Archon stared at nothing, ears bleeding.

Michael scrambled to his feet and found Ellunias amidst his color guard. "We need Malthus on those catapults!"

The Commander of the North Gate was staggering to a rise and beating back his color guard with a fury. He smacked flaming pitch from his vambraces and coughed. "He had orders to circle the front and hit the rear."

More volleys roared overhead, exploding with deadly effect. Loyalists screamed and burned, many tumbling over the Wall. Under cover fire, the remaining five siege-towers opened their hatches. From their topmost portals swarmed hundreds of rebel angels. They erupted in flights from the opened roofs of the towers, fanning out into swarms before arcing down onto the parapets of the Wall. Michael heard the rush of wings descending upon them.

"We need to get word to him, Commander," Michael shouted. "If those catapults aren't silenced, we'll be too suppressed to support our infantry if the Gate falls."

Ellunias pointed at the development. "And how do you suggest we do that, Archangel?"

Michael glanced at the closest siege tower. It was faced with heavy iron, yet where the trebuchets had beaten away the plating, the wooden frame underneath was aflame. On either side, wafting banners bore that wicked glyph, painted in blood and obscured by the rising smoke from the barrages. Within their ports, he saw angels rushing up the interior staircases to gain access to the roof, where they sprouted wings and flew for the Gate with murderous intent. There was a rabid fury to them which Michael had not anticipated. It soured his guts.

Portholes swung open from the front of the Wall. Gall-guns began sending banks of javelins into the rebels' ranks. Michael saw their meter-length shafts shoot out in an expanding square spread. Many of the low-flying enemies were run through by these projectiles, but most were too high to be affected. The rebels continued to pour out from the nearest siege-tower, like an abyssal volcano issuing forth a torrent of winged darkness.

"Yews," Ellunias roared, "let fly!"

On the flanks, the archers drew, nocked and loosed their fusillades of broadhead arrows into the swarms of rebel mobile infantry. Many dropped like stones, quilled like porcupines. Many more landed on the parapets, only to be met by the garrison infantry rushing from their hatches below the top deck. Furious fighting ensued across the breadth of the North Gate as rebel and loyalist infantry engaged in hand-to-hand combat.

Gabriel wandered through the melee, emerging from the ruck as Michael and Ellunias were enveloped by the color guard. Again, the catapults came on, erupting random points across the barbican's ramparts in vomitus sprays of naphtha. Faithful and faithless alike were consumed in the holocaust, whole pockets of angels incinerated by the flames. Those who survived were driven to the bloody stones by hails of arrows arcing high from the enemy below.

"Our skirmishers need to clear the air," Gabriel said. Michael turned to him. He was still wide-eyed and bleeding, saber in-hand.

"No!" the Cherubim Patriarch shouted. "Send them high and to the flanks. Hit their archers while they're still training volleys on us." As he spoke, two more salvos came in. Several of the artillery bartizans were blown to pieces, their crews scattered and burned alive.

"We're losing batteries, Archangels," Ellunias said. "Without the artillery, they'll cover the remaining ground unchecked."

"And their sappers will have free rein of the portcullis," Michael intuited. "Those battlewagons will be online before much longer." He threw a quick glance over the rampart. The rebel shield wall had encroached to within a few furlongs. He turned back to the seraphs. Smoke clogged the air, obscuring the fight as garrison legionnaires became embattled with the invaders. "Commander, concentrate your remaining heavy hitters on that shield wall; if we can make them vulnerable, they can't field as many troops into those towers. And they won't dare risk an open-air assault; our porcupines would shred them." He turned to Gabriel. "Consul, sally two thirds of the Cognoscenti and drive into their ranks once our artillery has created an inroad." Gabriel looked at him, confused. "Just relay the order, Gabe; they'll know what to do." He drew Virtue from its scabbard and unfurled his wings.

"Where are you going?" Gabriel yelled.

Michael stepped towards the ramparts. "To pierce this darkness and find Malthus. He's our only hope of stopping those machines down there."

"You can't detail him off those battlewagons!" Gabriel said.

"If those catapults aren't silenced then they won't need the wagons," Michael argued. "Commander Ellunias, can I count on you not to squander my Cognoscenti?"

Ellunias nodded. "If they must, I'll make sure they sell their lives dearly."

Empyrean Falling

"It should be me going after Malthus," said Gabriel.

Michael pointed at the throngs of rebel angels amassing behind the shield wall in a frenzy of malcontent madness. "Do you want to fight your way through that?" His brother followed his pointing finger out to the flatlands choked with the teeming ranks of the foe. The frontline had begun to separate from the catapults. Only their crews and a cohort of four hundred-eighty dark-armored angels remained with each battery. "I didn't think so. Take care of my Cogs and I'll make sure Malthus is reached. Equivalent exchange." Gabriel gulped at the scene before him and gave an imperceptible shake of his head. "Trust, baby brother."

Michael bolted into the air. He coursed through the maneuvering throngs of rebel flyers. Overhead, he saw the echelons of seraphim skirmishers arc into their pincer on the rebel archers below. He dodged incoming flights of arrows and enemy slinger stones. Javelins hurled past his head, tearing the air at his ears in a wicked scream. Catapult payloads unleashed their hellish comets into the sky before him. He darted under their arcing trajectories and cartwheeled around volleys of the foe's gall-guns. The wind pressed against his face and tore at his clothing, yet he drove on, Virtue in-hand as he gained speed over the shield wall and its amassing cohorts. Those who intercepted him were slashed to the ground. His altitude was low, but the satanic ranks seemed to stretch to the horizon. Some bore the sackcloth sigil of the Phoenix Empyrean. Most carried the burlap-and-blood banner of that infamous horned glyph.

Once past the rear-rankers, he trespassed into the vacant land behind the marching legions. The dead and wounded littered the turf amidst trenches churned up by the trebuchets. Broken bits of war gear lay scattered across the open terrain. Heretic seraphim sporadically relayed messages as their tribunes transited the acres in their armored war chariots. Around them swarmed their retinue of cavalry.

Ahead lay the first catapult battery. Their crews winched down the arms, loaded the pitch barrels, lit them, and unlatch the launch mechanism. They were a tireless orchestra of precisely trained methodical destruction. Michael fought the temptation to divert course and destroy them. He chose the more prudent, sacrificial part of valor. Time was not on his side, though the temptation called him.

Empyrean Falling

He instead flew until at last finding a shining silver bar on the horizon to the right. It transited the fields with a roll of distant thunder. Ahead of him several hundred meters off lay a cluster of battlewagons. Michael landed on the grassy flats and stabbed the air with Virtue; its blade radiated light. He looked again at the encroaching stream of glinting locomotion on his right. He saw the great plume of chalk rising in its wake and knew he'd found the Pegasun Centaurs. They diverted course and headed for his beacon.

Malthus cantered at the vanguard. When they neared, the executive officer raised a hand. The column behind him trotted to a halt. He was bloody in his regal heavy plate armor, his magenta plume dancing in the midday breeze.

Michael lowered Virtue. The gleaming quieted. "Commandant Malthus," he called with a dip of his scarred, sweaty brow.

"Archangel Michael," the cavalry commander replied with a tipping of his lance. He raised his thick, grilled visor to reveal a blood-spattered beard, curled and oiled to manicured perfection. Michael caught the hint of perfume on the wind.

"Consul Gabriel sends his compliments," Michael said as he furled his wings out of respect. "He requests you bypass the sappers' wagons and reroute your knights to the catapults."

Malthus jerked his attention past Michael's shoulder and gaped at the fiery specks arcing for the Wall. "I see. They have developed the situation. How favors the Radiant?"

"Commander Ellunias lives up to his honorifics."

Malthus nodded and yanked down the visor of his helmet. "Sapper wagons were a lark anyway; we were busting them like ticks. Have no fear, Archangel. Tell my lords I'll have these reprobates roasting on the kindling of their own siege engines by sunset!"

Michael smiled. "I'll range ahead, clear a path. And Malthus? First drink back in Zion is on me."

With that, the Cherubim Patriarch was off for the catapults. They never saw him coming as he smashed into their rear-rankers. Over a dozen died from the impact's shock. Michael swiftly began carving them up, dancing among their unprepared numbers. He battered their shields to kindling and broke their iron swords with

Virtue's blessed edge. Red sprays fountained from the creases in their armor. He ducked and weaved between them, one archangel deftly maneuvering through four hundred legionnaires.

They piled at his boots until he jumped into the air with his wings, repositioning himself at their backs and flanks. For the Sword of God, it was nothing more than a series of logic equations. He banished sentiment and focused on the work. He felled them in such numbers so swiftly that, before the catapult could reload, he'd worked his way to its epicenter and began slaying the crew.

Only the centurions dared challenge the archangel. They came at him in twos and threes, their trans-crested helmets marking them as hardened elites. He parried their blows, keeping them at bay. He stood next to the catapult's flaming payload, its pyramid of reloads at his back. The centurions encircled him, their legionnaires rallying at their armored backs.

"Blood feeds the flames," an officer growled. "We are Fallen."

"From the ashes our fires rise anew!" came the reply from the rebel legionnaires.

They rushed him. Michael fought them off, but the sheer press of their numbers pinned him to the wooden beams of the catapult. He buried his sword to the hilt in a centurion and punched the jaw off another. He bit and kicked and roared but they came on still, hacking and stabbing. His armor bent and warped, Michael repulsed them with one last momentous exertion. They flailed and landed on their backs. Except one. He scrambled to the catapult's burning payload and roared the chant again before bringing his centurion's swagger stick down onto the clay pot. It burst. The explosion's naphtha reached the reloads and cratered the landscape. Michael barely had time to dive for cover. The ground met him, and all went black.

Gabriel saw the explosion from his place atop the siege-tower. Behind him, the Cognoscenti rushed to re-form. They had taken the mobile engine by force from the air and were mustering to cleanse its innards. By virtue of the red tunics under their leather corsets and bronze cuirasses, no one knew if the Cognoscenti bled. They fought until they dropped, never uttering a word save commands and the battle hymns they used to keep time. How many had perished from their wounds, Gabriel could not say, but they marched on, each phalanx a thresher of spears, interlocked shields, and greaved hobnail sandals stomping all underfoot. The inroad had been achieved. Though outnumbered, the Cognoscenti were carving up the rebel shield wall.

The archangel looked out and saw the Pegasun Centaurs cantering from one catapult battery to the next. Many erupted into violent explosions that killed horse and rider alike. But most were silenced in a swift galloping overhaul. Confident Michael fought with them, Gabriel took the Cognoscenti and plunged into the bowels of the siege-tower. He fought his way through the cramped stairwells, overcoming any angel who opposed him with his twin sabers. He struck and parried, lopping off limbs and taking heads in a gush of marrow. The Cognoscenti were right behind him, covering the archangel with their eight-foot ash wood spears. It was brutal, frantic work; the towers were as tall as the Northern Wall proper. By the time he emerged from the entry ramp, the sun had begun its afternoon descent. Yet in moments the acre surrounding the war engine's base was engulfed by conflagrative bombardments.

"Scatter!" Gabriel ordered. He lunged clear of the mushrooming explosion. A sulfuric wave cooked his greaves as he escaped, only to crash into another angel. He landed on his breastplate, the wind leaving him. When he rolled onto his haunches, he beheld a fearful sight.

One of Satan's black-armored guardians lay across from him, his legs entangled with Gabriel's, their swords strewn. A terror seized Gabriel as he faced the daunting blackheart. The two reached for their weapons and clashed blades in a resounding tempo of ringing metal.

Suddenly, two bare pair of arms laid hold of the villainous elite. Before Gabriel could rise, a spear plunged overhead, burying itself in the deathly guard's exposed eyes. Blood sheeted down his face as the iron leaf-shaped blade was retracted. When the foe expired, the attacker moved into view. Gabriel breathed with relief as three Cognoscenti, utterly begrimed, took up a ward. Two swiveled to the fore, spears ready, while the third offered Gabriel a hand.

"That's how you deal with a Death Guard, Archangel," the surly cherub said.

Gabriel rose and thanked him. "Where do we stand?"

"Our rebel brothers are stacking up. If something's not done, there will be a breach."

Gabriel followed them in flight. Before he could spit, he was embroiled in an evasion of arrows so numerous only the most dramatic of aerial maneuvers saved him until he descended upon a rampart near another siege-tower. Enemy lancers poured from the war engine, pushing back the beleaguered Cognoscenti. By Gabriel's estimate, less than a hundred scarlet clad elites defended a space of ninety cubits, breastworks of the slain rising before them. Beyond, another siege-tower was flooding rebel angels onto the battlements.

He then caught sight of Malthus' cavalry and lost heart. The twenty thousand Pegasun Centaurs were down to less than half their number. In their wake, at least a dozen catapult batteries laid silent amidst charred rubble and grey columns of smoke. But the heavy cavalry had lost momentum. Pike-wielding rebels worked in concert to dismount the majestic riders. Those not pulled from their horses were slain in their steel saddles, pikes hooking them in place while all manner of weapons punctured the kinks in their armor. Blood streamed from their wounds, dashing gore upon their pristine plates and the valiant steed straining underneath.

Surrounded, they dismounted to fight as mobile infantry, resigning themselves to die on their own terms. Gabriel scanned their ranks for the magenta plume of Malthus. He found the Commandant and his color guards still mounted and hacking their way clear.

He turned from the scene of impending heartbreak and looked upon the Cognoscenti's dwindling ranks. By the time the North Gate's garrison sent legionnaire reinforcements, the rebels would overrun the position and gain a foothold inside the Northern Wall. Malthus' elites were a hardened crew who feasted on the hardships of their occupation. Plus, Gabriel trusted Michael to reinforce them.

"We could use your help, Consul," came the voice of a grizzled sergeant at the Cognoscenti's fore. "But if you choose to leave then, by blood and brimstone, we'll hold the Wall to the last."

Gabriel regarded the sergeant. They were a mere remnant now, less than forty. To the left and right, angels rushed to occupy the smaller, mobile gall-guns loaded with arrows. They made ready to swivel the decks with what meager fusillades they had left.

Empyrean Falling

Another siege-tower lumbered forth, spitting firebrands. Gabriel's mind ached in the throes of indecision. "Cogs," he said with a sudden flair, "would it shame you to hold these consecrated stones with a seraph a while longer?" A cheer answered him. "Then gather spares...and pray an archangel can make a difference."

The Seraphim Archon made for the nearest siege-tower. He leapt from the ramparts and swung around to land on the monolith's rear. His impact sent a shockwave into those inside, crammed into the narrow stairwells doglegging the interior. Their lances were useless in such stacked ranks. Gabriel sliced his way through them, a storm of screams bathing the innards of the mobile war machine. Clusters of Cognoscenti cheered his emergence from the charnel tower, brandishing arms from behind their breastworks of piled bodies.

The Cognoscenti's cheers were stymied as an uproar from the rebel legions pierced their paean chorus. Gabriel's triumph was unstrung as he saw the source of the malefactors' jeers.

The sun's heat beat down onto the embattled angels as they fought bitterly for control of the Northern Wall. The ramparts were ovens. Angels suffocated in the crush. The whirlwind of arrows and smoke created a haze as Satan's legions disintegrated into a mob vying to ascend via the remaining towers, torn banners wafting in the fog of war and the horns blaring over the murderous cacophony.

Beyond the Wall, Michael was pulled from the darkness by a cataclysmic quake. He blinked and struggled to find his limbs. Dusk light pierced ruddy thunderheads. Concealed in roiling blankets of smoke, he could hear the roar of lost legions. He saw the low position of the sun and knew hours had passed. Rising to shaky legs, he found Virtue and unfurled his wings.

Soaring over the battlefield, the sight greeting him was one of stupefaction. The Wall was breached; the North Gate's barbican had imploded. Around it pressed such a multitude, he could barely see what remained of Satan's force. They poured through the bottleneck in dizzying masses until being checked by a bulwark of upturned sun-hats plugging the breach. Armored columns of Northern Defenders received the onslaught. Michael spotted the loyalists' vanguard, where a magnificent band of seraphim moved with such grace and temerity that they could only be Ellunias' color guard.

Empyrean Falling

When he finally reached them, the urban cohorts and Cognoscenti had repelled the apostate angels, aided by archers on the broken battlements of the Wall. Angered, Michael descended amongst so many rebels crowding the breach that he could hardly maneuver through the crush. Even in the gloom, he could tell they had lost heart in the siege. The archangel dove into the nearest cluster, who fled upon sight of his apparition. He hunted down and cleaved them all.

The sunlight died. Stars peeked through a purple sky. More arrows found their marks in the beaten backs of the enemy. Panoplies were cast aside as the disenfranchised besiegers withdrew. Those cohorts of rebels standing their ground were massacred by the Holy City's faithful cherubim. Atop the Wall, loyalists swiveled porcupines and onagers onto them, trapping hundreds of their helpless prey in the bailey. Hemmed in and cut off by the faithful stalwarts, the enemy angels were slaughtered to the last. The whole thing lasted minutes.

When it was over, a tension descended onto the survivors. Bodies stacked dozens high all around them. Vacant and exhausted, Michael moved through the morbid harvest. A laceration along his jaw oozed blood; a gouge clotted on his left eyebrow; his healing chest wound ached from the exertion.

Gabriel stood across from him. The Seraphim Archon looked ashen and ghoulish; his right cheek filleted and blood sluicing from a linen wad stuffed into his right pauldron. His sabers dripped red gore. Behind him, angels shucked their gear and worked to pry apart the stone rubble that once was the North Gate, while azure-cloaked urban cohorts formed a ward with the remaining Cognoscenti phalanxes.

Michael regarded him in the aftermath's hush. He paid no heed to the queries of officers or petitions of valiant pursuers. Even the sporadic propulsions of friendly artillery meant nothing. For the first time in months, all he cared about was his younger sibling. Michael sheathed Virtue with what strength he had left before reaching up to wipe the blood from his eyes.

"Looks like we've made it again," Michael said. He wanted to move closer but something in Gabriel's demeanor stayed him.

"Where were you?" Gabriel asked.

"I tried to silence the artillery ahead of Malthus."

Gabriel scoffed. He coughed and spat red at Michael's boots. "Bloody good it did us."

Michael surveyed the battlefield. The Northern Defenders looked no better than their deceased brethren. Detritus littered the riven field like a landfill; siege-towers rose from a gruesome quagmire, ringed by the butchered and obscured by tendrils of illuminated smoke. "So," Michael said, "this must be what Hell is like." He turned to Gabriel. "Did Malthus quell those batteries on the right?" A grim silence met him. "Gabriel?"

"He's dead."

Michael winced at the guilt. "Does Ellunias know?"

His brother's eyes burned holes through him, jaw set and his good fist clenching a bloodstained saber. "I'm sure he does," the Seraphim Archon rejoined with a grievous excoriation, pointing to the mound of rubble where teams of angels scrambled in a frenzied state. "He's dead too."

Empyrean Falling

Chapter VI

"...He makes His angels winds, and His servants flames of fire."
—Hebrews 1:7

Ural stood quietly in one of the many unfinished alcoves deep under the Bastion. The arched stone lanes and wide halls above were once reserved as a place of recreation. For ages, the angels blew off steam and communed there. Now, the interior of these archaic institutions was being gutted to make room for the Mausoleum. In place of fencing halls and gymnasiums were epochal crypts riddled with sepulchers lined with etched bronze placards bearing the names and deeds committed by Zion's bravest seraphim.

He watched Gabriel's choir inter their dead. He whispered prayers for the angelic processions flooding through the low stone archways. Many limped in their dress uniforms and armor, many more were maimed; the Siege of the Northern Wall had taken its toll.

The air shifted over his shoulder. "An unorthodox place to meet, I know," came a quiet voice.

Ural smiled at the familiar baritone at his back. "Why you chose it, no doubt, Patriarch." He turned to see Michael leaning in the shadow of the arched threshold.

"Sorry to keep you waiting," the archangel apologized as he rounded the corner.

"I always saw waiting as a gift," Ural said casually. "It gives time to reflect and pray."

Michael mock-saluted him. "Melphax has no doubt learned much from you in your time together, Ural. I see why you two are such good friends."

Ural chuckled. "I've learned more from him, I assure you." He watched Michael's attention drift to the funeral procession plodding through the far hallway. "I hear the Wall is in bleak shape. The North Gate demanded a high price."

"It could've been avoided," Michael mumbled with a distant tone. His eyes locked onto the train of seraphim bearing caskets draped in their unit's banners. With a jolt, he snapped back to the moment. "I have to make this quick; the Council wants a debrief, and I'll be damned if I'm going to let Gabriel stand there unaccompanied."

"Well, how does that saying go, Patriarch?" Ural said with a lighter tone. "You don't choose your family. But you can't really replace them either."

Michael nodded and squared up on Ural, eyes focusing on him. "I'm sending you out. Muster your Concordia legions and march into the Northern Plains. If Satan is there, hold and send word. If it's Mazerrel like we suspect, judging from the banners we saw at the siege, crush him. Retake the Aphaea River and hold it, if you can."

Ural's eyes widened. "I suppose this isn't sanctioned?"

"I'm about to find out."

"Between permission and forgiveness," Ural cautioned, "I'd say that pit of crowned vipers will grant you neither. But their venom is nothing next to the tonic of the Lord's will. Just you wait and see." Ural winked and saluted him. Michael saluted back and departed.

An hour later, Michael was passing through the Hallowed Causeway, headed for the Council Chambers. He met Gabriel at the threshold. Before them, the Council of Elders sat in their marble-tiered thrones, reviewing last-minute preparations for the hearing. All eyes fell on Michael in a mixture of consternation. His stomach tightened as they came up to the dais.

"Who approaches the Council?" Metatron heralded out of formality.

"The Sword of God and Second Born, Archangel Michael."

"The Voice of God and Third Born, Archangel Gabriel."

Metatron waved them forward. "We've summoned you to review the siege of the Northern Wall," he announced. Gabriel shot Michael a wary glance. "I know it has only been a matter of days, but this congress must address certain issues to avoid future mistakes."

"And what mistakes might those be?" Michael asked irritably.

"Not just mistakes, Archangel," Eldar Asmodeus crooned, "but curiosities, as well."

"If we're to come under scrutiny, have Eldar Sariel nominate the charges," Michael countered. "I won't face prosecution from those who don't know the arena of the crimes."

"Calm thyself, Archangel," Asmodeus replied. "There hath been no talk of prosecution."

"Yet," Michael shot back.

"Still, we must conduct an inquiry," Metatron said. "Why were your archangelic powers over the elements not employed?"

"Many lives could have been saved," Asmodeus added.

"Any raising of the terrain would've given the invaders redoubts to cower behind," Michael told them. "Fires would've screened their movements. It wasn't an engagement capable of preternatural interventions."

"And what of lightning?" asked Sandalphon.

"It was a cloudless day," Michael explained. "Tempest alone controls the storms."

Asmodeus smacked his lips. "And Lucifer."

Michael shot him a look. "Lucifer is gone." Asmodeus averted his eyes. "The use of God's gift isn't a precision weapon; we would've suffered casualties as well."

"It seems anything would've been preferable to the catastrophe that took place," Archangel Michael," Asmodeus chided. "You should be reprimanded."

"You're calling it a catastrophe?" Michael sneered.

Asmodeus raised an eyebrow. "Perhaps we should let the facts speak for themselves. Consul Gabriel, what is the status of our Northern Wall?"

Gabriel cleared his throat before stepping forward to address them. "Of the eighty-four myriads, twenty remain. The artillery is spent of munitions; they're bone dry. Ellunias is dead, along with his color guard and the entirety of the Pegasun Centaurs."

"Please be so kind as to report on the details of the Radiant's demise," Asmodeus requested with barely contained glee.

Gabriel ignored his rancid tone. "The rebels, or Fallen, as they are called now, were on the cusp of defeat, their siege engines aflame. Yet they persisted, advancing right up to the Wall. We were holding our own—winning even—until sentiment got in the way of duty.

"I think the major asset of being a faithful angel is retaining a heart, something these Fallen know how to exploit. They captured Malthus while he was attempting to silence the artillery batteries. In a gruesome display of malice, they paraded my Commandant before their lines, torturing him with whips and chains before their tribunes drew and drew and quartered him at the Gate. They lopped off his head and hurled it over the barbican. Ellunias lost it. It took minutes to dissuade him from abandoning the ramparts and leading his knights and the Cognoscenti out on a sortie of vengeance."

"We heard reports it took his own color guard to contain him," Metatron declared.

Gabriel nodded. "That's true. That's when the Fallen made their move. My escorts on the left flank watched as the enemy bombarded our plinth, billowing smoke over the ramparts and driving away all but the Cognoscenti. The asphyxiation created a vacuum in our lines that the Fallen's siege towers exploited. They poured their cohorts over our Gate."

"And this commenced well into the day?" Metatron asked.

"Correct," Gabriel answered. "There's more though. Ellunias wasn't anywhere near this disaster but, when he caught wind of it, he rushed his cadre back and descended on the invaders. No doubt the battle there was furious as they blindsided the vast arrays of rebels. Inspired by Ellunias, the deserters rallied to their posts while their

Commander held the gap. Yet before anyone could reach him, something else happened."

Metatron sat up in his throne. "What more could befall you?"

Gabriel took a breath. "Something was in those sapper battlewagons. I don't know what, but their incendiaries razed the Gates before our eyes. The Fallen stormed the bailey. But Ellunias wasn't called 'Radiant' for his armor alone; his mind was as bright as his countenance. I'll boldly declare Ellunias ingenious and industrious; he gave us precious time to reorganize."

"And where was Archangel Michael in all of this?" Asmodeus questioned.

"I was out trying to silence the remaining catapults on the left flank," Michael replied.

"Remarkable," Asmodeus scoffed. "Thou hast failed us once again, Archangel."

"We're straying away from the path of this inquiry," Metatron stated, "which is to determine what could be prevented." He looked at Gabriel. "Consul, if you please, continue."

"Of course," Gabriel replied. "The Fallen threw themselves at us. The Cognoscenti repulsed the fore-rankers but it wasn't long before their spears broke, forcing them to 'skin the iron,' as their saying goes. I swore I heard Ellunias call for Malthus' revenge, but it took all we had just to hold the line against the enemy flux. I spent my time trying to plug the siege-towers.

"Ellunias stood defiantly at the fore of the engagement, where the carnage was thickest. Some of my seraphim reached him, begging the Commander to send for aid. But he refused nine times, stating if he couldn't hold the Wall, none could. Of course, when I heard this, my heart burst but, alas, I was compelled to respond lest I lose my vaunted hero.

"Despite their losses, the rebels brought up a fresh division. It was meant to intimidate my seraphim. So, Ellunias took the initiative and did something that spat in the Dragon's face. He charged. But the overwhelming surge of Fallen managed to rout us. All except Ellunias. He and his color guard held the line while our enemies rushed past. His knights sacrificed themselves to preserve the line. Of all the Northern Defenders, I call them foremost among valiants."

"We have reports stating Michael arrived after this," Asmodeus announced.

"Yes," Gabriel confirmed, face darkening. "By then, it was sunset. The Cogs formed a breastwork of bodies in front of our meager line, but not even the greatest of virtue can save the doomed. I'll never call the Northern Defenders cowards, for none shrank from their duty. But I can call them exhausted and overwhelmed.

"The Fallen swarmed the gap, preventing anyone from aiding Ellunias. We saw the Radiant get pierced through the collar with a lance. Then we heard the explosion. In desperation, his color guard collapsed the North Gate's barbican. It toppled onto the advancing multitudes, sealing the breach. They bought us time to regroup. That's when I arrived."

Metatron leaned forward. "You saw it?"

"Unfortunately."

"Then what happened?"

"We were repulsing the last of Satan's forces with the help of the urban cohorts when Michael arrived. Ellunias had broken the siege's momentum. When night fell, the Fallen lost their resolve and routed. Thankfully, we reorganized our tattered lines, set up pickets, and moved our wounded to the urban hospitals. With the Wall temporarily out of harm's way, we set our engineers to work salvaging the debris. We found Ellunias' body under the rubble an hour before dawn, surrounded by his remaining color guard."

"And where was Satan during all of this, Patriarch Michael?" inquired Israfel.

"Never saw him," Michael replied.

"But he *should've* been there," Gabriel interjected. Israfel asked him what he meant. "Because I fought one of his so-called Death Guard."

"I suspect he wasn't there at all," said Michael. Beliel asked him to explain. "The Fallen's formations were sloppy; they lacked tactical sophistication. Once engaged, their legions were easily picked apart. If it weren't for their sheer numbers…"

Metatron tapped the arm of his throne. "You think Satan is elsewhere?"

Michael shrugged. "I don't know, Head Eldar. But he wasn't at that Wall."

A tide of reflection rolled through the assembly.

"What does Heaven's aristocracy suggest?" Metatron asked.

"The Gate must be rebuilt," Gabriel proffered. "Satan's army may be licking its wounds in the Northern Plains, but our defenses are bled out and leaderless."

"Most of the Cognoscenti were wiped out as well," added Asmodeus, his snide tone driving nails into Michael's skin. "We must not forget their presence will be sorely missed." He turned to Michael. "And what do you recommend, brave Archangel?"

Michael's eyes shot to Asmodeus. "Pursue them."

A wave of scoffs erupted from the Council's majority.

"Our Wall stands on the brink, and you want to send out a sortie?" Asmodeus decried.

"The best defense is an attack, Eldar Asmodeus," Michael replied with as much humility as he could muster. "Allow me to send Ural as a first wave and I can crush this fleeing rabble in a week."

"I would not hazard to call Satan's army a rabble," Asmodeus warned. "Victory or not."

"Whatever you call them," Michael said, "they are retreating. We have a chance to secure roads between Zion and Lorinar, vital lines of communication and supply routes. The enemy's morale is decimated; now's the best time to strike. Battle Group Concordia can do it, with another six legions following in close support."

"We don't have the numbers to field such an expedition," Asmodeus observed.

"I'm asking for thirty-six thousand as a spearhead, with another six myriads two weeks behind."

"You'll get nothing," Asmodeus seethed. "You have proven yourself a failure twice…"

"Stop," Metatron boomed, vibrant eyes glaring at Asmodeus. "Michael has proven himself an archangel of deed, not diplomacy. We won't crucify our own here."

Asmodeus was silent as the two locked gazes for a beat.

"If strategy is our paramount concern," Beliel said, "send angels to reclaim the Aphaea."

Metatron audibly inhaled. "It's rumored a formidable army holds the River."

"I'm told Mazerrel leads them," Asmodeus added.

"All the more reason to act now," Michael insisted. He turned to Metatron. "If Mazerrel holds sway over the Aphaea, it will take more than a static defense to dislodge him."

Metatron massaged his amethyst eyes. "Can it be done with the three legions of Battle Group Concordia alone, Archangel?"

Michael weighed his options. "No. We need an expeditionary force of real numbers."

The assembly reeled. Asmodeus and Metatron exchanged stern expressions. In the end, Metatron spoke, "We must look to our own defenses. Ural goes alone for now."

Israfel indicated Gabriel. "What of him?"

"Our Consul has held the Northern Wall thus far," Metatron declared. "God willing, he can hold it still." With a wave of his hand, the archangels were dismissed from the dais and its encircling tiered thrones. Michael and Gabriel hobbled for the marble exit.

"Oh, one more thing," called Asmodeus. The brothers faced him. "I have a report here indicating that a small legion left the South Gate less than a week ago. Tell me, Archangel Michael, where is that little protégé of yours, the one you've so craftily hidden from us the past two years?"

Michael's stone gaze faltered. Gabriel turned with a glare.

Asmodeus raised his eyebrows expectantly and stared down at Michael. "Where is he now?"

And far beyond the Council Chambers, leagues south of Zion and its contested Walls, the rebel angel Belphegor spurred his dapple mare through the marsh, his broken wings spurting blood and feathers in the chaotic tumult.

Behind him, the Southlands were awash with the mangled bodies of his Fallen army. He cared neither for them, nor for the legion of seven thousand Faithful angels with their blinding pearly armor, nor the mountain which the mysterious cherub raised and dropped onto his massive army, nor even the grisly fate that surely awaited him and the hands of Satan.

All that mattered to Belphegor was escaping that terrible cyclone of wind and fire that devoured his legions, and the golden-maned, emerald-eyed bane of his Fallen who strode atop it to the cries of "Raziel! Raziel! Raziel!"

Empyrean Falling

Chapter VII
"But the subjects of the kingdom will be thrown outside, into the darkness, where there will be weeping and gnashing of teeth."
—Matthew 8:12

Mazerrel's legions were packing it up. As the moon waxed overhead, the ranks of the rebel angels formed their cohorts and crossed the River Aphaea.

Gi'ad Althaziel maneuvered through the crush of armored columns assembling near the bridges. He watched the rangers unfurl their wings and follow their sergeants into the clear, starry night. Their echelons rose over the crystal oscillating surface of the Aphaea to vanish beyond the western riverbank. Under them snaked the long column of legionnaires flanking the oxcart baggage train, their horned glyph sigils and legion totems held aloft in endless succession.

Nelgleth approached the bridge's abutment behind him and stood on the landing beside the stone bridge. "This whole thing is like a dream of something you've always wanted, but you know is not right," he said. "And if you take your eyes off it, it'll vanish."

"Seems a crime to abandon our position, after all that we've done," said Althaziel dourly.

"I've known Mazerrel for a long time, Gi'ad," Nelgleth replied. "Whatever he tells us, it comes from the top. That should be good enough for us here."

They watched the legion transit past them. On either side rose promontories of discarded armor and broken weaponry. Beyond them, great bonfires sent acrid towers of smoke slithering up into the night. Gi'ad repulsed from the stench and noticed only the wounded who could travel, fight, or be of use to the war effort remaining. He looked again at the bonfires. Their stench was singular.

"Subject to the needs of the service," he said bitterly.

"What we do tonight is far greater than any mercy misconstrued as cruelty on our fallen brethren," Nelgleth told him. "We must look forward, Gi'ad. Maneuver warfare dictates such."

"I wonder how those drunk on their faith will perceive it, should they win the day." Althaziel nodded towards the south. "You know that's what they call us now? Fallen." He scoffed. "I'm sure from their illustrious eyes, we're beyond the mercy seat of grace."

"What need have we of grace?" rejoined Nelgleth. "We *are* Fallen, fallen into the flames of our sacrifice to rise anew as something greater, something afire, something Empyreal."

He led Althaziel back to their transportation pool. Ten forty-wheeled flatbeds were each loaded with several enormous vats, concealed by a sackcloth tarp secured with ropes and mooring hitches. Around them was a sparse escort of eighty angels, all with tar-covered armor and sheathed spears. They looked like unholy eidolons milling about in the shadows.

Sammiel was there, inspecting each vat's cargo. Althaziel threw him wary glances under moonbeams as he slathered his armor in camouflaging tar. He found his guard always up around that angel. He never trusted those who had a propensity for water.

With the final inspection complete, Sammiel gave the order and the teamsters whipped their oxen south across the networks of bridges crisscrossing the Aphaea. Their caravan moved against the flow, while overhead, the starry night swarmed with redeploying auxiliaries. They pressed past the angel-choked road, eighty angels armed to the teeth in plate-mail armor covered in tar, their ten flatbeds drawing more than one curious onlooker. Sammiel paid the passersby no heed, even as the keen-eyed rebels inquired as to their contents.

It took over an hour to clear the first legion. By the time they reached the eastern riverbank, the moon had turned. They made their way through the army's abandoned camp and came upon a southeasterly bend, where the waters of the Aphaea were highly concentrated. They drew up their column and posted pickets. Steam rose off the oxen's back as they strained against their yokes in the sultry late summer night.

Gi'ad and Nelgleth held counsel at the vanguard.

"What fortune earned us the task of posting on a bridge while the army falls back?" Althaziel groused.

"The siege failed, Althaziel," Nelgleth murmured. "Mazerrel's force is under orders. And though we may have just beaten them in the field, but I suspect there are other things afoot."

"But we crushed what they sent against us," Althaziel said. "It took us weeks to do it, yes, but have command of the Northern Plains. He's taking an enormous risk."

"You are not the Chief Weapons Master anymore, Althaziel. We must earn our place in this new Empire the Dragon is building. Sammiel will have his cargo unloaded by dawn. Go to the pickets. At sunrise, you'll link up with the rearguard."

"Yes, Captain," Althaziel growled sourly.

The surly Nelgleth turned and signaled to the troupe. "What we do today will live in infamy, Althaziel. It's an honor what he's given you."

Althaziel watched him slink back to the flatbeds before drawing his attention to the ground. In the muddy turf was a broken totem of the recently defeated faithful battle group. He knelt and scooped it up. The golden staff was heavy, its intertwining twin serpents snapped in places. On its axis was a silver cornucopia. Under it were medallions depicting libation bowls. He knew their leader; it made it easier to defeat them. But it made it harder to accept. In a flash of heat on his brow, he cast the busted totem to the earth and stomped off towards the picket.

Empyrean Falling

The sun rose as it always did. In Zion, the River Aphaea broke into several streams. Upon this delta, the Holy city was built. Every morning, Michael stood at the window of his Citadel office and watched the crystal waters run their course through the urban aqueducts. But that morning was different; there was no time. He had renamed his office the War Room with the intention of teaching his brother how to do his job. Often Gabriel elected to send his aide-de-camp in his stead, electing to spend more time answering the Elder's questions than leading campaigns against the Dragon's army.

The Cherubim Patriarch stood hunched over his desk. On the far wall, a large etched map of the Lower Realm had been hung. On it were all the topographical sites, along with every hamlet, monument, fort, outpost and city. He stared at it for hours, moving swatches of black and blue blocks around the terrain as legions and garrisons maneuvered or changed hands.

He shook his head. "Nearly a month for this." He ran a rough hand across his bare scalp and scratched the dark topknot at its peak. Over the past weeks, he was forced to scrape the Holy City for cherubim to fill the ranks of the Northern Wall. Each dawn saw him plumbing the garrisons and urban cohorts for reinforcements. It was exhausting. But he had no choice. The door opened. "You're late."

A commotion scrambled into his office. He turned to see a pair of angels bearing one of their brothers in a trundle. Their breathing was labored. They looked haggard. Michael took in their bloodied, malnourished apparitions with a hand on Virtue's hilt.

"Forgive us, Archangel," one of them rasped, hands on ragged knees. "He demanded to be brought to you." The harried angel indicated the trundle-bound comrade, who was curled into his litter in a state of catalepsy. "We found him near the Citadel of Glalendorf's ruins. He said his message was critical and for your eyes only."

Michael eyed them and, after a fashion, took his hand off Virtue's hilt. He knelt before the litter and looked at the invalid borne therein. "What do you have for me?" The angel did not respond. Michael observed his condition. "What am I missing, seraphs?"

"He stopped speaking a few hours ago," one of them replied. "There's a scroll there."

Michael reached into the litter and found a small bit of wrapped parchment in the angel's seized hand. He did not react as Michael plucked it from his cramped grip. The archangel took the scrap of paper and gave the angel one last look before unrolling it. He stared at it, motionless. His thoughts turned to Melphax, Paladin and even Deledrosse. As if awakening from a nightmare, the Sword of God stood up and looked down at the bedraggled seraphim pair.

"Leave." He tried to sound stoic, but the quaver in his voice betrayed him. He masked it with anger, as he always did. "And tell your Archon what good work you've performed."

They hastened from the Citadel office, bearing their catatonic brother behind them.

When the door closed, Michael became unstrung. He nearly fell over the desk in vexation. He clutched his chest, not from the scar Satan had left him, but from the fresh wound driven into his heart beneath. His soul felt lacerated. After a fashion, the archangel staggered around to the other side of the desk and took a drink from a stainless flask he kept hidden in a drawer. He stared into the warped reflection of the flask for several minutes. He would need his composure, that much he knew.

There was a knock at the door. Michael took a sharp breath and exhaled. It was Zophiel. He compartmentalized and pressed on. He was the Chief of the Armies of God once again.

"About time," he said, striding back over to the battle map mural. "We have work to do. Lorinar was assaulted the same day as the North Gate. Gilgamesh's Lightning Legion held them off with Unoth's garrison. They rejoiced until they found out what happened here; it was a diversion meant to keep them from reinforcing us at the enemy's backs. Anyway, I've redeployed their Thunderbolts further up north to perform quick-strikes on their interior lines. They should link up with Galeth in Prein by week's end. As for the Northern Plains, I cannot say. My scouts have not reported back to me and—" he turned to Zophiel. His slack-jawed expression made Michael's veins hammer. "Pay attention, adjutant! These lectures aren't going to be wasted." He ripped off a square swatch from its place in the Thousand Peaks and crumpled it in his fist. "I know your Archon is too busy dancing on a pinhead for the amusement of the Council, but by blood and brimstone if I have to teach him how to do my job through you, then you will pay attention!"

"What...?" Zophiel finally pried loose.

Michael shoved the scroll into his hand. "Read it, Major."

Gabriel's aide looked down and unraveled the small rolled parchment. The note was scrawled in a nearly illegible script, but its simplicity belied a dire content. It read simply:

Umbra Tempest has secured Northern Plains, Hundred Foothills, and Thousand Peaks.
Amin Shakush has fallen.

Zophiel looked up at him, the same aghast expression blanketing his features. Michael ground his teeth and set his jaw. "Wipe that ashen look off your face and let's get started," he said demonstratively. "War does not wait on sentiment, Zophiel; we'll mourn them later. For now, put your pain to work."

"The River."

Michael stopped and turned to him. Zophiel's face lengthened in terror. "Being Consul means little rest, Major. Decisions had to be made. No doubt the Council watches us. We have to make every move count if we're—"

"The North Aqueduct," Zophiel breathed.

"The War is here, Lieutenant," Michael asserted, stabbing his right hand at the wall. "I cannot be everywhere at once."

"Please, Archangel."

With a twining of his guts, Michael belted Virtue and followed the seraph. In seconds, they were flying for the North Aqueduct. Through whistling winds, his archangelic ears picked up a distinctive wail, a tide of cries flooding up from the urban district. But he did not have to reach the aqueducts to see what aroused such vehement alarm.

From their high altitude, the crystal streams flowing through Zion had a ruddy tint, flanked by aggrieved onlookers crowding the tiled metropolitan streets. Michael's sore legs fouled his landing on the brick causeway lining the riverbank.

Empyrean Falling

The currents before him were stained with angelic blood.

He turned to question Zophiel, but the aide refused to descend. Michael drew his blue gaze back upon the stygian torrent before him and reeled in disgust.

Punctuating this crimson river were shapes stretched and mauled as they bobbed and tumbled in the marbled waters. Michael peered into the rapids' cresting breakers, heart seized at the macabre revelation. One of the shapes rolled in the pinkish foam. He saw the twin hollows of eye sockets and the gaping cavity of a mouth.

They were the skins of angels. The cornucopia blue banners of Battle Group Concordia were tangled amidst them, interspersed with the desecrated and mutilated dead legionnaires.

Michael felt his knees crash onto the gilded stone promenade. The grisly waves boiled and waxed as the flayed corpses surrendered their gory fluids. Michael's hand absently dipped into the current. When he pulled it out, the bronze of his skin was stained garnet. The breath rose in him until his lungs were compelled to birth such a scream that nearby onlookers, already horrified at their violated river, snapped their attention him.

When at last his sorrowful fury abated, the Cherubim Patriarch slumped where he knelt, head bobbing between shuddering shoulders and topknot falling over his collar. All held breathless, staring at him. Zophiel remained aloft, but it was another who dared to brave Michael's proximity. He felt a gauntleted hand rest on his shoulder.

Gabriel.

"I've sent for the Council," his younger sibling gently whispered. "Surely after seeing this, they'll grant you—"

"To the Oblivion with your Elders!" Michael rounded to his feet and tore free his brother's hand. He glared at the Gabriel through eyes drowned in tears. He pointed to the charnel river as evidence. "What do you think of their sanctimonious mandates now?"

The two locked gazes as their lesser brethren gathered around, fearfully absorbed by the scene until their gazes drifted back to the thundering rapids brimming with fleshy detritus. Sensing their arrest, Michael spun on their huddled masses, face flaring in his choler.

"Fetch Arkadia! Tell him to bring me my armor!" He turned back to Gabriel and jabbed a finger in his face. "This suspension mandated by your Elders is unendurable, Gabriel; I'm through with the Council. Mazerrel's barbarity won't go unpunished! I'm going to the Aphaea and I'm going to purge his armies, with your Council's permission or without it."

Gabriel opened his mouth to speak but his brother had already turned to the scores of trembling loyalists. "Faithful!" Michael bellowed into the crowd, froth gathering on his goatee as he raged in the deafening silence. "These holy brothers are worthy of righteous justice! Cinch up armor and brandish whetted arms, for the scourge who committed this sin awaits divine retribution! I'll crush this league of fiends and send Mazerrel to the Burning Hells!"

They chanted for Mazerrel's head. Then their ranks began to part at the rear. All heads turned to see Arkadia atop an oak and onyx carriage, lined with silver and drawn by Michael's sable warhorse, Andreia. Michael's fury waned at the magnificently quartered paragon of equestrian breeding. Horses trembled before him and angels were transfixed by his noble countenance. This vision evoked a measure of relief throughout the ranks of peerless defenders. Andreia's appearance was so majestic that it alleviated whatever nauseating malady had stricken those formerly gawking at the Aphaea.

Yet such momentous gallantry went unheeded by Arkadia. The Chief Hammer leapt from the carriage's post, tied the reins, and crossed the paved thoroughfare to Michael and Gabriel, careful not to let his eyes train to where the unholy torrents raged. With a solemn bow, the cherub presented himself to his archangel.

"My Patriarch, in this bleak hour of desecration, I come to you with a gift imbued with the strength of Faithful myriads and presented now as hallowed alms." Michael motioned for him to stand, but the angel refused, stating that as a sacrament for his crimes, he would not rise lest his archangel approved of the illustrious atonement.

Accepting him with honorable brevity, Michael crossed the promenade to his august horse and the carriage which he confidently bore. He drew close to Andreia's muzzle, touching the valiant charger's cheek to his own and stroking the nasal bridge at the fore of his chamfron. Michael's burning sapphires locked with Andreia's

Empyrean Falling

russet-ringed obsidians. That was the hallmark of his power; the armor encasing him was superfluous compared to the power of his spirit.

Michael parted from his mount and rounded the carriage. When he opened the doors, the spectators gasped. Made of the same substance as the Seventh Column's armor, the panoply housed within shone like pearl. The body of a winged lion holding a curved sword was embossed on its breastplate, its eyes set with diamonds, its roaring mouth filled with onyx, and the wreath about its head laced with sapphires. Flames were etched around the borders of the cuirass, its motif mirrored on the greaves, lamed tassets, pauldrons, vambraces and accompanying kite shield.

The archangel picked up the cuirass and held it aloft. It gleamed. Turning from its apex of artisanship, Michael addressed the cherubim held in its thrall.

"This work of dedication is a boon that protects my flesh with its alloy and guards my spirit with its endowment," the archangel said. 'But it's not through faith in me you stand here! This flesh coiling my soul is a gift from Father. And this armor is a sacrament to our King!"

Arkadia rose, tears streaming down his soot-caked cheeks.

"You provide this heroic legacy so that I may do that which the Almighty has set before me. Unto the Lord I dedicate this armor, not for myself but for those of you whom I would deem Faithful!" Approbations erupted from their multitudes. Michael set down the cuirass and turned to the waters. "Let not this sinful act dissuade you from your oaths. Villains reside beyond our Walls. With this armor I proclaim to you a new oath: I will contend with the Fallen on your behalf. I will perish to preserve the lives of any one of you! You are my brothers! I won't forsake you. Take up the broken sword of our Father. Strike down the darkness. And together we will find Ural's survivors and make this Scourge of the Faithful, Mazerrel, pay!"

Empyrean Falling

Chapter IIX

"...at the taunts of those who reproach and revile me, because of the enemy, who is bent on revenge."
—Psalms 44:16

The sun burned away the frost of the Northern Plains as they rode. Ahead lay the shimmering twisting line of the River Aphaea, gleaming silver on the horizon as Michael galloped Andreia towards its eastern riverbank. Behind him flocked nine thousand volunteers from Zion, armed and angry. Their zeal had not slackened in the several weeks it had taken to force march from the North Gate. They gleamed in their plate mail armor under the autumnal morning light as they winged behind their archangel. At his call, they touched down on the slick verdure and began assembling in ordered arrays of battle.

Michael's vanguard was a series of cavalry wedges two thousand angels strong. Over the past month, they had ranged throughout the verdant fields with a furious resolve, gathering pockets of survivors where he found them as they methodically pushed north.

They could see the remains of Mazerrel's encampment on a series of low hills ahead. He raced with his vanguard for the position of weathered wood and piles of melted armor and bones. Already he could see his airborne pickets soaring in echelons overhead, their javelins, darts and slings poised. The legion trumpets blared behind him. The infantry cheered their archangel as they re-formed on the grassy fields. Their front stretched to over a league in both directions; their plate mail gleamed and their forests of spears glimmered in the midday sun. Tribunes rode their chariots between the legions' inseams, their hawkish gaze ensuring no mistake from their underlings impugned their honor.

Out front, Michael saw movement behind a hillock's crest, just between them and the Aphaea. He whistled and slowed to a canter. At his signal, the vanguard re-formed to closed order and matched Andreia's speed. Small, hunched shapes meandered behind the low gradient of the hillocks ahead. Beyond them, abutting the eastern riverbank, the abandoned encampment still smoldered. Michael squinted at the movement. As he neared, they began to take shape.

At two furlongs out, he could make out the tattered blue remnants of their legion tunics. They were beaten and threadbare. He stopped counting at sixty. Several waved their lacerated arms at his vanguard while one lifted the blue cornucopia standard and fluttered its ragged cloth back and forth. Michael drew upon them at a trot.

They bowed and lifted the battle standard again. "Hail, Patriarch!" shouted the color sergeant, his fist squishing blood through his fingers as it gripped the cornel haft of the flagpole. Michael marked him by his trans-crested helmet.

The archangel turned in Andreia's saddle. "Bring water! Get a medic up here!" He turned back to the legionnaire as others began to come from their concealment and gather around the battle standard. The segmented strips of their armor hung in shreds, their blue tunics mere bloody rags. "Rise, Concordias. What news of your general?"

"Alive but unconscious," said the color sergeant. "We attempted a night raid but Mazerrel cut us off and proceeded to mob us. Ural made a last stand and challenged him to single combat, hoping to buy us time to escape. He was badly maimed."

Michael leapt from his saddle and approached. "Show me."

The officer took them into a dugout the Concordias had furrowed. "Bedlam ensued and it was all we could do to pluck him from the ruck. We've been on the run ever since."

Michael nodded. "You did Heaven a great service by your bravery, Sergeant."

"For what it's worth, Patriarch, the rebels range all over these parts, and Mazerrel's angels have devolved into a rabid throng. Far more crazed than what we faced at the North Gate."

They wound their way through a series of fighting holes and dirt hovels to a bedroll where Ural lay, his large frame wrapped in blankets. A bloody bandage wrapped one of his eyes; one of his legs was in a splint. Michael knelt before the old sagacious general and observed his condition. He stroked the venerated cherub's ring of white hair and placed a hand on his broad shoulder.

"How many of you are there?" the archangel asked.

"About four hundred," the color sergeant answered. "We tried to escape but they cut our wings before we were able to slip out of their camp."

Michael stood. "We've found several groups like yours. But the enemy has eluded us."

"It won't be enough, Patriarch," the color sergeant warned. "We see many dark shapes in the night; they've kept us hemmed in close to that blasted encampment. Every sunset we hear screams of our brothers being tortured and executed."

"Mazerrel has shown himself to be a pestilence," Michael said darkly. "We'll flush them out." He turned and made for his awaiting cavalry. With a seamless motion, he was back in the saddle. "I have two legions inbound, Sergeant. Rotate Ural and our wounded to the rearguard. If you fight, I have a detachment of Concordias such as yourselves who have elected to push on for a rematch with Mazerrel."

He spurred the cavalry towards the eastern riverbank. They thundered past the knot of Concordia survivors, kicking up great clouds of chalk on the Plains. Michael entered the camp at a trot, Virtue drawn and his vanguard in closed order around him. They snaked through the rising promontories of charnel refuse. Bodies, rotting flesh, and bones still smoldered. Piles of melted armor crackled in intermittent flames. Slain officers were flayed and nailed upon crosses, "Faithful" scrawled on placards nailed to their chests. Charred skulls were piled in pyramids twice the height of their horses.

Empyrean Falling

The corpses of slain war elephants were vivisected and arrayed in a cultic circular pattern in the central parade ground. Michael took in the grisly holocaust. He looked down to see one of the broken golden totems of Battle Group Concordia, half-buried in the soil. His stomach soured at the tension borne in its silence.

"Father be with them," he whispered. He looked back at his legions. They were closing in. Behind them, a blanket of fog began to form on the Northern Plains. Something darted out of the corner of his eye. He whipped about to see a fox race out from one of the piles.

The promontories exploded around them. Great sonic concussions bowled over the condensed ranks of his cavaliers. The knights screamed, their horses reared in murderous agony as jagged shards of bone and metal ripped apart whole wings of his cavalry. Michael spurred Andreia, dodging the horrific blasts erupting throughout the abandoned camp.

His two legions moved to the double-quick. Their tribunes had the colors flying high. His skirmishers were nowhere to be seen. Michael galloped for the tribunes, shouting for anyone able to hear to get clear of the kill zone. Around him raced the heavy cavalry, each desperately jockeying to escape the trap. He heard the singular note of a horn from behind; it pierced the ringing in his ears. He reined Andreia about in time to see it.

Over the eastern riverbank swarmed a flood of Fallen. They came in waves, surging up from the bridges along the Aphaea in dark-armored columns. Their pikes bristled overhead, surmounted by the low-and-fast swoop of their airborne peltasts. The riverbank choked with their numbers, a vomitus issue of rank-and-file heresy marching for the encampment. Michael scanned their ranks for Mazerrel, his eyes burning for the Scourge of the Faithful, but the monstrous cherub's silhouette was nowhere to be seen.

The archangel turned and caught sight of his tribunes. They were racing for the networks of bridges to the north. The legions were trailing a few furlongs from the riverbank. They overtook the Concordias' dugout. Michael tried to rest in the knowledge that Ural was safe. But his heart burned for vengeance. He galloped for the nearest tribune, already whipping his majestically adorned war chariot across the Northern Plains. Michael stabbed Virtue into the air. The tribune replied with his scepter, his personal guard and command staff encircling him, apace with their leader.

"Praise the Lord," the regal seraph proclaimed as the cadre slowed to meet Michael. "We saw the explosions. I have the lads moving in force to retrieve survivors."

Michael shook his head. "Mazerrel has left an ambush for us, but they number less than two thousand. We should be able to sweep them from the field in minutes." Andreia danced under Michael, whinnying and champing at the bit as he fed off his master's mien. "Re-form your cohorts into a concentric circle; envelop them. Have your yews move to the air to ward off their skirmishers. And redeploy your Cogs to the left oblique. I want no one escaping today."

The tribune saluted and Michael was off. He raced down the inseam of the nearest cohorts until coming upon the second legion's tribune who, in his zeal, had ranged too far ahead.

Similarly adorned, the other tribune wore bronze heavy armor and a silver crown, a scepter in one hand and a spear in the other.

"Tribune!" Michael hailed. "Stack your cohorts in three staggered lines. When contact with the enemy is made, I want your rear echelons to sweep right and envelop these felons!"

"As you command, Archangel!" the tribune said with a cumbersome bow, his regal crown dipping less than a hand's breadth.

"And Tribune? I want no prisoners." The tribune dipped his brow again. Michael eyed him before saluting and rushing back to the fore. The remnants of his cavalry had rallied on a flat and were reconnoitering the field. They met him just south of the camp.

"Where is he?" Michael growled.

The cavalier captain raised his helmet's shining steel visor and spat. His eyes were blue fire. "No sign of the Scourge, Patriarch."

"Damnation," Michael cursed. The sky darkened. They looked up to see the Fallen skirmishers circling over their position like vultures. "Clear the field!" Michael shouted.

Andreia brayed, and the cavalry rushed out from under the airborne peltasts. Javelins and slinger bullets bit the dirt around them as they spread their formation and galloped for the protective cover of the first legion's archers. They transited the marching fronts of the

Empyrean Falling

second legion's cohorts. Four-hundred-eighty angel strong groups marched with large shields and heavy plate steel armor, their helmets and lugged war laces shining like a sea of glass under the sun. Potshots were taken at the blocks of Faithful infantry, but they formed the testudo with their shields and easily turned the missiles. A volley from their own honeycombed banks of archers sent the Fallen peltasts retreating amidst a cloud of arrows.

Drums kept the beat of those marching; archers ascended and worked their yews; dispatch riders raced to-and-fro; centurions called out orders; and trumpets blared.

By the time Michael and his band of seven-hundred-strong cavalry reached the archers, the foremost Faithful legion had crashed into the enemy front. He heard the crack of the clash and looked from his mounted vantage. Spears and pikes lowered as the Fallen re-formed into a trio of wedges, bunching together as the centurions ordered their legionnaires to close the rows. The intervals between their spears shrank as they swept down and vanished in the thrust. They shouted for vengeance, chanting "Concordias! Concordias! Concordias!" The initial attack was a furious collision as each ordered front stepped with mechanical discipline into the awaiting thresher of their foe. Screams erupted amidst blasting horns and pealing trumpets.

Michael watched the rear-rankers press into the backs of their comrades, using their sheer mass to gain an advantage. The press worked. He saw his volunteers gain ground, purchasing one cubit at a time in buckets of blood. He knew the scene: they were locked into the crush, grinding away at one another with razor-edged polearms. Angels died by the dozens, suffocating in the crush. Arrows rained from above. Slinger stones caromed off shields. The second legion's fore-rank met the ordered wedges of Fallen infantry at an enfilade, turning the abandoned encampment into a barrier-riddled battlefield.

The Cherubim Patriarch led his cavalry through the inseams of the second legion's stacked heavy infantry, hastening for the leftmost flank of the first legion where his Cognoscenti volunteers held in a refused line on the grassy flats just before the networks of bridges. Their bronze heavy armor and shields shone in contrast to the pristine silver gleam of their line-fighter brothers. Michael threw a glance back south, where the fog had manifested. The baggage train was two miles off, safe from the conflict. Already medics were ferrying the wounded back into the mists. Ural was there too. He clipped Andreia's spurs and found the first legion' tribune embroiled in a ferocious duel with a knot of Fallen at the fore. The color guard was skewering rebel angels with their cavalry lances and smashing them with their warhammers.

Michael joined the fray, mopping up the isolated cluster of Fallen in heartbeats. "Tribune!" he called to the blood-splattered commander. "Send your First Cohort across the River. I'll take the cavalry across the bridge and meet them on the far side."

The tribune reined in a circle. "Right behind you, Archangel."

The two Faithful legions enveloped the Fallen ambushers. They made short work of them on the upslope. The fighting was furious but methodical; no Fallen raved as they did at the North Gate. Michael considered the Concordian color sergeant had gone daft, but he knew better than to question a member of Ural's battle group.

Michael led his cavalry across the bridge. The Faithful archers had regained command of the skies. Arrows rained onto the heads of the rear-ranking Fallen, quilling the upswept turf of the Northern Plains' eastern riverbank. The archangel watched his First Cohort expand its front and fly over the battle. They leap-frogged to the western riverbank and converged on his position, marked by Virtue's sunlit gleam as he brandished it overhead.

From the other side, the battle looked over. The Faithful volunteers had encircled the two thousand strong Fallen force. Their resistance was token at best. Though every lost cubit of ground cost loyalist lives, the rebels were losing numbers, nearly pressed into the waters. They screamed and shouted. Their commanders rallied with the infamous Fallen chant. Michael watched their hopeless struggle with satisfaction marred by the tension in his guts that any moment their formation would break and route. And when they did, he and his detachment would be waiting for them.

The rout never came. The Fallen died to an angel. The legions worked their bloody havoc in dire detail until every one of the rebels was a squirming heap of meat and metal.

Empyrean Falling

The tribune whipped his chariot across the bridge to Michael's position, his pace slowed and a triumphant grin beaming his features. "Let not the taste of victory turn to ash in thy mouth, Archangel!" he bayed. "We have carried the day!" He rode up to Michael's flank, his color guard mixing with the surviving heavy cavalry. "Though they did seem to have found their grit at the last possible moment," the tribune added with the adrenal aplomb of a victor.

Michael nodded in tacit agreement, silent with a furrowed brow. "These weren't Mazerrel's cohorts," he stated cautiously. "They were far too ordered compared to what we faced at the North Gate. And not one of them carried the glyph banner." The tribune hummed in his throat. "Mazerrel has given us the slip," Michael growled. He sheathed Virtue. "At least Ural is safe—"

There was a horn blast from the south. Michael strained to look over the bloody forest of his legions' lances as they re-formed on the eastern riverbank. Auxiliaries picked their way through the charnel mounds of the battlefield across the River, executing wounded Fallen and plucking Faithful casualties from the muck. He sprouted his wings to take flight and gain a better vantage, but Andreia bucked and kicked every time his seat left the saddle.

But he had no need; in seconds he saw it. From the mists that had gathered in the south, a wall of pikes encroached upon the Northern Plains. From their flanks, he saw wings of cavalry dart out of the fogbank. Before the hedgerows of tall pole-arms were honeycombed banks of auxiliaries. At their vanguard manifested a banner; its sigil was a poison-tipped dagger on a blood moon. Only one angel in Heaven used that curved dagger, a master of assassins who had turned foxy general. They were cut off. Michael's blood thundered in his veins.

"They're working in concert?" the tribune decried.

Michael wiped the sweat from his upper lip and snarled. The baggage train. Ural. Zion. "No." He unsheathed Virtue. "This is worse. This is competition."

Empyrean Falling

Chapter IX
"You should fear the sword yourselves; for the wrath will bring punishment by the sword, and then you will know that there is judgment."
—Job 19:29

    Satan readjusted in his saddle, enduring the blistering wintry winds as he sat atop his sable mare, Nyx. Beside him rode Vuldun, the captain of his personal guard. Behind them trailed the column of black-armored guards, their numbers stretching over a league across the frozen tundra. Winter had touched the West. Around them rose the broken obelisks of their former Empire, buried in snowdrifts to their scarred apexes. Behind them, the collection of ziggurats crumbled beneath tons of ice, slowly receding into the distance.

    "We're nearing the site now, my lord," rasped Vuldun atop his gelding. He was invisible in the chilling night. His uncanny armor concealed all but his vibrant green eyes under a moonless eve. Behind him rode the bulk of their force, shades withered to skin and bones and armor as they plunged deeper into the forgotten lands now blighted with wintry storms. "Our rangers tracked the clutch of Faithful to an oasis just over that ridge." He pointed to the night-shrouded horizon. Through intermittent gales, a rise could be seen arcing in the distant skyline. "Reports say they were last seen lowering something into a cistern."

    A frigid gust coursed over Satan's gaunt face. His shoulder-length hair lifted in the flurry, more black than crimson now. He refused to tug at the mantle whipping about his jagged black armor; he would endure this vile cold as the paragon that he knew himself to be.

The weeks had dragged on, growing more perilous with each mile. It could be tasted in the air, like the fetid stench of a slaughterhouse's rot. Even Vuldun felt its dreaded pall sluice through his spirit. All felt the bitter sting of their enterprise. Yet Satan pressed on, refusing to relent even with the winter's ill tidings.

"What word from my lieutenants?" Satan asked. Vuldun hesitated, only the rumble of legions and the howling winds filled the void. "Captain?"

Vuldun sighed. "Mazerrel's still out there. Word has it that his legions have flocked back to him, lulled by the call of their 'Scourge.' He spurned them in hatred, nominating only those veterans whom he deemed worthy to prey upon every coastal hamlet and village to the north. He did his work well, so I'm told; they fear him. They should be back at the North Gate by now, working havoc on Zion."

Satan grinned mirthlessly at that and took a deep, icy breath. "And Umbra Tempest?"

"Fled to the Northern Plains. When Michael evaded him at the Aphaea, he gave chase all the way back to the Northern Wall. I guess the master of assassins wished to succeed where Mazerrel had failed. But the North Gate's new commander, Nicolae, repulsed him. His attack failed, though only barely, and mostly due to trickery."

"He was under orders," Satan said blandly. "Pressure must be kept on the Holy city lest they feel confident enough to sally in force into the East's terrain. We're outnumbered, Vuldun; I cannot allow our adversaries to employ their numbers. We must think strategically. We must pick the ground to fight upon. We must isolate them in pockets before our zeal wanes. And we must keep them hemmed in. So, our brothers have adopted Mazerrel's new title?" Vuldun nodded. "Good, it shows esprit de corps. Embracing the hatred of your enemy can be like a warm stole amidst the winter gloom."

"I suppose that is the bright side to all of this, my lord."

Satan smiled insidiously. "You think my excursion out here is nothing more than a detour?"

Empyrean Falling

Vuldun shook his head. "I don't begin to question your unerring wisdom, my lord, but I fail to see the function of this enterprise that has nearly a million of us forging into a blasted wasteland, so far removed from the war."

"Trust me when I tell you that every element thus far has landed into place in the East. Our cause here is paramount, otherwise, I would not bother with this lethal cold. And I certainly would not put you, the flower of my army, at risk. It is an honor what we do, far more than the fire and bloodshed that drench the Eastern Kingdom. And when what I seek is found, this enterprise will come to fruition and you'll behold such a spectacle of disarmament as to make our conflict a brief, unpleasant memory."

Vuldun shuddered, tugging at his sackcloth cloak as another gale harried them. This far out in Heaven's badlands, the nights were merciless. Snows mounted with such frequency as to bury half the column in their camps. New paths had to be shoveled daily. Angels expired by the scores from the freeze while others went mad from their reckless plunge into the abandoned border of the Realm. They dared not muse on how close they had drawn to the Oblivion's edge.

Satan knew they desired the pandemonium of the East over the blight of the West. The tales of Mazerrel escaping Michael's retribution fueled them. They spun theories on how he disappeared into the Northern Shores and regaled one another with tales of him ravaging every city he could lay his meaty claws on. "To ride with the Scourge" became a slogan for the downtrodden. They sang dark odes to his glyph banner when word came of his atrocities.

In his absence, so they were told, Tempest led his cavalry to the North Gate. Under orders, their nocturnal assault lasted three days without pause. Though it failed, the Fallen under the Dragon's banner knew it had done its job in keeping the Faithful locked in Zion.

The stories kept them sane. And Satan knew it. He demanded his disciples live up to their titles. In a show of encouragement, he had winged above their massed numbers and shouted with supernatural force, "In the East, they call you my Death Guard! But here, with me, I call you my Imperial Flames. You will be the first to rise! You will taste the shores of the Empyrean before any other! Let no angel—loyalist or revolutionary—doubt your conviction! Though Mazerrel and Umbra Tempest contend for my favor upon sacrosanct redoubts, virgin plains, and crystal rivers, fire your hearts with the knowledge that you are my elite! Unto you, I give the keys to everlasting light!"

But another story made its way through their column. Even the former Cognoscenti were silenced by its malady. The elites drew up in fear at its whisper. No rumor incited the chill of dereliction more than the Bane of the Fallen, or "Raziel" as he was called. The reports on this progenitor of holy wrath cut their courage to the quick. The survivors of the Southlands' disaster who reached them cataloged the angel's deeds; such mysterious, unquenchable destruction, the mere mention of his name evoked shivers around campfires. To squelch whatever mirth cultivated among the huddled angels, all one had to do was threaten them with a confrontation against the Bane. And none could muster the grit to deny his existence.

That this angel's identity remained an enigma proved an ominous portent to the superstitious rebels. Scuttlebutt was that it was the spirit of Morning Star returned to face Satan. Others declared him to be Michael waging a secret war. While others—estranged from their comrades—claimed it was some unknown angel demolishing their southern army.

But Satan knew. He remembered how the angel fought but, more importantly, he knew how the angel thought. Often he would embolden them by saying it would only be a matter of time before this Bane, this "Myth from the South," would meet his end at the tip of Hadar. But first, Satan knew he had to prove his resolve.

"Bring me the prisoner."

Vuldun twisted on the horn of his saddle and signaled to an awaiting seraph. In minutes, a detail came thundering towards the column's vanguard, murmurs trailing their wake. The Dragon turned to see a troupe of Imperial Flames hauling an angel shackled and bound to a dapple mare. His clothes were tattered and covered in sludge, his bare skin shivering in a pallid, frostbitten blue. The horse's lips frothed, its flanks caked in mud. The withered beast teetered under the frail weight of its chained, beaten rider.

Satan sidestepped Nyx over to him and lifted him by his scalp. The archangel took in the gaunt visage of the prisoner, his slack-jawed cheeks so hollow, they filled with the scum of his trek. He regarded the angel with a grim eye.

"Behold," Vuldun said with a proffering hand, "Belphegor."

"How far have we fallen," Satan said with a gesture. At his command, the entourage took hold of Belphegor's bare shoulders, cut his bindings from the horse, and cast him to splash face-first in the slush. Satan turned to Vuldun. "Bring me Baal."

With a nod, Vuldun disappeared from the vanguard. The Dragon turned back to Belphegor, who was prone and quivering under the gaze of his fellow apostates.

"Two million, Belphegor," Satan said. "That is what I gave you. Not to kill, steal and destroy, but to occupy, divert and distract. The Southern Wall was depleted. Your orders were simple: attack their garrisons, draw attention away from the North Gate. Yet even this task proved too much." Eons seemed to pass as wintry gales howled through the mounted caucus of pitiless elites. "Rise, Belphegor, and face your destiny as an Empyreal Phoenix."

Belphegor struggled under the weight of his chains. His thin limbs quaked as he dragged himself to his knees. Broken, bruised black and purple, and shivering, he felt the cold sting of shame surmount the winter as his master leered down at him.

"I am, however, not without an iota of magnanimity," said Satan. "So, I'll allow your apology."

Belphegor leapt upon this with temerity. "Thank you, My God!" he cried, vigorously animated. "You must believe me, no matter how crazed the tale. One angel! He came to us from the swamps, riding a cyclone of wind and fire. Nothing stopped him! He turned our numbers; our weapons failed to find the mark; every one of our disciples lost hope! Those who escaped his wrath were mowed down by his legion!"

"He had a legion?" Satan inquired.

"Yes, my god," Belphegor wheezed, "seven thousand shimmering angels, armor so blinding we couldn't face them! By dawn of the second day, I'd lost two thirds of my force!"

Empyrean Falling

"But *two million*, Belphegor," Satan reiterated. "Surely with such a host you could mount an attack or have pathfinders lead you around this preternatural hazard?"

Belphegor shook his head. "He used our control over the elements to terrible effect, my god. Not even the archangels have shown such a display as what we saw!" Satan glared at him for that. "Fire erupted from the same spot of ground as jets of water; those who weren't turned to ash were drowned in the deluge. Hail and bolts fell from a clear sky, freezing winds tore the auxiliaries to pieces. But that wasn't the worst of it…a mountain—he plucked a whole mountain from the bedrock and dropped it on us! We laughed when he took to the field, so small and void of escort, but now? Now my nightmares are fraught with his specter!"

Satan exuded a serenity. "Mercy is not forgotten in my Empyrean, Belphegor. You saved my life at Min Thralr. For that, I shall spare yours." He dismounted and knelt before the angel. "Umbra Tempest warned me not to elect you for such a task, but I neglected his advice. Recent actions made his intentions suspect; I feared his motive was not pure. I must admit, though, I'd unwittingly spurned clever counsel. For shame, Belphegor; I would have very much liked to see you prove him wrong. But alas, fate's fearsome fortune persists, and I have yet to sit upon my Throne." He turned back to Nyx and reached into his saddlebag. From the leather flap, he produced a small black velvet pouch. "So, we must forge a new path."

Vuldun arrived with Baal in tow. The burly, malformed angel rode atop his bull, Moloch, a scythe tethered to his bare back. The angelic monster had horns which spanned the breadth of his beastly mount, his deformed snout huffing steam through flared nostrils. They were a ghastly mirror of mutated devolution.

Satan motioned to him. Baal dismounted and strode to Belphegor's horse.

"Though spared your life may be," Satan said, "blood must be shed to atone for this lamentable obliteration." Terror darkened Belphegor as the bestial cherub Baal regarded him with a pair of beady red eyes and raised his scythe. "Embrace your punishment, Belphegor."

Empyrean Falling

In one swift motion, the scythe's blade fell and decapitated Belphegor's mare. The Imperial Flames' mounts whinnied and frisked as the equine flesh went sloshing into a goopy mix of sinew, fluids and snow. Blood steamed the air as it showered over a cowering Belphegor. Before him, the dapple mare's body flailed before expiring in the muck. The Imperial Flames gathered around to watch.

Satan waved back his dark knights. He stood over Belphegor and the horsehead in the clearing. From the velvet purse, he produced a red shard no larger than a grain of rice. It gleamed ruby in his pale hand. Breaths caught in throats as the mounted elites beheld it. Belphegor screamed from the light, scratching at his sullied face.

"I'll give you this one solace," Satan declared. "Your life shall be spared."

"Yes, thank you, my god!" cried Belphegor. "All praise be to your name!"

"You shall seek death," Satan warned as he held the glowing red shard before them, "but death shall flee from thee."

The kernel of light rested in the palm of his archangelic hand. With the other hand, he pressed upon it while humming melodically. His fingers etched a fiery glyph in the frozen air. Black flames emanated forth, slowly lapping over Belphegor and the severed head of his mount in consuming shadowed waves. Belphegor screamed as the darkness bent light around him, engulfing the writhing angel in torturous cries and an unholy radiance made of imperceptible shades, obscuring him in a cloud of acidic heat. The intensity grew until the tension popped, the shockwave knocking Satan back on his haunches.

They heard Belphegor wail, limbs thrashing in the lapping black waves. The black cloud fell to the slush, leaving a smoldering effluvium. The sight before them churned their innards. The smoke cleared. Belphegor was no longer a bedraggled surgeon-turned-general; he'd been transformed. Coarse, dark hair covered his body. Hooves dug at the slush. His appendages ended in something resembling more claws than fingers, scratching at a snouted face. He blew phlegm and gurgled blood. The horsehead was gone. At first, they thought it was Baal, worked up to a frenzy. But the bullish angel held untouched on the flank, Moloch licking the blood from his scythe as he peered on the grisly scene with beady glowing eyes.

Empyrean Falling

Satan stood proudly before the grotesquery that was Belphegor. "Cursed you are, Belphegor, for destroying that which I hold most sacred. May you live out your days as a skulking imp. Contempt will be your mantle; cowardice will be your food. I damn you to this shade of foul putrescence. And should you live to see my victory, I shall send such a force to hunt you down as to chase away the stars with its wrath."

Satan turned and got back on his horse. He turned to Vuldun. "Bind him to the dregs of the baggage train. When we near the Oblivion, send Baal with a detachment and have him hurled into the void, lest my work here spoil."

Empyrean Falling

Chapter X

"For our struggle is not against flesh and blood, but against the rulers, against the authorities, against the powers of this dark world and the spiritual forces of evil in the heavenly realms."
—Ephesians 6:12

Michael walked along the repaired barbican of the North Gate. Snow fell in blinding flurries. The cold made his bald head ache, his topknot damp and heavy. The wolf pelt cloak hanging about his frame weighed him down, but he was supremely grateful for it amidst the deep blizzard. He transited the breadth of the Northern Wall in the predawn, inspecting the battlements and artillery bartizans, blanched and blanketed in the wet white of a harsh and sudden winter. He sometimes wondered if surviving Umbra Tempest's ambush and the months it took to fight his way back to Zion was worth it.

Each morning he elected to patrol the freezing Northern Defenders, emboldening their armored huddled ranks with his apparition and encouraging them with his words. It was his favorite time of day. One could hardly decipher who benefited more from the routine. The cherubim infantry would shovel snow from the ramparts while the seraphim crews chipped away at the ice congealing around artillery batteries. Yet they would each, in turn, stop at their labors to bask in the warmth of the archangel's presence.

Empyrean Falling

They relished any relief from the dreaded scene taking place beyond the Wall. Though the brutal and unrelenting conditions of the early winter took its toll, what occurred out in the fields of the Northern Plains was far worse; a dark tent city had been erected. Palisaded pavilions rose in grisly torment just beyond the range of the Northern Defenders' artillery bartizans. The nights were filled with arrhythmic drums, discordant dirges, mocking blasphemies, and minor chord melodies played in disharmony. They hardly slept.

The days were spent in weariness as noxious cook fires sent their grisly smoke wafting up over the Wall. The Faithful knew what the rebels ate. Mazerrel's rangers snuck through the night to lash the mutilated bodies of their prisoners to the broken siege engines of their failed assaults. With each sunrise, the horned glyph sigil would show up, painted in cruor. One could hardly look over the ramparts without seeing a sea of iced-over, busted engines congealed in a purpled sea of blood that stretched in hellish vista. Many abstained from looking, desperately trying to salvage what was left of their constitutions.

Michael refused to avert his eyes or let his shivers be seen. He would stand at the crenelated stone lip, wind and snow battering his squinting visage, and stare into the madness. Mazerrel had made his presence on the battlefield known. The predawn light washed the Northern Plains before him a sheet of blues. They were out there; he could feel their eyes upon him. So he stood and watched, every morning and every evening.

"I can't tell you how much it warms my heart to see you alive," he said to the grey colossus lumbering up to his flank. He felt the salute at his side and turned.

"Any day above ground is a good day, Patriarch," Melphax replied with a wink. The giant cherub was decked out in his full plate armor, looking no less haggard than the rest. He played with the jagged hole in his lamed tasset as his archangel regarded him.

"I'm sorry for what happened," Michael said quietly, a pursed-lip smile and furrowed brow marking his stark features. "Amin Shakush was supposed to be safe."

Melphax shrugged. "It's war, Patriarch; no plan survives first contact with the enemy, especially this one. I'm sorry we failed. But Tempest failed too. My lieutenants saw to that."

"Paladin and Deledrosse left a noble legacy," Michael said. "Ma'igwa too, if we're being fair. Their sacrifices won't be in vain. A pinprick of light in our dark night of the soul. Father knows we need every boon we can get these days."

"Speaking of which," Melphax said, indicating the icy horrors in the fields below and the snowdrifts that steadily rose up the height of the Wall, "if we don't break this stalemate, Mazerrel's psychological warfare is going to accomplish what no catapult could."

"Those damned horns and drums," Michael snarled, reminded of the noise beyond the Wall. "The notes are so flat or sharp, you could metronome the winces with every keening beat and bend."

"We could do without the effigies of the Son as well," added Melphax in a hushed tone in between wintry gusts.

Michael nodded to the side. "Walk with me." The two strode west along the Wall. Michael spoke in low tones when they were not inspiring their weathered subordinates. "I wish Ural were here."

"Is he still unconscious?" Melphax asked.

"Mazerrel did a number on him," Michael replied. "He's in a coma. I have Rafiel checking on him once a week." He adjusted his wolf pelt cloak to hide a shiver. "How his Concordias escaped Umbra Tempest's legions, I'll never know. Hell, how *we* escaped, I'll never know. That was a solid two months of protracted evasion."

He passed a checkpoint at the barbican's exit. An angel busied himself breaking stalactites off the stone awning, his armor wrapped in soggy rags. Michael nodded to him before passing the watch post. The sentries saluted. He thumped their pauldrons. They smiled. So did he. When he moved on, the smile vanished. "Though it wasn't without its cost. Gabriel never lets me forget, especially after Umbra Tempest tried his hand at siege warfare. Morale was a real problem in the aftermath. Still, had I never sent Ural to face Mazerrel…."

Melphax touched his archangel's frosty vambrace and looked him in the eyes. The archangel appeared feral in his armored wolf pelt guise, topknot falling about his pauldrons. But Melphax knew the cherub's heart. "Fury evaporates, Michael, but damage abides."

The drums' tempo increased. Michael spat over the rampart. "As much as our spirits gain salient jubilation from you," he told

Empyrean Falling

Melphax, "this cold war of Mazerrel's threatens to unstring us. Commander Nicolae has proven to be a competent regent of the North Gate, but I fear even Alrak's return with the Seventh Column is but a steaming breath in this whiteout."

"You have chosen the Radiant's successor well."

"It may not matter whom I choose," Michael rebuffed. "Speak candidly, Pillar of Iron. What is the condition of our Northern Defenders? I've been ensnared by politics, a system that feeds on victory yet deprives me of achieving it."

Melphax sighed. "Well, you've certainly hit the crux of it. We can't defeat them without you and yet, without the merit of triumph, they won't release you from the advisor's aegis."

"It's worse than a switch-back," Michael lamented.

A trumpet blasted from the bailey. Michael looked behind him to see a flight of seraphim messengers winging through the cold air to even intervals along the Wall. He saw them land and pick out the garrison officers. Furious, animated arguments were held. In minutes, the seraphim stationed on the Wall began packing their belongings and forming up. He watched as myriads slung kits and winged it east. The activity brought the North Gate to life. Many forgot the cold.

"At least Gilgamesh's Lightning Legion is still intact," Michael said wistfully.

"Looks like we could use the Thunderbolts right about now," Melphax commented. Flights of seraphim began to evacuate the Wall.

"Well, I sent them north with orders to infiltrate the Dragon's Lair and raid their supply depots," Michael said. "At this point, all we can do is hamper their war effort; this winter has brought us to an uninvited armistice." He saw the flocks of seraphim mustering into regiments and taking flight under cherubic protests. They receded in droves, vanishing from the Wall. "This has the stink of my brother." Melphax cleared his throat. "What do you think of Consul Gabriel?"

"To put it blunt as ball bearings, my Patriarch, I'm concerned. Our Consul is capable, no doubt. But I'm troubled by his actions in recent months, what's happening before us being chief among them."

Empyrean Falling

Michael gestured towards the sky with a forefinger over a sarcastic grin, indicating the wintry air choked with corps of seraphim flying away from their posts along the Northern Wall. "You mean?"

Melphax nodded. "Many of his angels have been slain but this devotion to his choir reeks of avarice. It's pathological; the Scourge looms within bowshot. Atrocities are committed wholesale. Not even the hooves of Umbra Tempest's siege equated to this abomination. One can hardly sleep for the blasphemous rituals Mazerrel performs under the moon. And during the day, there are acts of such sickening cruelty visited upon his hapless prisoners that it's all Nicolae and I can do to keep the rank-and-file at their posts. But our words are losing their potency, Patriarch; the Northern Defenders are cracking."

Michael watched the seraphim. "I'll do my best, but—"

He was interrupted by a familiar angel winging for his position. In the tumult of seraphic withdrawal, Weir landed on the paved stone of the battlement, his face flushed. "Patriarch!" Michael waved him in. He surmounted the ramparts before his archangel, rosy cheeks huffing. "It's Polemarch Sivad, sir. He's holed up on the spire of Carthanos." The cherub pointed in the direction of the sprawling metropolis. The Great Library could be seen piercing the landscape. "He nearly broke my back when I petitioned him to come down."

"Just leave him be, Captain," Michael said with a deep and abiding sigh. "Whatever's troubling him, I'm sure it'll pass."

"He says he's done fighting."

Michael pinched the bridge of his nose. "Tell him…" Melphax tapped the lamed tasset guarding the archangel's thigh. Michael looked up to see Melphax raising a finger. They listened. Silence. Mazerrel's drums had ceased. They looked at each other, trepidation searing their faces. Michael looked out to the enemy camp. He thought he saw the faintest glimmer of metal amassing before the palisades. "We don't have time for this."

"Shall I finish rounds and submit my report?" Melphax asked.

"No," Michael answered. "Get Nicolae up here." He turned from Mazerrel's tent city and the frozen hinterland beyond the Wall. "Captain, summon the Seventh Column. I'll take care of Alrak." The archangel sprouted his wings and bolted south for the Library.

Empyrean Falling

"Patriarch," Melphax called. Michael stopped midair. "Go easy on him; you were new once too." He winked at his archangel. Michael considered it before flying off, transiting the flights of withdrawing seraphim. Melphax regarded Weir. The cherub's face belied any mustered composure. "Rest easy, Captain," the former leader of Amin Shakush said. "If ever there was an acolyte of truth and logic, it's your Polemarch. Trust in the power of family."

The sky was ablaze in early morning titian scarlets. The clouds looked afire as Michael endured the bitter wind and landed on the Great Library's rooftop. He found Alrak sitting on the stone lip facing east where the sea shimmered beyond Zion. His mane was a golden pennant at half mast, lifted by the breeze.

Michael approached softly, his wings catching pockets of air from the chimneys as he glided over the roof's shingles. He felt the brooding cherub sense him, though his young reflexes refuse to acknowledge it as he squinted into the nascent sunrise.

"Why does it have to be like this?" Alrak asked him.

"What do you mean?"

Alrak turned his squint on him, angular cheeks rosy in the cold and emerald eyes blazing. "You know exactly what I mean, Michael." He stared at him as Michael descended to the stone parapet next to Alrak. "I slaughtered those angels without mercy in the Southlands. Their screams fill my dreams every night. Why?"

Michael furled his wings and folded his arms, eyes downcast. "When we started all this," he sighed, "the 'Dragon' was supposed to be this otherworldly thing, an agent of chaos from beyond the Realm. We never considered it a philosophical, moral failing. Of course, the irony is that we set a trap for ourselves."

Alrak sneered. "Do you really think God needs protection from Lucifer?"

"Of course not," Michael said. "But you saw what happened at Benediction. What am I supposed to do, let them raze Zion and kill everyone who stands in their way?"

"The Lord could stop this whenever He wants. Why doesn't He restore harmony?"

Empyrean Falling

"Well," Michael began, "one thing the Son taught me was that He wants us to be complete. That means growth, and, like muscle, we must be stretched and torn so that we may be made stronger."

"I wish the Son had that talk with Lucifer," Alrak lamented.

"Lucifer never bothered coming to the Son, Alrak. Love requires trust, humility, sacrifice." The archangel sighed. "My brother lost sight of this a long time ago, blinded by his own radiance."

"So, we fight and die to protect a collection of stones?"

"God doesn't care about that."

"Right," Alrak said sarcastically, "like God doesn't care about you training us to fight only to turn on each other; like He doesn't care about angels trying in known vanity to capture His White Throne?" He smirked. "Like He doesn't care about you having to kill Lucifer?"

"Enough!" Michael barked, his voice cutting through the howling gales. The archangel rounded on Alrak, his fur mantle bristling in the wind. "We don't contend in this storm of fire and bloodshed to prove our fidelity to God or to protect Him!"

Alrak's stomach churned. He looked up with a blank stare.

"Flesh comes at a price, Alrak," Michael admitted, crestfallen. "At times, I wish we'd stayed in the Empyrean; we would have never known power and all the faults it inherits. But this flesh, this war," Michael revealed, "is our crucible." The young cherub shook his head, tears welling in his eyes. "Alrak, how do you make a vase?"

"I don't see what this has to do with—"

"Just…humor me."

Alrak sighed. "You mold it."

"And how do you do that?"

"Add water."

"Good, and how do you get it to stay in the shape you desire?"

"Heat it in a kiln."

Michael nodded. "Exactly." He smiled at his protégé. "After it's heated, it's in the form you need, yes?" Alrak slowly nodded. "And then you have a magnificent vessel, don't you?"

"So, you're saying this war is shaping us?"

Empyrean Falling

"Far from it," Michael answered. "I'm saying *this*," he extended his arm, "is the potter's wheel and Father is our water." He placed a hand on the angel's gore-caked armor. "This age of flesh is molding us, Alrak. Because of our dispensation here, we know how majestic life was in the Empyrean. We were formless clay, cosmic mud clutching with infantile necessity to God's bosom. We needed shape. We needed character. We molded ourselves into loving vessels, but the Prophecy of the Dragon was meant to harden us."

"I just wish He'd let us return to the Empyrean."

"But what a travesty that would be to know only perfection! One day, we'll return to that Upper Realm, but first, we must choose between vanity and passion. Life's about pursuing the mystery. Only by going through this tribulation, can we align our hearts with God."

"But can we ever truly have that idyllic homecoming?"

"Yes, when and the Dragon is finally defeated."

Alrak was silent, his mentor's harsh insight taking root.

Finally, Michael spoke. "So, now you know the truth." Out on the seaside horizon, the first rays of sunlight burst forth, painting the clouds and formations of seraphim. "We wrestle with the evil of fear which festers in our hearts. That's why we bear this flesh." Alrak's glowing eyes trickled drops of tears. Michael smiled and wiped his cheek. "Take heart, dandelion; we will know the Empyrean again."

With that, the archangel climbed to the parapet's stone lip and spread his wings. The wind howled. His topknot and fur mantle dangled between the feathered expanses.

"What now?" Alrak asked.

Michael eyed sternly. "Fulfill your role in this War."

Alrak's eyes bulged. "Has the time come already?" Alrak's eyes looked like a binary constellation in contrast to the cresting sun. He choked down a smoky lump in his throat.

"The Scourge of the Faithful will find you at the Gate," Michael revealed. "Now go, and beat the Hell out of Mazerrel."

Empyrean Falling

Chapter XI

"...act with courage, and may the Lord be with those who do well."
—2nd Chronicles 19:11

    The sun ascended. Angels shivered in their plate armor. Michael felt the bite in his bones as he touched down on the North Gate's barbican. To either side, cherubic line-fighters hastened to their posts, lugging spears, swords and shields. Squires hauled bundles of arrows for what remained of their archers. Gunnery crews loaded gall-guns and ballistae. Officers barked over the drums as maniples beat to general quarters. Michael saw gaps in the line on both sides of the Wall as seraphim continued to evacuate amidst the marshaling clamor. He was grateful for the sunshine's radiating invigoration, but they still saw their breath in the midmorning cold. His wings furled into the slits on his backplate to the tune of heavy infantry dog-chomper cleats scraping the barbican's stones under the jostle of metal panoplies.

    He found Nicolae at the ramparts, standing among his color guard like a bronze statue while the angelic sea crashed around him. His long, braided goatee dangled in the wind as he adjusted his spiked conical helmet and cinched the leather straps of his scale mail armor.

"Interim Commander," Michael greeted with a salute. "Praise Father. Glad to see some seraphim have remained at their posts."

Nicolae furrowed his heavy brow and fingered the pommel of his gilded spatha. "We have no auxiliaries and our gunnery crews are cut in half." He pointed to the encampment. "Mazerrel's horns have filled the air for twenty minutes; he's mustering." Near the enemy palisades, they saw the burlap-and-blood glyph banners. Nicolae turned to his color guard and began handing out orders. Their numbers dwindled as they sprouted wings and flew down the length of the Wall. Michael observed him with a look of obvious concern. "Our communication lines are broken up and down the Wall, Patriarch."

Behind them, another pair of wings disturbed the air. Nicolae's color guard turned in a defensive posture but Michael recognized that angel's sound. And could smell the oil of freshly cleaned armor.

"You know," Alrak said with a light tone as he landed among them, "you put vinegar in an archangel's mouthwash one time, and he never forgets it." He looked over the ramparts and pointed to the icy fields before the Northern Wall's plinth. "Michael, look."

The archangel approached. He peered over the crenellation. The ice bulged and broke in snaking lines through the snowdrifts, leading back to Mazerrel's camp. The lines ended less than a hundred yards from the Northern Wall. "They masked their work with the noise," Michael realized. He faced Nicolae. "They've tunneled to the battered plinth of the North Gate."

Nicolae's eyes turned to blazing amber discs. "Yews, up!" he shouted. "Sergeant Major, divert the First Cohort to the bartizans! Get the ice off those trebuchets!"

"There's no time!" said Michael. "The equipment's frozen solid and they're already inside our batteries' range. Abandon the artillery and put the crews on our machicolation points inside the Wall. Use the tar, oil, gall-guns, caltrops, whatever they can muster."

"Won't matter," said Nicolae. "Without Gabriel's seraphim, we're silk on the filature."

"What are their numbers?" asked Alrak.

Nicolae shrugged and continued to send off his color guard with missives. "There's no way to be sure. Last count had them at a hundred-eighty thousand, but that was days ago. Who knows how many more have flocked to Mazerrel's banner since then." He pointed to Gabriel's departing battalions. "We have no rangers, no scouts, no peltasts, and no messengers. How are we supposed to coordinate our defenses without the Archon's choir?"

Michael saw the last flights of seraphim under the rising sun. "Alrak, come here." The cherub bounded over the stone battlement to him. Michael's baritone was barely audible over the arming myriads of loyal angels. "Listen to me. Now has come the time when you must face the Scourge. Do not shrink from him, lest your fear fuel his rage. Be nimble of foot and flight of flank." He forced a smile through the worry lines creasing his hard face. "You've been taught by the Princes of Heaven. This is the culmination of your work in the Southlands. You're ready, and I have faith in you."

Alrak grinned, his jubilant spirit easing Michael's burden. In the frigid sunup, his emerald eyes waxed in ardor's brilliance. "Then why do you fear, Patriarch?" Michael couldn't find the words. Alrak casually shook his head. He laughed, his smoky tenor echoing through the crisp air. He threw his head back, blonde hair cascading down his pearly-armored cuirass. Michael pursed his lips. Alrak rapped his breastplate with his knuckles. "Don't make me an excuse for another bottle, you gnarled old knot."

"We have Fallen slingers inbound, Patriarch!" Nicolae warned.

Alrak instinctively unsheathed the cruciform meter of honed steel slung at his waist.

"No," Michael halted, waving down the cherub's weapon. Alrak lowered his broadsword and looked at his mentor, confused. "Find Weir and regroup with the Seventh Column. After that, link up with Melphax. Make sure he's shoring up some weak point on the Wall." Michael unfurled his wings. "I'm going to find Gabriel and recover the seraphim."

"Don't take long," Alrak warned. "Seventh Column or not, we can't hold them forever."

Michael's eyes darted from his protégé to the trenches of Fallen streaming from Mazerrel's camp. Their lines gleamed in the ice as the sunlight reflected off their massed shields and spears. "Just pray my brother hears my words, dandelion." With that, the archangel flew east, trailing the echelons and vanguards of seraphim.

Alrak lifted his chin at Nicolae. "Where do you want us?"

Nicolae fidgeted with his lamed tasset. He unsheathed his single-handed spatha then just stood there, staring at the rebel legions advancing through their shoveled networks.

Alrak grimaced. "Fine, we'll take the left." Nicolae nodded absently, transfixed by the enemy host. The roar of his color guard could be heard thundering up the stone-worked steps of the tiered battlements. They would be surrounding Nicolae in seconds. "Good luck, Commander. If you need me, just send word." Nicolae failed to respond. Alrak saluted anyway and was gone.

He darted through mustering blocks of line-fighters as they formed their maniples under the sun-hats. Trumpets blared, spurring the cherubic companies to their posts. Alrak found Weir and Ables dressing the lines of pearly-armored elites as they waited in formation on the up-armored courtyards behind the Wall.

Weir spotted him in the general mill. "Timetable, Polemarch?"

"They're at the plinth," Alrak replied. Weir cursed under his breath. Alrak admonished him with a glower. "Everyone's ordered to the Gate; it's a full call-up."

"Then let's get to it." Weir motioned to step off the line.

Alrak intervened. "Not us. We're posting on the left flank. Keep our reserves in the bailey."

"I suppose you're going to make me sit in the shade?" Weir said with a frown.

"Oh, I'm sure we can find a spot for you on the Wall," Alrak smiled. Weir perked up. They both looked at Ables, whose scrawny, scraggly form lingered at the sun-hat's fore. Alrak and Weir led the main force in flight to the ramparts, leaving a grumbling Ables with the reserves under the cover of their sun-hats.

When they crested the Wall, the Seventh Column beheld the Fallen marching against them. Fear captivated their hearts.

From his station, Alrak rounded on them. "Alright lands, six months ago, Mazerrel's Fallen toppled our defenses and killed Ellunias the Radiant. But we were not there; we could affect nothing!"

He scanned their faces. All glowing orbs were locked onto his spritely form. "The enemy breached our Gate once. Will the Seventh Column allow them to do it again?" A chorus erupted from the glimmering legion. Alrak grinned. "Then replace fear with faith and we'll turn this tide of blasphemous renegades on their heels!" A forest of spears oscillated in the fervor, heralded by seven thousand triumphant voices.

Alrak looked over the ramparts. Mazerrel's forces were coming under attack from the machicolation points. They hurled pitch bombs back at the Northern Defenders, the sticky flames billowing smoke over the Northern Wall. Gunners inside the Wall reeled from its effluvium. Alrak snarled and turned to Weir.

"We have to stall them." Without missing a beat his alabaster face whipped back to observe the amassing Fallen. He tested the weight of his sword and unslung his kite shield.

Weir groaned with resignation. "Am I to stay here?" There was no answer, only an impetuous cherub's prayer and a leap off the ramparts, wings fanning as he dove for the foe's columns. Weir hoisted his spear and turned to one of his seraphim. "Tell Lieutenant Ables that Polemarch Sivad has gone into the trenches to stop these buggers, and I'm going to make sure he doesn't raze the place with his gifts or get skewered in the process."

The Seventh Column seraph saluted and departed for the bailey. Weir could already hear the frantic sounds of combat wafting up from below. Somewhere down there, Alrak was carving up the enemy. Weir hoped he was lucky enough to convince the cherub of backup. He knew Mazerrel wasn't one to be trifled with and Polemarch Sivad had already gained a reputation of overconfidence.

Michael, however, was there for none of that. He pumped his wings under the soaring hordes of seraphim as they flocked to the East Gate. He landed on the stone-carved path of archways leading to the barbican's innards. Seraphim flooded around him, their officers taking census under the meridian sun. In the crush of teeming angels, he spotted no familiar cherubic faces. Pressing on past the seraphim, he burst through the bronze double doors of the armory. The seraphic guards stammered for him to halt but he paid them no heed.

The armory was a blockade of paperwork; gone were the weapons racks; the tiled floor was piled with towers of reports. Out beyond, the sea could be heard crashing against the shoreline just beyond the Eastern Wall. Michael saw Gabriel's slender frame meandering between the haphazardly stacked documents.

"So, the Archon has traded his trumpet for a shepherd's staff?"

Gabriel kept his nose buried in a scroll, flanked by towers of paperwork. "I don't want to hear it, Michael."

"And I don't want to say it," his brother replied, "but it looks like I have no choice. What are you thinking?"

"It was our determination that redeploying the seraphim to the East Gate in exchange for the cherubim stationed here would be a more judicious use of resources." Gabriel looked up from the scroll before moving on to another stack of papers. Michael trailed after him in the converted armory. "Are you here to report on my envoys?"

Michael tilted his head. "Envoys?"

"I sent epistles to Mazerrel," Gabriel said absently, busying himself with another ream of lists. "I thought if we could entreat with him, it might buy us time to pull in Lorinar's garrison for a pincer—"

"Mazerrel has begun his attack on the North Gate," Michael stated flatly. "No doubt whomever you sent to grovel before the Scourge has been flayed and cannibalized."

Gabriel looked up at him. His mouth opened for a trice before returning to his seraphic rosters. "I want to be prepared if there's a flanking attack from the sea."

"A seaside attack?" Michael sneered. "Look around you, Consul; no one would ever think to assault this fortress's choice beachfront property. Their landing craft would come under range of our artillery before they even reached the strand. Mazerrel is throwing his full force at the Northern Wall. If we don't repel him now, then they could be inside Zion by sundown. I have the Seventh Column and Melphax up with Nicolae, but it isn't enough, and you know it."

"You have *Raziel*," Gabriel said snidely as he plunged deeper into the stacked files. "What need have you of my meek seraphim?"

"Without reinforcements, they will fail, and you know it."

Gabriel wheeled on him. "You'll find no more sacrificial lambs in my flock, Michael. I've already given my golden fleeces to the altar of your bloody pride; I will relinquish no more. Surely,

Empyrean Falling

there's room in Hell for the likes of Keyleas, Mealdis, Ellunias and Ma'igwa to torture us for our sins against them."

"I think there's a special place in Hell for us if we dishonor their memory by cowering," Michael rejoined. "We've turned a blind eye for far too long."

"Would any of us have chosen this if we had known?" Gabriel mused. "We will be the stewards of sarcophagi and tombstones before this is over." He turned his back and wandered deeper into the lanes lined with crates of paper.

Michael lingered near an archer's loop. He stared out at the crashing waves, resilient against the winter cold. "The only merit it has is in the not knowing; it's our test of faith."

"Enough with the platitudes," Gabriel said. "I'd gladly stand in the gap of Hell's maw for His name." The ceiling rumbled with seraphim taking their newly assigned stations.

"Yes, but if He asked, would you order them to stand in that gap?" Michael challenged.

Gabriel sighed from across the room, checklist falling to his thigh. "If He asked? Yes."

His brother drew near. "He *has* asked, Gabe. The Three have been cognizant of this since before the founding of the West. It's the founding principle of the Eastern Kingdom. Otherwise, we'd never know the nature of evil, the wages of sin, or the temptation of power. Will you stunt your growth now, when all hangs in the balance?"

"And how do you expect me to grow?" Gabriel said. "By sending my choir to certain death in the teeth of our enemy? The Dragon is ravenous. How many do you think he'll devour before we defeat him, if we even can defeat him?"

Michael's face grew hot. "Proximity to Elder tiers has wormed cowardice into your heart, disguised as prudence."

"The Council has its purposes," Gabriel muttered.

"I don't suppose the likes of Metatron have given their blessing," Michael inquired, "to divert half our capable forces to a Gate whose very placement renders it impervious to assault?" Silence was his answer. "No, I didn't think so. Tell me, did you even give them the courtesy of divulging your intentions or did you just post the

Empyrean Falling

orders to your tribunes and let consequences be damned? I personally would've just done it," he said sarcastically. "It's easier that way."

"That's rich coming from you," Gabriel replied. "You tread upon honor's flagstones as if they were a path of vipers crushed beneath your dog-chompered jackboot. Asmodeus wasn't surprised to hear about Alrak's little escapade in the Southlands with seven thousand elites. Yes, brother, you have your secrets too."

"Then we're both drunk with the vices of our sins," Michael admitted. "I'm not perfect and neither are you. If anything, that should compel you to further virtues."

"Is not the preservation of life virtuous?"

"Every moment you elect to protect your seraphim is a heartbeat purchased by my cherubim's blood. Your misplaced virtue forces my choir to stand alone, and it's killing them."

"Your reckless feud with Morning star is killing them!" Gabriel boomed. "Do you even care about your choir, Michael?"

"I care enough to fight, Prince of Heaven."

Gabriel scoffed. "Tell me, brother, would you rather preserve those who have faith in your leadership, or would you rather win at any price, the weak drowned in this baptism by fire? Your conflict with Satan is nothing more than a competition with Lucifer. I won't abide such machismo, especially one that costs my choir their lives."

"No, *his betrayal* is costing them their lives!"

"Are we so sure that our ordained mission was to prove our fealty to God by staving off rebellion?" Gabriel sneered. "Perhaps Lucifer knew that all along. Perhaps this was his greatest gift to us: the fulfillment of our destiny."

"Our brother was a paragon," Michael said, his voice cracking as he fought back a sob, "but he was no martyr."

Gabriel crossed the lane to the archer's loop and stood next to Michael. He peered outside. "This War will claim us all."

Michael wiped an eye. "As stars burn and die."

Empyrean Falling

Chapter XII
"For I will defend this city to save it for Mine Own sake…"
—Isaiah 37:35

    Flurries fell on the Northern Wall. The snow mingled with the blood. Fires fed on angelic corpses. The Faithful were falling back. The North Gate flooded with Mazerrel's Fallen.
    Nicolae saw the horned glyph banners of the Scourge's legions stream over the ramparts. The afternoon sun was masked by a stinking haze, flights of winged rebels, and clouds of arrows darkening the sky.
    "Yews, to the fore!" Nicolae bawled from the front.
    The archers took up positions on the bailey and began loosing broadheads. The enemy's first- and second-rankers tumbled into the slush, the Wall turned wet by the heat of myriads of violent souls.
    Alrak watched the situation develop from his post on the left. The Seventh Column stood as a bulwark in a gale, their lugged war-lances dripping red before piles of Fallen bodies. He saw the Northern Defenders rout, leaving Nicolae and his color guard exposed.
    The Faithful cherubim had mustered in the bailey and re-formed their lines. Behind them, the supply depots were littered with wounded. Mazerrel's acrimony was fully realized as the medics

quickly ran out of water; the tainting of the Aphaea had rendered the Northern Aqueducts unusable. Nicolae gave the order to start repurposing sun-hats, carts and any debris they could salvage into a makeshift redoubt. Showers of arrows arced into the Fallen masses, drilling them by the thousands, but it did nothing to stem their terrifying tide as they came over the North Gate's barbican.

"Get to the gall-guns and sweep their lines!" Nicolae ordered.

The Faithful archers focused their fusillades onto the small antipersonnel battery emplacements along the Wall, clearing the way for courageous cherubim to rush in, swivel the crew-served launchers, and unleash their banks of projectiles into the enemy flanks. Scores of rebels thrashed in the muck, riddled by the javelins. Those legionnaires who stayed to reload and try again were hacked to pieces by the ravenous fiends of Mazerrel's cohorts. It was a desperate affair.

So superheated was the atmosphere around them that the snow turned to rain, spattering the pools of blood that ran rivers around charnel mounds of armored corpses.

"Captain!" Alrak shouted over the din. Weir turned to him, gore-splattered armor dripping red rainwater as he drew his lance from the throat of a rebel angel. "Put us in a wedge, double-front, and push on the Interim Commander's position!"

Alrak dodged a javelin that caromed off the bailey's flagstones at his greaved boots. He looked up to see what few Faithful peltasts remained engage in a furious duel, trading volleys as they nimbly maneuvered through the wet air. On the far right flank, he saw echelons of winged cherubim encroach on the North Gate. Alrak counted twenty-some-odd bands of flyers, all wearing the yellow tunics of the East Gate Garrison. They came in low and fast, swooping in to check the Fallen's advance with a shock-troop style attack. Mazerrel's horde caved to their assault just east of the bailey. Spears snapped in the clash as the cherubic reinforcements dove into them.

"Double-quick!" Weir shouted.

The Seventh Column leapt forward, their ordered ranks of pearly armor and bloody spears marching in time to a battle hymn. Out from behind the makeshift redoubts came phalanxes of Cognoscenti. They heard the glimmering elites' chorus and took up a madrigal paean. Into the promenade they surged. Their spears threshed the Fallen numbers, skewering them by the hundreds. Sans mercy or a slowing of pace, the scarlet-clad heavy infantry stomped over the rebel casualties, grinding them with their dog-chompers.

The two Faithful forces converged. They created a triangle of resistance that soon evolved into a mobile defense platform. Medics rushed into the protective gap to retrieve the wounded. But like the tidewaters flood around a strand, so too did Mazerrel's numbers come in behind this moving cyst of defenders, sweeping in and killing anyone they reached.

Alrak beheld Mazerrel's Fallen as they pressed upon his harried legion. From head to toe, they were covered in a paste of blood and ash. Their faces were mutilated with jewelry made of bone and jagged metal. They screeched from maws filled with teeth filed to points. Many bore tattoos of the glyph while some had faces stitched with bits of rotting flesh from their prisoners. They held no discipline, clawing and banging at the Seventh Column's shields with axes, mauls, spiked cudgels, war hammers, flails, maces and fighting knives. These were not the timid, untested legions of Belphegor's army. Nor were they the ordered ranks of Umbra Tempest's battalions. These angels were something mad, incongruous, deranged. Where they could not affect a breach by pulling away the Faithful's shields, they hacked at their lances until they shivered, forcing the Seventh Column legionnaires to draw their cut-and-thrusters. The knights called for spares but before Alrak could react, they had run dry, resorting to the close order tactics of the urban cohorts' thrusting.

The Faithful line-fighters ground their dog-chompers into runnels of blood, which sluiced through the broken flagstones of the promenade. Before them, the North Gate crawled with Fallen brethren like a hellish anthill spitting firebrands and slinger stones.

By the time Alrak linked up with Nicolae's color guard, they were about to be isolated in a sea of Fallen. His purple-caped retinue held in a circle while he commanded from the center. On the right, the yellow tunics of the Eastern Garrison had locked shields and were closing the gap. Alrak made his way into the protective ring of Nicolae's ward. He threw a quick glance south. The urban districts rose in snowy repose, waiting in silent, virginal dread.

Empyrean Falling

"We're going to be surrounded, Interim Commander!"

"We need to extend our line, Polemarch Sivad," Nicolae replied. "I sent orders for the Southern Garrison to be en route but—"

"Onagers inbound!" shouted their sergeant major.

Alrak turned to see incendiary rounds arc from the North Gate bartizans. The Fallen had commandeered the artillery and were turning them on the Northern Defenders. The fiery salvos unleashed havoc as plumes of pitch and shards of debris erupted at their greaves. Some of the Faithful were caught in the blasts, melting in their armor. The bailey turned into a conflagration.

The Fallen seized on this and took control of the North Gate's barbican, accessing the gears that allowed the giant portcullis to rise and the doors to swing open. Through this iron mouth vomited a crush of raving rebel angels, pikes in-hand and horns blaring.

"Extend the line and fall back!" Nicolae commanded.

Trumpets pealed over the deafening chaos. The Cognoscenti ground their way further on the left flank, while Weir ordered the Seventh Column to widen its front. On the right, the Eastern Garrison pushed back into ground they had already covered, fighting for every step against ten times their number. The whole line began a fighting retreat, that methodical rearward march that requires the utmost grit and disciplined resolve.

The rebels charged through the lapping flames, driven to a frenzy by the bloodletting and their own recalcitrant madness. More assaults from the captured artillery came in, smoking projectiles ejaculating from the Wall directly onto the Faithful lines. Hundreds died in the explosions. Weapons and charred bits of bodies shot around the loyalists as they backpedaled for the relative safety of the makeshift redoubts. The concentrated fire of the artillery hammered their position, killing them by the scores.

"Scatter!" Alrak barked as a concentrated volley shot for them.

The yellow tunics took flight south. Many of the Cognoscenti held their position, choosing to die on their own terms. The Seventh Column sprinted for the breastworks, knowing the air was deadlier than the ground. Alrak dragged a wounded legionnaire by his bevor to the secondary redoubt behind the sun-hats. He crouched behind the makeshift cover, wiping away sweat-matted locks.

When the Northern Defenders saw this, they lost heart and fled into the urban quarters of the Northern District. Furious fighting took place in the streets. Buildings burned. Holocausts of unmitigated fury followed for anyone who surrendered to Mazerrel's legions.

Alrak broke clear of the bedlam and found a bow and quiver. He sprouted his wings and shot high to a roof. He crouched behind the brick lip as arrows whistled past. To his right was a colossal cherub with a broad face and grey plate mail armor. He knelt behind the lip as well, plucking bits of flesh from his massive flanged war mace.

"Fancy seeing you here, Pillar of Iron," Alrak greeted cheerfully, "I hear you did quite well in Michael's poker game last week," he teased. Melphax stared at him, dumbfounded. "Who knows, might be able to afford another one of those journals I always catch you writing in."

"If we live that long," Melphax finally replied.

Alrak laughed and leaned over the lip's cover just long enough to loose an arrow. He ducked back down as several broadheads sang past him, so close as to take locks of his golden mane with them. He exhaled. "This is getting us nowhere."

"Use your gifts," Melphax urged. "We all have heard the stories. Send these buggers to the Burning Hells."

Alrak eyed him. "I can't control it. We need Michael."

"The Patriarch isn't here," Melphax countered. "If we wait for him to show up, we will surely die."

Alrak calculated the odds. "Okay," he said finally and threw a look back to the breastworks. He shot back over the lip and unleashed several arrows in quick succession. Melphax utilized the covering distraction and flung himself off the roof on broad fanning wings. By the time he glided down onto the makeshift redoubts, Alrak was right behind him. Melphax leapfrogged to Captain Weir's position, who stood guard over a wounded, delirious Nicolae.

"We have to clear the area," Alrak said as they sprinted forward, dodging murderous fusillades of arrows as he leapt over the rubble. "I've never tried to focus it before!"

"Weir, get behind the secondary redoubts!" Melphax shouted.

"What's going on?" Ables scowled.

Melphax began delegating recovery teams. "He shall sunder the earth and scorch the firmament!" he roared, pointing to Alrak as he maneuvered for the North Gate. "Tear flesh and purge sin, Raziel!"

Angels ran back and forth, relaying the message and pulling pockets of Northern Defenders from their last stands on the promenade. Even the Cognoscenti obeyed once they were told what was happening. Some chose to remain, making themselves targets of opportunity for the artillery so that the rest may escape.

When all were assembled, Melphax turned to Alrak. "The deck's been swept, Alrak! Let it rip!"

Weir tended to Nicolae. "I'll never get used to this," Ables moaned as he stuffed wads of cotton into his ears. Around them, the Seventh Column beamed in gleeful anticipation of Alrak's power.

Alrak darted to the crest of the breastworks. The promenade before him was ablaze with pitch fires under the dusk light. The bailey beyond was a landscape of stygian bogs and mesas of dead, lakes of blood pooling around the broken flagstones. Before him stretched the teeming throngs of Mazerrel's Fallen legions, a sea burning to crash upon him with murderous intent. Alrak's armor shone like a beacon in the fetid afternoon haze. He closed his eyes, knelt and prayed.

In a flash, it came. Faithful angels huddled behind their entrenched positions while static electricity crackled around Alrak. Light emanated from him until a distortion of blue energy overtook his petite form. It hummed and waxed, levitating his body above the grisly scene. Fire gathered at his feet. A tremendous thunderclap erupted. Jets of water spewed from the bricks, bursting enemy formations. The ground opened and swallowed dozens of the foe. Meteors fell from the overcast sky while pillars of flame shot from gaps in the tiles. Wind scoured the Fallen beneath bolts of lightning which cooked cohorts in their armor. No one looked. They did not have to; the noise told the tale. One could hardly hear the screams over the roar of Alrak's expulsion; it was a wholesale slaughter of cataclysmic proportions, an unquenchable elemental monster feasting on rebel meat. No one dared peek over the barricades.

Empyrean Falling

When the maelstrom ebbed, Alrak sank back to the breastwork, the cyclone of wind and fire dissipating. The flood of harrowing annihilation ceased as fast as it arose, leaving a vacuum of impenetrable silence in its wake. The Faithful's ears rang as they picked themselves up and hazarded a look. The promenade before them was a barren vista. Nothing moved. The piles of dead and pools of blood were washed away; only the bare, broken flagstones and cavities of bedrock remained. For the first time in winter, the golden streets of the promenade's courtyards were visible.

Beyond the busted Gate, they saw a carpet of detritus so thick with mangled flesh and armor as to rival the height of the Wall. Ragged guidons wafted in snaking tendrils of smoke.

Alrak stood at the summit of his impromptu talus, shoulders heaving as he breathed. Out beyond, all was still. Nothing moved.

Except one.

A shadow loomed in the Gate's barbican. Manifesting from the acre of swirling fog, a corpulent hulk sauntered in. Alrak saw it and uttered a word. "Mazerrel."

Weir, Ables and Melphax froze at the sight of his menace. The Scourge of the Faithful crossed the threshold into Zion. An instant later, the silence was broken by a noise from Alrak's direction, echoing throughout the thoroughfare. They broke from their trance to find him unfurl his wings and fly from his perch, sword drawn. It was all the officers could do to stand and watch, struck by the temerity of the Seventh Column Polemarch. The Faithful hazarded an emergence from their shelter. There was a rustle as the legions came back to life. Guttural barks of Fallen could be heard in the urban recesses.

"We still have work to do," Melphax declared.

They withdrew to the line of battered Northern Defenders and began the slow process of urban warfare, fighting building-to-building. They could hear the climactic duel still; it was enough to shatter any compunction they may have had to bear its witness.

Except for Melphax; he alone hobbled back to the North Gate. As twilight fell on Zion, so did its mirror of titian pitch fires turn to a warm glow. Ashen smoke choked the air. He wiped his eyes clear of their gunk and spat paste caking his mouth and clogging his nostrils.

Empyrean Falling

Lightning bolts struck the ruins of the Wall. Twisting wreathes of flame snaked into the firmament above the broken ramparts, punctuated by an enraged Mazerrel. Flashes of light blanketed the horizon, answered by Alrak's echoing grunts. They roared across the desolate wasteland of the barbican. Under the atmospheric reports, Melphax heard Alrak yelling and Mazerrel howling, spurring his impetus. To his right, the Seventh Column shone like a constellation as they protected the porous Wall. Farther back, he heard the smoldering crackle of fires feeding on the Northern Districts, the heat from their flames cooking his backplate.

Melphax arrived in time to see Alrak vault up onto a crumbled rampart, beckoning Mazerrel to commit with a sneering grin. The Scourge of the Faithful leapt upon the bulwark, propelled by membranous talon-tipped wings. A storm of biting metal and showering sparks erupted from their swords. When the two parted, they surmised one another and met again in a violent flurry.

Melphax saw them meld into a blur of pearly silver and rust, bathed in lightning and swirling plumes of fire. But it was the Bane of the Fallen who triumphed, breaking the Scourge of the Faithful and sending him flailing through a section of ramparts. The maniac coursed through the smoke until at last crashing into the Northern Plains, plowing up the soil until the bedrock raked his reeking flesh. He thrashed in defeat before rising to confront Alrak with a glare.

Alrak held atop the broken Wall while a beaten Mazerrel stared him down from his churned acre. Even at such a low and distant vantage, the Scourge exuded a potent menace. The two heaved beneath blood-splattered hide and dented armor. Yet just when Melphax thought the abomination would fan his wings and charge, the Fallen let out a bray of such blasphemous fury as to make every angel for a league tremble. The sulfurous rage enveloped his hirsute corpulence, summoned from his hooves. And when it ended, he turned and retreated into the clouds. Alrak watched him fade into the brume.

Mazerrel was a speck in the amethyst sky when Melphax got to Alrak's position. "What happened?"

Alrak's thin, flushed cheeks were a canvas of bloody scratches plastered with sweat and ash, billowing puffs from busted lips with eyes waned to jades. "He's fled," he breathed, "to continue the fight and prolong the inevitable. This will go on." He turned to Melphax. "We must pursue him. Tell Captain Weir to assemble the legion. We leave when they're ready."

Twenty minutes later, the Seventh Column was gone, several thousand elites leaving behind all but their weapons and whatever kits could be hauled under flapping wings.

Melphax propped himself onto a chunk of rubble. The stars winked above the desolation. Exhausted teams of medics scoured the veritable sauna which had become the bailey, tending wounds and sorting the living from the dead. Oxcarts trailed them. Melphax heard a pair of wings push the air behind him and furl into a backplate.

"I'll never get used to this," came a rueful, powerful baritone. "Such are the fruits of my labor."

Melphax slouched. Propriety had long since lost its appeal. Besides, his leg screamed in agony. "Another victory like this and we won't have to worry about our sorrows, Patriarch."

"I don't know which I fear more: the grave of defeat or the isolation of failure."

"If we fail," Melphax reminded, "even your protégé won't be enough to save us."

Michael pivoted to imbibe the scene. The bailey was pocked with scorched cavities, flagstones powdered in a semicircle fanning out to engulf the ruined barbican. Beyond the Northern Wall, a silent harvest of rebel corpses, salted in ash and marinated in blood, blanketed the churned fields. Patches of dead were so bloated, they burst. Others were burnt to a crisp, imploding into flaky piles.

Michael knew this handiwork. "Where is my dandelion?"

Melphax labored to face him, a sigh flooding from his barreled chest. He removed his helmet and wiped his large brow. "He's assembled his legion and gone after Mazerrel."

Empyrean Falling

Chapter XIII

"...thou shall not forsake him; for he hath neither part nor inheritance with thee."
—Deuteronomy 14:27

    Umbra Tempest watched them fly into the frosted heather. Their pearly armor was gore-encrusted but they moved with an uncanny efficiency as they bounded into the winter forest. He had tracked their flight for days as they headed into the frozen hinterlands north of Zion. The cold did not seem to affect them; they joked around campfires and maneuvered their several thousands with none of the chattering that plagued his own freezing legions.

    He thought of his brother Orean. Their bright mien reminded him of his twin sibling. He wondered where Orean was in that moment, if he were still alive, or if his insurrection's words had wormed into his brother's noble heart. A part of him missed Orean; Umbra Tempest knew what an asset his brother was. Having his twin watch his back with an extra set of spying eyes would have proven invaluable. But alas, the serpentine general worked with what he had.

    He left his army to roam the Northern Plains under command of his lieutenants, the Seven Serpents. Comprised mostly of cavalry, Umbra Tempest's legions were fast-movers but unable to maintain stealth for long periods of time. He let them work their havoc in the open tracts and grassy flats abutting the Hundred Foothills, rounding up Mazerrel's stragglers and harrying this unknown Faithful force.

These Faithful were chasing Mazerrel. And he had no intention of stopping them.

The Scourge of the Faithful had limped his way north towards the ruined Citadel of Glalendorf some days ago, with these elites nipping at his hooves. The reports from their captured survivors corroborated what Tempest saw he as spied on them. They were less than seven thousand, but they were formidable and uniform, with a spritely cherub for a leader. His golden mane and emerald eyes were striking enough, but what truly captured Umbra Tempest's attention was his charisma and expertise. Solace trailed in his wake. He addressed every angel's issue with eyes set like flint. He yawned through peals of laughter around watch fires and burned the midnight oil with tales and jokes. His legion adored him. Sometimes Umbra would find him sitting apart at night, observing their bivouacs with a glint in his exhausted jade eyes. First to rise and last to his bedroll, this unknown Faithful seemed nothing short of Lucifer reincarnated, endowed with all the training Michael had gleaned over the millennia.

What a prize he would have been for the Phoenix Empyrean.

He doubted the Dragon was aware of this protean, unparalleled legion. But information was the key to action. Thousands of routed rebels roamed the fields and forests, telling of the siege to anyone they met. Umbra had ordered his flyers to corral them for questioning, but this was a feint. He let his divisions be seen; they would channel this strange new group of Faithful along a path of his choosing. One angel could dissect them; ten myriads could not stop them. If this lone cherub could turn Mazerrel's siege, then he would wait.

Whitetail deer presaged them. He watched their flying chevrons enter from the gently rolling overcast horizon, intercut with fingers of woods and frozen creeks. He nestled into his perch in the leafless trees as their scouting party ranged past. As they bounded through the wooded upslope, Umbra listened, watched and waited.

"We could pursue this villain in our sleep," Weir said to Melphax, "were it not for the speed at which he moves and the cavalry roaming these hills."

"Still," Melphax replied as they maneuvered around trees, "we're vastly outnumbered here. Each step we take towards him is one that puts distance between us and Zion."

Alrak threw him a wry look. "Still thinking like a general."

Melphax winked. They heard flapping wings. All eyes shot up as they dove for cover. Umbra Tempest watched their vanguard vanish into the shadows of felled logs and snowdrifts. It was one of the rangers. The seraph touched down and furled his wings before approaching the formation. There was the hoot of an owl. Alrak answered with the call of a loon. The two crossed the interval and Alrak waved Melphax up.

Umbra Tempest crept closer. "Report," Alrak ordered. The seraph saluted then took a second to catch his wind. Alrak fidgeted, counterbalanced by Melphax holding off to the side, as a mountain endures a storm. No doubt Alrak's mind raced; Umbra Tempest could see his thoughts as he faced the violet sky burning on his right. He could smell the worry as their petite leader ran numbers, logistics, tactics and their overarching strategy.

Melphax placed a palm on Alrak's pauldron. He whipped around to lock eyes with the colossus. Though Alrak barely came up to Melphax's chest, Umbra Tempest noted the mutual respect in their posture. Melphax nodded. Alrak took a deep breath.

"Polemarch," the ranger breathed, "we found him."

Umbra Tempest watched Alrak light off with the ranger, leaving Melphax and Weir in the ravine with the rest of the legion. Dawn burned through the skeletal tree limbs. Melphax crested a hillock. A beat later, Weir was beside him, looking in the direction of Alrak's flight.

"I went last time, you know," Weir said to Melphax. "Besides, isn't that why our Patriarch sent you along?"

Melphax unlatched his war mace. "Looks like Michael has us both looking after his dandelion." Weir shook his head with a smirk. "Who are we kidding?" Melphax said with a burst of laughter, "I'm just here to make sure he doesn't get *you* killed!"

A trumpet pealed from the southeast behind them. Melphax turned to see another seraph circling above. Their rangers intercepted and escorted him to the wooded hillock. When he reached the officers, he bowed, tunic damp beneath a leather half-harness. "I come with an urgent dispatch from Zion." Melphax and Weir exchanged glances. "Archangel Michael calls for Polemarch Sivad to return to Zion."

"Under what pretense?" Melphax inquired.

"With all due respect, General," the messenger countered, "pretense is not my concern. I'm under orders from Consul Gabriel to escort Polemarch Sivad back to the Patriarch."

Umbra Tempest's ears perked at that. "A moment then," Melphax said. He touched Weir's elbow and the two receded out of earshot on the promontory's crest.

"This *does* come at the worst possible time," Weir groused, throwing a look to the messenger. Melphax huffed his compliance. "Mazerrel is caught. We can end this now, Mel."

"We've been away from Zion for nearly two weeks," Melphax observed. "Who knows what's happened? Events may require clandestine interdiction. Regardless, we're about to fall upon the Scourge, as Michael ordered." He spat. "This tries even my patience." Weir asked him what they should do. Melphax exhaled. "We break the news gently." Weir groaned. "Let him rage against me. I can weather his *sturm und drang*."

Weir stuck his chin out. "Too late."

Alrak came in low over the spindly limbs and dawn-scorched horizon, accompanied by a squad of Seventh Column seraphim. The crimson morning rays made their panoplies gleam like a prismatic galaxy as Alrak touched down on the crest, eyes burning at the news.

"Ables has him," he squealed. "He's holed up in Glalendorf. The rangers are surrounding the ruins now, but we must get the legion into position before I can pounce. Captain, put our cohorts into a concentric posture around the northwest flank. Keep hidden until my signal. When Mazerrel sees the approach, he'll think himself cut off and try to double back. That's when I'll intercept." Alrak's smoky tenor raced. "General, you should come in behind me and circle to the northeast side; ensure Mazerrel doesn't give us the slip. I'll need to know if there are any hidden passages; after all, it was built millennia before my incarnation."

Melphax and Weir held stoic through his orders.

"Alrak," Melphax said.

"He's bound to spot us if we linger," Alrak continued. "I'll need you to muster the Seventh as soon as you can."

"Alrak," Melphax tried again.

"There isn't a moment to lose—"

"Alrak!"

"What?" the archangelic protégé roared, face red and eyes drilling through the colossal angel.

Tension swelled over the summit before Melphax regained his composure. "There's word from Zion," he said soothingly, indicating the messenger behind them.

Alrak peered around Melphax's broad shoulder. "Who's that?"

The seraph bowed. "Consul Gabriel's aide-de-camp Zophiel, Polemarch." He rose to address the cherub. "I come with a dispatch from Archangel Michael. He says—"

"The message orders you back to Zion, Alrak," Weir burst.

"Very funny," Alrak chuckled. "Who put you up to this? Was it Ables? Melphax? Quite the joke, you two."

"It's no joke," Melphax declared. A smile clung to Alrak's face. The Pillar of Iron rubbed his stubbly cheeks. Behind him, Zophiel sighed with exasperation. "We've already argued the point, Alrak. His credentials are valid. Michael has ordered your return."

Alrak's mouth went slack. Umbra Tempest grinned behind his concealment. "What perverse ruse is this, General?" Melphax blinked. Alrak folded his arms. Blonde locks cascaded over his jaded lamps. "We're on the cusp here, Zophiel," he fumed, raking curled strands from his face and pinning them behind his ears to reveal a chevroned brow. "You don't understand what you're asking of me."

"I'm not asking," Zophiel said, "the Archangels are *ordering*." Zophiel's button nose went up. "Is this not a test of faith, Polemarch?"

At that, all presented groaned in annoyance.

"Two weeks pissed away on a fruitless chase," Weir spat, scratching a scruffy neck. "We've abandoned Zion for nothing."

Melphax focused on Alrak. "Not vanity. Obedience."

It did nothing to abate Weir's balking, but the Bane of the Fallen knew how to roll with the punches. "He's right," Alrak admitted, chewing his lip as he scowled at the turf. "Melphax, take the Seventh and keep pursuing Mazerrel, but don't engage. Weir will assist you." His gaze shifted south to Zion. He motioned to Zophiel and the two leapt into the air. Alrak held for a brace of heartbeats, lips pursed with the mocking baritone of satire and a flamboyant, mocking posture. "I shall return."

Moments later, he was lost to sight. Weir and Melphax held their humored vigil. Unbeknownst to them, Umbra Tempest had slinked away. His mission was complete, for the time being.

"Well," Weir said with a mischievous grin, "what do you say we hound an abomination?"

Melphax holstered his mace. "You're going to have to show me how to lead this princely band of swashbucklers, Captain. I'm not convinced they can handle my old school ways."

Weir peeled a roguish grin, "Oh, we might surprise you."

"Your lads look awfully pretty in your shiny new armor and your spiky black hair. You think they can keep up with an old salty stump like me? Are they willing to get those fancy new digs dirty?"

Weir flashed pearls and winked. "Try us."

Empyrean Falling

Chapter XIV
"When thou goest out to battle against thine enemies, and seest horses, and chariots, and a multitude more than thou, be not afraid of them: for the Lord thy God is with thee…"
—Deuteronomy 20:1

Michael slouched in one of his office chairs, massaging his forehead. On the desk before him lay a dingy papyrus map of Lucifer's Island. At his back was a bronze gong, placed in a wooden brace. Gabriel paced the tiles on the other side of his desk. Michael leaned on the corner of the map, face flushed as he mulled over trite details and rehashed debates. Their quarreling had persisted for two hours and, aside from telling Gabriel about Alrak and the Seventh Column, nothing had been accomplished.

A part of him was grateful just to have his little brother in the same room. He had sent so many petitions over the past weeks that his pages ran out of paper, each met with cold silence. The pain of lost seraphim was too much to bear in the face of an archangel who would only ask him to risk more. Michael's relief was incalculable when Gabriel finally did appear, yet it wasn't enough to split the wedge between them. The air hung thick in their congress.

"Consolidate our lines," Gabriel argued. "What use is holding the Wall only to field legions that get slaughtered like what happened at the Aphaea?"

"They're weakening," Michael said through a yawn. "They've been met with a slew of defeats. It won't be long before their constitution wavers."

"And are you prepared to be wrong?"

"Their pride won't cloud their judgment forever."

"No," Gabriel said, "but their detachment from the Lord will. The Council has seen the prisoners we've taken. The Fallen are becoming deranged." Michael eyed him wearily. "Look, all I'm saying is that you've defied the Council enough, and it's cost us."

"How, Gabriel?" he scoffed. "I've fielded the Seventh Column and, as a result, Belphegor's legions are destroyed. I broke Mazerrel's hold on the Aphaea. I sent Gilgamesh and Galeth to destroy their supply depots on the islands, and they've been met with success."

"You mean the ones you haven't heard from in a month?"

Michael pinched his nasal bridge. His fatigue gave way to morosity. "One from their expedition *has* returned. He bore grave news. I've tried to maintain faith but…"

"They're gone, aren't they?"

"The Lightning Legion has been destroyed."

"I suppose you have faith in Alrak too," Gabriel said. "Yet you reserve this confidence from the Elders? What mistakes they have made have been of the head, not the heart."

"They don't know war," Michael rebuffed, "Their conservatism will only get us picked apart. We must pursue Satan, especially now that Mazerrel's army has been routed." Gabriel reminded him that Mazerrel had a myriad's worth of survivors. "That doesn't bother me. What has me vexed is the Dragon's absence. He started this; why has he kept himself hidden?"

"Perhaps he felt his armies wouldn't be able to raze the Holy City?" Gabriel proffered.

"No," Michael frowned, "there's something more at work here. Something I'm missing."

A guard knocked at the door. Michael and Gabriel turned to face it. "Polemarch Alrak Sivad is here, Patriarch," the guard said.

"Admit him," Michael answered.

Alrak entered and stood before the archangels, arms crossed and jaw firmly set. He exuded a radiance, despite the glare burning in his lamps. His aura was aflame. Michael eyed him while Gabriel smiled wanly, perched with a foot braced against the corner.

"You're upset, I know," Michael began. "I've had reports on the progress of your hunt so spare me the rant. Trust me, I know."

Alrak ground his teeth. "Then why am I here?"

"You're aware of the Lightning Legion's infiltration into the 'Dragon's Lair', right?" Alrak nodded. "Well, I haven't heard from them in weeks: no carrier ravens, no seraphim, nothing. They've always somehow managed to get word to me, but when they stopped…well, I've tried not to concern myself with things I can't change, but yesterday my worst fears were confirmed. Gilgamesh and his Thunderbolts have been rooted out and slain."

A twinge of remorse cracked Alrak's indignant façade. "Again, I ask: why am I here?"

Michael rubbed his bleary eyes. "You know of the cherubic twins, Uriel and Nuriel?"

Alrak nodded. "Couple of gatekeepers, right?"

"What else do you know?" asked Gabriel from their flank.

Alrak turned to him irascibly. "That they were endowed with a talent for the manipulation of brimstone, big deal."

"They're masters when it comes to fire," Michael corrected. "And they're not just gatekeepers, Alrak; they hold the Keys to Hell."

"I never understood the reason for creating the Burning Hells in the first place," Alrak said. "I mean, why build a fiery prison? Just destroy the Dragon outright?"

"The answer seems obvious now," Gabriel observed. "Lucifer is Satan. The Morning Star is the Dragon. None of us have the power to destroy him; he must be contained."

"Hell must remain under our dominion," Michael added. "It is an utmost priority." He directed Alrak to a chair near his desk. "Sit, dandelion. We have much to plan."

Alrak acquiesced and plopped into the seat with a sigh. "So, what is it about these wonder twins that warrants me flapping all the way back here?"

"Uriel," Michael announced, "turned to the black flame of Satan. Nuriel, however, remained in the light, serving in the Lightning Legion. I fear he's either dead or captured. If that's the case, then Satan may find a way to gain access to the Gates of Hell."

"Which lead to Earth," Gabriel interrupted.

"And to Humanity," Alrak finished with a nod. "I see where this is going."

Michael stared at him. "If the Dragon gains access to the Gates then nothing we've done will matter; he'll roam free for all eternity or until Father intervenes. If he gains access to Earth, he'll kill the humans. We must preserve them at all costs, Alrak. We must secure the path to Hell."

"That's why I forsook the killing of Mazerrel," Alrak sneered, "to go on some rescue mission for an angel who is already dead?"

"An effort must be made," Michael tried. "I doubt more than a hundred of Gilgamesh's angels live, yet if Nuriel is among them, he must be found. You have to bring him back to us."

Alrak rose intractably in his seat. "Assuming the Seventh Column can be recalled in time, who's to say we'll be able to forge through the enemy-infested Northern Plains? Mazerrel's army may be shattered but we've heard nothing from Umbra Tempest since his early winter siege. All reports indicate he still controls the Northern Plains. It's because of him and his infamous Seven Serpents that we're holed up in our garrisons. Evading the cavalry and flyers of the one who mastered stealth will be difficult. I know; the Seventh has been doing it for weeks now.

"And even if we did," Alrak continued, "how are we to navigate the waters of Lucifer's Island? Assuming we can cross that leviathan-infested channel, where do we beach? Where was the Lightning Legion's last confirmed location? What about supply dumps for refits? Satan may be using his 'Lair' as a staging ground, but that doesn't mean they'll have the resources we need. And whatever millions of Fallen reside on the mainland, there are thousands more gearing up in his stronghold.

"It's an arduous campaign you ask of me, mentor. And if by some miracle we're able to track and rescue Nuriel, how will we affect our escape? Every bit of turf covered in infiltration will have to be retread; our return will be chock full of enemy legions deploying or maneuvering." His eyebrows shot for his scalp as he drew to the edge of the chair. "In short, the endeavor is unfeasible."

Michael's response was swift and assured. "You're right, dandelion. The scenario you've described is unfeasible. The Seventh Column can't marshal in time to deploy and they cannot infiltrate."

"Then for the last time," Alrak fumed, "why have I been severed from my legion?"

"Because," Gabriel replied matter-of-factly, "they're not going." Alrak blinked at him. "It'll be too tricky sneaking an entire legion through Fallen held territory."

"So, what am I supposed to do?" Alrak shrugged. "Word has it that Satan has mutated the topography into some perverse den. Am I to waltz into the heart of darkness alone?"

"Not exactly," Michael replied. "There's one who can successfully invade that apostate domain."

"Oh, good," Alrak muttered with a dour smirk, "reinforcements."

Michael turned and rang the bronze gong. A guard appeared. "Bring me the veteran."

A small, surly cherub made his way stiffly into the War Room. He was shorter than Alrak, with a permanent scowl and a topknot that hung to his waist. A deep scar ran the length of his cheek, vanishing into his grizzled goatee. Alrak spotted a dozen wounds, no doubt with a dozen more concealed beneath his battered, rusty field plate.

"Alrak," Michael said, "meet Shiranon. As far as we can surmise, he alone has survived the Dragon's Lair, and is all that's left of Gilgamesh's task force."

For the next hour, the four laid out their plan. Alrak's hazards were corroborated by Shiranon's testimony. The veteran irregular annotated Michael's maps for him. But there was another aspect of the operation that was revealed by Shiranon: Uriel was being held captive.

"Nuriel often spoke of it," Shiranon said. "He wept for his brother who danced on the edge of darkness. In the end, he was held prisoner by Umbra Tempest. He figured it was a failsafe. The wily assassin had orchestrated a contingency in case a backdoor to Hell was needed. Nuriel hoped to rescue him during our mission."

Michael perked at the proposition of saving the Fire Twins. For once, it seemed things moved in the Faithful's favor.

When the plan was finalized, the two angels departed, albeit under a cloud. Michael's stomach twisted at the thought of again ordering his protégé to dive into the teeth of death, but that was the price of excellence; his blessing was the curse that might doom him.

A heavy silence hung between the archangels after Alrak and Shiranon passed the War Room's threshold. Michael stared at the ornate doors, their shadowy hollow infesting his spirit with dread.

"He hasn't failed you yet," Gabriel murmured. "He has experience and now he has Shiranon."

"Maybe you're right. Shiranon's luckier than a cat."

"I'm sure some of those lives will rub off on our little Raziel."

"Perhaps," Michael said and returned his attention to the map.

Gabriel came around behind Michael. "Besides, there are more pressing matters."

"What do you mean?"

Gabriel rang the gong. "Guard," he called with preternatural force, "alert the Zealots." He rounded the desk and faced his brother, forcing a steely gaze.

Michael looked in confusion as the Elders Camiel, Azriel, Asmodeus and a dozen Cognoscenti filed into the circular War Room, bearing grim faces. He discerned the scene unfolding before him, suspicions confirmed by the shackles in Azriel's hands and the reluctance in his sad eyes. He turned to Gabriel and matched his gaze.

"Forgive me," Gabriel sighed, "but the Eastern Kingdom hinges on law and order; you must be held accountable for what has been done beyond the shadow of the Council's aegis."

Michael stared at Gabriel in disbelief. In a flash, he clutched the maps and flung them to the floor. He shot to his feet. "This is how you repay my labor, with accusations of treason?"

Gabriel backed away from his brother's rage. "The laws have been broken, Michael! Your pride has made you a hypocrite!"

"So, you'll bind and sentence me because I know how to wage war better than the bureaucrats?" Michael fumed. "Tell me, who will stand against the Phoenix Empyrean while I rot in a cell?"

"We shall find a way," Asmodeus crooned. "But the law is explicit. He who does not submit to our authority must answer to the prescribed judgments. You will stand trial."

Michael rounded the table and eyed the troupe one by one. "Very well." He presented his wrists, staring at Gabriel. Azriel advanced with a stiff gait while the Cognoscenti enveloped them. Michael made no motion to resist, holding silent as the manacles were fastened to his cuffs. He glared at his crestfallen brother as the irons clamped down. With the chains secure, the Zealots escorted Michael out of the War Room, a dreadful silence in the entourage's wake.

Alone and absent the heart to follow their procession, Gabriel shuffled over to the desk. He reached down and plucked the torn maps from the tiles. He sat in the chair and began poring over them. He rifled through stacks of papyri. But his concentration failed and, before he knew it, he was hiding his sobs in his hands and crying out to Parakletos. Whether it was for forgiveness, strength or mercy, he could not articulate. But he wept and prayed, all the same.

Empyrean Falling

Chapter XV

"...and be sure your sins will find you out."

—Numbers 32:23

  Michael stood on the Council Chambers' dais, surrounded by the stone-carved tiers. Seated in their marble thrones and robed in resplendent garments and shimmering tiaras, the Council of Elders watched in silence as the Sword of God presented himself, shackled and cascaded in the long amber rays of the afternoon sun. Dust motes illuminated in their waft across Michael's face as the Elders assembled their notes and hushed their last minute dialogs with one another. When all was prepared, Metatron rose to address the congress. He summoned their attention with a rap of knuckles.
  "Let us not waste time with idle torment, but hasten to our task so the grief of our judgment may be assuaged." He motioned to the attorney angel with a resigned sigh. "Make thy case, Eldar Sariel."
  The prosecuting angel descended from his throne and stood next to Michael, a scroll in his hand. "Cleave the iron of my will and you will know no trial vexes my heart more than this." His steady voice carried across the assembly. "But we must perform our duty." He unraveled the scroll. "Let us catalog the details of this archangelic treason and be done with the matter.

Empyrean Falling

"For keeping the insurrection of Lucifer a secret," Sariel continued, "for the clandestine raising and tutelage of Alrak Sivad; for the deployment of the Seventh Column into the Southlands; for acting in violation of the Council's judgment and usurping Consul Gabriel; for sending Ural's Battle Group Concordia to their deaths on the Aphaea; for leaving Zion's walls to punish Mazerrel; for allowing Gilgamesh and his Thunderbolts to launch an unsanctioned raid on the Dragon's supply depots, which resulted in their destruction; and for ordering Alrak Sivad and Shiranon on a rescue mission without first presenting the proposal to the Elders for confirmation…for all these indiscretions, we, the Council of Elders, elect Sons of God and the ruling governmental body of the Eastern Kingdom, hold Archangel Michael, the Second Born Cherubim Patriarch, the Lion and Sword of God, in contempt and violation of his princely station. We motion to declare him a traitor." Sariel's luminescent eyes could barely meet Michael's as he finished and departed his archangel's proximity.

Metatron stood again. "Verily, let the minutia of these charges be laid upon the altar. The floor stands ready to receive those compelled by Parakletos to speak."

Asmodeus wasted no time descending to the dais. Barely had his soles touched the base before his liquid tenor was crooning. "How thou art fallen in this dire hour, Archangel. Tell me, do you feel responsible for the carnage which drowns us, beating our host as a galley in a gale?"

"I've done all that I can to stem the tide, Eldar," Michael responded coolly.

"And yet you've lied to this Council, kept secrets from the Heavenly Host, and worked to cover both Lucifer's transgressions and thine own. Tell me, why should you be absolved of these crimes and not banished to the West? And spare us the maxim that without your guidance, we would lose this war. It has been Gabriel's decisions, based on our congress, that have kept these hallowed precincts secure. We have triumphed while you have plotted and schemed."

Before Michael could proffer his apology, Beliel spoke. He stumbled down the steps. His blushed countenance tried to focus on the blurry image of his archangel as he entered the dais. "Would I allow this grievous pursuit to transpire void of my rebuttal, I'd not be a cherub but a mongrel that hath spurned its master."

"Spare us thy misplaced fealty, Eldar Beliel," Asmodeus scorned. "Return to thy throne to wet thine pipe with the spoiled nectar of vice."

"Eldar Asmodeus," Metatron reprimanded, "honor Eldar Beliel and permit him to speak."

"It would be a dishonor for me to allow such drunken babble to foul our halls," Asmodeus rejoined. "I only seek to preserve our dignity." Asmodeus turned to Michael as the lush Beliel retreated to his throne. "Archangel, what defense can you provide for committing the very sins of treason that you've sworn to abolish? Convince us you are not a villainous renegade such as thy eldest sibling."

"Lucifer has Fallen into pride," Michael said.

"Ah, yes," countered Asmodeus, "but was there not some way to dissuade the Morning Star from the desecration in his heart? You of all should know how to divine that path."

"I never knew the depth of my brother's wound," Michael shot back, timidity purged by his temper's flare. "Who could divine the heart of the First Born?"

"Yet in all thy ages of fellowship, thou never saw this heresy?" Asmodeus asked.

"I knew of his discontent and estrangement," Michael replied. "But to insinuate revolt was unheard of; he led us out of the West. How were we to indict him? No, I tell you, Eldar Asmodeus, I didn't see this coming any more than any of you."

"Yet thou attempted to hide it from us until the very tiles of the Hallowed Causeway were drenched in blood!" Asmodeus fumed.

"I tried to spare the angelic host the pain of error," Michael said. "What if Lucifer's intention wasn't to rebel? Would our race ever recover? Could you ever trust the Three again?"

"At last, a worthy chord to strike upon in this tone-deaf apology," Asmodeus lilted. "But tell me, if presented the fortune, would you set upon the same course again?"

"With all my essence, no," Michael confessed.

"Aha!" Asmodeus barked, jabbing a finger at the archangel. "Then you admit the fault?"

Michael snarled at him. "I admit the failure but not the intent!" His booming voice caught them off guard. Even bound and void of armament, the archangel's flare had power behind it.

"You are overstepping your bounds, Elder Asmodeus," Metatron warned from his highest seat. "Eldar Sariel is our resident accuser. Allow him to do the questioning."

"My zeal doth hath the grip of me," Asmodeus acquiesced smarmily. He folded his thin arms into the sleeves of his red robe.

"An agreeable observation," Metatron grumbled from his throne. "Nevertheless, it is Eldar Sariel's duty to perform the rites of prosecution."

Asmodeus withdrew from the dais. Sariel appeared in his wake, hands clasped to his burgundy robe and his nose pointed at the tiled floor. A handful of stiff heartbeats passed as he summoned his faculties. "You have trained your entire life to combat the threat of the prophesied Dragon, yes?" Michael replied that he had. "And yet in all that time, did it not occur to you that perhaps the very creature who could presume to threaten the Eastern Kingdom was the most exalted created being?" Michael only sighed and drooped, his topknot falling across his chest. "Who else could wage war on God and hope to achieve any meaningful victory, save he who is unequaled in majesty? Surely you were suspicious?"

"How could such a thing ever find a foothold amidst our friendship?" said Michael.

"But surely there were signs."

"We would forgive them, as any loving sibling would."

"And what was Gabriel's opinion of Lucifer over recent millennia? Did he call into question certain dubious clues as to First Born's nature?"

"Of course," Michael replied with a flippant shrug, "and I would summarily defuse them."

The Council launched into an uproar.

"Because of my love for him, I chose a blinding path!" Michael shouted over them. "Not even Gabriel could give voice to the splinter of fear in our hearts. Not in our wildest nightmares did we portend Lucifer becoming Satan. We knew something was dreadfully wrong, but who dared to lay bare so deep a wound? We loved our brother, yes; but we feared him as well."

"So, you abstained?" Sariel inquired.

"We felt it wasn't our place," the archangel replied, "that it was a matter to be dealt with by Father. He was above us, if even by a hair's breadth it may as well be an impassable gulf. That's why I've taken every offensive posture I could, because we're given precious few chances for victory over Satan and his enthralled one third."

"And yet thou continue to heap sins upon thyself," Asmodeus shot from his throne.

"Silence thy tongue, Eldar Asmodeus," said Metatron. "You've spoken your peace. We need no more dictums from you at the moment." He turned to the dais. "Continue, Eldar Sariel."

The Elder attorney bowed to Metatron. "If you elect to follow Father's will," he said to Michael, "and you truly doth love our Deity, then surely thou shalt elect to honor the establishment He hath ordained for our Eastern Kingdom?"

"Not when it moves in vanity, as a blinded cripple drowning at sea," Michael replied, eliciting another crescendo from the tiers of Elders. "I merely wish to convey that my judgment on warfare is more astute than anyone before me. It's your job to make policy and govern the everyday affairs of the angelic host; it's my job to prepare them for the day when those policies come under threat from the Dragon."

"And is this the only prophecy for which we should ready ourselves?" Sariel asked.

"No," Michael answered, "there's the Prophecy of the Drowning Sky, the Prophecy of the Thorned Shepherd, and the Prophecy of the Broken Gate, just to name a few."

"And will you seek to counter our judgments when these conflicts arise?" Sariel inquired.

"If you fail to act as needed," Michael said, "yes." Another torrent of discontent flooded the delegation. "If you choose ill paths then I'll course correct. I'm no keeper of scrolls; I'm a warrior and by faith, one day, a soldier. Into you I trust our rites; into me, you must trust our protection. We are at war. Let me lead us to victory."

"Thou truly think thou knoweth better than we?" Asmodeus spat, his eyes flaring.

"In matters of crusade? Absolutely."

"And what of your brother?" Sariel continued. "Are we to allow thou undermining schemes to perpetuate, though they dishonor the Archangel Gabriel, who hath been elected Consul of the Eastern Kingdom's legions?"

"My brother is not equipped to be war chief," Michael replied flatly. "He can't order his angels to their deaths. Instead, he works to preserve their lives out of avarice. You knew this when you elected him Consul." Michael's chest swelled. "You'll lose this war; we'll pay for your lack of self-esteem and your arrogance!"

"Enough!" Metatron ordered demonstrably with a hum. The soundwaves pierced Michael in a state of paralysis. Azriel moved to his side, ready to sequester him. "I shall not allow our tongues to work spiritual violence against each other. Not from the Elders, and not from you, Archangel."

"What of the task force of irregulars led into the Dragon's Lair at thine behest?" asked Camiel. "Reports indicate their tongues have been withheld from Zion's ears. Their deaths are rumored in our halls. Wasn't this assignment another one of thine clandestine progenies, Archangel Michael?"

"Indeed, it was," Michael replied. "We were aware of the exigencies. Gilgamesh was tenacious in his pursuit of nomination, to the point of offense if I did not give it to him. The failure is ultimately mine, I know. But not every battle can be a victory, Eldar Camiel."

"What oath canst thou swear that such a costly disaster shan't befall us again?" the angelic judge asked rhetorically.

"None, Eldar Camiel," Michael replied. "But the longer we cower, the more deprived of resources we become. With the tainting of the Aphaea, we're left with precious few options. We will wither behind these towering Walls while Satan's lieutenants reeve the fertile leagues before us."

"And I suppose thou would risk an offensive campaign to rid this Council of the threat."

"Yes, Eldar Asmodeus," Michael replied. "If we sit and linger, we will only be waiting to die. But if we move to crush them in the open field, force them to commit to battle…"

"We shall leave Zion open to attack!" Asmodeus snapped.

"The Archangel makes a worthy point, Eldar Asmodeus," Metatron stated. "Nearly a year ago it was impossible to see but, now that we hath witnessed the objectives of the Dragon and his forsaken kin, we can behold the Sword of God's insight."

"Verily, but it doth not ebb the treacherous tides of war," Camiel observed. "Archangel Michael must atone for his crimes."

"Are they truly crimes?" Michael petitioned. "I've worked against the Council, yes, but for a greater good sanctioned by Father, especially concerning Alrak and the Seventh Column."

An outrage erupted that eclipsed all others. Michael's pleas were drowned in the storm of reprobation. Foremost was Agni, the mediator between the angels and God.

"How dare thou use Father's name in vain!" Agni decried. "I motion to have Eldar Azriel bind Michael and lock him away in the deepest recesses of the West. Exile him for blasphemy!"

"Our Archangel has fallen into delusion," shouted Asmodeus, "following the spiral of his eldest kin. Head Eldar Metatron, compel Eldar Azriel to silence him before our spirits are befouled by further violations of the tongue!"

"Shall we pluck the finest stock from our royal stable?" slurred Beliel. "Are we to assume that faith alone will carry us when we sever the greaved boot upon which we stand?" Grumbling rebuttals rose. "Michael taught us the virtues of bronze and steel. He's our chieftain, second only to First Born, whose traits were sundered by nobility's vice. Lucifer was Heaven's pride, but Michael is Heaven's valiant. Let us not be so quick as to cast away that heroic blade. Set a penance for him but don't forsake Michael as Lucifer forsook us."

"Get thee gone, thou cherubic churl," Asmodeus sneered. "And leave the labors of Heaven to those who are not mired in the vice of vines."

"A stiff drink would do us all well this day, Eldar Asmodeus," Metatron stated plainly. "But Eldar Beliel posits a goodly avenue of recompense. However lamentable such actions are, they must unto this day be held aloft." He regarded the tiers, a measure of levity coming over him. "Who among us could predict such truths would come from the mouth of one so boorish as our Eldar Beliel? I'd wager even the pious Eldar Urim could not have divined that."

"And what does our charitable oracle say?" Camiel asked. "Advise us in this darkened hour, Eldar Urim. What canst thou divine from Parakletos? Are we to excuse the accused or is it Father's wish to ascribe some punishment upon Archangel Michael?"

Urim sat silent and still in his marble cathedra. A gravitas fell upon the Council Chambers. He steepled his fingers to his thick lips, shimmering eyes waning as he focused on the voice whispering within. "The will of the Elders is a translation of Father," he said. "But Father is above us. If Michael declares that a holy reprieve was granted to him in the matter of Alrak's deployment with the Seventh Column, then I believe it best to trust him. His actions were done through conviction, not vice or vainglory. Let us prescribe this function: that Michael be sent forth from Zion, equipped in his panoply and accompanied by whatever force we decree. And he shall not be permitted within the Gates again until he stands victorious over the Dragon, or is interred in the Memoriam with his slain choir."

"Do not give the felon a single cohort," Asmodeus decried. "Thou shalt only condemn those who take up his lionhearted banner."

The other Elders disagreed, electing to equip Michael with a force to satisfy his vision for victory.

"What will the Council bestow then," Michael asked, ignoring Asmodeus, "so that I might conquer our foes?"

Asmodeus rose in his throne and glared at Michael. "Hath our lofty chants confused thee?" he raged. "Perhaps we should summon a page and transcribe it so that our thoughts may truly be conveyed on what is transpiring this day?"

"I only plead for a count of my legions so that I may know what tactics to employ," Michael said with forced humility.

"Legions?" Asmodeus repeated. "No, if thou be so desperate to violate our mandates and sally forth, then a single legion thou shalt have. And I surrender that much out of protest." Affirmations abounded from all save Metatron and Beliel, one too stricken with grief and the other too succumbed with drink.

"What can I do with a single legion?" Michael inquired indignantly. "Give me fifty myriads and I will defeat Satan."

"Never," snarled Asmodeus.

Michael set his jaw. "Give me twenty myriads, and I'll end this War for the Throne."

"Denied, Archangel."

Michael ground his teeth. "Give me twenty thousand and, in my desire to fulfill Father's will and please you patricians, I'll not return until our Enemy lies broken atop a mountain of his disciples' corpses. This I swear before you and Father, upon my release."

Asmodeus locked gazes with Metatron. Michael watched a silent debate unfold between them. All assaulted Metatron with some collective opinion, which he sternly rebuked. But when his eyes fell from theirs, it was apparent that the majority had won the mute debate. The Head Elder turned and stood from his elevated throne, looking down at Michael.

"Give the Archangel a campaign legion," Metatron said with a heavy tone, "and send him off." He turned to Michael. "Archangel, you may plead guilty to the crimes and accept this task force, or you may plead innocent and face the consequences of exile."

For many moments, Michael contemplated. He looked at them each in turn until their gazes broke from his. Shackled, they knew his power. "Guilty."

Metatron struck the arm of his throne, the resounding noise confirming the Council's judgment. "One campaign legion it is."

"Now be rid of this assembly," Asmodeus ordered. "Take thy fifteen thousand and get thee gone from our hallowed sight, and further not our harrowing plight."

Azriel removed Michael's manacles. The Cherubim Patriarch strode from the dais, his countenance held as high as could be managed under the weight of such an oath.

Empyrean Falling

    The trek back to Michael's mansion was filled with prayers. Even with his tactician's mind, fifteen thousand against Satan's millions was suicide. As he donned his panoply, he wondered who it would be that would elect—or be elected—to follow him. He prolonged the endeavor of preparation in his mansion; chances were he would never see his home again. He touched every weapon and ran a hand along every piece of furniture. For the first time, the trials ahead broke his heart in trembling fear. Trepidation gripped him and he fell against the terraced balcony, raising his arms to God.

    "Dear Lord," he wept, "abstain not from my spirit! I have been beaten by politics. Don't forsake me, as my brothers have. Bless me with clarity. Stoke my will. Embolden me to whatever end Your mighty kingship ordains. I'll stand and fall if that is what You seek, Lord, just please don't hold aloof. I've sinned and I'll bear its burden, but I beg of You, guide my heart, if not for my sake then for the sakes of those soon to be entrusted to me, unaware of their doom.

    "Do with me what You will. But if it's in Your wisdom, please don't spare the fountain of Your love. Help me to conduct myself as the Archangel I was created to be. Amen."

Chapter XVI

"Do not forsake your friend and the friend of your father, and do not go to your brother's house when disaster strikes you—better a neighbor nearby than a brother afar."
—Proverbs 27:10

There was no christening procession or fanfare as they departed the Holy City. The Faithful defenders of Zion hid their forlorn hearts behind stoic faces as the fifteen-thousand-strong column marshaled on the promenade and marched for the North Gate.

"Maybe it's just the spearhead?" some pondered as the legion passed them by.

"They won't get far," said others. "Fifteen thousand will barely be enough to hold the Aphaea."

"If that."

They knew Michael and his angels were being ordered to march out and die. The amount of discord it sowed between the choirs only deepened the animosity. No seraph attended the departure. Even those along the parapets kept to themselves.

Michael gawked at the number of heroes and veterans when he met them in the bailey. His heart swelled as he saw the medic Ariel amongst their ranks. On the hour of their presentation, the interim tribune of the newly mustered legion came before the archangel to cede his staff. But what surprised him most of all was their appearance. Though most were cherubim, all had shaved their heads, giving themselves topknots. On their panoplies were painted the lion's head symbol embossed by Arkadia onto Michael's breastplate. A legion of topknots and lions stood before him, armed and silent.

"I cannot," Michael stated, refusing the scepter. "This is a doomed path. We are not enough to succeed. You follow the Council's mandates to your deaths." He turned to their van in the shadow of the North Gate. "Why would the Elders be so fickle? They send me Heaven's exemplars in hopes it will give me an edge, yet they do not give me the needed myriads."

He wheeled to face their commander. "This is no insult, Tribune; Mazerrel's horde is maniacal; Umbra Tempest's forces are swift; and Satan's legions are vaster than the stars. No band of heroes can hope to succeed against such countless enemies arrayed against us. Return to your stations. Elders or not, I won't allow you to follow me in ordered condemnation."

As he spoke, they began to break down. A wailing erupted from them. Tears slicked the still-shattered flagstones. "Don't spurn us!" cried out. "Better to die in your shadow than live without Virtue's gleam!" The uproar filled the bailey's promenade.

"I would be a felon if I lashed you to my fate!" Michael shouted. "Dry your tears, champions. I won't permit the Council to squander you, the crown jewel of our armies. For in my absence, our Holy City will need your heroism to bolster their hearts!"

The tribune quelled his legion's anguish. With a knowing smile, he bowed to his archangel. "The Council has issued no such order, Patriarch." Michael furrowed his brow. The tribune leaned in, topknot falling across his field plate. "We're all volunteers. And we will follow you, with or without your blessing."

Michael was still in awe of their resolve, even as they struck into the enemy-infested Northern Plains. Yet he was haunted by grief. Lucifer had abandoned him. Gabriel had betrayed him. The Elders had banished him. The thought of suicide burned in his breast each day as he led his angels north into the hinterland.

But Umbra Tempest's brigades kept his mind occupied. Michael's legion endured raids on a near-daily basis as his Faithful tried to maneuver to a safe outpost. Harassed by forward elements, the archangel was still unsure of his mission. Being whittled away by Fallen cavalry and flyers would bleed out his resources. But plunging into the flatlands to deal with Umbra Tempest head-on would get them killed. And if the serpentine general had made amends with Mazerrel, then his Faithful did not have a prayer.

They picked their way precariously north for three weeks, laboriously reconnoitering to maintain their formation and dodge enemy cavalry. But when they had reached the River Aphaea, they received a boon that would launch them on a focused enterprise.

It came in the form of a Faithful supply vessel crawling down a tributary, a single-sailed flatbed ship named the Winged Fury. Its skipper, a seraph named Erodantes, confessed that he'd ferried some of Gilgamesh's Thunderbolts from the channels around the Dragon's Lair to the coastal settlement of Bleoshed. This was no small feat; rumor had it that Satan had enthralled the leviathans, bending them to his will so they would attack any vessel. Michael leapt upon the news, devouring every detail the mercantile captain could recall. Invigorated at the prospect that some of his choice irregulars still lived, Michael felt a glimmer of optimism.

But whatever rays of hope added light to his glowing eyes were quickly clouded by an addendum from Captain Erodantes. Upon their landing, the crew of the Winged Fury and the surviving Thunderbolts beheld a sight so horrifying, it emptied their stomachs. Bleoshed was in ruins. What was worse, the Scourge had personally done the job. His sigil was emblazoned upon Bleoshed's wooden walls, painted in a paste of blood and ash before a landscape consumed by blankets of smoke. None survived the holocaust. It became apparent that Mazerrel wasn't content. He wanted more. He was razing the coast for a second time.

It was then that Michael had his epiphany. "He's coming back for Lorinar. Could it be any clearer? We *must* finish the Scourge."

Further inquiry revealed that Mazerrel had summoned his myriad-strong force for the assault, culled from the survivors of his sieges on Zion.

Empyrean Falling

"The Lorineans have less than a thousand angels to post on the walls, Archangel," Erodantes said before leaving. "They'll be lucky to hold the Stone City for an hour."

Michael's volunteers dumped the baggage train and packed up that night. Supplies were loaded onto the cavalry and chariots. The infantry kept only their panoplies and hastened for Lorinar in an airborne strike. Their archangel said a prayer of thanksgiving as he spurred Andreia eastward towards Lorinar.

Far in the West, however, amidst a sprawling cityscape of broken obelisks, crumbled temples, and weathered shrines overgrown with newly sprouted springtime foliage, the army of Satan continued its forced march. Their vanguard was a malevolent shadow plunging into the melting snows. At the head of their massive column was the Dragon, astride his jet mare Nyx and shrouded in an inky black cloud. His Imperial Flame armor soaked up the very fabric of night.

For weeks they had eschewed military precision in favor of velocity. But such extremity had taken its toll. The rearguard had been abandoned. Quarrels broke out in the camps. Some left their units during the night. Others committed suicide. Yet none of it concerned Satan; with each league of crossed terrain, he drew nearer to his prize.

The stars manifested in solstice numbers overhead. An officer glided in and landed next to Satan's vanguard. The Dragon recognized his soundless flapping posture as Kemuel, a former Temple Guardian. He reined and sidestepped to provide the angel a landing spot.

"Make it quick, Kemuel," Satan said curtly. "I'm nearing my prey and have much to plan. And spare me another dispatch pleading for me to quell the mutinies that threaten to unravel our corps. I've heard the petitions: 'relent or slack in the hunt's extremity'."

"I bear word from your lieutenants."

Satan perked up. "What news from my Scourge?"

"Raziel drove him from Zion, my lord," Kemuel said with a trembling voice.

Alrak, you darling dandelion, Satan thought, *you're becoming quite a* thistle. "No doubt Mazerrel is doing what he does best then. What is his proposed action now?"

"Lorinar, my lord."

Empyrean Falling

"While the Dragon is away and the Dark Storm rages in the Plains…" Satan growled. "They are falling into old habits."

"With all due respect, my lord, we could have that glory for ourselves if you wheeled this army about. If you desire Lorinar, then let's abandon this chase in this forbidden land and head East."

Satan's crimson eyes fell upon him with an arresting fury as he slowed Nyx to a halt before one of the forgotten tundra's oases. "You would like me to call off this hunt for the sake of play, you and the other whining mongrels who have second thoughts about electing me as their god? Do you truly think I care about Lorinar? Does the White Throne sit in the gardens of its Merciful Fate Ziggurat? No, our prize lies south. Our aim is behind the bloodied defenders of Zion and their foolish archangels. The road to Lorinar is swift and cheap, but the road to victory is long and dear."

Satan dismounted next to a circular stone pit. Throngs of guards rigged harnesses for the descent into the underground oasis. "Do you think my brothers tremble because they perceive the Stone City as the emerald of my scepter? Our struggle waits in Zion, and it will be that jewel which we pluck. But not until we have secured what our prey intends to hide." He indicated the well before them, cascaded in moonlight. He tied up his black-streaked locks and grabbed one of the harnesses. "These six Faithful we're pursuing are more vital than any city. When we capture what they believe to have spirited away and return to the East, you'll see why I've led the soul of my army into the West during the dead of winter. Spring is upon us and, with it, victory." He mounted the crumbled stone lip. "You must learn to trust me as I love you. Now, is there word from my Umbra Tempest?"

"Yes, My Lord," Kemuel stuttered, fumbling through his notes in the sparse light. Satan snapped his fingers and sparked a ball of flame to aid the angel. "His Seven Serpents have held the North and the broken fortress of Amin Shakush. The supply routes are secured, though disputed. The Seventh Column was spotted pursuing Mazerrel but their leader, Raziel, was recalled to Zion. General Tempest is headed south to attack the raiders at their source. He has devised a new plan for Zion. He should be there within the month."

Satan smiled as he secured a rappelling line to the harness and mounted the stone lip. "How will our trinity ever hope to endure? You now witness the dance of vendetta, Tribune Kemuel. Mazerrel seeks infamy; Umbra Tempest seeks redemption. Void of my presence, both enterprises will fail."

"All the more reason to make haste for the East, my lord," Kemuel urged. "We're countless leagues from our brothers. Their forces are outnumbered. What are we affecting rooting around in this fetid corpse-empire?"

Satan eyed him as his Imperial Flame guards double-checked his harness and began their descent into the oasis well. The archangel reached out with lightning swiftness and backhanded Kemuel with his rappelling line. The tribune sprawled across the tundra. Nyx neighed and bounded forth with a vicious kick. Satan halted his mare from finishing the job with a cluck of his tongue.

"My patience with you cannot endure forever, Kemuel," the Dragon seethed. "What we do here is vastly superior to any Eastern futility. We will gain victory tonight. Victory through the sword will come later. Trust in me, lest I lose trust in thee." With that, he grabbed the rope and vanished into the black mouth of the well.

Empyrean Falling

Chapter XVII
"By his knowledge the deeps were divided, and the clouds let drop the dew."
—Proverbs 3:20

At Lorinar, Michael's legion overhauled Mazerrel. By the time they reached the Stone City, winter had receded into spring. Under nocturnal cover, they assailed his rearguard, smashing through the throngs of besieging Fallen as they flung themselves at Lorinar's walls. A furious struggle arose; Michael joined the Faithful defenders holding firm in the Ziggurat capital at Lorinar's heart. For hours into the night, the two legions fought bitterly for control of the Stone City.

In the turmoil, Michael and Mazerrel dueled, the Sword of God and the Scourge of the Faithful matching blows with an unparalleled rage. But in the end, Michael pummeled Mazerrel through the urban blocks until he was forced to withdraw. He fled west with his ragged cohorts, scorching the flatlands in their wake. Relieved to find some of Gilgamesh's Thunderbolts still alive within the Ziggurat, Michael rallied the defenders and mustered to pursue.

In the aftermath, they were hailed as a corps of heroes, earning the name Lions for their stalwart ferocity and cunning stealth. Upon the ramparts of the Stone City's fortress capital, Michael swore to chase Mazerrel into the Oblivion, if that is what it took to destroy him.

Empyrean Falling

For days they hounded what was left of Mazerrel's army. His rearguard committed to a series of holding actions, stalling Michael's pursuit of the Scourge and turning the campaign into a protracted meeting engagement.

By the ninth sundown, the Lions had finally picked apart the last of Mazerrel's rear elements. They caught up with the bulk of his remaining force on the slopes of the Hundred Foothills, just east of the Thousand Peaks. The seven thousand glyph-waving maniacs erected a shoddy perimeter of upturned wagons from the baggage train, bristling with pikes and banners. Under an overcast small hours sky, they gathered on the string of upland hills with the sierra of craggy mountains at their backs. Michael's Lions marshaled on a crescent of fields adjacent to the hillocks, the wildflowers peeking through as spring showers washed away the last vestiges of snow.

The archangel had been advised to wait until dawn, that a night raid would be too difficult, given Mazerrel's nature. He refused. "Victory won't wait for the sun," he said. Michael beheld a vista of frantic movement as the enemy repositioned on the slopes under a concert of trumpets. Peltasts ranged above, descending from the grey night to hem in the Fallen before winging back into the thunderheads. Behind Mazerrel's recalcitrant malefactors towered the labyrinthine bulwark of the Thousand Peaks, piercing the night with their alps.

As the Lions dressed their lines, an ominous chorus emanated from the Fallen ranks. The baggage train before them was set ablaze. Michael turned atop Andreia to behold Mazerrel's legion taking up another one of their blasphemous paeans. Deep baritones and basses rose in sacrilegious concert from the rows of pikes. But this wasn't like before; every Faithful knew in their heart that the Fallen were trapped and outnumbered. The hunters had caught the scent; such acts of heretical intimidation would not shake their resolve that night.

The weather was almost balmy as Michael galloped down the brigades of marching heavy infantry. Visibly was hampered as he put them into a deceptive double-wedge formation, with the archers behind the protection of the line fighters' vanguards. He rode swiftly across the jagged front, spotting a familiar face amidst the small hours' fog and rumbling of dog-chompers.

"How's your lance today, Lantheron?" he shouted over the din of barking officers.

The tall lancer grinned, his chainmail coif shrouding cobalt eyes and tufts of dark hair. "My blade doesn't like this humidity, Patriarch! It prefers the weather of an enemy's guts."

Michael laughed. "Crimson is a more inviting hue than rust!"

"Aye, Patriarch!" Lantheron bellowed, seconded by his maniple's fellow cherubim.

Satisfied, Michael spurred Andreia down the line to the barren inseams, where chevrons of mounted knights were galloping to the flanks. Lances had yet to be couched but already the angels were pulling down their helmets' visors and readjusting the straps on their saddle-locked iron shields. He cantered up to their stacked blocks of equestrian fury and sought out their leader.

"Major!" Michael bawled through the clattering noise. The officer broke ranks and trotted over. With a quick salute, he raised his grilled visor, his azure crest dancing in the wind. "Hit Mazerrel's center as two fists simultaneously. Be mindful of their cavalry; if you get bogged down on their heavy infantry, their horses could outmaneuver your pincer." The major nodded in his unwieldy carapace of thick armor. "Focus on breaking their center until our line-fighters can close and finish the job. Do you need anything?"

The major shook his head inside his iron shell. "It's a good plan, sir. We'll be fine."

"Then may Parakletos guide your lance." He saluted the major before riding away.

The archangel withdrew to a prominent knoll behind the rearguard. The baggage train was situated there, with magazine dumps of spare lances and field medics under Ariel setting up under the intermittent amber play of the Fallen's conflagration. It was the best vantage he could find. He attempted to appear stoic but with each passing moment, a souring in his chest grew until, by the time he reached the baggage dump, he was staving off a sickening grimace.

The distant clamor wafted on drizzly winds as he crested the promontory. Michael pivoted Andreia next to a cluster of riders and racks loaded with bundles of spare lances for their brothers-in-arms.

Empyrean Falling

Scouts bustled around him, laden with last minute messages and materiel. The knoll was alive with quick response units.

The Faithful legion marched for the string of hillocks. Michael watched Mazerrel's forces re-form on the crests. Their front shifted laterally, cohorts of half a thousand rebels shooting forward of the flanks while banks of archers filed in front of the burning baggage. They set up their tall shields with lightning efficiency. The shadows of night and fire played tricks on Michael's eyes, but he thought he saw large shapes lumbering behind the condensed rectangles of infantry pikers. Arrows arcing into the wet wind could be heard. Seconds later, Michael heard horses neigh on the right. His cavalry was taking volleys. The velocity of Mazerrel's reaction was startling.

"So, this is how the Scourge will end," spoke a pure tenor from behind the Cherubim Archangel, "on a dreary night in the Hundred Foothills." Michael wanted to turn and draw Virtue, but he knew the rider sidling up to him. "This victory is long overdue, brother. Tell me, will it be as gratifying as you'd hoped?"

"The bear is most lethal when it's cornered and wounded," Michael replied darkly. "Mazerrel is desperate; his rebels will fight to the bitter end, Consul."

The Seraphim Archon tugged on the bevor of his pristine cuirass. He fiddled with his reins. "But your angels—the Lions, that's what they're called now, right? They outnumber the Fallen by thousands. You're in pursuit, invigorated...." His voice was desolate, sapped by their fraternal tension. "The Council guessed his contention with Umbra Tempest would manifest in another strike on the North Gate. But his nemesis has vanished from the Plains."

"You guessed wrong," Michael growled, his gaze on the developing engagement before them. "Is there a reason you're here?"

"I was about to ask you the same thing."

Both sides deployed rangers to the skies with phosphorescent bulbs that flared over the battlefield. Blocks of stacked infantry illuminated under the light as airborne duels began. The brigades of Faithful infantry encroached on the hillocks. Michael thought he glimpsed Mazerrel's hulking silhouette on the far side, but it was hard to tell with the billowing smoke. The rain picked up. Thunder rolled.

"I have less than eight living members of Gilgamesh's irregulars," Michael declared matter-of-factly. "If I'm lucky, I'll have one or two when it's all over."

"Then why aren't you down there, preserving them?"

Michael sighed and pointed to the right flank. "Listen."

They heard the blaring of trumpets and the whinny of panicked horses. To circumvent the Fallen archers, Michael's cavalry had overextended themselves on the flank by at least half a mile. The dragoon cavaliers could not see Mazerrel's war elephants waiting to spring their trap, but Michael's archangelic eyes could perceive the pachyderms' shapes in the shadows.

"I kept expecting his pachyderms to show up at Lorinar and then later when we overran their rearguard," Michael said, "but he never deployed them. Until now. I guess he was saving his trump card for the last stand. They stand twice as tall as our heaviest horse and wear half their weight in scaled armor. Their trunks are encased in steel and their mahout drivers will skewer any of my surviving dragoons with javelins. That's what you're hearing right now."

"I don't understand," Gabriel said.

"That formation wasn't there six minutes ago," Michael explained. "If I were leading from the front, I'd never see it."

He sent messengers to the First Cohort on the right flank, ordering them to angle back and use their shield wall of lances to protect the line against the rampaging war elephants.

"So, Mazerrel's got a few fleas under his fur, big deal."

Michael burned away Gabriel's flippancy with a glower. "His flight west has resulted in him overrunning old units left stranded from when Ural broke his hold on the Aphaea last summer. I don't know how many of these stragglers he's picked up or what their composition is; all I know is that he has reinforcements hidden until *precisely* when he wants to bring them into play." He worked his jaw, teeth grinding. "I can't afford to take chances. Satan is still out there and by comparison, this is just a bloodying of the nose."

"I'm sorry the Elders did what they did," Gabriel tried. "Surely this is all part of God's plan."

Michael turned back to the hills and nodded at the Lions, who were closing on the crest and its pike-crowned fiery hedge of Fallen. "Do you really expect them to believe that?"

The Lions' reserve brigades of dragoons threw their wedged formations at the elephants, hoping to buy time for their brothers to escape. More phosphorescent bulbs flared in the humid air, revealing glimpses of the heavy infantry lines tramping up the slopes towards the fired baggage train, their lances looking like moving manicured forests. The sound of arrows ricocheted off shields and armor. He heard the Fallen bray and jeer, thousands more voices than what could be accounted for by visibility alone.

The Fallen cavalry maneuvered through the breach on the right and found the Lions' dragoons. They smashed into one another, archers and infantry scrambling to clear the homicidal stampede of equestrian fury. Clouds of grime hazed over the crush. Behind them, the Faithful line-fighters fanned out, overlapping the enemy wings.

"They volunteered, Michael," Gabriel reminded, averting his eyes from the carnage as another bulb flared over the battle.

"Yes, they did," his brother replied. "And I'd hoped that you might bring reinforcements." He smirked. "But that would be asking too much; risky enough coming here at all, no doubt."

"Don't patronize me," said Gabriel. "We can barely secure Zion. And now there's the advent of Umbra Tempest returning. They're scared in Zion, Michael. We could use you."

"And I could use *you*," Michael snapped. "What do you expect me to do?"

"Flee this battle and hit Umbra Tempest from behind."

"You have millions in Zion," Michael fumed. "The Lions are less than z myriad. What possible advantage could we afford you?"

"The fear of your celebrity will break their resolve, coupled with the knowledge that you abandoned this salient triumph over Mazerrel to ensure their destruction."

Another flare revealed Fallen peltasts winging in from the clouds. They descended with lightning velocity and began shredding the Lions' left flank. By the time the Faithful archers could repel them, hundreds of line-fighters were riddled with javelins and stones.

Empyrean Falling

"See those angels there?" Michael said, indicating the harried left flank. "Another surprise like those rangers and the Lions' shoulder will break. If they're lucky, they'll be able to push the forward element off the hills. If they're not, well, the whole legion will fold and be rolled up from the left. I'll spend the next two weeks scouring the Northern Plains for what's left of my lionhearted valiants."

"You're not going to help me, are you?" Gabriel asked.

"Do you know what'll happen before sunrise?" Michael asked. "First, our cavalry will be surrounded by line-fighters. What few of them survive will be stomped by the pachyderms on the right. If they're lucky, they'll punch through the foe's oblique inseams before getting skewered. Then the melee will commence. Order will collapse; this soggy terrain bogs down both sides. Cohorts will overlap and outpace each other until there's no form left to either legion. Hundreds will die from the press alone. Confusion will kill scores more before discipline is regained. These Foothills are too wet, but we have no choice; we won't get another chance at this."

Already the Lions' rear-rankers were hoisting banners, signaling for the seraphic intermediaries to relay the first batch of spare lances for delivery to the front. Riders galloped around them, grabbing bundles to relay up to the rear-rankers.

As the Lions' front charged up the hills, Mazerrel's Fallen pikers leapt over the burning baggage train and met them on the slopes. The rain saturated the terrain. The infantry's dog-chompers proved their worth as the legions trudged through the muck, their momentum flagging. The clash was a drawn out, sporadic labor. Angels tripped in the mud only to be over-trodden. It was sickening to hear them engage piecemeal instead of the preferred unison clash. A crackling sound tickled Michael's ears, like a building imploding from a blaze, a far cry from the cathartic thunderclap of uniform collision.

Lightning heralded the storm. Dispatch riders bore the same messages to Michael: *need assistance; re-form!* Michael's responses were identical: *hold fast; press on*. Messengers dumped their blown-out steeds and resorted to their wings. Signal banners waved along the obscured battlefront, their silver and blue pennants calling for aid. The knoll's racks went bare. Mazerrel's army was putting up a fight.

Empyrean Falling

"You can't perceive the battle's epicenter," Michael began in a dire tone as droplets of rain began to ring off his armor, "but I can tell you that my dragoons are being hacked to pieces. They're unable to evade, sandwiched by the infantry. To wit, every one of them will die tonight. I knew it when I planned the attack. I knew it when I met their officer on-field. But they had to bait Mazerrel's pachyderms and prime our line-fighters to affect a breach."

His brother shook his head. "How can you risk so much?"

"This is war, Gabriel; you're going to lose angels."

The pachyderms were turned by a concert of the Lions' First Cohort and concentrated volleys of archers. They ran amok, thrashing into the center. Hundreds were trampled before their mahouts could produce the spike and hammer and kill them. Fresh screams and neighs erupted, letting Michael know that his cavalry was now truly being massacred.

"I just can't reconcile their deaths."

"Then reconcile yourself with this," Michael spat, "every hour you hesitate, you put my volunteers at risk. Without support, we will die!" His brother's fervor beat upon Gabriel until he found solace only in the battle; it was easier for him to look upon the mayhem of carnage than it was to match lamps with Michael. "The Fallen know how to concentrate their numbers so that we fight at a deficit. They strategize better. That is why you must commit, Gabriel. You *must*."

The Fallen pikers took to the air long enough for Mazerrel's archers to shove the flaming wagons from the baggage train down the slopes onto the unsuspecting Faithful. They followed with broadsides of superheated barbed arrows, armor-piercing warheads that thrummed point-blank into the Faithful legionnaires. Their advance was repulsed. Chaos ensued.

The rain began to beat down on them. The night fled under the sky's flashing electricity. Fallen cavalry thundered into the Lions' left flank as the Faithful angels floundered in the gulley at the base of the hills. Cohorts busted and line-fighters routed. The archers were overrun, cut down by the dozens in the rain's masking darkness. Neither archangel saw the development, but they could hear it. Michael's eyes welled with tears as he looked at Gabriel.

"Help me," he urged. "Please. I'm begging you; I can't win this war alone."

Medics raced from the knoll to intercept the wounded as they limped on comrades' shoulders across the barren turf. The open terrain became littered with casualties. Dispatch riders darted through their bloody clusters, desperate to evade the oncoming fusillades of Fallen peltasts who sought to work further pain on the wounded. More messages filtered in, all pleading for archangelic intervention.

Michael heard an all too familiar roar and turned to see what remained of his cavalry surmount the hillock. They hooked around the banks of archers and shot for what could only be described as the command post. They had found Mazerrel. A vicious, oppressive hammering of the earth ensued as the Scourge began beating the dragoons to death. In moments, a token smattering of them were bypassing the archers again, in retreat back down the hills.

"How can we expect to achieve victory, Michael?" Gabriel whispered. From the corner of his eye, the archangel saw the right flank finally give way. Angels fell in heaps along the Hundred Foothills, maniples caught on all sides by their enemies. Those who tried to fly away were piked by screeching rebels. Only the tribune managed to escape the slaughter and envelop the Fallen's rear lines, making a mad dash for the archers and Mazerrel. But again, the Lions were checked. Gabriel leaned in his saddle, his armor creaking as he drew to a brace of cubits from his brother. "Can we truly tempt the death of the Heavenly Host for vanity?"

Michael's restraint fled. "Vanity?" he roared. "Cowardice rules your heart, Gabriel! Commit the whole of your choir. At least then we might have a chance!" His gripped Virtue in preparation for the draw. Andreia fought the bit, feeding on his master's anger. "Fight, Gabriel! There's no time left for reservation!"

With that, Michael slammed his spurs and galloped down to his retreating Faithful. Rain splashed off him as he maneuvered through the trickling stream of stumbling wounded.

Gabriel slumped in his saddle and watched his brother draw his sword. In moments, the Cherubim Patriarch was nothing more than a speck lost in the downpour. Water ran runnels down the Seraphim Archon's cuirass, soaking his padded gambeson. He heard

Empyrean Falling

Michael shout orders for his Lions to re-form. A part of Gabriel screamed to unfurl his wings and fly to his aid. But he knew no words of his could match those of his brother's. However, he could still help.

Gabriel knew he should not; the glyphs were dangerous. Only Lucifer could use them with confidence. Michael never had a talent for their employment, and even Gabriel only used them sparingly in their heyday. But it was all he could think to do. He drew a fiery sign in the air and sent the wind westward, pressing at the faces of the retreating Lions until they were compelled to turn and follow their archangel. The banners lifted and fluttered towards the enemy.

With each torrential wave, the Lions rallied to Michael more until they held such force as to overturn the Fallen's crowning momentum. The tides of battle shifted as an undertow founders the crest of a wave, and as quickly as Mazerrel's maniacs gained command of the field, they were sent in a frenzy back up the crests of the Hundred Foothills.

The Lions pursued the rout with furious efficiency. In the early morning gloaming, Gabriel watched Michael gallop in a zig-zag, Virtue slicing through rebel backs and necks as Andreia staved in chests and stomped skulls. No Fallen was left alive in their wake; the hilltops turned to bloody mounds piled with bodies. Mazerrel's forces bolted, their discipline unstrung by the miraculous Faithful rebound.

Gabriel reined about and made for the long road back to Zion. He trotted through the pockets of medics. Squires rushed about, plucking all manner of resources from the caches. The knoll had fallen into disarray as the steady flood of butchered angels poured in. Their resilience struck him in that harrowing moment. Even those whose arms were hacked away or legs crushed refused to cry out, grinding their broken jaws in the sting of treatment. None wept.

Such nobility elicited tears from Gabriel's luminous golden eyes as his horse slowed amidst the ghoulish nightmare. Wounded and dying writhed on all sides, enduring the agony in an eerie quiet. He could hear snippets of these heroes malign their forced exclusion and the price their subordinates had paid for their errors on-field.

The surgeons tending their rueful patients weathered the self-flagellation with embraces and prayers, where sutures and tourniquets failed. These were the last moments of those angels' corporeal lives; it was all they could do to tend them with palliative honor. Gabriel buried his face in his hands, the downpour masking his sobs. He heard Ariel's voice in the storm, directing the medics and striding between aid stations. Though a seraph, his heart both broke and burst to think of the heroism displayed by the first protégé of Chief Surgeon Arkiel. Gabriel had failed to prevent Ariel from volunteering for the Lions in time, but he took solace in knowing that his twin, Rafiel, was safely in Zion, overseeing the medical wards of the garrison defenders. They had struck a deal; Ariel would protect Gabriel's brother, and Gabriel would protect Ariel's brother. The covenant gave the archangel hope.

When he recovered, the Seraphim Archon clung to the knowledge that Mazerrel's army was finally smashed. The Scourge of the Faithful was alone. With him would perish nearly all threats to Lorinar. But it was of little comfort; his brother's words had cut Gabriel to the marrow. The echo of his gravelly baritone still gripped the Voice of God's heart as he rode home.

Michael cantered as the Lions flew pell-mell up the highlands leading into the Thousand Peaks. The steep slopes were peppered with racing lancers while, overhead, swarms of Faithful took excited pot shots at the surviving foe's backs. He leapt into a cluster of sprinting Fallen. Virtue sang and heads rolled, marrow gushing at the severed mandible. Andreia matched his blows with thrusts from his spiked chamfron and kicks from his massive flanks. Showers of blood splashed in the predawn rainstorm until not a rebel was left standing.

The Lions cheered as Michael brandished a sullied Virtue into the drenching sheets. Fallen corpses twitched in the mud at Andreia's hooves. Michael's eyes waxed as he bawled a war cry into the roaring dawn. Andreia reared on his hindquarters, black mane splaying water.

"Their defeat isn't enough today," Michael declared through the howling winds. "They've been beaten before! Slay them to the last, lest they return anew!"

Lantheron descended from the torrential skies. "My Patriarch," he heralded, bringing his bloodied lance to rest across cracked pauldrons and saluting through the rain. "Scouts report less than a thousand rebels fleeing into the mountains."

"And the Scourge?"

Lantheron spat red into the rain. "He fled when their lines shattered. The Fallen are breaking into the passes. Mazerrel is headed for the Valley. We can either finish off the last of these curs or bypass them for the Scourge."

Other Lions had gathered around them. Through peals of thunder and charging angels, they could see the decision fomenting within Michael. He looked to the crevasse. Rain sluiced down the walls and gushed into the rocky slopes like a terrestrial mouth funneling the sky's fountain. Beyond lay the dilapidated Amin Shakush…and what it hid. Michael thought of the fleeing villain. Again, his guts soured. The epiphany hit him just as a bolt of lightning illuminated the path's interior. Then he understood; the missing piece fell into place. It all made sense now, and it vexed him terribly.

The archangel whipped to Lantheron and the waiting cohorts. "If ever a cause was worthy of our names, it is this: that we must catch the Scourge before he reaches Amin Shakush. Beyond this diluvial gate flees our prey. But take heart, my Lions, the storm will mask our own gale of faith and fire! He will be destroyed!"

Empyrean Falling

Chapter XIIX
"...as a thief in the night..."
—2nd Peter 3:10

    Satan's forces traced their way back through the treacherous paths of the Western Empire. Steady winds beat at their armored backs, swirling their cloaks as they trekked past the last of the crumbled edifices. It had been nearly nine months since they had entered that forbidden land, whipped and prodded by the Dragon through countless hazards, snows and mutinies as they followed him towards an unknown end. But when their god found his prize, they rejoiced, for they knew their trial might at last be complete.

    Their slithering monster of an army returned, mounted myriads of heavy cavalry flanked by brigades of scythed chariots. At the front were Satan's Imperial Flames, dwindled to half their strength with the legions of infantry in column behind. None were left to question why they did not fly; all knew the purpose of the trek's hardship.

    Countless stars winked at the legions, joining with the crescent moon to reflect off their armor. The wind whispered prideful haunts as they rode between the dilapidated mirror plating of the once majestic monuments, sprawled like the corpse of some blasphemous, entombed giant reminding their depraved hearts of halcyon days. The sight of

Empyrean Falling

their beloved idols crumbled with neglect fueled the indignation burning in their breasts. Each Fallen snapped his reins and clipped his spurs that much harder.

A rucksack lay across the horn of Satan's saddle. His crimson eyes fixated on the prodigious mountains piercing the thin nocturnal horizon ahead. The ire driving his army east burned upon his nape, like the breath of some malicious gorgon. Moonbeams glistened off strands of his jet-black hair, draped like silk between his black pauldrons and hanging like a cowl over his skeletal pallor. Gone was the flush regality of his titian youth.

Kemuel rode beside him. He handed Satan a scroll. "Vuldun's sacrifice at Glalendorf has bought you the time you need, my lord. The watchtower kept Michael from hooking round our flank. Your Flames will be waiting at the staging area by midnight."

"We're less than two leagues from the Thousand Peaks, Captain," Satan replied icily. "Your elites may have secured camp west of the mountains, but it's far too early to gloat."

"General Tempest's Seven Serpents report that Mazerrel fled to Amin Shakush a month ago," Kemuel reported. "They say it wasn't long before Michael's legion encircled him."

Satan grinned mirthlessly. "My brother recalls what he had hidden in that fortress temple."

"Perhaps he's deciphered our scheme?"

Satan's face looked ghoulish in the pale moonlight. "He has deciphered nothing that I do not wish him to decipher. Vuldun made sure of that before he died." He felt Kemuel's eyes upon him. "Don't let it vex you. I sent Vuldun there to die. Of all the officers in my stable, I knew that he alone was both expendable and capable of stalling Michael. My Phoenix Empyrean is beauty from ashes. Eternal safety awaits, Kemuel, but first, you must earn it."

"It'll be easy, my lord," the new captain of the Imperial Flames casually boasted. "Michael commands little more than seven thousand volunteers, all holed up in the Valley. They'll make their valiant stand and we'll stamp them into the sod."

"My brother may be weakened, but God's Lion is most dangerous in his final mortal hours, when he knows there's one last chance to prove his valor." Satan's smile faded. "And if my youngest brother's anxiety continues, then it'll stay that way. But if it doesn't," he turned to burn his underling with a level gaze, placing a spiked gauntlet on the rucksack across his lap, "we only have to reach the Iron Temple to succeed."

"The Faithful fought hard to keep that from us," Kemuel remarked. "Their leader, Jehuel, really gave us a slog when we overtook him in those subterranean gardens."

The Dragon nodded, oily strands of hair falling over his gaunt face. "They fought harder to elude us. My brother picked his champions well, but the error is in his lack of perspective; he has no inkling of what truly matters in this war and therefore commits perpetual folly."

"Mazerrel has proven a worthy interdictor," said Kemuel. "He and Umbra Tempest have worked diligently to hem in and break Zion. They've laid sieges, killed hundreds of thousands of Faithful, held leagues of vital land…but all under false pretenses?"

"I'll tell you a secret, Captain," Satan intimated, "one that none know and few dream of in their nightmares. This is where the real war is fought. Here you've divorced yourselves from the tenets of your piety. You've followed me to the ends of Heaven. The battles in the East are nothing more than a clever distraction for egomaniacs, a bonny farce that will sting bitterly when my brothers realize it. Those who follow Mazerrel and Umbra Tempest know nothing of true dedication. They are swept up by the whirlwind of warfare's fever.

"In this realm of abandoned glory, you've won the war against yourselves," Satan continued. "You will always be your most daunting antagonist. What follows on the morrow will be the result of that internal struggle. You have proven yourselves to me, but more importantly, you've proven yourselves to you."

"We strain to serve you," Kemuel said. "I've even sent some of the Imperial Flames with Althaziel to infiltrate the Lion's camp. Their orders are to free Mazerrel by dawn or die."

"I do admire initiative," Satan said with a nod. "Impressive. Now let's hope they succeed, for I won't tolerate failure at the eleventh hour." He heard Kemuel gulp. Satan's lips tugged upwards.

Empyrean Falling

"Victory doesn't lie within the Walls of Zion, Captain." He patted the rucksack. "Half our triumph lies here."

"And the other half?" Kemuel asked. Satan tapped his nose. "And Umbra Tempest?"

"He has his orders," Satan replied, throwing him a glance as he palmed his prize.

"What's in that sack, my lord?" Kemuel finally asked.

"The key to leverage, my witless worm, the key to leverage."

"Leverage over what?"

"Not what," Satan declared. "Whom."

"The Faithful?"

Satan shook his head and sent a glyph into the stars above a mottled sky. "The King."

Many leagues to the east, those same stars winked over Zion.

The Holy City was aflame.

Gabriel flew through the Hallowed Causeway. Blood dripped from his battered armor onto the marble tiles below. The drapes wafting in his winged gusts still bore the lingering stench from the Battle at Benediction nine months ago. He could still pick out its gruesome catastrophe in the renovated perfection as he flew.

His panoply was dented, scratched, and smeared in layers of gore, melted by the still-raging fires of the razed Gates. A gash traced a jagged line from his right temple to his chin. Boltered hair stung the raw flesh of open wounds.

It had been weeks since Mazerrel's defeat. Gabriel rested in the comfort that Michael was not under threat from Umbra Tempest since the wily fox had been turned from his latest siege of Zion only minutes ago. It was a paltry comfort; the assassin general had come within a hair's breadth of breaking the Faithful defenders.

His eyes burned with adrenaline as he furled his bloody wings into the slits in his backplate and touched tiles at the base of the Forty Steps. A deep laceration on his left calf fumbled the landing, his dog-chompers scraping the marble.

With each gold and silver step, the Seraphim Archon fought to divorce his spirit of the lingering images of the crumbled Walls, the flaming promenades, the streams of dead seraphim floating in a bloody ocean in the streets, and their killer's masked, domed helmet. He forced his mind to embrace love, strength, faith and mercy; to imagine those still alive and the ones he could still save. He begged Parakletos to pacify the aching hearts of those dying outside.

When he reached the Foyer, Gabriel saw the Temple Guardians standing on either side of the Doors, their identities shielded by immaculate panoplies. One look at Gabriel's shattered armor and wounded gait sent their forms rigid with anxiety.

"Who comes into the presence of the Everlasting Almighty God?" the new Keeper boomed.

"The Voice of God, Archangel Gabriel."

The gruff Keeper's sapphire eyes narrowed on him. "State your purpose, Archangel Gabriel."

"I seek counsel with the Lord Almighty, to discern the fate of the Faithful."

"Death still lingers in Zion," the Keeper said, rising to his full, average-sized height. "Is this the best place for our Consul?"

"I'm here to argue the case for my brother," Gabriel growled through blood-blackened teeth. "Now admit me before it's too late to save your Patriarch."

The Keeper motioned for his three subordinates to open the Doors. They slung their shields and took up the prescribed stations. "We heard them from our posts, Consul," the Keeper said as he grabbed the handles. "Some seraphim reported the districts ablaze."

"The noise you heard was Umbra Tempest's cavalry," Gabriel said. "Many city blocks are engulfed in flames, but the Fallen have been repulsed and sent beyond the Gates."

All eyes locked onto the archangel. They held a collective gaze for a span of heartbeats before remembering their job. White light spilled onto the Foyer and Gabriel's soiled frame. A rumble rattled his cuirass. Radiant beams cascaded as he strode past the cherub-flanked threshold into the Inner Room.

He knelt on the glowing floor, bathed in the wreathing wheels of fire emanating from the White Throne. He bowed his head into the illuminated mists, trying to discern a righteous path upon which to set his spirit. Temptations swirled inside. He wanted to demand answers. He wanted to gnash and weep for the destruction Umbra Tempest had wrought. He wanted to wail and beat his bruised breast at the cost of their narrow victory. The toll equaled nearly a tenth of his choir, their valiant deaths a salient burden. *No! Purge their faces*, he thought.

A shadow passed over him. "Share with Me, My son."

"It may not be enough, my Lord," Gabriel's tenor cracked.

"Rise, child."

Gabriel looked up at the fiery Throne, his yellow eyes dim as amber by comparison and clouded by runnels of tears coursing through the paste of grime on his cheeks. As he rose, the image of the Son gently burned them away.

"I'm not my brother," he said ruefully. "The Elders have entrusted a task to me that I'm ill-equipped to carry out. I was never the archangel meant to bear this mantle. He's the fighter; he's the chieftain." There was contempt in his voice. "I'm just the princeling."

"Into you, I have gifted the power of compassion and discernment, Gabriel," said the Son. "Michael is assertive, and Lucifer was brilliant. But in them there was a restlessness. Into you, I've given tranquility. Do not think ill of traits which I've bestowed upon you simply because they don't mirror your siblings. You're an archangel for a reason. You're a seraph for a reason. Your choir is as sanctified as your cherubic kin. Do not squander your gifts because they're different. Such are sins against My love for you."

A sob welled inside Gabriel. "I never meant to—"

"I know," the Son said, saving him the pain of apologies. "What will you do now?"

Gabriel sighed and steadied himself. "Of the millions that once garrisoned the Walls, nearly half are dead or incapacitated. The Seventh Column came back to hit Tempest's rear lines but, without Alrak, most of them were cut down. Had it not been for Nicolae's sacrifice, that serpentine rogue general would have triumphed."

"But he didn't."

"No," Gabriel conceded, "he did not." He shifted on his dog-chompers. "But Satan's elites are still missing from the action. It perplexes me. Michael's legion is a paltry bunch, for sure; however, the Dragon has been such a non-factor in this conflict."

"You must be wary, Gabriel," said the Son.

"I want to help my brother but…"

"But?"

Gabriel shrugged. "I have my orders." His heart surged with a wave of frustration. God remained silent. "The Elders elected me Consul, what else can I do?"

"Even the Anointed Cherub strayed from the path of righteousness," cautioned the Son.

"You mean we were wrong to punish Michael?"

"Mistakes will be made," the Son told him. "The question is: what can be done to rectify them?"

Gabriel squirmed. "But what if I race to my brother's aid and leave Zion vulnerable in its darkest hour? How can I be sure Satan's army will even attack?"

"Have you been sure of anything in this war, Gabriel?" the Son asked. Somehow, through the gleaming mists, the archangel sensed God's empathetic smile. "In the end, the choice is yours. But know I'm the God of love, not the God of judgment."

Gabriel fell to his copped knees and palms. "Have I disappointed You, My King?" he sobbed.

The Son leaned down and touched His lips to the Seraphim Archon's matted hair. "You are on the path I have set before you. My faith in you abides."

Gabriel's form shivered. He trembled in the catharsis of the Son's divine kiss. Reinvigorated, he rose to depart. As he strode away, the Son called after him.

"Gabriel." The archangel turned. The Son stood before the White Throne, its revolving, fiery wheels and beams of holy radiance throwing His simple, white-robed form in bold relief. "I miss your symphonies the most."

Gabriel smiled, a genuine, warm grin. The first in months.

Empyrean Falling

Chapter XIX
"Let the stars of the twilight thereof be dark; let it look for light, but have none; neither let it see the dawning of the day."
—Job 3:9

Michael sat in his command tent, ringed by his closest officers and their aides-de-camp. Before them, a map of the Valley of a Thousand Peaks was draped over a makeshift campaign table. It was well into the small hours.

No one had slept in days, their anxieties provoked by a trapped Mazerrel, who pounded the innards of his temple prison of Amin Shakush. At first, they checked the skies for thunderclouds. But the unceasing rage elicited more than one grueling night watch. Such psychological bombardments were reminiscent of the Scourge's wintry siege; many of the Lions were coming unglued by the maleficent juggernaut's constant hammering roars.

None suffered this malady of deprivation more than Michael, who slept less than anyone and made a point to perform his duties closest to Amin Shakush, lest Mazerrel escape.

News of the force of Imperial Flames encamped on the outskirts of the western mountains had come to them an hour ago. Satan's main column would not be far behind. It vexed Michael's exhausted cabinet as they convened in the command pavilion. Even

Empyrean Falling

Alrak and Shiranon, fresh from their rescue of Uriel and Nuriel, felt the oppression of Mazerrel's raging imprisonment.

Michael's suspicions were confirmed when Melphax, Weir and Ables breathlessly entered the Lions' camp with the remaining portion of the Seventh Column, nicknamed the "Wolf-workers" after their tireless tracking of Satan's army in the West. They numbered than three hundred and had barely survived to tell of the Dragon plucking the Tome half from Jehuel's corpse in the Western oasis. Mazerrel may have been trapped, but they drew no solace from it.

Satan was coming for his lieutenant. Michael knew his own defeat would simply be a pleasant addendum. It made the Cherubim Patriarch's rows of traps and pickets in the Valley look like a cruel joke. If any of Satan's myriads got behind the seven thousand Faithful and freed Mazerrel, they would have to fight on two fronts. They stared in weary, grim silence at the battle map.

Michael raised his head from his hands to meet their ember gazes. "If they come at dawn, we can maybe hold till midday."

"We could fall back to the Iron Fortress," Shiranon proffered, pointing to the mountain castle at the southwestern ridgeline of the Valley. "It would afford us enough elevation to nullify his cavalry."

Melphax shook his head. "They'll just hook around to Glalendorf and cut us off from any potential reinforcements from the Eastern Kingdom."

"Or wait us out," Lantheron added.

"Or free Mazerrel," said Ables.

"Then things will really get hairy," Alrak joked. This time, none laughed at his unfazed lightheartedness.

Weir stared at the map. "Either way, it seems Mazerrel won't be lodging there for long."

After a tense silence, Shiranon grabbed his broadsword from the weapons rack and stormed out of the headquarters. No one challenged him; everyone understood his frustration; to be successful in surviving and accomplishing so much, only to be beaten now.

"Have we petitioned Gabriel?" Alrak asked.

"I doubt it'll matter, dandelion," Michael sighed. "I could use a drink. Think there's still some mead in your hall, Mel?"

Empyrean Falling

"Who's to say Father's finished with miracles, Patriarch?" Melphax proffered. "We may be using that mead to celebrate."

"Why must God put Himself in a box at the epicenter of a City?" Michael bemoaned. "Remember the days, Pillar of Iron, when we could walk freely in His company?"

Melphax rubbed his chin. "I remember the days when we didn't have to walk at all, when days were not days, and all was light and energy…and love."

"Times like these, in our nadir's descent," their archangel stated, "I burn for the nostalgia of that Age."

"We're the better for it, though, Patriarch," replied Melphax.

Michael's armored shoulders rose and fell like bellows. "Assuming we survive."

"We're the better for it regardless, my friend," the Pillar of Iron said with a reinforced assertiveness.

The archangel, face hidden in his hand, extended an arm to touch the general's vambrace.

"But survival would be nice," added Ables, scratching the scruff around his jaw.

"So, what do you want us to do?" Alrak asked.

Michael rose from his campaign stool. He leaned over the map, hands on the table, his topknot falling like a rope across his breastplate. "We'll keep setting trammels and caltrops as close to the western ridgeline as possible. Melphax's salvaged Sunbursts will be placed at the outskirts, where the trees are densest. Post the peltasts in the ferns above, ready to skewer the Flames when they flounder. Hopefully, the fires will force their cavalry to go it on foot. If we can take away *that* advantage, then we might stand a chance at fending them off for another couple hours. But the trick will be holding them at the mountains. Once they get into the Valley…"

"And they *will* get into the Valley," Ables reminded.

"Yes, and we'll be ready when they do," Michael nodded. "Have our engineers dig spike pits at close intervals half a league back from the mountains."

"Satan will be expecting that," Alrak declared.

Michael nodded again. "But he won't be expecting our use of it. The trap won't be in the pits; that's just the diversion. Once the faux sod collapses, the Fallen will funnel into the lanes between them, condensing their ranks for our yews. This is one time where we must conspire the way they do; raw strength won't proffer our salvation."

"Where do you want us Lions, Patriarch?" asked Lantheron.

"Here," Michael replied, tracing a longitudinal line along the western ridge, "and here." He drew another line behind it, in the open ground before Amin Shakush. "I want good interior lines, no overextension. Lantheron, you and your contemporaries from the Thunderbolts—Shiranon, Orean and the like—will be placed on the extreme west. Keep the line in check." He shifted to the Iron Fortress. "Alrak, you, Melphax and the Wolf-workers will post directly in front of Amin Shakush. The baggage should be moved to the eastern Peaks. A picket is all we can spare to guard them, but we must have someone watching our extreme rear, lest we get outflanked. Never forget that Mazerrel is their objective; we're just the lucky dessert." He stood there for a long moment before rising to his full height.

"Is there anything else?" Melphax asked.

The archangel drew a hand up to his goatee. "Yes," he finally replied, looking to Alrak. "Where are Nuriel and Uriel?"

"In the custody of the Seventh Column remnant," he answered. "I was about to send them with a detachment to Lorinar for safekeeping before news came of the Imperial Flames' encampment."

"No, we need them sent to Father immediately," said Michael. "They must descend to the Burning Hells and secure the Threshold. If Satan is slain and sent to the Infernal Realm, he could devise a way to breach its Gates and push into Earth, powers intact."

"Can Uriel be trusted?" Melphax asked Alrak.

"He worked as hard as we did to ensure his escape," Alrak told them. "He's repented of his sins. I don't think he'll betray us again."

"Pray that he won't," Michael warned, "or all we've strived to protect will unravel at our backs." He rounded the table and stood over his pupil. "Alrak, are you sure?" The angel nodded. "Then I'll draw up the order and make libations for your way through the

Tempest-darkened Plains." He strode past the assembly, threw back the tent flap, and emerged into his Valley ward.

Stretching from the acres in front of Amin Shakush to the northeastern end of the Valley of a Thousand Peaks was a veritable sea of tents, palisades, weapons racks, and baggage. Lances glistened in the pale moonlight like a starlit forest of steel. Those that could not sleep made use of their time with calisthenics or the baritone underscore of paeans. Yet over this orchestra, Mazerrel's bashing of Amin Shakush's interior waxed in prominence.

Michael made his way to his bivouac, gathering what little strength he had left to ensure his gait would not belie the wracking fatigue. As he began the short trek over the muddied slopes, a cherub intercepted him. The angel's armor bore all the familiar signs of recent combat. Without breaking momentum, the cherub flung himself at Michael's boots and bowed.

"My Patriarch," he breathed, "I bear urgent news."

"Speak, Lion, what is it?"

"We have something," he said excitedly, "that is, we've captured someone whom you must see."

Michael arched an eyebrow. "Who?"

The cherub looked up at his archangel with a foreboding expression. Before he knew it, Michael was following the angel up the dusty track southwest beyond Amin Shakush. His mind raced, trying to piece together what it could be as they flew low in the waning night, skimming over the left flank of the Lions' camp and past the towering mountain-castle of iron that was Amin Shakush.

Ahead lay a column of smoke. A smoldering fire died in a wheat field atop some minor plateau on the eastern ridge. They reached their destination when the cherub descended near a cluster of armed, battle-worn Lions gathered around some rocky outcropping. Some of them spotted their chieftain and, like a wave, they turned and bowed. It was then, when everyone dropped to their armored knees, that Michael saw the thing which had enraptured them.

Gi'ad Althaziel sat on his hindquarters in the dust, bound with hide and bludgeoned purple and bloody alongside two other Fallen. He was stripped to his trousers, his thick chest and arms sheeted in cruor. The Fallen Chief Weapons Master's face was a shadow of its former dignity. Gi'ad had crudely stitched scars running down his cheeks and another over his left eye. His face was withered and wrinkled, drained of sinew so the skin sagged between pointed ears. His once shorn scalp sprouted a sickly grey ring of hair.

His companions hardly looked better. Michael identified one by his uncanny black armor. There was a gash across his brow where someone struck the weak spot with a saber. The other one Michael barely recognized. He was short and stocky with a beard that melded into his hair, like some grotesque patch of facial fur. A pair of beady eyes glowed through his hirsute scowl as Michael neared.

One of the cherubim pointed with a bloody sword to the Fallen in the center. "We caught them sneaking in to free Mazerrel. They almost had it done when our pickets spotted them."

"Good thing it wasn't Umbra Tempest," another Lion stated over the gallery of armored topknots. The party laughed darkly.

Michael's eyes locked onto Althaziel as he approached the trio of rebels. The ring of Faithful parted to allow his entry. Those closest to the prisoners withdrew the lance heads from their poise over Fallen throats. Michael knelt in the dirt across from Althaziel. A hush descended over the Faithful as they waited on bated breath to hear what their Patriarch would say. Michael glowered sharply in the moonlight. Althaziel resembled a bronze idol. Their stillness made the two look like a grave monument, a warrior's repose for hatred's sake.

"Just tell me why, Althaziel."

The Fallen cherub searched his archangel's eyes. "Would it change anything if I did?"

"I don't know," Michael confessed. "It might bring me peace."

Althaziel nodded in compliance. "All these millennia I've been honing the warlike coils of this Heavenly Host, and for what, so we can prove our love to Father? Lucifer promised a return to the Empyrean. Who better to lead me out of the doldrums of training half-wits than the First Born of Heaven?" He chuckled. "And who am I to argue with *peace*?" His laughter swelled until he crowed, doubling over in a fit of madness.

Empyrean Falling

With a swift fist, Michael struck his former friend in the neck with the top two knuckles of his fist. Althaziel fell onto his face, choking in the dirt. "Forgive me," the archangel said, "but I have no time for lunacy, Gi'ad." He rose and leered down at the villain. "I'll give you this one chance, Gi'ad: repent, and there may be clemency."

"To Hell with your clemency," Althaziel snarled. "I'll take my honorable chances on the chopping block."

"Then the chopping block it is. And there will be no honor."

Gi'ad rolled onto his knees and spat blood at Michael's boots. "That'll be judged by the victors, and you know it."

Michael signaled to the captors and departed. He could hear the Lions descend upon their prisoners. They hauled them to their feet. He knew the sounds well. They would strip them to the waist and bind them to wooden posts. By dawn, Gi'ad Althaziel and his comrades would be decapitated. The archangel put the notion out of his mind as he made his way back to his bivouac. If he was lucky, he could catch a couple of hours' sleep before dawn.

The constellations faded. The first crack of sunrise was beginning to illuminate the indigo horizon. The eastern ridge dissolved into jagged, purpled shadows as the sun rose.

Out of its birthing radiance descended a speck. Michael caught sight of it and watched it grow to reveal a winged angel. Unchallenged by his Lions, the angel came within twelve cubits of Michael's position. In the predawn gloaming, Michael spied the bronze panoply and iron weapons. He wore only greaves, a cuirass, a red horsehair crested helmet, and a red cloak. His spear and short sword were slung across his bare, scarred shoulders as he winged down.

A Cognoscenti. He landed gracefully and in one fluid motion furled his wings, gathered his cloak, and bowed. He laid his weapons flat on the turf under scarred hands and bowed his head. "Patriarch Michael," his gruff voice sang. "I bring word from Zion."

Michael rushed to him, motioning for the Faithful to stand. "By all means, rise and report. What news from my vaunted elite?"

The angel rose to his dog-chompered sandals, slung his shield, and drove the butt-spike of his spear into the dirt with authority.

"What few of us are left," he announced, turning and pointing to the east from whence he came, "are with you."

Michael peered into the rising sun. From its august blaze, thousands of garnet and bronze wings dotted the titian horizon. He had to steady himself, overcome by the eleventh-hour boon.

Melphax manifested on Michael's flank. He traced the eyes of his archangel to the Cognoscenti. He followed the elite's arm pointing to the east. A whistle escaped Melphax's peppered beard as he saw what looked to be a full corps, close to eighty-five hundred angels, emerging from the sunrise.

"You've been reinforced," he observed with a wry charm and crossed arms. A grin creased his weathered, aged face. He placed a hand on his archangel's pauldron. "See, Michael? There's still time for miracles; the constellations yet conspire for us."

Michael sucked back tears and clasped the Cognoscenti's forearm. "They do indeed."

Empyrean Falling

Chapter XX

"And if ye go to war against the enemy that oppresseth you, blow an alarm with trumpets; and ye shall be remembered before the Lord your God, and saved from your enemies."
—Numbers 10:9

It started in the predawn.

Michael fared a couple hours of sleep. But it seemed no sooner did he lay topknot to bedroll than his tent flap was thrown open.

"The baggage dump's been hit, Patriarch," a familiar sounding cherub reported from the opening. "We don't know how many, but they're cavalry, well hidden in the mists."

Michael peered at him through blurry eyes. The angel was tall, his plate mail doing nothing to thicken the slender frame that housed his baritone. After several deep breaths, Michael dragged himself to his armor stand and began dressing for battle. "Why can't our pickets search above the mists, Lantheron?"

"See for yourself," he replied, pointing with his lance to the morning rays in the east.

Michael lumbered from the tent to behold a fearful sight.

The sunrise burst through the mountains like a blinding nova, auburn light illuminating banks of swirling fog. Even from their long vantage, it hurt to look upon such a brilliant vista. The Lions' camp sprawled before them. Maniples marched in files to mustering cohorts.

Empyrean Falling

Wedges of airborne rangers patrolled the outskirts. At the eastern edge, the baggage dump appeared as a cluster of mounds hugging the foggy bottoms of the Thousand Peaks. Beyond these, the shining orange haze obscured all. It was there that combat was already joined.

"Your orders, Patriarch?"

Michel rubbed his eyes and squinted into the east. "Move all spare kits into the camp and fire the baggage dump. I won't have some phantom cavalry reaching the Scourge while our backs are turned. The fires should foul their formation." He turned to Lantheron. "Besides, the dead don't eat much."

Thirty minutes later, the Lions were marshaling in the Valley. They deployed in a snaking line along the apex of the western ridge, the gleam of their spears' warheads hidden amidst the springtime verdure of trees. On the left flank, Lantheron and Shiranon posted among the line-fighters. Behind them, Alrak Sivad was stationed with Weir, Ables and the Wolves directly in front of Amin Shakush.

The Cognoscenti were given an ancillary position to afford some measure of rest before battle was joined. Alrak and his officers stifled smirks as they observed the Cognoscenti's dour reaction to Michael's orders. But they empathized; it was never easy for valiant hearts to abstain from an opportunity for sacrifice.

Michael met Alrak at his post before the collapsed iron barbican. They were cool and cozy in the shadow of the mountain. He approached his protégé, tightening the straps of his gauntlets before pulling his silver diadem from the silk wrap at his waist. His pearly panoply hummed as a mirror to the Seventh Column across the way. They were a stark contrast to the rusty dilapidation of the Iron Fortress towering at their backs.

"How'd you sleep, dandelion?" Michael asked.

Alrak eyed him with a mischievous expression. "Heroes don't sleep; we just douse our lamps so as not to keep our lesser kin awake." He thumped Ables' breastplate. "He needed his beauty rest." The spry seraph growled a playful rebuff.

Michael regarded them both. "I have every bit of confidence in you, but this is someone's home. I think it best if he were here to aid."

Empyrean Falling

Melphax landed in their midst. He strode over and took up Alrak's side, his grey armor as battered as his lost abode. He looked skyward to behold the crumbled ruin that was once his imposing pride and joy. His large chest rose and fell beneath its smoky cuirass.

"Derelict from my home," he said, "I always dreamt the state of disrepair would be tolerable. But now that I've returned, the grief is almost too much to bear." The rightful owner of Amin Shakush shook his head with a rueful grimace. "But it's *still* my home," he rumbled, eyes falling to meet Alrak, "and you can count on me to defend it, no matter the toll."

Alrak set his jaw and squinted a smile of approval at him.

The three stood there in the open shade, silently observing the last phalanxes of Cognoscenti maneuvering into position on the flats at their oblique. Their armor glistened as the sun beat down. A cool wind coursed through, filling their nostrils with the aromas of honeysuckle and pine. They imbibed the blissful, fragrant moment.

Michael turned to Melphax with a pensive tilt of his head as he observed his hounds of war. "Will we ever know peace, old friend?"

The Pillar of Iron huffed. "It may take a miracle, Patriarch."

A stir emerged from their front as a flying wedge of Faithful drew in from the western mountains. Curiosity filled their wake as they flew to Michael's position. Many on the ground pointed their lances at the cluster of Lions, captivated by something hidden in the knot of airborne infantry.

Then Michael saw it. A black armored mass was at the center of the blue and silver crests of his centurions. Their blue capes curled about their armor as they knelt with hands on hilts. The uncannily armored villain stood proudly in their center.

The flight's officer bowed and raised the visor of his helmet. "My Patriarch, the Dragon has sent an envoy."

Michael's jaw clenched as he glared at the Fallen elite. Though he was flanked on all sides by wary cherubim, he possessed an air of unwavering pride. "Allow him to speak."

The Imperial Flame took a step. The centurions tightened their grips. "Patriarch of the Cherubim," the elite began, his voice the quality of acid on gravel. "My god, Satan, seeks to preserve you, the flower of Heaven's warlike wreath." There was an oily tint to his speech. "He desires no bloodshed and hopes the loyalists of his younger brother will pledge allegiance to the rightful heir of the White Throne. You have fought valiantly, Michael, but it's over."

Michael thought he detected a smile behind the strips of armor overlapping his face.

"Let us not build where no foundation may take root," the Fallen continued. "You've defeated Mazerrel, yes, but you're seven thousand with, what," he leaned over in mock observance of the Cognoscenti forming in the acres behind, "eight thousand in reserve? My master commands millions, Lion of God. Under a lesser Fallen's generalship, you may very well devise some clever ruse that carries the day. But you've never faced the Dragon in open battle. With all due respect, you're outnumbered, outclassed and will soon be outlived should you continue this stubbron show of defiant futility."

Michael endured him in silence.

"He implores you, mighty chieftain," the envoy said, "admit his army into the Valley, relinquish your bloodless grip on Amin Shakush, and you shall be inducted into his Phoenix Empyrean with honors. He misses his brother, Archangel," the angel said candidly with a narrowing of his titian eyes. "Please, don't squander the jewel of Zion's crown on a vainglorious cause."

All eyes turned to Michael.

"Tell your master this, blackguard," he said quietly. "My loyalties are to my family. Let the passion of my honor be weighed upon *that* scale. Better to perish in the light of the Throne than to thrive in the shadow of a petulant, traitorous demagogue."

Michael motioned for the centurions to escort the envoy back. He stood on the vacant ground before Amin Shakush, flanked by Alrak, Melphax, Weir and Ables, still as statues amidst the storm of bustling Faithful and the aftermath of the Imperial Flame's visit.

Alrak observed the stark blue canopy above, amused and undaunted. "It's like, on a scale of one to ten of bluishness," he remarked out of nowhere, "the sky's a seven."

Laughter rose from his contemporaries. The Seventh Column Polemarch pushed long golden strands out of his face and looked down, returning his emerald squint and a pursing of his lips to those around him with a tongue-in-cheek smile.

Michael shook his head, suppressing a grin as Melphax let out a chuckle. "You're an odd one, dandelion," the archangel told him.

Their levity was broken by a herald galloping up to them in a frenzy. His severed wings dripped blood. His armor was hacked away, revealing gored flesh. Both rider and mount looked deranged. But when he spouted his message, Michael knew the angel was lucid.

"Those Fallen in the mists," he barked. "They're all cavalry! Umbra Tempest leads them!"

Before the words had left his mouth, explosions from the western ridge shook the grass underfoot. The Sunbursts. Already the Lions had sprung their first trap.

"Stations!" Michael bellowed. He turned to Alrak and Melphax as the trumpets and drums transmitted signals. The archangel jabbed a finger at the Iron Fortress. "Remember, no matter what happens, *that* is their prize. Let no one reach it." He donned his silver crown, sprouted his wings, and flew towards the mountains.

Michael coursed low and hard until arriving at the frontline. A leather-clad squire held Andreia's reins at the summit. He landed on the saddle and plucked a lance from one of its four corner holsters. He looked down and saw the enemy. Satan's vanguard was all cavalry and chariots, spitting projectiles up the slopes as they charged.

The conflagration had achieved its desired effects; the Fallen were scattered before the rolling tide of acidic, gelatinous flames, the rear-rankers entangled upon their writhing comrades. Order dissolved in tandem with their uncanny armor. They quickly became prime targets for the Faithful peltasts hidden in the trees. Death rained down upon the disorganized enemy, killing hundreds. In time, mounds of corpses littered the foot of the western ridge, coiled by acrid columns of smoke rising from pyres of mutilated bodies, melted together by the Sunbursts' naphtha concoctions.

Over this tangle of boiling flesh and metal leapt the Fallen cavalry. They cleared the sizzling chasms while the chariots were forced to divert to the flanks. Peltasts and yews assaulted them with salvo after salvo, but the Imperial Flames' armor repelled the missiles.

"Aim for the eyes!" Michael heard one of their captains bark from their place of observation above.

The storms of projectiles changed trajectory, arching at shallower angles. Michael watched with satisfaction as the onrushing elites jerked from their galloping mounts and flailed backward, faces bursting in splays of blood as arrows and slinger bullets found their marks. Yet on the Fallen charged, their numbers an unwavering black tide climbing up the ridge.

"Shields to port," Michael ordered. A crack of thunder and the entire line moved to the ready. "Level the iron!" Like a wave rippling from the archangelic center, the Lions lowered their seven-cubit long lances into the horizontal. Affirmations came from Faithful officers, rising over the din in a series of last-minute maxims meant to bolster their resolve.

"Steady, lads! Wait for them!"

"Mind your intervals!"

And then it came. Satan's elites threw themselves on the flanks first, their vanguard clashing with the center heartbeats later. Thousands of horses thrashed in their deaths, chests tearing on the honed edges of the Lions' pole-arms. Riders catapulted from their perishing mounts into the forest of lances.

"Chew them down! Aim for the faces!"

For twenty minutes, chaos engulfed the ridgeline as the lances rippled in unison against the up-rushing Fallen dragoons. When at last the Imperial Flames seemed exhausted upon the whetted hedge, a stillness arose as the breadth of the slopes writhed in shredded horses. Blood hung in the air like a rusty haze. But from the tumult emerged a harrowing sight. The Imperial Flames rose from the flailing equestrian carnage, their black armor slathered in gore. Without hesitation, they marshaled into orderly ranks and advanced on foot.

"Re-form!" the Faithful centurions bawled down the line. "Prepare to grind!"

The Lions consolidated their ranks to form sturdier shield walls. Michael saw the impenetrable curtain of smaze rising from the trench. The crack of arms and armor pierced his ears. In one uniform collision, the Imperial Flames met the Lions, their black-souled ranks outnumbering the lionhearted topknots three-to-one. The two cadres ground away in that violent shoving match indicative of massed heavy infantry combat.

Michael spurred Andreia into the fight. His color guard fought to keep up as they collided with the enemy, their lances shivering on the faces of the foe. Michael wheeled, thrusting his second lance into the eyes of his opponents. Yet on charged more. Before he could take another breath, Michael was on his third lance. Members of his color guard rushed to him as he drew another, but Andreia had him protected, kicking and staking with his spiked chamfron.

But the press of the enemy overwhelmed them. The Lions fell back, the concert of tactics useless against such masses. They backpedaled through the trees, setting fire to the crest's woods in an attempt to stall their attackers. Michael and his color guard were the last to abandon the ridgeline. As he fell back, he caught movement near the Sunbursts' terminus. The putrid curtain of smog hung like a grey wall, but something thundered behind it. Out from the haze-burst legions of Fallen infantry, encased in black mail and flying in ordered wedges. Red and black guidons of the Dragon fluttered through the smoke. Michael reeled in horror as hundreds of thousands of them poured forth, choking the air with their myriads.

For a split second, he regretted not taking the Fallen envoy's offer. Purging the thought, he spurred Andreia into the Valley, joining the beleaguered Faithful. In two hours, the western Peaks were stained with blood. Corpses littered both sides of the ridge, gathered in rising mounds at the nexus of fighting. Above this charnel carpet, the forest burned, spewing smoke and ashen sparks into the morning cerulean.

The Cherubim Patriarch cantered across the breadth of the Lions' van, extolling them with exhortations. Before leaping into the fray, he hazarded a look to the flanks. The left held, bored with inactivity. The right, however, was beginning to buckle.

Before he could shift the line or thrust his way free of the enemy crush to reinforce them, the Lions' right wing collapsed. Hundreds sprouted their wings and soared to gain distance.

But Michael never had to issue the order. The Cognoscenti were all over the situation. As he shattered his last lance and drew Virtue, he beheld the full battalion—eighty-five hundred bronze-and-scarlet speedsters—unfurl their wings and shoot across the terrain towards the broken flank. Like one massive machine, the force of Cognoscenti leveled their eight-foot spears and raised their shields to mid-port. A chorus resonated over the field as they took up a paean.

They slammed into the onrushing Fallen just as they came off the slopes. Furious fighting picked up as fresh phalanxes collided with waves of Imperial Flames. The re-grouped Lions quickly rallied and charged back to their posts, emboldened by their Cognoscenti peers.

But hopes were dashed when Michael beheld the mainstay of Satan's army flood over the western Peaks like a swarm of scarabs, rolling over the craggy, corpse-littered precipices. The sheer volume of their vicious numbers shook the sod at Andreia's hooves.

Then the left flank was hit.

Michael's stomach twisted as the chariots hooked around the extreme left, furlongs away from Amin Shakush. Alrak's Wolf-workers braced for the attack, but a few hundred prodigies were no match for the mobile assault platforms. Michael faced a dilemma: remain at the embattled center and hope Alrak and Melphax could hold, or abandon the Lions and preserve that which he knew Satan wanted most, Amin Shakush.

Alrak Sivad answered for him. Michael watched as boulders and iron rubble were plucked from the mountainside and hurled down in front of the speeding chariots, fouling the enemy's cohesion. They crashed into one another, teams playing out on the mountain's shoulder while Weir and Ables hemmed in the flanks, darting in and out of the chariots' diverted paths and hooking their wheels, mounts or riders with their lances.

Michael turned to the fray at hand. "Fall back to the Cogs!"

Again, the Lions backpedaled, the agonizing withdraw that wasn't a retreat but a fight in reverse, a battle to preserve cohesion. Once an interval was gained, the Faithful flew with all haste for the Cognoscenti. The Fallen pursued, hot on their airborne dog-chompers. From the left swept the chariots, attempting to hit the Cognoscenti at the oblique. From the fore charged the ravenous myriads of Fallen infantry. And yet the elite Faithful never blinked in their baleful stare at the countless onrushing attackers.

Empyrean Falling

Michael noted the Fallen's disorder. Satan's angels were rabid, shouting and howling, brandishing their weapons, and clambering over the terrain with bouts of false bravado. They were a malevolent deluge of warped, malnourished, deranged, black-hearted, venomous hatred, intoxicated by blood madness. Their spirits were as decayed as their cadaverous forms.

Then the acres of fallow fields opened up a furlong in front of the Cognoscenti. The foe's numbers collapsed under their own weight and plunged into the spike pits. Like the breaking of waves on a shore, the fore ranks of Fallen were impaled in the ditches. On the avenues in between, the bewildered survivors funneled into a chaotic press. The Cognoscenti sang a hymn of praise. Behind them, the Lions erupted into peals of exultation.

As Satan's infantry clogged on the turfed bottlenecks, the Faithful archers emerged from their concealment behind the Cognoscenti. Overhead sprang the rangers, taking to the air to pelt the infantry and duel with those who fluttered to the sky only to be struck down by the hundreds.

But still, the press of their numbers burst through the bottlenecks and into the flats ahead. Even the Faithful's hedgerows and caltrops failed to stop them. They met the Cognoscenti full bore, colliding with their ordered phalanxes under such momentum as to shatter their spears.

Into this the Lions rushed, exhausted but determined to not let their brethren fight alone. Michael rode at their helm. When he rushed into the fore, it was no longer a shoving contest, where ground is purchased with arms and dog-chompers, but a melee of swords, shields and butt-spikes. In the midmorning humidity, the warring factions kicked up such a haze as to obscure all luminous vision. Michael fought in the crush, slicing through countless Fallen.

It was then that Satan appeared, circling overhead with wings blacker than pitch. The Cherubim Patriarch looked up and placed a hand over his scar, protected as it was by the ornate cuirass. A heartbeat later, he unfurled his wings and prepared to bolt.

Andreia bucked in protest.

Empyrean Falling

Michael leaned down to his horse's ear. "You'll want no part in this one, my friend. Stay alive; I'll need you later." He stroked the horse's mane and vaulted from the saddle.

Satan beckoned him with Hadar. "It's been a long time coming, brother," he shouted over the madness. "Show me how sharp the Lion's claws are!"

Michael brought Virtue up and struck. A flash erupted. Thunder rang as Virtue's silver edge bit Hadar's black ore. The archangels collided midair, breastplate-to-breastplate.

What came next was a supernatural duel. Lightning crackled and fire wreathed, terrifying the warring angels below. They abandoned their hard-fought spots of turf to avoid getting caught in the mix. The two archangels brought their fight to less than a few spans above the ground, plumes of fire and gales bursting from them with each strike. Whole formations of angels were consumed. Michael fought to keep his adversary's fury contained, gritting his teeth until the blood hammered in his ears. But the Dragon was crafty. A jab from his sword sent Michael sprawling as the evil weapon pierced his bevor. Momentum carried him so the blade traced a carving path down to his lamed tasset. He let loose a horrendous scream and plummeted to the battlefield below.

Satan took hold of him as he fell. "Join me, brother!" he growled as they grappled.

Michael answered with a fist to Satan's neck.

The Dragon blocked the attack and grabbed the Lion's severed breastplate. "So, be it!" With an anguished cry, he hurled Michael high and fast across the churned Valley until he crashed into the side of Amin Shakush, shaking the mountain with his meteoric impact.

A great clamor sprang from the Fallen as all beheld the Sword of God's collision. The Faithful waited in tense silence as Michael tumbled down the side of Amin Shakush's lower tiers. *Surely*, they thought, *our archangel is dead*.

Then a second fear was realized. Michael's impact created a crack in the side of Amin Shakush. Out from the fissure burst forth Mazerrel. The fiend squirmed and writhed from the hole until at last, his corpulent, hirsute mass shot free, sending tons of iron onto the angel-filled acres. His roar carried over the Valley.

Holding a patch of hillocks in front of Amin Shakush's barbican, Alrak and Melphax watched as the Scourge circled the sky, invigorated by the wanton butchery.

"If ever you wanted to inherit the mantle of Patriarch," Melphax shouted to Alrak as they fought, "now's the time!" For once, the protégé had no answer.

In Amin Shakush's crumbled bailey, Michael staggered from the piles of debris. His limbs quaked. He found his feet in time to see Satan and Mazerrel soar in. No sooner could he raise Virtue than the two were forging a tandem assault amidst the ruins.

Satan darted to Michael's right while Mazerrel roared on his left, his membranous wings billowing clouds of smoke into Michael's face. The Faithful archangel backed up, trying to keep them at frontward oblique angles. A hesitation arose in their lethal triangle.

But it was Mazerrel's avarice for revenge that initiated the fight. He roared and lunged, bringing his scimitar down like a cleaver. A stroke from Michael and the attack was diverted into a section of wall. Satan rushed him from behind. The Dragon was swift. He swept Michael's feet out from under him, sending the archangel onto his back. He wasted no time and sheared Michael's silver diadem, grabbed him by the topknot, and cast him beyond the rusted ramparts.

What followed was a half hour of desperation. Mazerrel and Satan were ruthless in their duel. It took all that Michael had to stay alive as he was pummeled across the battlefield.

By the time the spring sun had reached its zenith, the Faithful had less than a thousand able-bodied angels capable of withstanding the ever-growing legions of Fallen. A meager defense was erected behind a breastwork of bodies and rubble in Amin Shakush's bailey. Alrak, Melphax and their junior officers fought at the barbican in known vanity. Even Alrak's preternatural powers were not enough.

They saw Michael entangled between Mazerrel and Satan as the two most powerful Fallen hurled him into an abandoned section of the Valley where he landed on a mound of detritus, the backplate of his pearly cuirass saving him from being impaled on shivered guidon hafts and jagged war implements.

His limbs turned to jelly, breath shallow and labored as the blinding sun beat down. A pair of dark shapes intercepted the light. Standing over him was the imposing shadow of Satan. He crowed, his red eyes burning like sinister constellations next to Mazerrel.

"My Phoenix Empyrean won't be the same without you," Satan said proudly.

Michael's vision darkened. He readied himself for the blow that would end his life. Time slowed. In the distance, Mazerrel brayed.

He heard Satan's domineering voice through the roar. "Where is Umbra Tempest?"

"Carving his way to the Iron Fortress," Mazerrel replied.

"Give me my prize and you may have what you seek."

"I'm forever in your debt, master," said Mazerrel. "I have it."

"Then you've done well, my friend," Satan told him. "Now hand over the Tome half so that we may fulfill this war's purpose and rid ourselves of an unjust God."

They began to laugh. Michael's heart ached as the two congratulated one another.

Suddenly, the revelry ceased, overridden by a distant, abrupt noise. Michael braced for a death blow that never came. The blast came again, clear and distinct, with a piercing tone. It rode on the wind with a melodic evanescence, surmounting the din of battle.

"What in the Burning Hells is that?" Mazerrel growled.

"I know that sound," Satan seethed. "We have a problem. Summon the reserves."

Michael heard the two sprout their wings and flee the grisly promontory. For a moment, all he could do was breathe.

He clawed his way to his hands and knees. The vista before him was one of absolute failure. Death abounded. All those who followed him seemed to have met their painful doom. The Fallen controlled the Valley. His heart broke and he wept.

Then a ray of sunlight warmed his face, and he looked up to the east. Tears of agony turned to tears of joy, and his sobs segued to the catharsis of laughter. Overcome by the development before him, he thrust his arms into the air. Never before had he seen such a spectacle of heart-bursting spiritual rejuvenation.

The eastern horizon was filled with myriads upon myriads of flying seraphim, radiantly gilded in sunlit glory. Their Archon flew at their helm, blaring his trumpet until the robust brass notes filled the Valley, echoing off the Thousand Peaks and rattling angelic armor. And under them, every cherub from Zion rode on fully-armored battle mounts, flooding down the eastern ridge.

Then came the words that no cherub ever expected to hear but now, in the nexus of crisis, were sweeter than manna. As the seraphim flew for Amin Shakush and their beleaguered brothers, they courageously shouted, "Switch-back! Switch-back!"

Like a cleansing flood, they descended. The remaining defenders turned to employ that one tactic they had forsaken, yet the seraphim had embraced, eschewing ego and tossing armaments into the air, only to be caught moments before the crash. The seraphim grounded in a protective line in front of the surviving Lions, Wolf-workers and Cognoscenti.

Michael's heart wanted to leap out of his breastplate. He looked for Satan, eyes drifting to the western ridge where the rest of the Dragon's Fallen myriads were racing in a rabid fury for Amin Shakush. His eyes traced to the Iron Fortress' ruins, and he knew.

Empyrean Falling

Chapter XXI

"And they were trampled in the winepress outside the city, and blood flowed from the press, even unto the horses' bridles, by the space of a thousand and six hundred furlongs."
—Revelation 14:20

All of Heaven was in the Valley of a Thousand Peaks.

What had once been a battle in the vicinity of Amin Shakush soon turned into a monumental struggle encompassing the full circumference of the Valley. The entirety of the angelic host, myriads upon myriads, poured into the fight. Whole legions were devoured in the press of warfare. Fires spread over leagues of terrain. No dog-chomper cleat trod on a stitch of turf but, instead, ground away upon a slippery, shifting sea of corpses rising in swells of charnel cupidity.

The valley overflowed with angels as Satan and Gabriel's armies met. From the west, the Fallen hauled columns of battlewagons clad in iron and lugged by files of oxen. Their teamsters cracked the whip as they lumbered with oaken wheels and sally ports issuing fresh centuries of infantry. Above the monstrous mobile war-carriages, Fallen archers hurled volleys. The battle's intensity redoubled as fresh waves of carnage were added to the already teeming hurricane of steel-shrouded flesh and iron-willed violence.

Andreia found Michael on the promontory, bearing Ariel and Rafiel on his back. The medics examined him and stitched him up as

Empyrean Falling

best they could. Before they could issue a reprimand, the archangel was astride his charger and racing for the Iron Fortress.

He rode beneath the maelstrom until the sun burned off his stupor. When his wits were about him, he leapt into the gritty air, dodging fusillades of arrows. He locked onto Satan, who transited the skies amidst the pandemonium. But as he pursued, something caught his eye below. Though obscured by the haze swirling around thickets of pole-arms, Michael bore witness to a terrifying amalgamation of elemental gifts being unleashed on Amin Shakush.

Fiery hail rained down on the crumbled castle walls; the earth moaned as it gaped to swallow Fallen legionnaires; bolts of lightning struck out of a clear sky; jets of water sprang from the dry soil; baleful winds froze teams of chariots; arrows were turned by gusts; and shards of ice fell from thin air. A preternatural violence was being unleashed wholesale.

The archangel recognized the cherub riding atop a cyclone of wind and fire in the eye of this storm and knew that Alrak was desperately attempting to stem the tide of enemies surging upon their position. Behind him, the surviving Lions, Wolves and Cognoscenti gathered and brandished their spears in the bristling domed formation known as the hedgehog, flanks secured by the dilapidated barbican.

A league away, towards the center of the Valley where fresh battalions collided in a homicidal catalyst, Umbra Tempest carved his way through the rear ranks of Faithful. His helmet was discarded, white hair sullied to the same purplish black as the rest of his staved armor. Bereft of pauldrons and greaves, his battle skirt hung in shreds beneath a punctured breastplate. Yet on he fought, alone. He made short work of anyone who failed to escape.

His cavalry was gone. Only the assassin remained, striding into the embattled rear-rankers and challenging them with a point of his curved longsword. A vacant acre around him foreshadowed his presence on the battlefield. Angels parted in mobs to get clear of him, and those that did not were dead in the span of seven breaths.

He tread on a carpet of bodies until at last surmounting a great plateau of corpses half a league from Amin Shakush. All shrank from him, their formations fouling only to be met from the front by Satan's Fallen. All, except one. Though a head shorter, the angel donned the same domed helmet and facial shroud as the assassin general. The Faithful pointed one of his short swords at him and Umbra recognized his constellation partner and twin, Orean, as the lone Faithful who dared to challenge him. A great contest arose between the two but, in the end, Umbra Tempest slew his twin brother.

Inspired by his example, one by one the Faithful went up against the Fallen terror, and one by one they fell until he stood alone, triumphant in his mastery.

"Tempest!"

From behind the villain came such a cry as to raise the hackles on his neck. He turned to see a small cherub rush him, broadsword high and gore-spattered kite shield pumping on his arm. The Faithful angel was far shorter than him, with a topknot trailing behind like a pennant. Umbra Tempest saw it was none other than Shiranon. He turned to embrace the attack, and thus his greatest trial commenced.

Their duel was one of abject barbarity. Shiranon, grief-stricken over the many deaths of his friends, fought with the spirit of a wild creature, casting away restraint. His opponent's celebrity meant nothing to him. His mind clouded in anger; all he knew was to cut and stab and beat and bash until Orean and the others had been avenged.

They moved at odd angles across the morbid plateau, each trying to outmaneuver the other, while overhead, gales of fire rippled as Gabriel and Mazerrel fought. Far off, the sounds of Satan and Michael's climactic second duel thundered in echo as they ranged all over the Valley. The archangels and the Fallen leaders burned the air and consumed thousands in their collateral fury. But where Umbra Tempest and Shiranon dueled, there was no fighting; all eyes were locked on the display of martial prowess unfolding before them.

The two bit and slashed with their blades. And when those failed, they punched and kicked, their armored limbs moving with such velocity that onlookers could hardly assimilate the strikes. Breath was stolen as all saw Umbra Tempest barely match Shiranon. He caught a bash from Shiranon's kite shield on crossed vambraces and wheeled his longsword to meet the Faithful's broad blade. He drew in close to the cherub, swords inches from their faces.

Empyrean Falling

"Are you so desperate to join my foolish prey?" Tempest hissed at the surly little ranger.

He shoved Shiranon and dropped low, working his sword over the lip of the Faithful's shield and slicing its wrist strap. It fell to their feet. He attempted to duck behind his foe, but Shiranon was ready and in one stroke severed the Fallen's sword hand at the gauntlet.

The two twirled apart, unfurling their wings and withdrawing to a safe interval. For a heartbeat they held, savoring the tension and catching their breath.

Tempest pressed his bleeding stump to his chest. He pulled his reserve dagger from the small of his back and lunged. Shiranon kicked his shield and fouled the attack. He frogged the general with his sword pommel, drawing blood from the foe's scalp. The Fallen dropped to one knee and kicked in a daze, a last desperate strike of the serpent. Shiranon juked and drove the tip of his broadsword down, parallel to his interclavicular notch. Blood gushed from his sternum and in one twisting motion, Shiranon retracted the blade and decapitated him. Umbra Tempest's head tumbled in a gory fountain.

A cheer erupted from the Faithful; Shiranon had slain the cunning terror Umbra Tempest.

Back at Amin Shakush, Alrak and his remnant fought a battle beyond their powers. Bodies fell from the sky, riddled with projectiles. Blood rained as thousand fought in the airspace, only to plummet and be impaled on the pikes and lances of those shoving below. The Valley grew shallow with the stew-like purchase of war; a veritable winepress of carnage.

The battlewagons reined in a column perpendicular to the ramparts. The lead war engine was afire, stalling the van. Fallen auxiliaries swarmed overhead, trying to provide cover.

Undeterred, Melphax saw the development and sought to affect their salvation. "Cognoscenti," he shouted to the thousand remaining cherubim holding at the bailey, "move at my signal!" At once, the bronze-clad elites disengaged and thundered into the ready. "Hedgehog! Hedgehog!" The heavy infantry drew into their knot of shields and spears. Melphax turned to his junior officers. "Weir! Ables! I'll hold here. You handle those boxes!"

Empyrean Falling

With a pair of nods, the two beat clear the fray and sprinted for the lead battlewagon.

"Climb aboard," Weir offered Ables with a derisive grin, indicating the exposed teamster's rig at the fore of the wagon.

Ables grimaced at his superior and clawed his way to the top. Weir was right behind him, shielding his face from the pitch fires burning alongside the wooden hull. The armored oxen were still alive, their iron plates battered but intact. Weir grabbed the reins and began snapping madly as archers harassed them. Arrows thwacked into the battlewagon and the flanking mires of blood and entrails.

"No, no," Ables squawked over the noise, a smirk on his face as projectiles whistled past. "You're doing it wrong. It's two quick cracks and one hard one. That'll—" He hurtled back against the driver's seat, slammed by the impact of an arrow piercing his breastplate. He regarded the wound with a touch and a bloody cough. "Surely you jest." Before his wide eyes could blink, another arrow landed below his sixth rib and a third in his neck.

Weir took one look at his dead friend before throwing himself from the wagon, his vacant seat riddled with arrows as the gruesome marsh rose to meet him. He nearly blacked out and would have drowned, were it not for Melphax plucking him from the quagmire.

"We're heading for the Temple," the Pillar of Iron said as more arrows thudded around them. He dragged the captain to his feet as Alrak's elemental storm raged not a furlong away.

"Last stand?" Weir yelled. Melphax nodded gravely before raising his mace and trudging through the pressing mill of combat. Weir stumbled to keep up. He floundered in the knee-high goopy pool, his leg broken. He looked on helplessly as Melphax's massive back grew less distinct in the miasma. Determined not to let another friend sacrifice their life for his folly, he leaned on his good leg and set his jaw. "A good soldier need not run," he said, recalling the maxim, "only stand and fight." He drew his twin fighting knives from their sheaths and turned to face the nearest oncoming host of rebels, knowing there was no escape.

Not half a league away, Gabriel endured Mazerrel in the air.

Empyrean Falling

The Scourge proved vicious in his exhaustion. With every strike of his scimitar, his odious maw belched a roar amidst fiery wreaths from spiked wings. His bleeding chest heaved as he cursed.

Gabriel's face was a tapestry of cuts and burns, his cheeks etched with soot and cruor. He sucked air as he hovered, twin sabers gleaming in the sunlight.

"Even if you manage to beat me," Mazerrel said, "you can't defeat my master."

Gabriel's mind raced. He heard Mazerrel laughing with derision. Michael's voice pierced the gloom of his inward path. *Replace fear with faith*. Over and over again, it ran in his mind until he found himself drawing breath and lunging for the Scourge.

With a move of archangelic speed, he cast one of his sabers at Mazerrel, piercing the beast's right shoulder before he could bring his scimitar to parry. A howl of unimaginable wrath burst forth. Instantly, Gabriel was on top of him. He sliced the Fallen's sword-carrying wrist and slashed at his neck. The collar bone snapped, spilling marrow down the Scourge's hairy chest. In the frenzy, he managed to lop off the tip of one of his strange horns.

Mazerrel grunted in agony as Gabriel plucked the weapons and vaulted off the chimera's back. Before his flesh could manufacture the hamstringing fear, Gabriel was hurtling for him again. He hit the beast between the bleeding shoulder blades and the two went sprawling. They plummeted to the battlefield below. Their impact on the Valley was like a falling star. A shockwave issued forth as the two slammed into the corpse-covered muck and rock. Dead bodies scattered in all directions, obscured by a great torrent of showering fluids.

Back at the Iron Fortress, Michael and Satan faced off on the parapets high above the Valley.

Below them, the Battle of a Thousand Peaks raged with an unquenchable ferocity. Under a ruddy murk, winged dots rose and fell in clouds too thick to be counted. All that could be seen in the fog was a vista of spears, guidons, plumes and crests stretching from one horizon to the other.

The two champions collided atop Amin Shakush, their swords sending sparks down on to the writhing sea. Michael fought with a renewed vigor, but with each swing of Virtue and hammering deflection of Hadar, he felt his focus waning. He struggled valiantly, using every lethal martial trick he'd mastered, but Satan was ready for them all. He gagged as the breath was knocked out of him, another strike flailing him back across the parapet.

"Face it, Michael," Satan declared casually as he strode across the battlement. "You're stretched beyond your means here. Why bludgeon your crest against my heel? Just hand over your sword and we'll forget about this ugly, petty defense."

The Cherubim Patriarch mustered his resolve and rushed his nemesis, using his wings to propel him. The two met in the air, reaching the very heights of the firmament with strike upon strike of archangelic power. The air shattered in sonic blasts, the battle below tamed in a frightened hush as all beheld their masters' duel.

Michael set his jaw and continued to swing and stab at his older brother's husk. And when that failed, he employed every part of his body, from bloody forehead to broken feet, in an attempt to gain an edge over his superior. Even though every menial victory was a pyrrhic one, he could not stop. He would not stop.

They fought as falcons, as phoenixes, as a Dragon and a Lion high in Heaven.

Satan managed to get behind Michael with a flurry of blows, turning the predator into prey. "I have an affinity for the old wound, brother," he shouted into his ear over the howling winds. He gouged a long cut down Michael's chest, feeling for the scar. The Patriarch screamed, giving Satan just the distraction he needed. In one seamless motion, he cut the hinges off Michael's ornate cuirass, sliced open his scar, and sent him crashing onto Amin Shakush's Pinnacle. Michael landed on his bleeding chest. Seconds later, the Dragon was there.

"Alas," Satan announced, raising his sword for the final blow. "It's come to this." He brought the blade down with a hideous grin.

Suddenly, Alrak was there, intercepting Hadar with blinding precision. Satan drove his weapon through, cleaving the protégé's sword with a growl.

"Raziel!" he barked. "I always knew you'd be trouble."

Empyrean Falling

Alrak held his defiant posture in front of Michael, broken sword glinting red in the fire and sunlight. The Polemarch's pearly armor danged in shards, encrusted with chum and dirt.

"So, you wish to preserve your mentor," Satan observed with a ghoulish gleam. "Don't you see I'm doing you a favor, dandelion?"

Alrak peeled a mischievous half-smile and winked. The two fought, each attack more blinding than the last. They were twin blurs. Alrak sundered the buckles of Satan's wicked cuirass. It hung by the pauldrons. With a snarl, the Dragon tore the armor from his torso and flung it over the battlement. Alrak capitalized on his fortune and lunged. The Dragon ducked a swipe and spun, Hadar finding its home through Alrak's breastplate.

Silence hung in the air. Alrak's mouth hung open, blood trickling from the corner of his lip to meet the lake wound in his chest. A look of disbelief coursed over his keen features as his eyes dimmed to jades. Satan looked on pitilessly. A swift side kick, and the protégé tumbled over the broken rampart.

"I guess you didn't teach him that little trick," Satan remarked to Michael. "No goodbyes," the Dragon smirked, gesturing towards the spot where Alrak fell. "Only the end."

Michael's eyes clouded. It took all he had to pry his vision from the parapet. Sorrow drained him. He raised Virtue limply and prepared for the bout that he was sure would end his life. When the two crossed swords again it felt hollow. Michael had already lost in spirit; it would only be a matter of time before his coil of flesh followed. They clashed in exhaustion. Satan seemed taxed. Michael believed it until his face was smashed into the iron wall and he was flung overboard to the bailey below. When he landed, he saw the Tome half lying next to him. He rolled over to see Satan lunging.

Alrak manifested from the gloom and lumbered forth, still clutching his broken sword. He leaned in, blood pumping down his belted waist, jade eyes dim.

"Haven't you had enough, little star?" Satan barked. Alrak shambled forward, clutching a stomach painted in crimson and his face ashen white, but he faltered and slammed face-first into the muck. "At last," Satan sighed mockingly.

Suddenly, a terrible impact met Satan; the breath left his unarmored chest as he flailed onto his back.

Michael stood over him, Virtue's tip a hand's breadth from the Dragon's unguarded heart and the Tome half-lying in the muck. He inhaled and tensed his arms, ready for the blow.

He blinked. The Dragon was no longer there. In place of his skeletal, black-shrouded visage was the First Born, glowing majestically in his flowing raiment. His countenance was hale; his eyes shone brighter than all but the White Throne; his mane was the color of the august sun. "I'm your blood, Michael," Lucifer's voice pleaded. "Please."

Michael fought to pierce the vision. He wanted so desperately to drop Virtue and embrace his lost sibling. But the din of war wafted up, and he remembered the past nine months, the past millennia. "No," he said gravely, "you have only ever loved yourself."

Satan's eyes flared. "Don't you see what I've done, Michael? We knew what it would take to teach the choirs fidelity! That was the Three's dirty little secret all along. Can't you see that I've become that passion? I've given myself so that you may fulfill your destiny. I'm the catalyst for your faith. I'm Heaven's martyr!" Michael stared at him. "Can you kill me now, in the cold embrace of revelation?"

Around them, the massacre reached its apex; sheer butchery ascended to a supremacy unequaled in the War of the Throne. Carnage reigned as king.

Michael saw a shimmer behind Satan's prone form. A figure stood silently, the hem of His white robe untouched by the death surrounding them. His dark beard and hair did nothing to contain the fire in His eyes as He looked back at Michael. The quiet turned his wild heart to something deeper. A peace came over him.

Michael answered with Virtue. He plunged it towards Satan's exposed chest. It pierced the Tome half in the muddy rubble next to the Fallen archangel's head, diverted at the last moment. Satan's eyes bulged. He looked at the blade, then at the one wielding it. Michael's eyes held on the apparition. Satan turned and looked. He too saw the Son standing there, unsullied and silent as the world dimmed.

They all beheld Him.

Empyrean Falling

Many stood bewildered. Fighting sporadically halted.

Gabriel straddled Mazerrel, twin sabers ready to scissor-cut the Scourge's head off. Compelled by the holy vision, he raced to the Tome half that had been in Mazerrel's possession and plucked it from the mire. He thumbed through the arcane pages until he found the right one. With a grunt, he ripped it out and with a mighty breath, drew his final glyph on its topaz-encrusted surface. It burned into the living air for all to see. Gabriel grabbed his trumpet from its place on his belt and blew into the glyph.

Behind him, the Elders winged in to bend the knee and lend their voices. Metatron led them in a tandem canticle with the archangel while Arkadia stood boldly nearby with his hammers.

A mighty sound burst forth from Gabriel, accompanied by a blinding radiance magnified by the Son. It had the melodious hue of a madrigal as it channeled through the Seraphim Archon. From its sacred notes, a nucleus of holy rays blinded the Valley. Light beams shot forth from the slender Seraphim Archon's body and exploded across the war-torn, riven landscape, swirling up into the smoggy cope. The Voice of God became consumed by the light, swallowed and enveloped by its incandescent nova. The sun eclipsed in that moment. Roiling waves of energy, deeper than the fabric of the cosmos, uncoiled in billowing, undulating flames from the airy canopy. In a moment of pure revelation, the veil was torn by the Upper Realm's emergence. God's essence harmonized with Gabriel's voice until the sky vanished under the eerie, numinous light.

It was a glimpse of the Empyrean.

Time stood still.

Thought fled. The angelic host fell to its knees.

Michael stumbled backwards and landed on his haunches. Tears streamed down his face.

Melphax froze, mace held overhead ready to deal a brain-splattering blow to a Fallen archer, while Weir stared on in cryptic approval, his lifeless body propped against an overturned chariot.

Satan reached for the Empyrean. A shadow intercepted him. He took the Dragon's hand and pulled him to his feet, serene eyes never leaving the apostate archangel. No one would be able to recall how long they stood there or what exactly transpired between them. Only that, in the end, the archangel nodded. The Son wiped away his sullied cheeks. And Hadar was cast to the ground.

The Fallen surrendered.

As quickly as it came, the Empyrean receded like a scroll. Its conduit through Gabriel vanished. He sank to the clearing beside Mazerrel, unconscious. Arkadia caught him just in time.

The Faithful rose. What followed would forever be known as the Hour of Binding. They shackled their recalcitrant brethren with ropes, chains and even banner cloth, so little did they resist. Michael clapped Satan in irons, unable to peer into his fiery eyes.

When he was finished, the Cherubim Patriarch searched the rubble. He found Alrak sprawled over a patch of bare rock, still and pale. Michael sank to his knees beside Alrak's broken body, the spritely cherub's golden hair draped over hollow, dark eyes. A scream tore from his breast. Holding his protégé's corpse in quaking arms, the archangel felt the full woe of his duty. No one could say for sure whether his cries were for Alrak or for all those who had gone before.

Slowly, through the fog of war, the Son approached.

Michael looked up at him, tears flooding down his cheeks. "Not him," he pled. "Not my dandelion." He buried his face into Alrak's cold, limp form, shoulders shuddering in the breakdown. Overhead, the sky lingered in an aurora.

"No," the Son replied. "You're right; not him." He turned His back and strode away.

Alrak coughed and sputtered, jade eyes opening. Michael felt the air rush into his young lungs. Fresh waves of tears sprang from his sapphire eyes as he embraced the revived pupil.

Alrak pushed him away and looked up with an arched eyebrow. "Did I say the sky was a seven?" he mused through a daze. "…Looks more like a nine."

Michael wept till he laughed.

Alrak Sivad lived.

Empyrean Falling

Chapter XXII

"...and prevailed not; nor was their place found anymore in Heaven."
—Revelation 12:8

It was like a dream. Hours blinked past. Seconds stretched for ages. Memories would forever be spotty at best in the recollection.

Under the watchful aegis of the Elders, Arkadia unveiled handcrafted chains imbued with divine properties. Fires of the Empyrean swirled in their oily metals. Their links hummed with an ethereal luminescence. At Gabriel's command, he dispersed them to the Faithful, who employed them on their Fallen siblings. The ad hoc bindings were replaced by the true manacles of containment. No one could escape their adamantine grasp. No one tried.

The Hour of Binding was complete.

They took them back to Zion.

Silence hung like a pall over their journey, even as they entered the Holy Temple.

The archangels furled their wings, ascended the Forty Steps, and opened the Doors to the Inner Room. Holy radiance burst from the threshold, echoing what they had seen in the Valley. Michael hauled the Dragon to the altar, his mighty chains unable to afflict his pride. The Fallen stood behind the Three, contained by their Faithful captors. All were battle-scarred and gore-begrimed, yet Gabriel alone had the presence of mind to call forth the custodians. They brought out a modest wooden bowl filled with water and draped in a white linen towel. A vial of oil sat on the towel's taut surface.

The Son stood at the black speaking dais, looking down at Satan and cascaded in the light. "You have turned My kingdom into a charnel house," He said. "Why?"

Shackled and beaten like his remaining insurgents, Satan rose to his full height. "You can't imagine what it's like to labor for the affection of that One whom you love most, only to have Him turn and create something new because He's dissatisfied. You have no idea the pathos such malfeasance induces."

"Actually, My Son," He replied, "I do." Satan averted his eyes, unable to match those of the Son. "But My Father is the shepherd of love. And no recalcitrant ram can stray so far that He would not brave the winding goat track to retrieve him." He descended the Forty Steps and stood next to the custodians. At the Son's behest, they placed the bowl at His feet. "Wash the blood from your hands. Abandon this First Born host, Enemy of My Father, so that I may cleanse his feet and anoint My precious Morning Star's head with oil. Ask forgiveness, Lucifer, and I'll atone for your sins and welcome you back to My flock. Flee these Heavenly Realms, Satan, so that My Anointed Cherub may take his rightful place at My Father's side."

The archangel stared back at the Son. Behind him, the Fallen cried in unison for their master to plead their case with the same eloquent conviction that had beguiled them so long ago.

"These stains are a testament to my sacrifice," Satan declared. "I would rather be a martyr to my Phoenix Empyrean than serve Your red right hand. My place is on that Throne, not beside it."

"So, be it," said the Son. A great sorrow resonated from Him as He turned and ascended back to the speaking dais. "Here is your judgment: cursed you are, with all your disciples, to spend the length of Humanity's history on Earth, stripped of your glory to live as shadows. Given unto you will be the influence of your voice alone. Only behind the veil will you find substance to wage war. You will be carried by the air, swept by the tide, and buried beneath the stone, powerless to escape. You will burn to destroy My Creation but denied you shall be of the strength to raze its splendor. You will be banished to that place you despise most; you and all who followed you shall dwell in this prison planet, unable to escape."

The Son gazed down at Mazerrel, a barely conscious hulk laced with chains cutting into his raw flesh. "Except for you, Mazerrel. You, the Scourge of the Faithful, tyrant of the Fallen and fiend of the West, have committed sins for which few punishments are fit. The atrocities you have embraced, and the litany of crimes you have perpetrated are viler than any in Existence. Unto you is bestowed a special judgment. You will be banished to the cold depths of Space for the length of this Universe's time, divorced from all sentient life. Then, when your isolation has given you final malice, you shall be hurled into the Lake of Fire to join your master."

The Son turned His attention to the Heavenly Host.

"Such shall be your fates as well, Fallen myriads. Cast from Heaven you shall be. Barring your deaths on the ethereal planes, when Humanity has reached the last of their days, you too shall be cast into that antechamber of the Burning Hells. This is the judgment of the Lord, which I pronounce with a broken heart."

A great cry arose from the Fallen throngs.

"Do you have any final words before your exile, Lucifer?" the Son asked. "Does Father's love not abide even for you?"

Satan raised his head to behold the Almighty. "I swear to You, I'll bring back the Empyrean. Damnation *will not* bar me."

"Very well," the Son said. "Let it be. I always loved you, Son of the Morning. That cannot change, no matter what Dragon has sunk its talons into your once holy heart."

In the blink of an eye, the Son transported the Heavenly Host back to the valley of a Thousand Peaks. Under the waning sun, at the Iron Temple of Amin Shakush, they gathered. Gabriel and Melphax recovered the Tome halves among the debris and brought them to the Son, while Alrak and Michael guarded Mazerrel and Satan.

The Son combined the two halves and led the archangels in opening a pathway to Earth. A blue translucent gap opened on the same rocky hillock where Gabriel had ushered forth the Empyrean.

Empyrean Falling

Scorched black as obsidian and bare of anything but substratum, the round hillock gave birth to a vertical fissure. It crackled and burned, awaiting their entry.

What followed became known as the Exodus of the Fallen. Every rebel angel, from Belphegor to Mazerrel, was herded at the end of a blade into the portal's shining vortex. It was sung among the Fallen in forlorn tenors, baritones, and basses:

"And thus of stars reproved, Heaven's canopy dim; and loss of brothers most bitter dear, constellations die of burning whim."

The angels wept bitterly, for the full debt of their war's purchase was paid.

Michael and Gabriel flanked the portal, gazes steady as the Elders took a census of the Fallen. The rebels were ushered through. When it came time for Satan to trespass the interdimensional gateway, Michael's constitution visibly wavered. Even Alrak shrank from him, for once his celebrity eclipsed by that of another.

"Just ask yourself this," Satan said to his estranged brother, "were the past nine months of labor pangs worth it? It took all this for us to catch a glimpse of that which we had lost. Imagine the full price of admission for Him to dwell amongst us again. What horrors would it require for us to truly return? What does that say about Him? I hope He doesn't beat you too harshly…when He's not neglecting you."

Michael's countenance held rigidly. "I'll miss you, Lucifer."

The Dragon looked at him, a solitary tear breaching his crimson eye and running the length of his bruised, bloody face. "You always were a dimly lit star, Michael. My name," he said, resigned at last in one cruel, authentic moment, "is Satan."

The first archangel stepped into the portal and vanished.

As the sun set on the Thousand Peaks, the myriads-myriads of Faithful angels sprouted their wings and flew for Zion. All fled the battlefield's stark, unnerving tranquility.

Except Melphax. He could not bring himself to depart his home. He patrolled the corpse-filled Valley, wings outstretched to navigate the sinewy mires. He traced a slow path through Amin Shakush, running a cramped hand over the rusted wall and dreaming of the day when he could repair it. He sat in the long-abandoned Temple, inhaling its ruinous musk.

When he had his fill, the cherubic general emerged from Amin Shakush and expanded his wings. He vaulted up and glided towards the eastern mountains, intent on returning to Zion with the rest of the Heavenly Host. As he ascended, he saw a lone figure cascaded in titian beams. Whoever it was stood atop a prodigious promontory of detritus and dead, where the fighting had been its thickest. Melphax descended to investigate, unlatching his war mace. He landed at a safe interval, vision obscured by the play of august rays and shadows.

"Who goes there?" he called, his deep voice rumbling in the Valley's grisly winepress stillness.

"Now that I have peace, Pillar of Iron," came a familiar forlorn baritone, "I don't know what to do with it."

Melphax relaxed. He saw Michael standing with his back to him, facing the dusk. He hobbled near the archangel and holstered his mace. For a long time, the two stood there, watching the sunset amidst the ghastly carnage.

"We'll rebuild, Patriarch," he finally stated. "And bear this Kingdom into a halcyon age." Michael nodded. Melphax tried to think of something edifying to say which might console his esteemed friend but, in the end, he came up short. He never considered himself a poet. Perceiving his archangel's desire for solitude, Melphax patted Michael on his steel pauldron and strode away. Moments later, when he was several paces down the charnel slope, the Pillar of Iron turned back to face him. "At least it's over."

Michael pivoted around and looked at Melphax, indignation searing his features. "Over?" He turned back to regard the gloaming and shook his head. He squinted into the bathing warmth of the stark alpenglow horizon. "No, my dear Melphax," he exhaled. "I'm afraid this is just the beginning."

End of Tome III

Empyrean Falling

Epilogue
"...repent, for the kingdom of heaven cometh."
—Matthew 4:17

...What flashed before my senses wasn't so much a dream or vision but an experience, one in which residual effects still lingered. My tongue tasted the acrid flakes of ash; my nose smelled the pungent effluvium of the battlefield. I heard the chorus of angels singing their dirge as the Fallen were led, beaten and chained, into the portal outside Amin Shakush. I could feel the cool dusk breeze and see the sun's crimson inside my eyelids.

When I surfaced from this tide of memories, I beheld Gabriel patiently watching me from his place in the leather chair. A smile creased his face, pursing only to admit the deep merlot in his hand. Apparently, he went for a refill while I was entranced with the epic. I saw him differently, then, as one who looks upon a stranger only to realize they were gazing at a long-lost friend who had matured in their absence. When lucidity returned, I was left anchored to the harbor of Gabriel's odyssey with questions.

"So, angels died?" I asked.

"Not any more than you do," he replied, savoring the wine. Despite myself, I eyed him. Had I not just beheld a saga where angels perished upon the points of whetted steel? Had I not just gawked in terror at the far-stretching vistas of carnage? Gabriel winked at me. "As I said before, we're immortal, but so are you. The only difference is the degree of separation. You have an entire dimension to traverse when you shuffle loose your mortal coil; ours is far less drastic. But of course, even in our physical state, we weren't given unto death as penance for our sins like you humans are now. Your bodies may be mortal, but inside, you're all luminous eternities."

"Timelessness is still a hard concept to grasp."

"It is," the archangel conceded, "because it's inaccurate." All I could do was frown. This invigorated him. "Wherever there's action, movement, or change, therein exists 'time'. If a thought occurs, then there's time. If a heart pumps, then there's time; for is not the interval between two beats—the space between two actions—what you consider time? 'Time' is simply the cataloging of eternity. You humans live in the same progression as angels, but your flesh is finite. There's no such thing as 'timelessness' as long as there exists a thing and then no-thing. Otherwise, it would be a frozen state, and Heaven is far from static, for better or worse."

"Is that why you swore off the glyphs?"

"No," Gabriel answered, "they were residual touchstones to the Empyrean. We used them to infuse the Western Empire, but we swore them off when it collapsed, cognizant of the perversion of power they provided. Temptation takes many forms. I guess Michael had his vices, and I had mine. Only Lucifer and I could use them, perhaps one of the few traits which we truly shared. But he lost his ability when he Fell and, after the Battle of a Thousand Peaks…whatever conduit I had to the glyphs was fried. But don't forget what will happen, Markus. Earth's history becomes Heaven's history. Zion will one day descend. We're all moving towards that charitable end…and end which is not an end but a new beginning. There is no end, only the closing of dispensations."

"But the War for the Throne ended," I argued petulantly.

He eyed me with those golden lamps of his. "Just because a war goes by an alternate name doesn't mean it's finished. The War for the Throne will rage beyond the end of human history. Right now, we call it the War of Souls because that's the object of their ire. We work to protect you."

"Why do you do it?" I asked sincerely. "Why do the angels fight to preserve us?"

Gabriel smiled. "We stand in the gap because Father loves you and we love Father." He considered me for a trice before taking another draught of wine. "And we love you as well," he admitted. "That's why we fought so hard at the Battle of a Thousand Peaks."

"It wasn't just your devotion to God?"

"Without that, we would've failed long ago," the archangel admitted. "But we knew that if we failed in the Valley—if Satan and Mazerrel combined the Tome halves inside Amin Shakush's Iron Temple—then Humanity would be vulnerable. It would break God's heart, but it would break ours as well. We love you not just because Father loves you but because you're beautiful, unique and innocent in your potential."

I dared to scowl at the Seraphim Archon. "Innocent?"

"We've led you at Father's behest, and others have led you astray at Satan's behest; beyond these influences, you're as pure as babes. The sin in the Garden changed all that, of course, but we're endeared to you because of your inherent lack of culpability."

I couldn't help but shake my head. "So, we've always been at the center of this war." A wave of guilt crashed over my heart; I suddenly felt as if our naiveté had cost the angelic host many of their brothers. I wept quietly. "I'm sorry, Gabriel."

"Don't be," he comforted. "It was bound to happen sooner or later. Lucifer saw Creation as pride wounded and couldn't bring himself to take his concerns before the Throne. He felt self-righteous enough to stew behind everyone's backs. Such was the nature of the Morning Star. Such was the sin of my eldest brother: prideful self-pity. An irony, for sure." He sighed. "The point that needs to be taken to heart, though, Markus, is that the Anointed Cherub had a choice. He knew what the consequences were if he continued to harbor his misgivings, yet he did nothing. Father set up the flaw in Morning Star's personality to test him and, much to everyone's sorrow, the

Empyrean Falling

Grand Patriarch failed. Thankfully, Michael and I triumphed…I guess 'two out of three ain't bad', as the saying goes."

"But still, how can you excuse so much slaughter in the name of the White Throne when the whole war was a ruse?"

"It was all we could do. If there's a known threat in front of you and an unknown threat looming on the horizon, you deal with the one staring you in the face first. We had to fight the battles, even though we secretly suspected that Satan knew he couldn't defeat God. What kept things in perspective was the fact that he could defeat us. The angelic host was quite vulnerable. Each battle was a pitched affair, every fight a desperate one.

"Despite their malcontent, I have to hand it to them: Mazerrel and Umbra Tempest were extraordinary generals. The Scourge knew how to strike fear into our hearts. That was his strength. Umbra Tempest, on the other hand, was clever. He knew how to confound us with tricks. But we knew God could defend himself. We fought out of faith as well as principle. Besides, you don't train for an age to fend off a Prophecy only to throw up your hands and cry vanity when it comes. It wasn't about protecting God. It was about selflessness, about protecting our angelic brothers and human cousins. The sad part, Markus, is it didn't have to happen that way.

"The real test was whether or not we could accept mankind's prestige. That was the only debate Father forced on us. What followed was the result of our decision. Each angel had to decide for himself. Most saw it as God's benevolence. Some saw it as an infringement upon their sovereignty. The War for the Throne was what resulted when the proud challenged the judgment seat. Why do you think the prodigal son story is relevant? Pay attention to the older brother; his resentment was his sin."

"But Christ told Michael that this was all ordained," I refuted cautiously. "Wasn't it fate that compelled Lucifer to become Satan?"

"No," Gabriel denied with a shaking head. "As God said, He knows all the avenues that we may take. But He blinds Himself, allowing our Free Will to determine which path to tread. Only He can know the future. All that we know is that which is given to us as tools to aid our missions. Never forget, Markus, Heaven is simply another dimension. We follow the same chronology. It's just that our flesh is considerably less corporeal than yours; it doesn't wither and perish of its own accord."

With that, I felt the matter was settled.

"What about Alrak?" I asked. "Is he still fighting?"

"He's made cameos since the First War," Gabriel replied, considering something before expounding further. "Poor Alrak, sometimes he just can't stand to be out of the spotlight."

"What do you mean?"

"You might find some of his exploits in Second Samuel…chapter twenty-four, I believe."

"There's another bit in the Book of Daniel that rings familiar," I added, "somewhere in chapter ten. Was that him, too?"

"No, unfortunately not," Gabriel frowned. There seemed to be a twinge of embarrassment in his tenor. "That was me." He wore a sheepish grin, though it was hard to pierce that glowing countenance. I recounted the story and confessed that I figured this to be Alrak. Apparently, I was wrong.

Gabriel caught my surprise before I could mask it, human reflexes being nothing compared to archangelic senses. "You have to understand," he said, "that back then the 'prince of Persia' was a pretty nasty villain. We're thankful that a lack of belief has put him into a subterranean coma. The past couple millennia would be much harder fought with that monster still in the fray."

"I'm sure he's not the only demon you've had to deal with."

"He's not a demon," Gabriel corrected. "No, is he a Fallen. There's a difference."

I knew at once what he meant, for it confirmed in me a long-standing debate. "But demons are monsters," I rebuffed. "Surely the Fallen can't be viler than disembodied spirits?"

"The Fallen are insidious fiends, deranged felons worthy only of contempt. They've elected their plight willingly out of vice, vanity and hatred. Pride, jealousy, selfishness and a lack of discipline all became paramount in their hearts because they chose those tenets over love. They're tantamount to the worst of the worst and will stop at nothing to bring us all to ruin.

"You cannot truly imagine what it was like to face them. They were unhinged. They fought with evil weapons and when those failed, they bit and clawed like rabid beasts. The only tactic we had was to hack them up until no life could be sustained. Now they roam this plane as exiled convicts. Few of them reside in Hell."

"I hope that time has slackened their lunacy."

"Quite the contrary," he answered. "Some wounds don't heal with time; they fester. Being divorced from the presence of the Almighty is one. Which is why you need to be wary now more than ever." He leaned in close. "The Enemy knows I'm here. They've been preparing for my arrival. Forgive me, but such occasions are rather high profile. You've probably sensed their presence in the past few years. Haven't you noticed things have been…difficult lately?"

I nodded, dizzied with revelation. Suddenly, all my recent troubles fell into a soothing perspective, as did the value of my current measures taken to fix them; to wit, my fast.

"The Fallen have been working on you for many years, Markus," Gabriel continued, "all in the hopes of thwarting us both. We've fought for you, just as we fought for others, but it's a losing battle. Your lack of discipline has given them quite a foothold.

"But now you've turned a corner; you've become receptive again! That's what fasting does—never forget that. God honors sacrifice and faith. Just ask Job, Abraham, Moses and Paul." Gabriel relinquished a bit, his fervency replaced by a levity. "You'd be surprised to hear what Isaac has to say about it all," he laughed. "That man will ramble for centuries about sacrifice if you let him."

"Ironic," I mused.

Gabriel considered that with an amused nod. He took another sip of wine. "Irony is powerful," he declared. "You'll experience your own bit of it before the end." I looked at him incredulously. "Like I said," the archangel defended, "we can't see into the future, but Father will often gift us with visions of what might occur, in order to aid us in our assignments. What I know about you, I know not because I can move through time, but because God knows it will help me to convince you of what lies ahead."

"But why me," I ask earnestly. "What do I have to offer?"

"The end is approaching, Markus. Time is running out for this Realm. As your race hurtles along towards its tumultuous climax, it grows more callous to Heavenly whispers. This is more dangerous than you realize. I want to give you every bit of currency with which you may ensure your redemption. I am the Voice of God; I have a responsibility to speak the truth. But I won't counsel the deaf. I have chosen you because you have an ear to hear."

He drew to the seat's edge, his luminous vision heating my face. In his passion, the archangel touched my knee. It warmed me to the bone. "If only you humans would *listen* to us when we speak," he urged, "you could be saved from such pain. Father wants us to grow on our own, but He loves us. If pain can be eluded, He wants to offer the detour. That's where the angels come in, where we earn our keep. We strive for you because we love you. Is that not worth requiting?

"You know one of the reasons why we clothed ourselves in flesh? Because it afforded us the opportunity to experience sin."

"So, that's why you went to war," I asked, "so you'd know the price of fealty?"

"Yes," Gabriel answered. "But there's more. We suffered so that we may know every trial, fear and tribulation you humans would go through. How can we minister to others if we cannot fathom their pain? There's nothing new under the sun, Markus. We've been there. We know. Satan lied at the Battle of a Thousand Peaks: the Three's dirty little secret is that we knew the War for the Throne was necessary to bind us to Humanity."

"But why so much attention on me?"

"I've chosen you because you'll listen when others won't. Anyone could attain the experience you've been given today, but so many of them refuse to open up to God. You've humbled yourself and sought out Father, therefore I've been granted the opportunity to make a prophet out of you. But when men become jealous—and they will— you must remind them that it's only your brokenness that allows such glory. You'll be a voice in the dark, my friend, a trumpet on the battlefield. And while we rejoice that you've heeded Father's call, we gnash our teeth at the sorrowful vista of unrepentant humans who squander their gifts on hardscrabble pleasures. What will be given unto you is something that could be given to anyone, if only they would turn to the quiet and heed Parakletos.

"It breaks Heaven's heart when Humanity refuses to hear us. It's unrequited love of the most heretical acme. But you've elected to entreat Father's guidance, and, for that, there will be blessings. It may be painful and it may not end in bliss, but it is sacrosanct."

"I'm afraid of martyrdom, Gabriel."

He waved this away with a casual grace. "If it ever happens, you won't be scared for long; lucidity sets in after terror. That's how you know you're about to die! After all the millennia of watching your kind perish, I've witnessed my fair share of fatal heartbeats. I'll warn you, though, if it ever comes to that—and it may—you'll experience a wave of fear like no other; the flesh knows when it's on the chopping block. But don't worry, we'll be there, waiting to escort your soul as it migrates to the Firmament."

"Can I put in a request?"

Gabriel shrugged and said why not.

"Can Alrak be there?"

He exhaled with a squint. "Alrak's going through a tribulation of his own right now," he stated. "Hard to nail that one down, to be honest." His gaze settled on me. "But I have faith in our dandelion. If he can't pull himself out of the mire, who can?"

"What's going on with him?"

"He's chafing under this Second War's rules of engagement. We pray and counsel with him, but I fear the strain of this conflict's stricter maxims may compel his heart to grow derelict. We are not what we once were." Before I could even finish my question, he had the answer. "Oh yes," he nodded, standing and finishing his wine. "How we fight now is different than how we fought before. Most have adjusted to the changes. Some, like Alrak, have not."

"Well," I smiled, "after all you've shown me, I can't imagine the mighty Alrak Sivad succumbing to sin. He'll pull through."

Gabriel watched me as I finished my scotch. The archangel's eyes appeared sad, as if no words spoken had ever rang hollower than mine just then.

"I hope so," he admitted. "I truly do." He pointed to my bedroom, his slender limb sliding out from the glistening emerald fabric. "My hour is up. It's time for you to retire. There will be much work ahead. You'll need your sleep in these end times."

I started for the bedroom. Halfway past the laundry room, I stopped and turned, hesitant to speak. Gabriel watched me from my living room. In that breath, he didn't seem like the archangel in my revelation. He was strong, confident, unshakable.

"Um," I stammered, fidgeting with my shirt tail. "So how does this work? Do I bow before I go?"

A smile swept over Gabriel, dissolving his hard veneer. "No, my dear Markus," he chuckled. "It is I who bow to you…" The Seraphim Archon, the Voice of God, Archangel Gabriel, sank to a knee and lowered his head, golden locks falling over an ageless face. "…as we did all those millennia ago."

It was then that I understood. This was what separated the Faithful from the Fallen. Lucifer would never bow to a human.

When he rose, I hazarded another query. "Can you divulge Alrak Sivad's tale?"

"Someday," Gabriel answered, "but not today." In the dawn's low light, his image dissolved amidst my furniture, an eidolon waning from radiant opaque to glowing translucent. "That," he said in a tenor that faded with his gossamer eidolon, "is an epic for another time."

An End

Empyrean Falling

Glossary

Angels: (The created beings that comprise Heaven's ranks)

Ables: (A-blz) (Cherub) Serves as an aide under Captain Weir and Alrak Sivad.
Agni: (Ag-nee) (Seraph) One of the **Eldar** and judicator between God and the angels.
Alrak Sivad: (Al-rack-Si-VAD) (Cherub) Michael's secret protégé and successor should he die. Other titles: Bane of the Fallen, Myth from the South, Polemarch, dandelion and Raziel.
Apollyon: (A-pol-lyon) (Cherub) Joins **Mazerrel**.
Ariel: (AR-ee-el) (Seraph) Medic and protégé to **Arkiel**.
Arkadia: (Ar-KAY-dee-uh) (Cherub) Chief Hammer in Zion; in charge of all forges.
Arkiel: (AR-kee-el) (Cherub) Chief Surgeon of Heaven; has two protégés: **Ariel** and **Rafiel**.
Asmodeus: (Az-mo-dee-us) (Seraph) One of the **Eldar**; "raging judge" with an infamous temper.

Astaroth: (AS-tar-oth) (Seraph) One of the **Eldar**; nominated by God to watch over the animals.

Azazel: (a-ZAY-zel) (Cherub) One of the **Twelve** under **Jehuel**; survives the War.

Azriel: (AZ-ree-el) (Cherub) One of the **Eldar**; "God's strong gofer": a field agent for the Elders.

Baal: (Bale) (Cherub) A cattle breeder.

Beliel: (BAY-lee-el) (Cherub) One of the **Eldar**; a scandalous judge; drinking is his vice.

Bellator: (Bell-ah-TOR) (Cherub) Captain of the Temple Guardians. He holds the night watch over the Doors to the Inner Room with **Dealleaus**.

Belphegor: (BELL-feh-gore) (Seraph) Officer and surgeon in Satan's army.

Camiel: (CAM-ee-el) (Cherub) One of the Eldar; "the Just".

Dealleaus: (Dee-ALL-lee-us) (Cherub) Guardian of the Doors to the Inner Room; serves on the same watch as **Bellator**.

Deledrosse: (Del-e-DROSS) (Seraph) Second lieutenant to **Melphax**; in charge of Amin Shakush's garrison.

Ellunias: (El-LOON-ee-us) (Seraph) "The Radiant"; Commander of the North Gate Garrison.

Erodantes: (Erro-DAWN-tes) (Seraph) Mercantile skipper of the Winged Fury.

Galeth: (GAY-leth) (Cherub) Unoth's lieutenant, a jovial scoundrel with a penchant for gambling and drinking.

Gi'ad Althaziel: (Gee-ahd AL-thaz-ee-el) (Cherub) Chief Weapons Master at the Cherubim Citadel; an expert on all arms.

Gilgamesh: (GIL-gah-mesh) (Cherub) "The Great"; one of the **Fourteen**; general of the **Lighting Legion**, also called the "**Thunderbolts**."

Goldruum: (Gole-drum) (Cherub) "Swift"; serves under **Mazerrel**; later in Tempest's **Seven Serpents**.

Israfel: (Iz-rah-fel) (Cherub) One of the **Eldar**; in charge of music under **Lucifer**.

Jehuel: (JEH-hue-el) (Seraph) One of the **Twelve**; leads his cadre into the West.

Kakabel: (KAY-kah-bell) (Cherub) One of the **Eldar**; nominated by God to watch over Space.

Kedlarn: (KED-larn) (Cherub) Leader of **Forty Hammers** at **Amin Shakush**.

Kemuel: (Ke-mu-el) (Cherub) A member of Satan's elite.

Keyleas: (KAY-lee-us) (Seraph) One of the **Fourteen**; escorts **Lantheron** to the Valley of a Thousand Peaks.

Lantheron: (LAN-ther-on) (Cherub) One of the **Fourteen**; escorts **Keyleas** to the Valley of a Thousand Peaks; under command of **Gilgamesh** in his **Lightning Legion** and later in the **Lions**.

Li'ithnu: (Lee-ITH-noo) (Cherub) An angel of Mazerrel's.

Linghal: (Leeng-gal) (Cherub) "The Silent One"; a scout for Mazerrel; later one of Tempest's infamous **Seven Serpents**; works in tandem with **Goldruum**.

Ma'igwa: (MAY-gwa) (Seraph) Chief Librarian at Carthanos; later becomes one of the co-leaders of the **Twelve**.

Malthus: (Mal-thus) (Seraph) Head of the North Gate's cavalry, **Pegasun Centaurs**.

Mazerrel: (MA-zur-rel) (Cherub) "The Scourge of the Faithful"; Lucifer's aide.

Mealdis: (MALE-dis) (Seraph) Approached by **Lucifer** following the Creation Coronation.

Melphax: (Mel-fax) (Cherub) "The Strong"; General of Amin Shakush; called "Pillar of Iron."

Metatron: (Met-ah-tron) (Seraph) Head Eldar; the ruling body of the Council and appointed by God to watch over Man.

Nelgleth: (Nel-gleth) (Seraph) An officer in Mazerrel's army, he serves with **Gi'ad Althaziel**.

Nicolae: (Nick-oh-lie) (Seraph) Interim Commander of the North Gate after **Ellunias**.

Nuriel: (Nur-ee-el) (Cherub) Twin of **Uriel**; possesses the Keys to Hell's Gates; a talent for Fire.

Orean: (Or-ee-in) (Cherub) One of the **Fourteen**, serves in the Lightning Legion; twin brother of **Tempest** and friend of **Shiranon**.

Paladin: (Pal-luh-den) (Cherub) First lieutenant of **Melphax**; oversees the Forty Hammers.

Rafiel: (RAF-ee-el) (Cherub) One of Arkiel's two protégés.

Raziel: (RA-zee-el) (Cherub) See **Alrak Sivad**.

Sammiel: (SAM-mee-el) (Seraph) One of Mazerrel's angels with a propensity for alchemy.

Sandalphon: (San-dal-fawn) (Seraph) One of the **Eldar**.

Sariel: (SAR-ee-el) (Cherub) One of the **Eldar**; in charge of prosecuting angels.

Seldax: (SELL-dax) (Seraph) **Death Guard** who accompanies **Vuldun** from the West.

Sheialla: (SHEE-alla) (Seraph) One of Mazerrel's angels; later a general under Tempest.

Shiranon: (SHEER-ah-non) (Cherub) One of the **Fourteen**; later in Gilgamesh's **Thunderbolts**.

(Umbra) Tempest: (Um-brah-Tem-pest) (Cherub) Citadel's espionage master; twin of **Orean**.

Unoth: (OO-noth) (Cherub) Garrison commander of the Stone City of Lorinar. His fortress is the Merciful Fate, also called the Ziggurat.

Ural: (YOUR-al) (Cherub) General of the experimental **Battle Group Concordia**.

Uriel: (UR-ee-el) (Cherub) Twin of **Nuriel**; possesses the Keys to Hell; a talent for Fire.

Urim: (UR-em) (Seraph) One of the Eldar; the Council's oracle; "Diviner of God's Will".

Usiel: (OO-see-el) (Seraph) Gabriel's armor-bearer.

Vuldun: (Vul-DOON) (Seraph) The first leader of Satan's Death Guard, see **Imperial Flames**.

Weir: (Weer) (Cherub) A captain under **Gilgamesh**; reassigned as Polemarch Alrak's aide.

Zodkiel: (Zod-kee-el) (Cherub) Michael's armor bearer.

Zophiel: (ZOF-ee-el) (Seraph) Gabriel's aide.

Archangels: (The three leaders of Heaven's angels)

Gabriel: (Seraph) Seraphim Archon; head of the Seraphim Choir and third most powerful being; known for his love and dedication to his choir's safety; has a natural preference for Wind. Other titles: Third Born Voice of God.

Lucifer: (Cherub) The most powerful created being; most beautiful, talented, intelligent, and charismatic of the Three; also, the eldest; in charge of all angels, relinquishes direct power to his two younger siblings; has a natural preference for Fire. Other titles: First Born, Anointed Cherub, Exultant Archon, Grand Patriarch, Morning Star, Lightbringer.

Michael: (Cherub) Cherubim Patriarch; head of the Cherubim Choir and second in power to Lucifer; known as Heaven's war chief and strives to be perfect in virtue. Other titles: Second Born, Sword of God, Lion of God, Chief of the Armies of God.

(**Satan**): (Cherub) The manifestation of evil. He retains all the powers of his host. Other titles: the Dragon, the Enemy.

Groups: (Specific units and orders of angels nominated to perform certain tasks)

Battle Group Concordia: An experimental multi-legion task force led by **Ural**.

Cherubim: The warrior caste of Heaven's Eastern Kingdom, Zion. Michael is their archangel.

Cognoscenti, **The**: Elite cherubim. They represent the old way; guardians of antiquity who rely more on quick wits and keen senses than armor. They forgo conventional plate mail in favor of the older panoply of bronze cuirass, greaves and helmet with an oak-and-bronze round shield. Their weapons are the ash wood spear, cubit-length sword, and dagger. Braver, more highly trained, and harder to dislodge, they never retreat. They are the cherubim's fearsome elites.

Council of Elders, **The**: A group of twelve elected angels that act as a congress over the affairs of Zion; made up of six seraphim and cherubim: (Seraphim) Agni, Asmodeus, Astaroth, Metatron, Urim, and Sandalphon; (Cherubim) Azriel, Beliel, Camiel, Kakabel, Sariel, and Israfel.

Death Guard, The: Satan's cadre. Also known as **Imperial Flame**s. They wear black armor laid in strips; impervious to almost all weapons. Upon their inception, they are one million strong.

Forty Hammers, The: The blacksmiths that work within Amin Shakush's Iron Forge, under the Iron Temple. Their leader is **Kedlarn**. **Paladin** is their overseer.

Fourteen, The: A special cadre of seven seraphim and cherubim sent by Gabriel and Michael to scour Heaven for Lucifer.

Imperial Flames: Satan's personal bodyguard, also called Death Guard by the Faithful.

Lightning Legion, The: "Thunderbolts". **Lantheron, Orean** and **Shiranon** serve in the small legion of irregulars commanded by **Gilgamesh**.

Lions, The: Michael's personal campaign legion assigned by the Council of Elders.

Pegasun Centaurs, The: Elite cavalry attached to the North Gate. Their captain is **Malthus**.

Seven Serpents, The: Seven Fallen once under **Mazerrel** then under **Tempest**; renowned for clandestine exploits. It is said they alone protected Tempest's flanks in the Northern Plains.

Temple Guardians, The: Angels chosen by Michael for their prowess in combat and a keen eye for security. Mostly cherubim, they protect the Holy Temple. Their captain is **Bellator**.

Three, The: The archangels: **Michael, Gabriel**, and **Lucifer**.

Thunderbolts: Nickname for The Lightning Legion. See **Gilgamesh**.

Twelve, The: Angels charged with the Tome of Descendance. Split into two groups of six, one led by **Ma'igwa** and sent to Amin Shakush and the other led by **Jehuel** and sent into the West.

War Implements: (Special weapons and terms used in battle)

Ballista: Stationary bolt-firing, torsion catapult. Bolt size is five cubits; can carry explosive tips; primarily used against infantry or armored siege-craft such as battlewagons and siege-towers.

Barbican: The focused defensive area behind a fortress's gate; the strongest point of defense.

Barbute: Close-fitting, open-faced helmet used by cherubim.

Bascinet: Iron helmet with a hinged visor; used by Legionnaires and Centurions.

Chamfron: Equestrian head armor; made from iron or steel.

Constellation: Two angels bound together, either as best friends or twin siblings.

Cuirass: Metal carapace of armor that fits around the torso, protecting both the chest and back, with two vertical slits at the back to allow the wings entry and exit.

Dog-chompers: Iron-soled cleats clamped onto the bottom of sabatons. Used by heavy infantry to gain footing in the muck resultant from line-fighting.

Dragoons: Official term for heavy cavalry; draft horses and riders armored in plate mail; armed with lances and small arms; serves as both shock- and mobile-infantry.

Dyad: A tactic used by **constellation** partners in dire circumstances to ensure survival, though in a crisis, any can form one, standing shoulder-to-shoulder with feet planted side-by-side.

Gall-guns: Portable stone-throwers used in sieges.

Greaves: Shin guards made of bronze or iron.

Hadar: "Glorious"; Satan's sword; made from an unknown metal; three cubits long; black; single-edged curved blade; two-handed grip; round handguard resembles a black flame.

Hadraniel: "Majesty of God"; Lucifer's sword since the West's inception; curved steel blade; ivory and gold handle.

Half-harness: Lightweight ancillary suit of armor; consists of a metal cuirass, greaves, and leather apron.

Lance: Dual-role term referring both to the tool and individual unit of heavy cavalry. Also, the primary weapon of heavy cavalry;

nine cubits of wood tipped with a cubit of steel; bronze counterweight added between the handle and the butt-spike.

Lamed tasset: Iron plate armor to protect the thighs.

Line-fighting: The mainstay of Heavenly combat; practiced by heavy infantry in massed formations; legions and phalanxes clash head-on.

Panoply: Generalized term used to describe any combination of arms, armor, and kit.

Pauldron: Metal armor fitted over the shoulder.

Poleaxe: A pole-arm four cubits long; hammer, axe, and spear at the head; wooden haft is wrapped in studded leather; metal pieces and a roundel protect the hands; pommel and butt-spike at the base.

Porcupines: Stationary javelin-launchers used in siege defense; loads 49 four cubit-long javelins into a single bank launched by torsion.

Sabatons: Iron guards that protect the tops of feet.

Sunbursts: A new machination of siege warfare. Two cylinders filled with gelatinous fire; can melt through all conventional protection; the invention is unstable. Only **Amin Shakush** has refined them to the point of implementation.

Sun-hats: Oversized palisades erected in a fortress's bailey; protects awaiting infantry from stray projectiles surmounting the wall during a siege; made of bronze and oak; held up by posts.

Switch-back: Tactic employed by seraphim; one group retreats, handing off their weapons to a passing relief force; used in the confusion of battle to ensure the front line isn't compromised.

Trebuchet: Stationary single-shot catapult used in sieges; operated by a ten-angel crew.

Vambrace: Armor fitted over the forearms.

Virtue: Michael's single-edged curved longsword. Four cubits long, it has a lion's body for a handle with two wings sprouting at the sides for the hilt.

Yews: Slang for archer auxiliary; the name derives from the wood used to construct their longbows.

Acknowledgments

Foremost, I must thank God. I've held my oath and run the course. I hope I honored Him.

Thanks to my parents, Lari and Carolyn; they ever-faithfully grasped for me when I Fell. I miss them dearly every day.

To Bob Williams, my mentor, who's remained a friend for decades, thus proving he's a horrible judge of character.

Also, gratitude proffered to Nicholas Goss, who dutifully helped with the publication of this monolithic work.

Very respectful gratitude to author Steven Pressfield; his works and correspondence have compelled me where others have flagged. I made it to the finish line in no small part due to his counsel.

And lastly, I must thank a certain woman whose edifying friendship led me back to Golgotha. The Lord used you in more ways than you know, KJD.

Made in the USA
Monee, IL
28 March 2021